Somebody's Baby

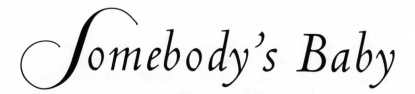

Somebody's Baby

A NOVEL

ELAINE KAGAN

William Morrow and Company, Inc.

New York

It is the policy of William Morrow and Company, and its imprints and affiliates, recognizing the importance of preserving what has been written, to print the books we publish on acid-free paper, and we exert our best efforts to that end.

Library of Congress Cataloging-in-Publication Data

Kagan, Elaine.
    Somebody's baby : a novel / Elaine Kagan.
        p.   cm.
    ISBN 0-688-15745-9
    I. Title.
PS3561.A3629S66   1998
813'.54—dc21   97-47244
                                          CIP

Printed in the United States of America

First Edition

1   2   3   4   5   6   7   8   9   10

BOOK DESIGN BY M. KRISTEN BEARSE

www.williammorrow.com

For Tom

Jenny

He had a tattoo. Maybe that isn't where to start, but what difference does it make where you start? I was rocked by the tattoo. It wasn't the first naked boy's chest I had seen, but it was certainly the first tattoo. An eagle, a large majestic blue eagle, majestic even with his wings closed, his head turned so you could see his kingly splendor in full profile. An eagle in repose, I said. I take that back: I didn't say it, I just thought it; I didn't say anything. There was just the shock of the eagle on the upper left side of his chest, a blue eagle under my fingertips. There was another tattoo on his right arm, a rose and leaves in a vine pattern that wound around a cross, and then another tattoo that said *Mother*, and then there were the letters that spelled out LETS FUCK, one letter each carved upside down on his toes. Four letters on four toes on the left foot and four letters on four toes on the right, no apostrophe. Those I didn't find out about until much later. I also found out later that he had carved those letters into his own toes when he was in jail.

Jail.

Not a word in my vocabulary. Jewish girls didn't know from jail then. Even Gentile girls didn't know from jail. In my neighborhood in 1959 in Kansas City, nobody knew from jail. They didn't even know from tattoos, much less jail. I had never spoken to anyone like him, not ever in my life, except for polite talk, hi and thank-you talk,

3

but not a conversation. I really didn't have conversations with *those* people, as my mother would have said, with her lips in a thin line and her chin at a particular angle. After all, I was a privileged daughter of the upper middle class. Jenny Jaffe, the sixteen-year-old only child of Esther and Mose Jaffe, five feet nine inches tall, about a hundred and twenty pounds, skinny and plain, with unruly brown hair pulled high and tight up into a ponytail in the hopes that that might make it straighter, pale skin and brown eyes. Loafers and stitched-down pleats and circle pins: the works. A midwest Jewish teenage girl, a quiet girl, one who hardly made a peep about anything, one who minded her p's and q's, not particularly popular, not particularly unpopular, just smack-dab in the middle of her senior year of high school—no edge, not bitter, just plain. The only thing different about me was that I thought I knew what I wanted, I had a dream. Not anything grand like Martin Luther King's, not anything that could change the course of mankind, just a little Jenny Jaffe dream. Of course, I had no idea how to achieve the dream, but that didn't seem to matter; even a dream without a plan made me different. Not too many people know what they want when they're teenagers—they didn't in 1959 and they still don't now—but I was sixteen and I had known what I wanted since I could stand. To be a dancer. A real one. Esther and Mose thought that their only child thinking she could be a dancer was a joke.

"Who goes all the way from Kansas City to New York and makes it? Don't be silly—you'll get lost in the shuffle there. You'll go away to college, and you'll learn to be something else."

I hadn't let either of my parents see me dance for years, not since I was a fledgling ballerina in a pink tutu at dancing school, the gawky big one with the stick legs in the back. "My daughter the ugly duckling"—my mother's hiss of a whisper and my father's quiet laugh in the dark recital hall—and from that time on, I never let them see me

4

dance. I kept my dream tucked away inside me. Maybe if it hadn't all happened, I never would have gone to New York and become a dancer. I would have scrapped the dream, run away with Will in the '50 blue Mercury, and danced only with him, in parking lots outside of country bars by the side of the road. But then you could also spend the rest of your life having a discussion about what is fate and what is your destiny and what has been written and what you can change. Nothing, if you ask me.

He was working at the Texaco at Seventy-fifth and Wornall, pumping gas into my friends' parents' cars; he actually stared at me while he washed the windshield of my mother's powder-blue Oldsmobile. I turned my eyes away and pretended to look for something in my purse. Then he was at Joe's, flipping hamburgers and washing greasy spoons—which was a joke, he added, smiling at my friend Sherry and me as he took the dishes off the table in the next booth. When he smiled, could it be that his eyes got bluer? Was that possible? And then twice I saw him working at the King Louie Bowling Lanes on State Line, renting bowling shoes to Friday and Saturday night dates. "Eight, right?" he said, looking at my feet, and I didn't answer him, and Mic Bowen said, "Yeah, right, eight," and took the shoes.

I was a senior at Southwest High School. He was an "I don't know what." I didn't know if he'd finished high school, I didn't even know if he'd ever gone. He was older than me, but I didn't know by how much—maybe just a few years older in numbers but light-years in life. William Cole McDonald. It was later that I learned his full name; at first I only knew *Will* because it was stitched in red over the pocket of his Texaco blue shirt.

"Hi there."

"Excuse me?"

"I said, Hi there."

"Oh. Hi," I said.

Riveting beginning. Embarrassing. Trapped in the car, my mother at the wheel, as Will walked around the passenger side to take the gas pump out of the tank. There was something wrong with his right leg; I noticed the limp as he passed my window. A limp and a smile and blue eyes.

"I only want to go to Harzfeld's," my mother said, "and maybe Wolff Brothers, but if they don't have it, I'm through. I'm not interested in an exhausting search for the right shoes."

I looked at her.

"I don't want an expedition. All right?"

"Okay."

"I want to meet Charlotte at the club by noon."

That's when he was cleaning the windshield, looking at me.

"One o'clock at the very latest," she said. "Where do you want me to drop you? At Sherry's when we're through?"

He was smiling, the red rag going back and forth across the windshield, his eyes behind it. I could feel my face turn pink.

"Jenny?" my mother said.

I rummaged around in my purse, my head down.

"Here you go, ma'am." He was at her window with the charge slip.

"Thank you," she said.

"You're welcome, and come again, ma'am," he said to my mother as she signed the ticket, and he looked at me. The sun was behind him, and his hair was so blond it was white. I tried not looking at him but I couldn't, I also tried not smiling—it required nearly biting through my entire bottom lip.

My mother turned the key in the ignition, and we pulled out of the Texaco.

"*Do* you want me to drop you at Sherry's when we're through?"

6

In the side mirror I could see Will waving at me, his hand in the air.

It wasn't as if I hadn't had a boy before. I'd had my share—a movie date, a burger date, even a prom. It wasn't like I hadn't been asked; it was that I didn't really care. Flirtations, rumors, and Saturday nights, that was the essence of high school then, who liked who and who went out with who and who kissed who and where. Nobody went much further than that, except in words. In words, every boy was hotly steaming up the windows of a parked Chevy, springing open a brassiere with just one hand, that hand touching bare skin on a vinyl backseat, but in deeds it was more chaste. Except for a few of us, the non-virgins. I was in a very select group: I had already had two boys and left them in the dust, and in 1959 that was a very big deal. In 1959 you were either a virgin or a tramp, and with David Greenspan and Mic Bowen I had crossed forever into the tramp category; I had gone "all the way," and there was no turning back. The difference between me and other girls who'd lost their virginity was that I wasn't in love with either one of those boys. I had no grand passion for David or for Mic; there was no romance, no betrayal, no nothing. David was Jewish, big and good-looking but borderline boring; he drove a 1957 red-and-white Corvette with crossed flags on the fender and was a starting linebacker for the University of Missouri, even though he was only in his freshman year. His neck was the size of my upper thigh; his penis, on the other hand, was not so lucky as his neck. Mic Bowen played basketball, was a senior at Central, had red hair and freckles everywhere, talked as fast as his basketball hands moved, and drove an old Ford station wagon that used to belong to his uncle Oscar, who did something with dog food; the smell of Mic's sweet Canoe aftershave was forever mixed with the smell of horsemeat that permeated the Ford.

Nobody knew I wasn't a virgin except the two boys and if they'd told anybody, I hadn't heard. I was the quiet one, the strange one; I had never really fit in. Nobody knew much of anything about me, since I didn't talk to anybody about anything; I seemed to be from another time or space. I didn't care about makeup or clothes or movie stars, like the other girls did, I didn't care about dating or who was crazy about who, and the only thing I felt about not being a virgin was that it was a secret, something I had done that made me mysterious and exciting rather than plain. As for the sex part of it, well, if *that* was sex, then I didn't understand what the big deal was. It was much more exciting to ride in David Greenspan's Corvette with the top down than to make out with him, and Mic Bowen had been more nervous and fumbly than I was. Both times had been in the dark. The dark of Mr. and Mrs. Greenspan's finished "rec" room in their basement, on an itchy couch that smelled of mothballs, and the dark of Mr. and Mrs. Bowen's front hall, on the icy floor. Both times had been silent, so the mothers and fathers could not hear. Both times had been fast. But they had happened, and I knew. On the outside, I'm sure I was considered too boring to not be a virgin. Jenny Jaffe. Who? Oh, that one, the beige one over there.

The first time I ran into Will I thought he just happened to be in the Gregory Drug Store, five blocks from my house. I hadn't seen him for about three weeks. You'd think that by now it would be hard for me to remember—and not just the beginning of it, not just the first moments, but all of it, the whole of Will and me: words, looks, spaces, and especially the holy purity of how truly young we both were. But it isn't hard for me to remember, and the truth is, that's probably because I never stopped thinking about it at all.

He was standing by the cash register, his head buried in a magazine, one piece of hair falling over his eye.

"Oh, hi," I said, when I realized.

"Hi there."

"Is that it, Jenny?" Mr. Sealy said.

"Hmm?"

"Is that all you need today?"

"Oh, yeah. Thanks, Mr. Sealy."

Will stood next to me at the counter. "What did you get?"

"Oh. A lipstick."

"Yeah? What color?"

"Pink."

"Let's see."

Mr. Sealy rang the cash register and handed me the bag. Will took out the lipstick and looked at it. " 'Pixie Pink,' " he read. "Here, put it on. Let's see."

"Now?"

"Sure."

Mr. Sealy was watching us from behind the counter, his arms crossed at his stomach, his thumbs tucked under his belt.

"I don't have a mirror."

"It's okay—I'll be your mirror."

I laughed. I laughed because I thought I might disintegrate. Will was looking at me like I was a movie star, he was looking at me like I was at least three years older, he was looking at me like Mr. Sealy wasn't there.

"Go ahead," Will said.

I put the lipstick on, looking into Will's eyes, while Mr. Sealy watched us, his face scrunched up into a tight frown. Mr. Sealy knew my mother and father; Mr. Sealy knew everybody in the neighborhood; the only person Mr. Sealy didn't know was Will.

"A little up on the right . . . yeah, that's perfect. . . . Boy, Jenny, you sure have a sweet mouth."

"Uh . . ."

"So you want to get a soda or something?"

"Uh . . . sure."

He held the door open for me like I was a grown-up lady, the tiny bell tinkled on the door of the Gregory Drug Store, and I was standing with this stranger at Seventy-first and Holmes.

We sat at the counter at Friedson's Pharmacy. I got a Coke, he got a vanilla phosphate.

"So how did you know my name was Jenny?"

"The guy said it at the cash register, the Mr. Sealy guy with the one big eyebrow straight across. He said, 'Is that it, Jenny?'"

"Oh," I said, laughing. I could hear the laugh; it was strangely high-pitched, somewhere up in the hyena range.

"You look like a Jenny."

"I do?"

"Yeah, it's kind of romantic . . . it fits you."

"Why? Do I look romantic?"

"Well, you look beautiful, that's for sure."

He looked right at me when he said it. I took a sip of my Coca-Cola. It was a toss-up—I would either choke, and Coke would come shooting out of my nostrils, or I would fall off the stool.

"So I thought maybe we could go out sometime."

My heart did this little zwoop thing up against my rib cage. "Okay," I said. I didn't even think about it, I just said okay. This was not like me. Not at all.

"Okay? Good."

"What's your name? I mean besides Will."

"McDonald. William Cole McDonald, ma'am," he said, the way a reckless cowboy would say it to the schoolmarm as he gets off his horse.

"I never knew anybody named Cole."

"Me neither. I used to get razzed about it a lot when I was little."

"Why?"

"Well, Cole McDonald . . . as in 'Ol' McDonald,' you know. . . ."

"Oh, God, I didn't even think of that."

"Yeah, there was a lot of 'how's your farm' and 'E-I-E-I-O'-ing whenever I'd walk by."

"And 'chick-chick-here'ing and chick-chick-there'ing . . . ?"

"Yeah, but I put a stop to it. I beat the you-know-what out of everybody until they forgot how to 'E-I-O.'"

Before I knew it, it was dark out and we had been sitting at Friedson's counter for three hours and I was late for dinner and nobody knew where I was. In those lost three hours I had told William Cole McDonald practically everything there was to know about me. I had no idea why. I could just talk to him—it was as if I had been waiting sixteen years for him to show up, so I could pull the plug out of my mouth. How I really didn't have any close friends, how I really didn't fit in, how I wasn't like any of the others and I didn't know why but I never had been, and he listened, he sat there settled on that counter stool with such calmness, his eyes locked into mine, and the more he listened, the more I told him, all the intimate parts of me that had never come out. I even told him how much I wanted to be a dancer, how I wasn't quite sure how to go about it, how I knew I would get no help from my parents since they thought the whole thing was a joke, how I thought it might have been easier on me if I'd had some brothers and sisters to take my parents' exclusive attention off me. Will told me having brothers and sisters didn't help much. He told me he hated one of his brothers so much, the brother who had always been mean to him, that when he was nine years old he went after his brother and tried to cut his throat open with a knife. I tried not to sit there with my jaw dropped, I tried to look as if I heard things like this every day, but it was clear to me that my heart was beating faster after he told me. When I was nine years old I was still playing with my dollhouse, when Will was nine years old he was playing with a Buck knife.

I told him how I had always been a good girl; he told me how he had always been bad.

"I guess it all started when I was in the first grade."

I tucked my left leg under me and swiveled on my stool to face him, sure that in this pose I looked very confident, very "older," very Natalie Wood. "Really? What happened?"

"They sent me home."

"Why?" I took a sip of my Coke.

"Oh, I told the teacher she had a green pussy, and for some reason she didn't like that, so she sent me home."

I choked. Coke sprayed out of me.

He was amazing.

We were together nearly every afternoon after school. I would leave Southwest and take the bus to Sixty-ninth and Mission Road in Prairie Village to Miss Lala Palevsky's School of the Dance, and Will would pick me up there afterward and drive me home. At night I was in my room studying English or math or American history, but from five-fifteen to six-thirty when my mother thought I was on the bus, coming home from dancing school, I was with Will.

He was so different from me: everything about him was different, everything that had happened to him was different—it was as if he had come down from Mars. I had been coddled and treasured in a wraparound cocoon world; Will had been thrown into life like a leaf on the wind. His mother had died when he was only five years old, and from then on, in many ways, he had been on his own. Will was the only child of his mother and father, but his father had been married a couple of times before Will's mother, and he'd remarried after Will's mother, and there were kids from all those marriages, plus kids the wives brought with them from their other marriages, and at one point, he told me, there were fifteen kids besides him in the house, but Will said that even though there were lots of step and half brothers and sisters, he always felt alone. "We never lived in a house like you know it, Jenny," he said, "more like half-torn-down houses, more like shacks, or trailers, and once," he said, "we were even living in some tents strung alongside the road." And they were always moving to places I'd never heard of, places called South Fork and Kernville and Pacoima, which were all somewhere in California. And a lot of the time Will had been raised by his aunt.

"My old man kept sending me away to Cleo 'cause he said he couldn't do anything with me, said I was too ornery and mean."

His mother had died from a carbuncle. I'd never even heard the word "carbuncle." Will explained to me that it was a sore like a boil, something that had looked like a virtual nothing until the infection spread and killed her. I remember the set of his jaw when he said "killed her"; I didn't take my eyes off his face.

"There was no reason for her to die except there wasn't a doctor around—*he* didn't get her a doctor until it was too late."

He didn't say any more and I didn't move in the seat, I just watched him. How could his father not have gotten his mother a doctor? Whoever heard of people who were sick and didn't go to a doctor? People who wouldn't call a doctor? People like that didn't exist in my life—we had a list of doctors with their phone numbers next to every phone in our house. I didn't say anything, I just studied him while he drove, his hands on the steering wheel, his fingers, the shadow under his cheekbone, the wave in his hair.

"I don't get along with my mother."

He looked at me. "You mean regular mother-daughter stuff or more?"

I squashed the forkful of coconut cream pie and pushed it around the plate. "More, I think . . ." I looked up into his eyes. How could I explain it? Will had been gypped out of having a mother, and I had a mother who didn't like me. It was true; I'd learned to know it, and the older I got, the clearer it became: no matter what I did, I couldn't measure up to the fantasy of who Esther had thought she'd have for a daughter, one who looked like her and acted like her, one who wanted the same things. The fantasy daughter always won out in her heart, she was always much better than me.

"What?" he said.

"I don't know . . . she just wants me to be somebody else."

"Who?"

"Someone different from who I am, someone who doesn't have dreams, someone plain." I laughed. "I *am* plain, I don't mean that, I mean . . ."

He put his hand on mine; it was the first time he'd ever touched me. We were in a big red booth at Allen's drive-in on Sixty-third Street, having coffee and pie. Will loved pie. I take that back: he more than loved it. "Pie is mandatory, Jenny, didn't you know that?" It was a Friday afternoon and black as pitch out, the middle of a big, loud Missouri thunderstorm.

"You're not plain, Jenny, you're anything but plain."

"Hey, I know what I look like."

"No you don't."

His fingers were still touching mine. I didn't move. My mother had practically made a career out of telling me I wasn't pretty *enough*; it was hard to believe she could possibly be wrong.

"Anyway, my mother wants me to be like her, I guess, the kind of person who doesn't want to go anywhere or do anything. She wants me to just stay put and make do."

"Well, she's gonna end up in a world of hurt, then, isn't she?"

I laughed. "Why? Do you think I'll do things out of the ordinary, Will?"

"I think you are a force to be reckoned with, Jenny. I think you're going to do whatever you want to do."

"Oh, Will, you're so crazy; everybody thinks I'm a boring, dull nothing."

"Well, then, everybody'll be surprised but me."

He took his hand off mine. I stabbed the bite of pie with the fork and ate it. "Yeah," I said, tossing my ponytail. "Maybe they will."

A force to be reckoned with is not exactly how I would have described myself in those days—in those days I had about as much force as those wispy white things that you blow off dandelions in the spring—but Will said I was, so I began to believe it. I began to exhibit my "brave."

"No, you cannot invite him to eat with us on Rosh Hashanah."

"Why can't I?"

My mother put the lid back on the soup pot and turned to face me. "Because he's not Jewish, because he doesn't even know what Rosh Hashanah is, because you don't know him, and because I said so."

"*That's* mature."

"What? What did you say to me?"

"I said it wasn't very mature. I said what's the point of participating in a religious holy day if you can't share it with your friends if they're interested and want to learn? You think God would rather I just said to him, Oh, I'm sorry, no, Will, not you."

"What do you mean, he's interested?"

"We were talking about the Rosh Hashanah and Yom Kippur holidays and he was interested and I thought it would be nice to let him come and see."

"He's not Jewish."

"We know that, Mother."

"Why can't you bring home a Jewish boy?"

I didn't say anything.

"What is he?"

"Nothing."

"What does *that* mean nothing? What are his parents?"

"Nothing."

"You mean nobody ever went to church? What kind of people are 'nothing'? I don't understand."

"His father never went to church, his mother died when he was five years old—that's all I know."

She frowned. I stood there. She turned and walked to the sink.

"So can I invite him?"

She didn't say anything.

"Mom?"

"You don't even know who he is, and besides, we only have family on Rosh Hashanah. On Passover you can have a stranger, but not on Rosh Hashanah."

"What? Is that a rule? Did Moses bring that down from Sinai—no strangers on Rosh Hashanah or you'll get a burning bush in your living room?"

Her eyebrow went up. "I don't like this, Jenny."

"What?"

"The way you're talking to me all of a sudden. Is that what you're learning from this boy, this Will, is that what you're learning from him? How to be rude?"

"I'm not being rude. I'm asking you if I can please invite him to come have lunch with us after services on Rosh Hashanah."

She turned her back to me, took a carrot, and began to chop.

"Mom?"

"Why do you always have to make trouble for me? I don't understand."

"Does that mean I can't invite him?"

Her shoulders raised. "No, you can't. I said no, didn't I? Why do you make me say it again?"

Not exactly a force to be reckoned with, but at least I stayed in the kitchen. At least I asked and I didn't fade. I thought of a lot of other things to say, snotty, stand-up, gutsy things, but I wasn't quite brave enough for that yet. I was just beginning to be a force, a little-bitty dandelion force, but I thought I was on my way.

I didn't tell my friends too much about Will; they saw him when he picked me up after school, they saw him when he dropped me off somewhere, but that was about it. I tried to keep him separate. I didn't want to let them know how close we were, I didn't want to share him or what we had, and I didn't think they would have understood anyway. They would have thought that my falling for an unknown boy who had tattooed LETS FUCK on his toes, without an apostrophe, was as crazy as Angie Singleton's falling in love with the "fairy mary" guy in Chasnoff's beauty shop who put blond streaks in her mother's hair.

"I'm not a virgin, Will."

"That's okay; neither am I."

I'd spent days worrying about how I was going to tell him, and he made it so easy. I just said it and we were through. No questions, no anything. I don't know why it was so important for me to tell Will I wasn't a virgin. It wasn't as if he'd tried anything with me, it wasn't as if he'd even kissed me—he hadn't even made a move—but it fell under the category of telling Will everything; it was important for me to tell Will everything about me, and so I did. Happy, driving downtown in that wonderful old blue Mercury of his—Will loved that car the way I'd never seen anybody love a car; it was a 1950, but you would have thought it was a brand-new Cadillac. He was constantly tinkering with it, polishing it, he even called it "darlin'." I sat beside him with the radio on my lap—he'd gotten a new radio and hadn't put it in yet, and there were wires connected to the dashboard from the radio hanging over my knees, a far cry from David Greenspan's red-and-white Corvette with crossed flags and butter-leather interior—and that wasn't all: I was listening to country music on that radio and country music on the clock radio next to my bed, people I'd never heard of, like Bob Wills and Kitty Wells and Red Foley were replacing Johnny Mathis and Dion and the Belmonts and the Flamingos in my heart.

"Where are we going?"

"To eat Mexican food."

"Will, I've never had Mexican food; I don't think you can get Mexican food in Kansas City."

"Of course you can, Jenny; you just don't know where to go. And after we eat Mexican food I'm going to teach you how to play pool."

"Pool?"

"Sure, with those legs of yours, you'll be halfway 'cross the table when you go to make your shot." He laughed and looked at me. "Those legs of yours go all the way to Montana, girl."

There *was* Mexican food in Kansas City. And there were pool halls, where everything was brash but strangely quiet, dusty stripes of light through waves of cigarette smoke, the click of pool balls moving in the dim, the smell of felt in my nose when Will leaned me over a table and taught me how to line up a shot. And barbecue places where you ate off pink butcher paper and there was no silverware and only beer to drink; and rowdy bars with country bands where the people were loud and pushy, girls crushed together at a filthy mirror in a too little bathroom, wearing too much lipstick, too much Maybelline and too few clothes. Short skirts and thighs and cowboy boots, sweat and whiskey and cheap perfume, breasts rising out of blouses tied too tight at the waist. A land where everybody looked as if there was a one-sheet drawing of them at the post office, near where you stood in line to buy stamps. And me, I was the foreigner, the newcomer with the Pixie Pink lipstick and the scrubbed face and the ponytail, the novice who had immigrated from the land of the country clubs.

I turned seventeen between Thanksgiving and Christmas, on December 4. Esther and Mose decided I should have a la-di-da soiree, with the girls in cocktail dresses and the boys in suits and ties. I practically used up all the breath in my body fighting them, but they were determined to have this party.

"I think it would be more exciting if the boys came in cocktail dresses and the girls in suits and ties," Will said.

"It's not a big deal; just get a suit or a jacket somewhere."

"How 'bout I just don't go? Why don't I meet you after the shindig? I'll wait in the parking lot."

"Why can't you borrow a jacket from somebody?"

"Okay. How 'bout Joe?"

I fell over laughing. Joe owned Joe's, where Will worked on weekends making hash-brown potatoes and chicken-fried steak with gravy and chocolate sundaes as high as your nose. Joe was maybe five feet tall, if he stood up straight, and weighed about two hundred fifty pounds, all his weight in his midsection, like a squat, puffed fire hydrant with skinny arms and legs sticking out. Joe's tuxedo would have been like a postage stamp on Will. Will was six feet two and lean, with muscles in his arms and wide shoulders and strong, callused hands and a little butt and skinny legs that went farther than Montana, probably all the way to Nome, and heart-melting deep-blue eyes and the whitest, thickest blond hair, so white that when he'd grown a mustache he told me that if the damn thing didn't shape up he was going to have to darken it with eyebrow pencil because it was so pale. He also had cheekbones, the most amazing cheekbones I had ever seen, which was because he was part Indian on his mother's side, Shoshone Indian, and all together it probably would have been a lot for any girl, even one with more moxie than me, but for me it was everything. I was falling in love for the very first time and it was with William Cole McDonald and there was nothing I could do.

"We'll get you a jacket, Will, and not from Joe. I'll ask Mic Bowen or somebody. Please."

"It won't fit, Jenny, and neither will I. I don't belong."

"Please, Will, don't make me have a birthday without you."

"You won't like it, Jenny. It'll be trouble."

"Please, Will . . . for me."

"For you . . ."

"For me."

His eyes searched mine. "Okay, I'll be there."

"You promise? Really?"

"What'd I say?"

I kissed him. We were standing in the parking lot next to the Jones store. It was about five-fifteen and getting dark out and we had been walking to his car. It was the first kiss we'd ever had. Up until then we'd stayed away from each other; all our intimacy up until that kiss had been in our talking, our telling each other everything we'd never said out loud before. I kissed him and he drew his head back and looked at me, he looked at me for the longest time, and I don't think I breathed. The sky was navy blue behind him, and I remember the parking lot lights, white neon playing on the asphalt, and how my hair was wet against the back of my neck from dance class and my cheeks were hot and the air was cold and I felt so small, all five feet nine of me, and my heart was beating fast against my ribs and Will's arms went around me and he scooped me up and pressed me into him and held me hard and kissed me again and again, Will's lips on my face and my neck and my eyes, Will's mouth on mine.

I'm sure the party was beautiful, looked at through someone else's eyes—a cold, clear Saturday night in December, clumps of brilliant stars in a black sky, frost on the windshields, ice and salt crunching under your high heels as you walked up the slick steps of Oakbrook Country Club, a big fire in the hearth of the foyer, the smell of oak burning and pine needles and perfume, the sound of laughter and music, champagne in stem glasses, a buffet dinner, candlelight, a band, everything my father and the Jaffe, Shafton and Blackman accounting firm could more than pay for. But I saw everything differently—I saw a pretentious, showy display of affluence, a waste, a sham. I didn't want to be there, I would have been happier eating short ends with Will at Snead's BarBQ, his thumb blotting the sauce off my chin.

I wore a red Chantilly-lace sheath dress, silk heels dyed to match, and my grandmother's pearls. I wore my hair down and wild, though my mother had more than suggested it should be in a French twist. They had already started the buffet line, and my mother had asked me twice why I was watching the door. I didn't answer. She didn't know he was coming; I hadn't told anyone.

He wore a black tuxedo and an impeccably tailored white tux shirt and a black silk tux tie and golden studs and black evening shoes—he'd rented the whole thing and hadn't said one word. It was the first time I'd seen Will in anything but his jeans and cowboy boots, except for a uniform or an apron when he was working, and when I saw him in the doorway, I had to hold on to a chair. He walked across the room to me.

"God, Jenny, you're beautiful," he said, and my mother appeared next to me as if she were attached to my body by boomerang.

"Will, this is my mother. Mom, this is Will McDonald."

"I believe we've seen each other at the Texaco station," she said, her eyes glittering. The only thing missing was a hideous cackle and one of those grotesque flying monkeys the wicked witch had.

"That's right," I said, "and he also cooks at Joe's, but you wouldn't eat at Joe's, now would you, Mom?"

Touché, Witch, I said in my head and took Will's hand. She saw everything, didn't miss a trick.

"What school do you go to, Will? Not Southwest . . ."

"No, ma'am, I'm all done with school. I'm out in the big world on my own."

"I'm starving," I said. "Let's eat."

"It works for me," Will said. He put his hand on my waist and steered me away from the witch. "Evening, ma'am," he said to her over his shoulder. It was as if James Dean had risen from the dead.

The fight started after the birthday cake. It seems that David Greenspan had the misfortune of making a bad judgment call and saying something to someone about my breasts. The misfortune was that Will was within hearing distance. Will's fist came crashing out of nowhere, and the starting linebacker for the University of Missouri was down. David Greenspan's nose was semipermanently crumpled up and inappropriately stuck somewhere to the left of his eyebrow, and he was unconscious and spread-eagled across my mother's per-fectly planned sweet table, his backside smashing the individual slices

22

of seven-layer chocolate cake and his head bleeding into the silver tureen of whipped cream. He narrowly missed the *Happy Birthday, Jenny* sign in black and gold. I never found out exactly what David Greenspan had said; I only knew it was about my breasts because Sherry's boyfriend, Bob Feder, heard that much. Will wouldn't tell me anything; all I could get out of Will was, "I didn't like the way he looked at you." That was all it took.

And that's all it took for my mother too, and she, of course, convinced my father, who did whatever she told him, and the edict came down loud and clear the very next day: From now on, there would be *no more Will.*

But it was too late for me. As far as I was concerned, from then on there was *only Will.*

"God, Jenny, I love it." It was a soft black leather belt with a sterling-silver belt buckle on which I'd had his initials engraved. He ran his thumb over the silver, pushed the belt through the loops of his jeans, and hooked it. "God, Jenny," he said again, his voice low. "I'm throwing the old one away."

"Merry Christmas, Will."

We were standing in the middle of a crowd of people, where Wornall Road comes up from the Plaza, where it makes that little rise and crosses Ward Parkway. Everyone was waiting: they would pull a switch somewhere and it would be officially Christmas; every tower and every building edge in the radius of the elegant Plaza neighborhood would be outlined against the night in colored lights. From then until New Year's, every plane that took off or landed in Kansas City after dark would circle over the lights.

Will took a tiny box out of his jacket pocket. "Happy Hanukkah, Jenny," he said.

Blue-and-white paper and blue ribbon, the curlicue kind that you run along the blade of a scissors, and a card with a menorah and a dreidel and a printed message from Hallmark that said, "May the eight candles of Hanukkah glow in your heart throughout the year." The shaky handwriting underneath read, "For Jenny from Will."

"Is it right? I got the paper and everything from the Gregory Drug Store. I asked old Mr. Sealy to help me so I wouldn't get anything wrong."

"Oh, Will."

"Open it."

I fumbled with the paper and lifted the lid, and in the center of the cotton was an exquisitely fragile gold ankle bracelet, two delicate chains wound together, so feminine and so beautiful; it was the most beautiful thing I'd ever seen.

"See, it's just like us," he said, cradling the dainty lace ribbons of gold in his big hand. "See, two chains," and his fingers touched mine, "you and me," and he leaned forward and he kissed me so gently and the crowd went "Ooooh" and the Plaza lights flashed on.

He put the bracelet on my ankle later, closed the clasp and kissed my ankle, and we wound ourselves around each other like the golden chains. It was the first night Will and I made love.

How silly we are to believe we can ever get there, get what we want. The odds are always against us. What makes people keep trying is beyond me, or maybe people try only when they're young and they don't know what's out there; maybe they learn to give it up the more they know.

I can't tell you what it was about William Cole McDonald, except everything. What I can tell you is that from the night of my seventeenth birthday until they destroyed us, I spent every waking moment

I could with Will. It didn't matter what I had to do or say—I did it or said it. My mother never knew where I was. I used every friend I had to lie for me, used every trick in the book. She caught me repeatedly. She yelled, she screamed, she implored my father, she forbade. It didn't matter. As far as I was concerned, she could have stuck a knife in her eye; there was no way I was going to give up Will.

But who could know the true power of parents? What they will do when they are faced with defiance. To what depths they will stoop. Who would have thought that despite a love as bright and stunning and meant to be as ours was, they could still win?

Or is that jumping the gun in this saga? It's probably not fair to cheat you out of the details of the romance. The breath-stopping, bittersweet romance of me and my William Cole McDonald and his blue tattoo. All the details that would explain to you how he was my passion. My true and consuming and only, only passion in the whole goddamn long and lonely fifty-three years of my big-deal, glamorous, uptown life. Do you want to hear how Will made me feel pretty? Me, Jenny Jaffe— plain, a truly plain girl, a beige girl, a practically nondescript girl if you saw me then—pretty? Talk about your long shot, your impossibility, your first . . . but he looked at me and I was pretty. Or do you want to hear how Will thought I was smart? Or how Will thought what I had to say was important? Or how Will turned things around in my head so that I began to believe in myself? To feel confident? Be happy? Feel changed? Or do you want to hear everything? How Will's loving me changed everything about me and everything in my life?

"I love you, Jenny, I will always love you, you're my girl."

God, what I would give to hear that . . .

He was everything to me and I gave him everything, everything I could. Nothing was sacred; no thought I had, no feeling, no part of me, body or mind, nothing I could do, was too intimate or wrong or frightened me in any way. We shared everything in the light. We were fierce with each other, intense and greedy, but I was the greediest. I was ravenous with him, I was a hussy—that's what he called me, and I was. I wanted to be, I wanted to do everything, I wanted to know what it felt like, I wanted to feel everything I could. I was seventeen and I was a hundred. I was a woman for the first time, just the emergence of a woman, the inaugural smatterings and smells of what it could be like to be a woman, and I was heady to think I could.

"Okay . . . okay . . ." He took a ragged breath. "That's it."

Laughing, looking down at him, straddling him, riding him, wet with sweat.

"What?"

"That's it, it's broke, it's finished—"

"No, no, I'll fix it—"

I slide off and take his cock in my mouth, the come of the two of us thick perfume in my face.

"It's no use, Jen, you broke it."

"Hey, don't tell me my job, mister."

I suck him.

"I'll be goddamned," he groans as he's hard again.

"Oh, shut up, Will," says Jenny the hussy, and I laugh until I'm filled.

Everything. We did everything. Things I'd only heard about, we did. And I said things. I mean words, words and phrases, things a lady would never say, came flying happily right out of my mouth. They couldn't be stopped; it would have been like trying to stop vomit. It was probably because I meant them that they came out of me with such strength.

"Eat my pussy, Will. Please."

Looking right at him. Eyes wide. Brazen. Defiant. I was someone else. Or—I take that back—I was just me, but I didn't know me, it was me for the first time.

"Wait right here."

He'd pulled off the road into the middle of a cornfield, what had once been a cornfield but had been mowed down by a Midwest winter, smashed-down stalks that went on forever, a brown field under a vast gray sky. It would have never occurred to me to pull off the road and park in somebody's cornfield, but that was Will. He got out and opened the door for me, held out his hand. He took a bag out of the trunk and walked away from me across the dirt.

"This is probably somebody's field, Will."

"Stay right where you are, Slim."

I leaned back against the Mercury and watched his stride across the broken tufts of amber, watched how his boots kicked up turf. When he got pretty far away from me he opened the bag, took out what looked to be cans and bottles, and set them up in a haphazard zigzag. I pulled my coat closer around me and jammed my hands in my pockets. The sky was moving fast and the wind was icy; any minute it was going to snow.

"What?" I said as he walked back and passed me, but he didn't answer, just touched my cheek with his hand and squatted beside the car. He lay down on the dirt and pulled himself under the Mercury.

"Will?"

"Yeah?"

"What are we doing here?"

"Just a minute, I can't hear you."

He was banging on something underneath the car, and then he slid out and stood behind me. He put his arms around me and pulled me to him, my back against the front of him; he buried his face in the side of my neck.

"What's the matter with the car?" I said.

"Nothing."

"Why did you put that stuff across the field?"

I could feel him through his blue jeans, hard and big against the back of my skirt.

"Will . . . ," I said, laughing, and he put his hand on my leg, the side of my left leg, and then around to the front of it, his hand up and under my plaid wool pleated skirt, the cold air hitting my skin. Kissing my neck and his fingers barely grazing my leg and then the crotch of my panties, just barely, hardly touching but still touching, his fingers brushing so lightly against the cotton that I staggered, but he held me and I tried to turn to face him but I couldn't move, he had me pinned there.

"Will, we're in the middle of a cornfield."

"Yep."

"What if somebody comes?"

"Only you're gonna come, my Jenny."

Will's breath in my hair and his lips on my ear, and his fingers moved aside the elastic of my panties, pulled it away from my flesh ever so slightly—I could feel the cold air, his mouth on my neck, his cock arched hard up against my butt—and then he brushed me with his searching fingers, gently brushed at me, and I was hot and wet under his fingers and my mouth opened and my eyes closed and he caressed me so lightly my legs trembled, and then he stroked faster and I didn't care that I was in a cornfield, I didn't care where I was. I took a step and I spread my legs open, I actually took a step and felt myself open and

Will's fingers were in me, oh, they were up in me, deep up and in me, high up in me, I was so wet and open and his thumb was touching, rubbing that little nub of me like velvet, and his fingers were sliding in and out and faster and sliding and harder and I slumped back against him, I thought I was syrup, I thought I would fall.

"Oh, Will . . ."

"It's okay, Jenny."

"Will . . ."

"Come on, my little sweetheart . . ."

I tried to reach my right hand behind me, to reach his cock, to get it out of his jeans, but he wouldn't let me. My fingers were empty, stretched out in the air.

"Let it go, Jenny."

"Oh, Will . . ."

"Let it go, my baby," he crooned. "I got you."

And I felt myself coming from farther away than the length of the cornfield, there was nothing but the sound of me coming, and Will held my stretched-out stiff fingers, laced his own fingers through them, and put the gun in my hand.

"My God." I was having trouble getting my breath, I was having trouble standing, I was shaking, he had to hold on to me. I looked at the gun in my hands. I had never seen a gun except on television, and there was a gun in my hands, a cold hard steel gun cradled in my fingers. I looked up at Will, and he was smiling.

"It's okay, baby, it's nothing," and he leaned down and kissed the tip of my nose ever so gently. "Come on, my little sweetheart, I'm gonna teach you to shoot before it snows."

• • •

I looked at myself in the mirror, I studied this new Jenny who could play pool and make love and shoot beer cans, stand in a cornfield, her legs wide, her feet planted solid, the wind whipping her hair back across her face, and the sound and the feel as a bullet pinged and the smell and the taste of the powder and the heat and the heft of the steel made her heart beat fast and the inside of her head roar as she blew beer bottles into smithereens. I looked at this naked Jenny. She looked familiar, but I didn't know her. Where was Miss Plain and Ordinary, where was Mose and Esther's beige daughter, the quiet one who had nothing to say? Who was this lanky girl with flushed cheeks and a blue mark that Will's lips had left at the base of her throat? A girl who knew what a .32 felt like slipped into the waistband of her pleated wool skirt, pressed hard against the small of her back. A girl who knew how to slide under a Mercury, the dirt and the weeds sticking into the flesh of the back of her legs as she learned how to hide a gun in a metal box that was welded to the frame of a car. A girl who'd walked through her mother's house smiling, with a bullet tucked tight in her fist. I looked at this naked Jenny with her wide eyes and I thought, Who is she? Is she the real me? And my mother yelled loud and clear from downstairs, "Jennifer, we leave for the club for dinner in ten minutes. You had better be dressed."

Showers.

Combing my hair in his shower.

Standing five inches taller, front-to-front with me, pulling a small black plastic Ace pocket comb through my thick, dark curls. Meticulously combing both sides and then tackling the bad place in the back at the top of my head where it always got so knotted, combing my hair as if I were five years old. Standing on my tiptoes gazing up at him in that skinny bathtub with the plastic curtain. Water dripping off my nose. He kisses my eyelids. Soap and shampoo. Steam. I spit toothpaste on his chest, right on the beloved blue stenciled eagle.

"Hey. What is that, Slim?"

"Oh, the eagle came."

Laughing. "Oh, he did, did he? I'm gonna paddle you."

"That's if you catch me."

"Hey, Jen, I already caught you."

He moves the soap across my breasts and my belly to my backside while he steadies me with his other hand. "Turn around, Punkin, I'll wash your back."

He had caught me, all right.

He had a list of names for me: Jen, J, Slim, Punkin; honey, child, kid, squirt, baby, sweetheart, little sweetheart; plus two Indian names: White Feather and Red Wing, depending on his mood. And then he got me my first cowboy boots and I never wanted to take them off and he called me Boots.

We were two but one, we never wanted to be with anybody else and we never wanted to be apart. Sometimes I even went to work with him. I'd sit at the Texaco pretending to read a movie magazine, but I'd really be studying Will's skinny legs and boots coming out from underneath a car while he did something to it with the hood up. I'd sit there and watch those blue jeans and cowboy boots, and this thing would come over me, this invisible happy net would just stick itself onto me the way chocolate sticks to an upside-down Dairy Queen. Or I'd follow him down aisle after aisle of auto supply stores as he read the labels on things he wanted for the Mercury, his fingers reaching behind him to grab hold of my hand. Or I'd sit at Joe's and drink vanilla Cokes and watch him flip a Denver omelet and catch it in the fry pan behind his back, my heart floating like the puffy yellow egg over his shoulder through the air.

"Did you see that? How was that, huh? You had no idea, did you, that I came from a long line of famous cooks."

Will smiling, Will laughing. Everything he did was important to me, and everything I did was important to him. . . .

Will watching me from across the room as I danced for him, I actually danced for him: he was the only one. He'd sit on the edge of the bed in his rented room, a serious look on his face, and watch my every move. Then he'd towel the sweat off me and tell me things until I could breathe.

"Someday I'm gonna build you a house, Jen, a big Victorian house with columns and lots of curlicues—"

"—and a porch."

"Of course. A porch that goes all the way around and you can dance on the porch and all through the house—"

"—in the middle of our land."

"That's right, in the middle of our land. . . . You were flying— nobody can dance like you, baby—I saw you fly. We're gonna go to New York, I'll take you, we'll go to wherever you need to go, and they'll discover you and then you'll dance for everybody—for the President, for kings and queens. You're gonna be a big star, my Jenny."

"I am?" I said, laughing, my breath ragged.

"You am," Will would say to me.

He believed it, he believed that I could go to New York or Paris or wherever it was dancers went to be discovered, and they would discover me. To Will, my dream wasn't silly; it was within my reach. He was the only person who believed in my dream, the only person who believed in me.

"It's enough already, you and this boy."

"Mom."

"You think he's the one for you because you haven't had anyone else and I know that you're seeing him, no matter how many times you tell me you're at Sherry's or wherever else you say. You're not fooling me; I know."

"I have to go."

I should have known there was a reason she was up so early. My mother never got up before I went to school; I had made my own breakfast from the time I could reach the cornflakes bowl, my mother stayed upstairs in her bed.

"Your father thinks you're not seeing him, but I know."

Her *g*'s all had a soft *k* sound, her accent still surrounding the words, a lilt of German, which is where her parents were born and the first language she spoke. German, English, Yiddish, and French— my mother spoke all those languages; she could be displeased with me in any of the four.

"I have to be at school."

She lowered her cup. "You're mixed up with that boy because you haven't had anyone else."

I was pressing my books against my chest, trying to keep myself from flying out of the room. "I'm going to be late."

"I don't care; you'll tell them you had a family matter. I'll write you a note."

I slumped back against the kitchen sink and looked at her. I found it shocking that my mother could be beautiful. Darker than me, her eyes, her hair; smaller than me, her bones, her frame, precise and fine and delicate; beautiful, that was the word, the beautiful Jewess Esther Jaffe. And her daughter, Jennifer, the ugly duckling, sticking up in the back. My height came from my father, also his flyaway wispy curls, his pale-brown eyes, his freckles, his gangly limbs, the shape of his face, his broad hands, his feet; if I'd inherited anything from my mother, I hadn't figured out what it was.

"You have plenty of time; you'll come into your own."

"What does that mean?"

I knew what it meant; it meant I wasn't pretty.

"It means you'll find someone who appreciates you for what you are."

We watched each other.

"There are lots of nice boys out there, nice boys from good families. You'll meet them when you go away to school."

"I don't want to go away to school, you know that."

"I'm not discussing that now. I'm discussing you and this boy."

I would definitely have a bruise across my tailbone, that's how hard I was pushing back against the sink. "He has a name."

She moved her lips but didn't say anything.

"Will," I said clearly, across her kitchen.

"It's a mistake, Jennifer. You're all mixed up with that boy because you're young and you don't know any better and I'm trying to make you understand."

"Why is it a mistake?"

"Because he's not for you."

"Because he's not Jewish?"

"Because he's not anything; he's . . . not for you, that's all."

"Why?"

"Because life has better."

"How can you say that? You don't even know him."

She tilted her head slightly to the right, her chin raised; the winter sun from the window touched her slippers at the toes.

"I know him, all right."

"No you don't. How can you say he's not for me if you don't know him?"

She didn't answer.

"Do you want to know him? Do you want him to come to dinner?"

Nothing.

"Mom?"

"I don't need to know him. He's a mistake, that's what I know."

Such confidence in my choice, such belief in who I was and what I'd picked for myself.

"I have to go."

"I'm telling you, Jennifer."

"I have to go."

I went to school, but I didn't really talk to anyone. I went to dance class and exhausted myself, and I saw Will. That was my new life. In between I lied to my mother about where I was. That's all I did.

"Why do you love me, Mr. McDonald?"

"Because you're my fantasy, Jenny, you're my lady, you're everything I always wanted, everything I thought I'd never get. You're just . . . my fantasy."

"Oh, Will . . ."

Me being somebody's fantasy. Hard to imagine, hard to believe unless you saw him, saw his face when he said it, saw his eyes when he looked at me, the *way* he looked at me, the way he saw me. Nobody ever saw me like Will. He said I was important, he said I was the first person in his life that he could count.

"What do you mean?"

"Because I don't trust people, Jenny. People turn on you."

"No, not all people; friends don't."

"I don't have friends. People say they're friends, but they only use each other. I don't need any friends."

"What about family?"

"Family are the worst."

"Will . . ."

"Hey, what'd I say?" His jaw set. "There's only you; Jenny—that's all I need, just you."

It's easy to say that I was too young, that I was inexperienced—what did I know? It's easy to say it was a first love and first loves never last, everybody knows that, they cough and fizzle and burn out and leave you with your guts spewed all over the floor. It's easy to say we never would have made it, that Will was wrong for me, that the sparkle would have dulled and dried up and I would have looked at him five or ten years after my seventeenth year and said, Holy cow, Chihuahua, what have I done? Easy to say, oh, so easy. But wrong. I have lived a lot of my life now. I am fifty-three years old now. I've had, maybe, most of what there is to have, and I know. It is silly to say who is right for you, because there's no way to figure it—it's the one who takes your heart away. There was never anyone for me but William Cole McDonald, no matter how many years I have spent being married to someone else, trying to love someone else, no matter what happened, the why, the how, of any of it. Will was the one for me—he bent my heartstrings and he stirred my soul.

January, February, March . . . New Year's Eve and Valentine's Day and Saint Patrick's . . .

April, May, June . . . April Fool's Day and May Day and graduation . . .

Ah, but June was so much more than graduation—how could I possibly describe June? What a shame that there's no word for the onset of the battle, the beginning of the war.

January . . .

"But why would you want to rob someone?"

"What?" His head is under the covers. It's very cold in his room and very loud—three portable gas heaters are blasting at once, but they don't seem to be doing much heating, they're just making a chorus of noise.

"I said why would you want to rob someone?"

"Mmm?"

"Will, come out from under there."

One blue eye, one cheekbone. "Huh? What?"

"Tell me."

"Squirt, excuse me, you want to talk about this now?" I move my fingers through the hair that's fallen across his forehead. "Uh huh."

"But I was about to get very busy."

"Tell me."

"I thought you wanted me to keep you warm."

"Tell me."

"What?"

"What I asked you."

He props his chin up on one hand; his elbow pokes into the mattress and makes a dent in the sheet as he looks at me. "It was never about someone, robbing *someone*, Jenny. It was more about . . . the doing of it because it could be done."

"The danger?"

"Well, maybe"—he shrugs—"but I never thought of that. I guess I never thought of anything. I just did what I did."

"And they caught you."

Then his head is back against the pillow and he closes his eyes. His finger trails the side of my thigh, his toes push against the top of my foot. I lean over him and kiss the blue eagle; he smiles at me, his eyes closed.

"And they caught you," I say again.

He kisses my shoulder as my right breast grazes his chest; he moves his hand to my breast, rubs his thumb across my nipple, and I'm wet. My heart lurches. He moves his hand slowly across my backside. I kiss the bone of his jaw, the light stubble across his cheekbones, his mustache. I inhale.

"And they caught you, Will," I say again.

He kisses my mouth and lifts me up and onto him with both hands. His cock is hard and solid and big under my pelvis. I ache, I want him so inside me.

"Twice," he says, looking at me.

I move my fingers across his chest.

"And what did they do with you?"

"They put me in jail, Boots."

"I can't believe it; it's so hard for me to believe it."

"Well, it's true."

I stare at him. His fingers are like velvet between my thighs. I can hear only the heaters and my heart beating—it's like an ocean inside my head.

"Will . . ."

"What?"

"Tell me."

"What?"

"Everything. I want to know everything."

I'm so wet beneath his hand. My hair slides along his chest as I lean over him, and we stare at each other as he moves up and makes his way inside me; we stare at each other as we each feel it, my breath catching as he makes his way deep inside. "You want to know *now?*" Will says as he dips his head to catch my breast in his mouth, but then he fills me and I can't say anything, I can only moan.

• • •

He told me everything. What he stole, how he stole it, how they caught him, and how he felt. He told me in painstaking detail because I asked him, because I wanted to know. Both times, he was sent away for armed robbery. For armed robbery they can send you to a prison for five years or for as long as they want. I sat there as naive as a new baby, biting my lip and glassy-eyed, hearing Will say words to me as if he were talking in a foreign language, words and phrases that I'd heard only in the movies, like "five to life."

The first time, he was fifteen years old and it was a liquor store; he stole one hundred seventeen dollars and fifty-three cents—he was specific about the money down to the last penny. I remember the look in his eyes, the irony, that you could steal only one hundred seventeen dollars and fifty-three cents and be sent away for eighteen months.

The second time, he was seventeen years old and it was a grocery store; he stole twelve hundred dollars and change, and he got sent away for "five to life."

He only had to serve three years, but eleven months into those three years they pronounced him incorrigible and they removed him from the vocational institution where he was serving, since he was still a minor and technically a ward of the state, and they sent him to a real prison. They deemed him incorrigible and sent him to a real prison because he had nearly killed a man named Newton Breen.

"We were up on this moving pile of dry wood as it made its way to the kiln, and I guess he thought it would be a cute trick to knock me off. He drop-kicked me from behind, and I fell a story and a half. I just sunk out of sight, honey, like that poor, dumb Wile E. Coyote in a Road Runner cartoon, and landed with my leg cracked under me like a toothpick that's been snapped into thirds. I spent three months in the hospital, layin' on my back with my leg in the air, and then they gave me two operations, stuck a handful of pins in me, and wiped their hands, said I'd always limp, that was the best they could do. The day they let me out of the hospital, I went to find Newt to make sure he knew I wasn't dead from the fall."

It seems Will beat Mr. Breen into a coma. It didn't matter that Mr. Breen had tried to kill Will first by throwing him out into the air to plummet over fifteen feet and crash into a cement yard with his leg broken under him; nobody cared. They deemed Will incorrigible and sent him to San Quentin. He served the rest of his three years there and was released on parole.

It was in the vocational institution that Will carved the letters LETS FUCK, with no apostrophe, in blue ink into his toes, but it was in San Quentin that Will grew up; whatever Will saw and felt on the spacious and lovely grounds of stunning San Quentin is what made him give up his robbing career.

"I will never be in a jail again, Jenny. I will never do anything that would put me in a situation where I'd have to go."

It had nothing to do with me that Will had determination, that Will had high hopes and believed that he had turned himself around. and could do anything. Will had faith in himself because of what had happened to him in his own life, it had nothing to do with me.

February . . .

"But what are you *doing* with him?" Linda said.

"Huh?"

"Well, you're certainly not going to *marry* him; he's not the kind of a person you could be married to . . . not that any of us are going to get married until we finish school . . ." And then she looked at me intensely. "Wait a minute—have you done it? Is that what this is all about? Have you gone all the way?"

"Linda!" Sherry gasped, and then stared at me. "She doesn't mean that!"

"I'm not a virgin, if that's what you're asking," I said.

"Oh, my God! You're kidding!" Sherry said.

I looked at Linda hard. "And neither are you."

"Oh, my God!" Sherry said. "She's not?" Her head swiveled to Linda. "You're not?"

"No," Linda said quietly.

"Oh, my God!"

Linda made three wet rings on the table with her water glass. "You better be careful, Jenny. At least I'm pinned to Alan, and we'll be engaged this summer and married when he finishes law school. You certainly don't want to end up with somebody with no future, do you? With somebody who works in a gas station, after all?" She laughed and ran her fingers through the bottom curl of her perfect pageboy, making sure each beige silk hair was tucked into the curve. "Really, how would you raise your children? And where? In an apartment above the Texaco?"

"I can't believe you guys!" Sherry said. "Am I the only one who's still a virgin?"

The waitress stood in front of us, her face flushed. She moved the hamburgers off the tray. "Okay, let's see, here—who had the vanilla Coke?"

"Me," Sherry said.

"And one cherry-limeade, no ice," she mumbled, "and a frosty malt . . . is that it?"

"Yeah, thank you."

Maybe it would be over now, maybe they would forget what we were talking about. I busied myself taking the paper off my hamburger.

"God, I was starving," Sherry said. "I thought I'd fall over in a faint."

"Me too," I said, and smiled at Sherry.

Linda took a bite of her double. "He's certainly not right for you—he's not exactly somebody who fits in."

"Could we just change the subject?"

"Linda, she doesn't want to talk about it," Sherry said.

"Because you know I'm right, huh?"

I shrugged. "Okay, I give up."

"He doesn't fit in."

"To what?"

"To our crowd, with us . . . you *know* what I mean."

"He doesn't?"

She raised her eyebrow. "Jenny, you're being *awfully* verbose."

"No I'm not. Verbose means wordy."

"It does?" Sherry said. "I always get verbose mixed up with obtuse—what does obtuse mean?"

"*Sherry,*" Linda said.

"What?"

I laughed. "Obtuse means dull, Sherry."

Sherry looked at Linda. "Well, then I don't get it. She's not being dull."

"Whatever the damn word is," Linda said, putting down her double and picking up a french fry. "You don't want to talk about him, you don't want to tell us. . . . Evasive, that's the word, you're being evasive."

"I'm not being evasive."

"Yes you are. Why are you spending so much time with him? It's not that I don't think he's good-looking and all, but why are you seeing *only him*? Because you—"

I spoke very clearly when I interrupted. "Because I love him."

42

"Oh, my God," Sherry said, dropping an onion ring. "You're kidding. You do?"

"You're making a big mistake," Linda said.

"Oh, my God," Sherry said. "I can't believe this."

I chewed my hamburger. I never should have said I loved him, I never should have said anything, I shouldn't even have gone to lunch with them, but there was a certain part of everything that was happening to me that was strangely lonely, and even though I didn't want to talk to them or even be with them, there was still an undeniable part of me that missed being what I had been. I'd just forgotten about Linda, how she was like a mosquito bite that wouldn't stop itching; she was never going to let this go. I wiped the corners of my mouth with a napkin, shook a lot of salt on the french fries, and made a small mountain of catsup on the side of the plate. I held the catsup bottle and thought about smashing it in the middle of the table. I wanted to call Will to come and get me; I wanted to go home and cry.

"Does *he* love *you?*" Sherry asked quietly, her eyes wide. She had a tiny mustard spot in that little dip between the bottom of your nose and your upper lip.

"Do you think we could just talk about something else?"

"I'm sorry."

I felt bad; it wasn't Sherry I was mad at.

"I don't know, Sherry. I think he does."

Linda shook her head. "You're being a jerk, Jenny. You're certainly not going to marry him, you're certainly not going to end up with someone like *that.*"

"You don't know anything about him."

"I don't have to; it's clear."

"What's clear?"

Linda didn't say anything.

43

"Yeah, what's clear?" Sherry said.

Linda glared at Sherry. "That he's not right for her, that he's not . . . I don't know . . . appropriate."

I laughed. It was clear she was searching and I had the upper hand. "You sound like your mother."

"Didn't he get into a big fight Friday night at the Leawood? Didn't he beat up some guy until he nearly died?"

I didn't know they knew about this. I took a sip of my limeade.

"Didn't he?"

"The guy had it coming."

"My God, Jenny, listen to you. Is that who you want to be with? Someone who hits people?"

"He didn't nearly die."

"I can't believe this."

"Hey, he cut Will off as we were turning into the driveway; he practically made us crash the Merc."

Sherry was staring. "What Merc?"

Linda went on: "Alan said Will beat on the guy until a bunch of guys had to pull him off him, till the guy was practically unconscious."

I didn't answer.

"Didn't he?" She waited.

"The guy didn't nearly die. I was there, I saw it."

"Is this your new life? You hang out with people who get in fist-fights and beat people up? He's crazy, Jenny. You'd better stay away from him."

"He's not crazy."

"Really, I'm sick of you acting like you don't know what I'm talking about. You know what I'm saying—Will's beneath you. You think you're in love with him? You honestly think that you can live happily ever after with somebody like that? Will's white trash, Jenny, and you know it; you'll spend the rest of your life living in a trailer park."

It was the first time I ever left Winstead's with half a cheeseburger still on my plate, and it was the first time I took the bus since we all got our driver's licenses, but I refused to get in Linda's car no matter how much Sherry begged me; I held fast to the bus-stop pole in spite of the fact that it was sleeting and freezing, and it was the last time I ever spoke to Linda Lubin in my life. Which, in retrospect, more than made up for leaving half a cheeseburger on my plate.

White trash. The same boy who said that at night we were never really separated, that if I looked at the moon from my bedroom window at the same time he looked at the moon from his bedroom window, then we were never apart. The same boy who kissed my eyelids, who watched my every move, who grinned as soon as he saw me, who was worried whenever I drove anywhere without him, made me call him so he'd know that I got there, made me call him again as soon as I got home, who was upset that I'd taken the bus home that day in such bad weather. "I don't want you slidin' around on the ice in some bus, Jenny. You're in trouble, you call me; I'll come get you wherever you are." The same boy who said he loved me so much that sometimes, when he looked at me, he was so happy his heart hurt. White trash.

And if that was white trash, what were we, then? Kansas City's finest petite bourgeoisie . . . the Jewish crème de la crème?

What was it Will said about friends? That they could turn on you? Oh, no—that was family, wasn't it? Or *was* it friends? It didn't matter; I didn't need any of it, and I'd never really had either of them anyway, so it wouldn't be such a great loss. Besides, why would I need anybody else now that I had Will? He was my friends and my family. I didn't need anybody if I had Will.

And March . . .

I put the receiver back and pushed open the folding door of the phone booth; the wind slammed it shut behind me as I walked away.

"What?" Will said, leaning against the Mercury. He had his collar up and his hands in his pockets.

"She's called Sherry's twice. Sherry's hysterical; she says she'll never do this for me again, that it's the last time. She said she had to make up this big cockeyed story because her mother was standing right next to her when my mother called; she told my mother that I went over to Mary Lou's house and she didn't go with me because she didn't feel well, and now Sherry's mother won't let her go *anywhere* because she thinks Sherry's coming down with the flu."

We both laughed.

"Poor Sherry," Will said. "I better take you back, Slim."

I pushed myself into him, burrowed my body into the front of his shirt. He took his hands out of his pockets, put his arms around me, and looked down.

"You know you're awful cute?"

"I don't want to go back."

"You don't, huh?"

"Uh uh."

He looked down at me, pushed back a piece of hair that was blowing across my nose.

"I love you, Jenny," Will said.

The first time. We were on the corner of Wornall Road and Seventy-fifth Street, at five-fifteen on the evening of Saint Patrick's Day, in front of the phone booth outside Jasper's restaurant. All of

Kansas City was drinking green beer, and Will held me and leaned against his Mercury and told me he loved me for the first time.

Ten o'clock. I was supposed to be home by eleven, and it was already a few minutes after ten.

"You think you got yourself a hot set of wheels there?"

Will was leaning out the window, yelling at the guy next to us, the guy who'd come out of no place, suddenly racing his engine next to us, moving his car back and forth as we sat idled at the red light, the guy who'd said something to Will under the roar of the motors, something I couldn't hear.

"Will . . . ," I said, but he didn't look at me.

"Huh?" Will yelled out the window. "You think that piece-a-shit Plymouth you got can make it to a Hundred Fifteenth?"

We'd just been driving, going for a beautiful drive in all the darkness, we were someplace way out in Kansas, farther west than Quivera, someplace I'd never been before, where it was all dark and deserted and there were no houses and no streetlights, just this skinny little moon way up high in the blackness and a sprinkle of stars. Will said it was a hawk moon.

"How do you know that?"

"I know lots of things that you don't know."

"You do?"

"Sure. Don't I know how pretty you are?"

I was sitting right next to him and he was holding my hand, rubbing his thumb against my fingers the way he liked to do, and I had my head on his chest. I looked up at him and moved my head under his chin, and he bent and kissed my forehead.

"I'm not pretty, Will."

"See? What'd I tell you? Look how much I know."

One minute he was telling me about a hawk moon, and then there was this guy, and then they were both screaming and Will wasn't holding my hand.

The guy yelled, "This Plymouth can make it all the way to Topeka, boy, and leave that shitass Mercury a yours in a pile of dust." He was smiling.

"Well, you're one ugly motherfucker," Will yelled, "and I got twenty bucks that says I can make you even uglier."

My fingers were holding the edge of the seat so hard. "Will."

"Shut up, Jenny."

Cold, stone cold, like he didn't know me.

Both cars skidded across 120th and turned onto a dirt road. Will slid to a stop and jumped out of the car, leaving the door open, pulled a twenty-dollar bill out of his pocket, and laid it on the hood of the Mercury. The guy was still smiling when he got out of the Plymouth, smiling and fat, with big arms; he was about the same height as Will.

"Will?"

"Shut your fucking mouth, Jenny."

"Yeah, shut your fucking mouth, little Jenny," the guy said, and Will went down. I didn't even see the guy hit him, but I heard it, a fist punching Will's face, and he was sprawled back against the grille of the Mercury, and then he hit Will two more times and I heard that sound too. I had my arms crossed in front of me and my fingers clenched flat over my teeth, and Will was just lying there and I thought maybe it was over, I couldn't get my breath, please let it be over, please make this all go away, and I put one foot out of the car and onto the ground.

Will raised up off the hood like he was a tornado and shot out at the guy, his fist across the night in the headlights, and the guy made a kind of *houphf* sound and staggered back and slid on the mud and went down. Then nothing happened. Both of them stayed there. All you could hear were crickets and both of them breathing hard.

"Okay?" Will said. "Enough?"

And the guy got to his feet and hiked his pants up like it was okay, like he thought it was enough too, it should be over and they should both go home. He took a couple of steps and shook his head like he was clearing it, and then he flew across the dirt and into Will like a bulldozer and Will went down. He was on his hands and knees and he was bleeding from somewhere, and I took a step forward, and the guy kicked Will underneath him, got the toe of his boot somewhere underneath him and kicked Will somewhere inside his rib cage, kicked him three times really hard—I could hear the sound—until Will couldn't stay upright. His knees buckled out from under him and his arms spread, and he was flat on the ground and he just lay there and it was quiet, but I knew I had screamed.

The guy pushed his hair back with both his hands, wiped at his nose and hiked his pants up, he took the twenty off the hood of the Mercury and tucked it into the pocket of his pants, wiped his nose again, and looked at me.

I was frozen against the open door of the Mercury.

"You wanna go with me, little lady?"

I didn't move. The guy laughed and took a step closer to where I was standing. I heard a low sound that I knew had come out of Will.

"Huh? Whatcha say there? What's your name? Jenny? You wanna go with me?"

I took another little step backward and grabbed the door handle.

"Hey, it's okay," he said. All I could see was that smile. I was so afraid.

"You touch her and I'll kill you," Will said.

He was up, I don't know how he got up, he was staggering, but he was on his feet, and suddenly all I could think of was that there was a gun in a box under the car. The guy took another step forward and I took another step backward and my rear slid along the edge of the car seat and the guy lunged for me as Will hit him and I slammed the big door of the Mercury as hard as I could and it closed on the guy's hand.

I was crying and Will was holding on to me and I was wiping his blood.

"I didn't want him to see you. . . . I didn't want him to know you were there. . . ." He was choking; his shirt was soaked with blood.

"It's my goddamn temper. I wouldn't let anything happen to you, you know I wouldn't, Jenny, my God—" And he was rasping, because something wasn't right in his rib cage; he had a hand to his chest.

"I love you so much, Jenny. I'm so sorry. . . ."

And I pulled his shirt off and he was kissing me and then my breasts were red from Will's blood and then I was bent over the fender of the Mercury like bending over the felt of the pool table. I couldn't get him close enough, couldn't get him deep enough, I wanted to feel him so hard, so deep inside me, that it hurt, I wanted him to ram me until I screamed, and then I was straddling him and my backbone was crashing into the steering wheel and my knees were smashed into the upholstery and I came and my eyes were open and Will came and his eyes were open and he was looking at me all the way to my soul.

And then I was laughing. I was crying but I was laughing, and somehow it didn't matter, not any of it. I didn't even know what had happened or who I was anymore, but it didn't matter. I guess I said goodbye to the rest of my life then—whoever I'd been before had disappeared, there was only this new Jenny, who belonged to Will, and we seemed so far beyond anything else now, there was no getting back, everything before now was gone.

And April . . .

"Did it snow in any of those places you lived in?" I whisper into the wool collar of Will's coat. Neither of us has spoken for at least twenty minutes.

It's too beautiful to speak out loud; the hush covers everything, like the twelve inches of new snow. It's too late to be snowing—it's April, it's supposed to be spring—but there it is, despite everything: snow on top of snow, on top of ice, on top of snow . . . everything covered in white drifts.

It's a little after six o'clock in the morning. My mother thinks I'm fast asleep with six other girls at a pajama party—she called me there twice before she went to bed—but Will picked me up when he got off at the bowling alley at midnight and I spent the whole night with him; I'd been awake for every second of it. It was the first time I'd ever wangled spending the night. The girls hardly included me in anything anymore, but this pajama party was at Sherry's, and Sherry had a generous heart. Me in Will's bed, lying next to him for a whole night—I couldn't believe how it felt. And then he said I had to see the dawn break. I thought he was kidding. I protested. I said the only time I ever went outside at five in the morning was when they dragged me off to Girl Scout camp or if I woke up with the flu. I said that he should go watch the dawn break at the window and then come right back to me in the bed; I said he would never get me out there— no, thank you—and I refused to open my eyes. He laughed and walked to the window.

"Jenny, it's snowing."

"It can't be snowing—it's spring."

"Spring or no spring, it's snowing. Come and see."

And now I look at him in front of the sunrise, all dressed and standing in the dark and the quiet, and I know we are the only two people alive in the whole world.

Streaks of red inching up into the blackness where there were still big, chunky white stars and then yellow, flaming yellow into dark blue, golden yellow lighting up the crystals of frost on every tree limb, like Tinker Bell touching everything with her sparkle wand . . . it all came alive in front of us, glistening, right there in front of us, a dazzling, silent ice show of white, pink, and gold. The two of us, breathless, not moving, caught up in the spectacle of the sunrise as if we were nailed to the ground.

"It snowed," Will whispers, "but I don't remember anything quite like this." His arms surround me. "Maybe it's because you weren't there."

"Not anymore," I breathe into his neck.

"No, not anymore, not ever. I'll never give you up, Jenny."

My eyes search his. "But why would you have to?"

"I don't know . . . but I never will."

We did not get on the sled and race down to the railroad tracks; Will said it was all too beautiful to damage. He tucked the sled under one arm and me under the other, we walked down "suicide hill." When I looked back, there were only our footprints, two sets of boot tracks close together, through the perfect crystal blanket of ice and snow.

"So why are you dancing so hard these days, Miss Jennifer?"

I turned and she was in the doorway. I was sitting on a bench, changing out of my character shoes in the girls' dressing room, and she was standing in perfect first position, her ballet shoes spread open at symmetrical angles, her cane planted firmly in front of her, her hands folded over the top. She wore a faded flesh-colored leotard, a scrap of chiffon skirt, matching tights, and cracked ballet shoes. A large white towel was tied around her neck and shoulders. White skin, white powder, red lipstick, black mascara, no rouge, dense liner circling her gray eyes. Miss Lala Palevsky, paragon of dancing teachers, complete with Russian accent, chignon, angry eyes, and fast hands—I knew the sting that could come if you executed a wrong move; a swift smack of that cane on the back of your calf or thigh would make you think twice the next time you stuck out your leg. Lala Palevsky believed in discipline and the dance; those were the only two things I had ever heard her speak of: the two *d*'s. I knew nothing else about her. Somehow, then, I believed she had no other life, that she spent night and day in the dance studio, existed only for the dance, probably didn't even need food, and if I pictured her doing anything at all that was remotely normal, it was possibly sleeping on the hard yellow wood floor. In her leotard, of course, without a blanket or pillow. Just lying there, pale and deathly still, her chiffon skirt finally at rest, her reflection repeated four times in the mirrored walls around the large room, a motionless toppled statue on the dusty floor.

Her body was small and precise and hard; the only thing that stuck out on her were her shoulders, her back blades, her muscles, and her knees. Small tight breasts, short fingers and many rings that flashed when her cane moved.

"Miss Jennifer?"

I was trying to find my voice, which had disappeared as soon as I realized who had spoken to me. I had never really talked with Miss Lala Palevsky, not in twelve years, not since I was five years old and first came to her dancing school—not unless you could count the endless repetition of the teachings of the correct execution of an ara-besque or a plié, a leap or a combination, an interpretation, or the unfortunate discussions of the incorrect angle of my hand or foot, sticking out in the air.

"Something has happened to you?"

I stood up. "No, Miss Palevsky."

"Yes, I think."

I looked at her.

"So? What has happened?"

"Nothing."

"You are different."

"I . . . uh . . ."

"You are different now, I am watching. Do not bite your lip, Miss Jennifer; it is not food."

"Yes, ma'am."

"So, you will tell me?"

"Uh . . . I don't know, Miss Palevsky."

"You don't know." She pursed her mouth. "Something."

I stood there, didn't know what to say. That I was different be-cause somebody loved me, believed in me, for the first time? That somebody believed I could be a dancer and so now I believed it too? Her eyes were like the coals that children imagine Santa will leave them if they've been bad. Could she read minds, could she see right through me to the wall on the other side of the room?

"So, now you are serious about your dancing."

"Yes, ma'am."

"Yes, ma'am," she repeated. "So, that I see. It is time you are serious about your dancing."

Neither of us said anything. She watched me.

"You can be a dancer, Jennifer, if you don't let anything stand in front of you, nothing to stop you in your way."

I tried to hold her eyes, I tried not to move but still to breathe. Not an easy thing, being a piece of Russian steel.

"So," she said, and then there was a small lowering of her shoulders as she looked at me. "That is all you wish to say?"

"Uh . . . yes, ma'am, I guess so."

And then she did something that astonished me: she moved her lips into something that resembled a faint smile, and she turned and walked away.

I nearly fell on the floor when I let my muscles go loose. Okay, so she could read minds, that was clear now. I was serious about my dancing. Before, it had been a dream and talk, but now it was more than talk, and that never would have happened without Will. Will believed in me so much that now I believed in me—but what if she thought loving Will would be the thing that stood in my way? As far as I was concerned, she had no personal life; as far as I was concerned, she lived only for the dance. I wanted to live for the dance *and* Will. With Will I could be anything; without him I would be through. I knew that, in my heart I knew that. What if she thought it was impossible? I certainly was not going to tell her, smile or no smile. I didn't need anybody else against me; I wasn't about to discuss my love for Will with anybody, it didn't matter who. I had nothing to say.

May . . .

"Why do you carry a gun?"

"Shh, honey."

"Will, nobody can hear me."

We were in Joe's. I was sitting at the counter eating a hot fudge sundae and Will had catsup bottles marching in front of me like soldiers, upside down on top of one another along the counter. It was a Saturday afternoon during the quiet stretch between lunch and dinner, when he got everything ready for the next meal—chopped lettuce for the dinner salads, filled sugar bowls and salt and pepper shakers, consolidated catsup, and printed the specials in block letters on the front and back blackboards.

"Joe's in the back with Becker."

"Yeah, but they can't hear me; they've got the radio on and they're arguing about who makes better soup."

He wrote SALLSBERRY STEAK WITH MASHED POTATOES AND GRAVY on the blackboard.

"Salisbury is s-a-l-i-s-b-u-r-y, Will."

"It is?" His face got red.

"What's the matter?"

"Nothing." He erased SALLSBERRY and put SALISBURY. He frowned at the blackboard and then at me. "Is that how you spell gravy?"

"Yep."

"You sure?"

"Of course I'm sure."

"It doesn't have an *e* in it?"

"Nope." I put a big spoonful of fudge in my mouth.

He smiled. "Okay. Sometimes I don't spell so good."

"Me neither."

"Yeah, sure."

"I don't."

"Uh huh. You want some more fudge, Slim?"

I held out my glass dish. "Yes, and another cherry. Will, tell me . . ."

"Hmm?"

"Why do you carry a gun?"

He filled the bowl with fudge and a cherry and put it in front of me.

"Because you never know."

"What?"

"What you could run into. Maybe I'll get hungry and have to shoot me a bear."

"Will . . ."

"Or maybe a Russian will come out of nowhere, a KGB Russky who wants to steal our atomic secrets, and I'll have to blow him away—you can never trust those Russians."

"I'm serious."

"Okay. To protect you."

"Okay, never mind."

"I'm serious."

"No you're not."

"I am."

He leaned forward and bent down till his eyes were even with mine. "Because I'd never want to be caught without one. I'd hate to use it, but I wouldn't want to be caught without one."

He looked at me hard.

"Because life is a constant threat and you never know what you'll run into. Do you understand?"

He stood up straight, and took his red-and-white "Joe's" hat off, ran his hand through his hair.

"A gun makes me feel more secure, Jenny."

He put his hat back on. "You want more ice cream with all that fudge?"

I didn't say anything.

"Jenny? You want more ice cream?"

"No, that's okay. I'm full."

And May . . .

"Your mother is worried about you."

"No she isn't; she's mad."

"Sunshine, hand me the gasoline."

"Daddy, why do you want to clean white sidewalls with gasoline? Isn't it better to use cleanser?"

"Since when are you such a car maven?"

I handed him the can of gasoline; he poured some on a rag and attacked the grease on the right rear sidewall of my mother's Oldsmobile. "Your mother cuts too close on her right turns." He looked up. "She's not mad; she's worried."

"Uh uh, she's mad. You're addicted to gasoline."

He smiled. "Okay, she's mad. . . . *I'm* worried."

"Why?"

"Because you're my baby and you're living another life."

"I'm right here, Daddy."

"That's not what I mean." He stood up. "It's about you and that boy, Jenny. It's no good."

I didn't say anything.

"Of course, pretty soon it'll be over. It's just like I told your mother: it's a passing fancy, how much damage could it do? Come June you'll graduate and then there's summer and then, come September, you'll be off to Mizzou."

"Daddy, I'm not going to M.U. I only want to study dance."

"Another passing fancy. It's the same way you felt about being a twirler—remember? We thought you were going to spend the rest of your life in that cute little outfit with the white boots." He laughed.

"It's not the same."

"Sure it is. And you got over that, didn't you? Whatever happened to those boots anyway? They had the cutest little tassels—"

"Dad . . ."

He walked around the car. "Well, I'll be damned . . . she's got a little dink on her fender and she didn't even tell me. I'll be damned."

He stooped to check the fender, disappearing behind the car, mumbling. I'm sure he didn't hear me walk away; he probably didn't even realize I had left him in the driveway until he asked me to hand him the gasoline. My father adored me, but he didn't know me anymore; he didn't realize I wasn't the same.

And good old June . . .

I suspect I wasn't the only one who graduated from Southwest High School in a normal cap with a tassel and with a baby inside her, under her gown. Of course, it's only a suspicion, but in my mind I always liked the idea of it, a whole line of pregnant seniors. If everything hadn't been such a secret in those days, we could have all thrown up together in the john down the hall from the auditorium, holding hands . . . or heads; we could have held each other's heads over the toilet bowls in a perfect daisy chain.

"It'll be all right, Jenny, don't worry. I love you, I see how scared you are, but don't you know how much I love you? I'm gonna take care of you, it'll be fine. We'll go to Bakersfield or maybe further north; we'll get married and we'll go back to California and have the baby. It's beautiful there, you'll see; you'll love it. God, Jenny, this is everything I ever dreamed of, you and a baby . . . Jenny, I love you so much."

He was intoxicated, he was joyous. My being pregnant wasn't a problem for him—it fit perfectly into his life.

"Everything will be wonderful, you'll see. I can get a good job doing construction there—no, driving a truck. Yeah, I'll drive a truck . . . maybe up in the wine country. Would you like that, Punkin, to live in the wine country?"

Wine country? What wine country? Okay, sure.

So I'd have a baby. I'd marry Will and I'd live somewhere called the wine country and I'd have a baby with Will's blue eyes and he'd drive a truck and I'd stay home and cook and clean and take care of the baby and wait for him to come home. It sounded good. Didn't it?

Wait . . . what home? No, don't worry about it, Jenny, shut up, any kind of home, who cares what kind of home? But could I do it? Could I live in a tent by the side of the road? Is there a kitchen in a tent? Is there a bathroom? Is it big enough to hold a crib? Hey, don't get crazy; he said he'd take care of us, didn't he?

"I knew it, I told you this would happen," she says, looking at my father, and then her eyes move my way. "How could you do this to me?"

I guess I knew my father would tell her, but I was so scared and he was looking at me with such love in his eyes that it slipped out. Of course, now I know there are no slips, you tell what you choose to tell and I needed to tell because I was chicken, so I told him and he told her and she went for me in the kitchen while the food stuck to the plates. You'd think my mother could have come up with something more original; after all, she did have a degree in English Literature and had been an actual teacher once upon a time; and it's not as if she even included my father—not "how could you do this to us" but "how could you do this to me."

"I didn't do this to you."

She pays no attention and looks back to him. "My God, Moe," she says to my father, "we'll have to call Dr. Bart and see if he knows someone . . . oh, my God, where will we go?"

"What do you mean? Go to do what?" I say.

"Go to fix this," she says, her voice rising, "to fix this . . . what you've done."

"What do you mean, fix?"

She stops stirring her coffee. The spoon skids and clatters across the kitchen table. She stands up.

"Mom?"

She walks to the sink, keeps her back to me.

"Are you talking about an abortion? Is that what you're talking about? I'm not having an abortion." My heart is slamming against my rib cage; I'm having a hard time staying in the chair. My mother says nothing.

"Daddy?"

My father has turned a sick, bleached yellow since the beginning of this conversation. He doesn't look at me but keeps his eyes focused on his cup.

"I'm going to marry him," I say clearly, my head banging.

"You most certainly are not." My mother spits out the words as if they are individual bullets being propelled from her mouth.

"I'm going to marry Will and have his baby."

This is the first time that I actually believe I will do this; it is when I hear myself say these words that I know I will marry Will.

"I will not allow you to ruin your life."

I look at my father; he doesn't lift his eyes. I touch his hand.

"I'm not ruining my life," I say to the top of my father's bent balding head. "I'm going to have the baby, Daddy, and marry Will."

"You don't know what you're saying," my mother says.

My father says his words very quietly. "I don't want her to have an abortion, Esther; that's not what I want."

"Oh, really, so now you're talking. So tell me, what do you want, Moe?"

He touches the coffee drops on the brown wood with his finger, and then his hand covers mine. "Not an abortion," he says again, and he looks at me for just an instant and then at her. "Maybe she could have the baby. . . ."

"Have the baby? Are you crazy? What is she going to do with a baby? Take it with her to college? Leave it here with me? And what are we going to tell everyone? *The baby fell from out of a tree?*"

I can feel myself panicking, I can feel myself about to scream. "Please don't make me have an abortion, Daddy. I'm having the baby. I'm going to marry Will and have the baby. Please."

"And ruin your life, ruin all of our lives—my God, what have you done?" she says, and a sob comes out of her; from somewhere deep inside my mother I hear a sob.

And my father stands up from the chair, but he doesn't go to her, he stands motionless like a fence between her and me, and then I'm crying—God knows I didn't want to cry, but then I'm crying—and I'm going to run from the room and the house and all of this, but she's in front of me, my mother has crossed the room and planted herself in front of me like a battleship—like the USS *Missouri*. She comes at me, loud and clear.

"You'll do what I tell you, Jenny," she rages, her flags flying. "You don't know what you want; I'll tell you; you're too young to know."

Ah . . . too young to know. Not too young to get pregnant, not too young to love somebody, just too young to know.

But first things first here, let's not forget our priorities. First, my mother was going to make sure I had an abortion, and lest we forget, an abortion in those days was not something you could just drop in and get one sunny afternoon at Baptist Memorial Hospital, not something you could order up from your local gynecologist; in 1960 an abortion was illegal, and in order to get one you had to offer up your daughter to a filthy butcher who did his slaughtering in a condemned building somewhere around Thirty-first and Main, or Seventeenth and Paseo, or maybe on the Kansas side, way out south, or, on the Missouri side, way down by the stockyards, or—wait a minute— Tijuana perhaps? We wouldn't want to forget about all the abortions that were done then in the countries of our neighbors south of the border, and I'm sure it was lovely there that time of year.

"They can't make you do anything, Jenny, they can't make you— listen to me."

"I'm listening, Will."

He's pacing back and forth at the foot of his bed, where I sit. We've been doing this for at least three hours. "They can't make you. I won't let them," he says.

"I won't let them either."

"Okay, then."

"Okay."

It's quiet in the room. And hot. Two fans are going, blowing my hair around, and I'm wearing cutoffs and a sleeveless blouse. I feel the threads of the ripped jean fabric brush softly against the insides of my thighs and I'm barefoot and I have chipped orange nail polish on my toes. I see that and it occurs to me I have to fix that when I get home, that's what I'm thinking about: not that I'm seventeen and I'm pregnant and what's going to happen to me, but that it's important I get my bottle of Revlon Orange Crush to fix the chips on my toes, and the shade is flapping against the wood of the windowsill and Will has on Levi's and boots and no T-shirt and there's a piece of blond hair that keeps falling across his eyes and he runs his fingers through it and tucks it up again and my heart moves and I realize I'm thirsty or maybe it's queasy and I'm going to get up and get a Coke and somebody honks their horn out in the street somewhere, and then he stops and turns.

"They can't make you do anything—they can't because they won't be able to." Three long steps and he's in front of me, grasps my hands in his and clasps them to his chest. "We're gonna be outta here."

Tall and standing there, planted in front of me, his legs wide, his skin hot and smooth under my fingertips, those blue eyes never wavering as I stare. "I won't let them do anything to you, Jenny."

"Will . . ."

"We're going to go to Oklahoma and get married."

He grabs me, lifts me up to him, until I'm on my knees on the foot of his bed, my breasts pushed hard into the muscles of his chest, the edges of his ribs pressing into me, his heart banging solidly against me, so close that I think it's my heart beating inside my skin, so close, the blue and the blond blur of him, his lips against mine, butterfly wings touching my mouth. "I won't give you up, Jenny. I love you."

"Will . . ."

"They'll separate us."

"No they won't."

"Yes they will," he says, and pulls his head back. "They can and they will—but not if we're married: they can't hurt us if we're married."

The fan makes its half circle and blows hot air across the top of us, chills the sweat on my neck, and I shake. The piece of hair falls back in Will's face. I lift my hand to touch it, his face now six inches from mine. His eyes don't blink as he speaks.

"Marry me, Jenny," he says, and the horn honks again and the shade flaps hard as if it's angry and I distinctly hear a drop of water from the kitchen faucet hit the soaking fry pan in the sink, and my eyes don't blink either and I don't even know if I'm happy or sad, I just hold on to him and I say, "Yes, Will."

·   ·   ·

The best-laid schemes o' mice an' men
Gang aft a-gley;
An' lea'e us nought but grief and pain,
For promis'd joy.

Good old Robert Burns.

Will would pick me up after he got off work. He'd go to work and pick up his checks and at six o'clock he'd be at Lala Palevsky's. I would go there as if I were going to dance class, but I wouldn't go to dance class, I would wait in the parking lot, and at six o'clock he would show up in the big blue Mercury and we would drive away. My wedding dress was stuffed inside my dance bag, a plain white sheath I'd bought at Harzfeld's, standing barefoot and alone in the pale-peach dressing room, studying my body over my shoulder in the three-way mirror, smiling at the new back of me and the new sides of me in a dress two sizes bigger to accommodate the baby growing at my waist; and under the folded dress a pair of cheap white peau de soie heels I'd bought at Chandler's to match the dress. And stockings. And a white garter belt to hold up the stockings. And a new bra. And a slip. And this little veil thing that had a ribbon and these sweet tiny fake rosebuds, to put on my head. And a nightgown, most of all a nightgown, white and elegant and not really see-through, but cut so that there was no doubt I was the only thing on the other side of the silk. And all of this bounty I had charged to my mother. I believed this was not only fair but fitting: if she hadn't been such a maniac about who Will was, she probably would have made my father buy me a wedding bigger than the Missouri State Fair. I bought my wedding ensemble alone. I'd thought about taking Sherry with me, but in the end I figured the whole thing would be too much for her, keeping such secrets. Me and Will running away into the night to get married, peau de soie shoes, and pregnancy—it was all too much for Sherry; she would not be able to contain herself; she'd crack and spill the beans. And I didn't want any slipups. If no one knew, then there was no way my parents could know. No Esther and Moe on horseback, at the head of the sheriff's posse. "They went thataway," yells my father, on one knee, his head bent close to the ground of a Kansas wheat field, sniffing the chaff as he deftly picks up the scent of gasoline from Will's Mercury while they track us by night. It was hard to imagine my father hovering over a wheat field instead of over an officeful of bald accountants, and even harder to imagine my mother on horseback, but I made myself—Esther Jaffe straddling a pinto, wearing a pillbox hat, a simple Dior suit, high-heeled pumps, and gloves. Oh, and a red-and-white bandanna tied casually at her neck.

I was very excited. I was more than excited—I was thrilled. I loved him. I loved him so much that there was nothing to say or do, there were no questions, I had no doubts. We would get married and then we'd tell them, and if they didn't want to help us, we'd do it on our own. After all, I had a high school diploma, I could work, I could do something—wait tables, type in an office, sell something in a store. Maybe wine: I could sell wine in the wine country. How 'bout that? Somebody has to sell wine in those wine-country wine stores, don't they? That was our plan, our scheme—to go back to California, to the northern part of California, and settle there. Our delicious best-laid scheme . . .

And then comes the "gang aft a-gley" part, because as hard as it is to put the words together and as much as I never want to say them or hear them or ever believe them, the words are: Will didn't show up. *Didn't show up.* I repeat: *Will didn't show up.*

Just picture it: A young girl stands in front of a dancing school on a hot summer evening, stands quietly clutching a canvas bag that holds her neatly folded wedding dress; hopeful, happy, she stands on one foot and then the other, moves the bag occasionally from arm to arm, moves her heart occasionally from her throat to her gut, sometimes leans back against the lamppost, takes equal turns looking to the left and to the right of her, praying for the glorious front end of a blue Mercury to glide into view, checks her face in the mirror, puts on lipstick, fiddles with her hair, walks up and down in front of the dancing school, does a little turn at the end of the brick walk, sings softly to herself, thinks about his face and his eyes and his hands on her, thinks about their life together and all she dreams of, tries not to notice as the light in the sky changes, tries not to panic or be afraid, talks to herself, tells herself how much he loves her—he loves me, he loves me, I know he loves me—and finally resorts to those sickening, silent Dorothy Parker prayers, the ones that if you heard them out loud would cause you to retch or weep: Please, God, let him come and I'll give you everything, please, God, let him come and I'll never ask you for anything, please, God, don't let this be happening . . . and when the moon is sharp in a black night sky, when the chimes ring clear from the tower of Saint Anthony's twelve times, twelve unholy times, announcing to her heart that she's been standing there six hours, not counting the twenty minutes for her early arrival because she couldn't wait, and her knees buckle and she lies sprawled on the curb, sobbing so hard against the canvas bag that the zipper leaves a miniature railroad track across her cheek, we know then that she will never see the blue Mercury, that she will never see the blue eyes or the blue tattoo, we know then that a piece of her has been damaged beyond repair. I knew then that a piece of me was dead and through.

"I'll pick you up out front, like always, six o'clock, in front of Lala Palevsky's, six o'clock, my little sweetheart, I'll be there."

Why would Will leave me?

Kissing me, holding on to me so tight, that look, that set of his face, that smile.

Why would he run away?

"Six o'clock?"

Crushing me up against him, kissing me and kissing me. I leaned back and looked up at him. "Six o'clock?"

"Hey, Jenny, what'd I say?"

Six o'clock. I heard him.

After all, this was *his* plan, running away to Oklahoma, to get married in Oklahoma, of all places, it was what he wanted, so where did he go? I was his fantasy, remember, his dream come true. And I believed it. I knew in the deepest part of me that it was true. Will loved me. So how could he just vanish into thin air?

My father wasn't in the house; it was just her and me. Four days later, four days of fog and waking and sleeping, not knowing anything around me—days, weeks, years, it didn't make any difference how long it was, I had no idea. In my room, in my bed, not knowing anything except, suddenly, that something must have happened to him, he couldn't have just left me, not without saying something, not without explaining, not without anything: not Will.

Joe knew nothing.

"Well, I just don't know, Jenny. He finished his shift like he always did, hung up his apron, said so long, and was out that door. I was making a triple-decker butter crust for that dumb broad who works at MacLain's Bakery, you know, the one who gets off at four, the one with her hair stickin' out all over the place, looks like she did it with a Mixmaster, and she was talkin' a mile a minute, and even though I wasn't paying no attention to her, what with her mouth flappin' like that and the chili boiling up and the goddamn cooler that went on the fritz . . . well, I don't know, Jenny. I heard the Merc, but I didn't even raise my head."

Mr. Boyer, who owned the Texaco, was also a wealth of information.

"Well, let's see now. He picked up his check, all right, but he didn't say nothin' else. Nope. Not as far as I know."

Mr. Boyer, standing in front of his gas pumps, his shirt starched and pressed as if he were going to a nightclub, the red rag in his pocket folded into a perfect square, the lines at the top of his nose deepening as he frowned and shook his head. I wanted to ram the toothpick he had clamped between his teeth right into the side of his face, hard.

And who else was there? Nobody. No friends, no family, nobody. The furnished room was furnished with nothing of Will's except his clothes, but his clothes would be gone because we were leaving, wouldn't they? Everything I knew about him I knew only in my head: stories, memories of his that he'd told me, pictures of people I had conjured up from his describing them, names that weren't in any phone books, no leads, no clues, no way to know where to go or what to do. . . .

I had to call the police. A person doesn't just disappear when he loves another person, when they're running away to get married; something had to have happened to him. I would call the police and they would get to the bottom of this, they would find Will.

"Put the phone down, Jenny, you're going to make a fool of yourself," the wicked witch said.

"Mom, get out of my room, please."

Notice the "please"—oh, the ever polite Jenny.

"There's no reason to call the police."

"Something happened to him."

"Nothing happened to him."

"Leave me alone."

I dial. I had a pink Princess telephone; it was quite the thing then; the dial made this sweet little rickety-rack sound as your finger pushed it around.

"Nothing happened to him," she says again.

"You don't know that."

Silence. She stands in front of the window, a dark silhouette surrounded by backlight. The sheer ivory voile curtains on either side of her blow out from the open window like the wings of an angel, but this is my mother we're talking about here, my beautiful mother, who is supposed to love me: I am her only child.

"Hang up, Jennifer. Nothing happened to him."

"Good afternoon," the male voice on the other end of the telephone says in my ear. "Seventy-fifth Street Police Station, Officer Stanfill here, how may I help you?"

"Nothing happened to him, Jennifer, I *know.*"

Smug and certain and sure of herself, and it is clear like a knife slicing through me that she *knows* what happened to Will.

"Hello? Hello?" Officer Stanfill says.

I look at her. "What do you know?"

"Put the phone down."

"What do you know?"

"Is there someone there? Hello?"

"I know he wasn't any good for you, that's what I know."

"What did you do?"

"Me? I didn't do anything. It was his choice."

I feel the cool round plastic of the Princess telephone receiver sliding down my chin. Poor Office Stanfill is getting nervous. "Hello, do you have a problem there? Is someone on the line? Hello?"

A problem—do I have a problem? I guess you could call it a problem, but I can't say that to him; all the words have flown out of me. I drop the phone.

"What did you do to him?"

"It's not what we did to him, it's what he did to you. That's the important thing."

We. She has decided to include my father. The blood rushes into my ears. I can hear it, loud, like I'm standing inside a waterfall.

"Tell me, Mother," I say to her, and I get up from my bed with sudden strength and she sees it and I think the only reason she answers me is because she's afraid I'm going to cross the room and hurt her. "Tell me," I say again, and I'm looking at her, and she says it right to my face.

"Did you think I would stand still and do nothing while he talked you into running away? Do you think I am stupid, Jennifer? That I would let you do that? Let you ruin your life?" Defiance crosses her face. "We offered him money," my adoring mother says to me. "We offered him money to leave you, and he took it and he went away."

Oh, you can try to fix that, turn the words around so that when you repeat them to yourself, year after year, day by day, maybe they'll get to be more palatable, easier to chew. But the truth is, no matter how you say it, it doesn't matter, it still adds up the same, so you finally just say it to yourself the way it was. Will left me because they paid him. How 'bout that for something to stick inside you? Money. My mother and father, the ever popular Esther and Mose Jaffe, my beloved parents, offered my William Cole McDonald money to leave me, and the corker is he took it and he went. No "Goodbye, Boots," no "See ya, my little sweetheart," no "Adios, my Jenny, I love you but I gotta go . . ."

Try to swallow that one. What happens? Ahh. Enter: Bitter. Oh, yeah, and betrayal. Oh, yeah, and rage.

That was before I even asked how much. What could it have been that they gave him? Tens, hundreds, thousands? A new Mercury and a pony? Two ponies? Three?

I never, ever asked how much they gave him. I couldn't ask that. I did the next best thing. I took aspirin. I don't mean "take two and call me in the morning"; I mean the bottle. All of them. Well, however many there were in the bottle—a handful? How many is a handful? Not enough.

It is not easy to kill yourself. It is also not easy to kill a baby floating around inside you. These things I know. The baby part is really only an afterthought, something I tell you in retrospect, because I certainly wasn't thinking about a baby then; it was only me I was trying to get rid of. In my clouded head, once Will left, the baby didn't exist anymore: there was no baby, there was no more Will, there was only me, alone. I'm just saying that in the movies, Scarlett can do a swan dive down the grand staircase and the baby is kaput. In real life, if the baby wants to stay, it stays. No matter what you do to yourself. I did plenty, and that baby held on to me like it was fixed to my insides with Krazy Glue, and remember, Krazy Glue wasn't invented then. When the bottle of Bayer failed—after the stomach pumping and the charming stay in the hospital, with Dr. Bart bringing in the psychiatrist that I refused to speak to and whose name I can't remember—I tried starving myself. After they got me home, of course, and after I tried to slit my wrists. You have no idea how much courage you need to actually pull that skinny blade through the pale, thin skin of the underside of your wrist. Not the touchdown, but the pull. I got through the touchdown part, then I stared at the blade, willed it to move, and when the thinnest line of red blood came to the surface of the skin, I lost my nerve. Or maybe it's true what they say about suicide, how females visualize how they will look when they're discovered, so they try to pick something not too messy, not too disfiguring, no gunshot wounds or razors to leave a very unattractive corpse. Of course, I did like the idea of blood splashing all over the bathroom, wreaking havoc on my mother's good Fieldcrest towels. Males, on the other hand, don't give a damn what they look like to whoever discovers their body—they just take a shotgun, pop it in their mouth, and blow out their brains. In the kitchen, in the bathroom, in the bedroom—what do they care? Or maybe it has nothing to do with being a male or a female; maybe it's just more proof that I wasn't a force to be reckoned with, that I never was, that Will was wrong. Maybe starving would be the easy way out, the coward's way but definitely easier, especially because they were watching me. Since the bad deed with the aspirin, they didn't stop watching me, the two of them, my adoring parents, taking turns watching me as Dr. Bart had told them to. How could I get my hands on a shotgun when I had two prison guards? Better to try starving.

It's amazing how you can push food around a plate and make it look like you ate some of it. I know how those young girls do it: it's a little Houdini trick, only instead of using rope and handcuffs, you do it with mashed potatoes and peas. You can go a long time without eating. That's another thing I know. Of course, eventually you pass out, or actually you have trouble standing, but it's a long time before any of that happens, and a very long time, I'm sure, before you starve to death—for me it was only enough time for Esther and Moe to realize that the whole thing was bigger than both of them, that they really didn't know what to do. It had become too late for Esther's abortion plan; she had to come up with something new.

Clever Esther.

I would be sent away. Removed and banished. I would be exiled to the Stella Maris Home for You-Know-Whats in Los Angeles. It would have been a lot easier to just stash me at The Willows, right in Kansas City, right off of Wornall Road, but one doesn't keep shame that close to home—Not if you're Esther and Moe Jaffe; one don't. When I was little and we girls passed The Willows, there was always a lot of whispering, and when I was a bit older, there was pointing, jabbing with elbows, and giggling. I have no idea what happens now. Maybe The Willows is gone. Or maybe there will always be a Willows, a place for wayward girls. That's what they called them then; wayward, as in drifting, aimless, as in stray dog. My clever mother found out about Stella Maris from Father McCaffrey at Our Lady of Lebanon Maronite, who played golf with Rabbi Bierman from Temple Beth-Am, who played golf with good old Dr. Bart. Ah, the ways of grown-ups; just a handshake between the diverse medicine men, and a knocked-up kid could be shipped away, and to California, of all places, Will's California, but what did my mother know.

"You'll stay there until you have the baby, Jenny, and then you'll come home."

Okay, sure. But wait, can I just go up north first and see the wine country? Maybe just take a little look around? I didn't say that; I didn't say anything.

"It's very nice there, the father said so."

What father? *My* father? That old man sitting over there? And what happened to him, why does he look that way? It never occurred to me then that what I had done had made my father turn suddenly old.

"It's just like a hotel."

I did not ask her if they had room service or a piano bar; I just watched her lips move as she spoke. She had a beautiful mouth, my mother, lips that were full and round, lips much more fitting for the 1990s, as if they'd been shot full of collagen. I assume she still has a beautiful mouth; I decided not to look at her lips or any part of her years ago.

"It won't be so long. Four, five months, and then you'll come home."

Did she think I would just come back as if nothing had happened? And what did you do, Jenny, since last summer? Oh, not much—I just went to this place in California, had a baby, and came home. Yeah? Where's the baby? Gee, I don't know . . . it was here a minute ago, uh, let me see now . . .

"Jennifer, are you listening to me?"

Watching me, she and my old father watching me. I shook my head, but I couldn't say anything, which was in accordance with my new plan: I would never say anything to anybody again.

My roommate's name was Rose. She was four months younger than me, two months more pregnant than me, and much more grown up. Her claim to fame was that her baby had been put there by an astronaut (what an astronaut was doing in her hometown of Fond du Lac, Wisconsin, was beyond me). He was an astronaut none of us had every heard of, a backup astronaut, I guess, for when all the others were busy flying around. Rose had a picture of herself and the understudy astronaut proudly displayed on the little table between our two beds. He had a crew cut and his arms were around her; the American flag was clearly evident on the pocket of the uniform jumpsuit he wore, proof that he was who she said he was. He also had a wife, three children, and the entire brass of NASA; he wasn't about to have anything to do publicly with a baby he'd made with Rose.

Clumped together by age, we were two to a room, just like in a college dorm. Well, not exactly. We were not supposed to divulge our last names, we were not allowed any phone calls unless specifically arranged with Nurse Rae Lee or Sister Angelica, and we were not permitted to leave except for our nightly excursion outside the gates, a quick walk around the block, preferably not stopping at Mr. Bernstein's corner grocery store to use the pay phone, which I would never do since I had nobody to call. A huddle of pregnant wayward girls walking together quietly in a clump. After all, we were pariahs in hiding, we weren't really supposed to be seen stinking up the neighborhood even though everybody knew we were there, concealed behind the gates, and over the wall, the bad girls "with child." Actually, childs, since there were twenty-eight of us, twenty-eight at all times, because as soon as a girl would have a baby and leave, another would arrive to take her place. Stella Maris was filled to capacity, never a room to be had, because of her good reputation as a place to send your very own wayward girl. It was a sprawling whitewashed stucco building, very California, very Spanish, with a red tile roof and cute green trim, a place where Santa Claus and the elves would have fit right in. On the top floor of the hacienda were the delivery room and the clinic where we went for our checkups. This was separate from the church. Church. I had been transplanted into the land of Catholics about as far from my upbringing as if I had been plunked down in a small village somewhere in Japan.

I arrived on a Thursday and was picked up at the airport by my social worker. Mrs. Havermeyer of the sad face and thick ankles, she accepted me from the stewardesses, who had probably been paid by my father to watch me for fear I would throw myself out of the plane or commit hara-kiri with a plastic knife from the TWA snack. Mrs. Havermeyer picked me up as if I were a parcel post package and passed me on to Sister Berl. I said nothing to either of them, except "yes" and "no" and "thank you." Yes, I had a fine flight; no, I didn't want anything to eat; and thank you for showing me to my little room.

Two beds with blue-yellow-and-pink-flowered chenille bedspreads, a tiny table between the beds, one lamp, one desk, one chair. And a window overlooking a garden Sister Berl called Saint Robert Bellarmine's patio, where we girls could have a picnic if we wanted, and one Rose. Rose was sitting on her bed, her back up against the pillows.

"Rose, this is Jennifer. Jennifer, this is Rose," Sister Berl said. Rose didn't move. We nodded at each other.

Rose had brown eyes, and short black curly hair, and sallow skin, and she was lost somewhere inside a man's extra-large pink oxford shirt with sleeves that hung below her hands. She didn't appear to be doing anything, just sat there staring. I put my suitcase on the other bed.

Sister Berl gave me an extraordinary smile. "Are you sure you don't want supper, child?"

"No, thank you."

"You ate on the airplane?"

"Yes, ma'am." My first lie to a nun. I waited for lightning to strike, but there was nothing; it must have been the same as lying to a Jew.

She glided a step backward; she didn't seem to have feet.

"Sometimes the first night is very difficult—it's hard to be away from home."

I didn't say anything. I was overjoyed to be freed from the grasp of the wicked witch and her old-man sidekick. I was thrilled to be away from home.

She stood there with her hand on the doorknob, the beautiful smile practically took up her whole face, what you could see of it that wasn't covered by the white thing that looked like crisp construction paper curving around the top of her forehead and pushing up against the sides of her cheeks. Eyes, a nose, and that smile—and then starched white cloth coming out of the white construction paper, which connected to black cloth all the way down to the floor. She moved, and two shiny black leather toe tips poked out from under the hem of her habit. I was relieved to see that she had feet.

I had never been this close to a nun, never spoken to one before.

One hand on the doorknob, the other fingered the black beads that were draped and knotted at her waist. Black beads and a big cross.

"If you want to talk to me, I'm just down the hall."

I didn't say anything. It occurred to me that her eyes were blue, a soft pale blue, and I could see Will's eyes and felt myself get dizzy. I dropped my gaze and looked down at the floor.

"Rose will show you."

She waited.

"Thank you," I said, my eyes focused on the bed's dust ruffle.

"Jennifer," she said, and we remained motionless until I looked up at her. "God loves you." Then she glided a little farther backward, her look encircling both of us. "God bless you, children," she said, and then the black cloth swirled and she was gone, without me having seen her shut the door.

Rose was watching me as I sat down next to my suitcase. It was devastatingly clear to me that proceeding with my plan was going to be more than difficult. It would be tough to try and kill myself again, tough to remain stalwart, anywhere within range of Sister Berl's smile. Neither Rose nor I said a word for five, six minutes. I heard nothing, didn't hear the sound of anyone crying, but I could feel the tears wash down my cheeks. Rose didn't speak until we both heard me breathe. Then she looked at me across the divide that separated our two nunlike narrow beds.

"Welcome to the land of the ghost babies," Rose said.

●　　●　　●

We came from everywhere, the twenty-eight of us, as far away as Italy as in Mia, who came from someplace called Parma, which was south of Milano, she said in this outrageous accent, "and we are important for our ham" and as close as Suze, who came from Ojai, which she said wasn't important for anything but was only an hour and a half away.

I tried valiantly not to let them get close to me, but there were things they knew that I didn't know, and they were persistent, and I was alone. They surrounded me like a small flock of birds.

"Jennifer, when Sister Theresa asks you, you don't want to work in the laundry."

Rose put down her fork and chewed on a piece of toast. "She's not going to talk to you, Suze. She doesn't talk to anybody, and she doesn't want to know."

I pushed my scrambled egg into my potatoes and sculpted a little yellow-and-white mountain with my fork.

"Oh, yeah, she does. The laundry's terrible."

"You think the kitchen is better?"

"Yeah, you get to eat all that food."

"God. How can you be around food? I can only keep toast down—everything else comes up."

"Well, that's pleasant conversation for the breakfast table." Suze looked at me. "Jennifer, you gotta pick someplace or they'll assign you—everybody's gotta do chores."

I picked up my juice glass and put it down.

"Hey, Suze," Rose said, "you want to hear pleasant conversation? My belly button has taken a turn for the worse—it's sticking straight out. Is that normal?"

"Dio," Mia said, shaking her head.

"It just better go back in the way it used to be after Buster comes out."

Words spoken by a true force to be reckoned with, not a mere dandelion.

Chores went on in the morning after breakfast, which followed six o'clock mass, if you went to mass. If you'd finished high school you had chores; if you were younger, you had school. I never said anything to Sister Theresa, and I ended up in the laundry; in the months I was there, I must have folded enough miles of never-ending clean white sheets to reach Kansas City and return. The smell of Clorox went everywhere with me, as did wrinkled fingertips and the hiss of a hot steam iron. Mia worked in the laundry too, which made it easier for me to continue my self-imposed silence. Though Mia understood more English than she was able to speak, our conversations about washing and drying ended up being the Italian-American version of *Pantomime Quiz.*

When I say there was no school for any of the older girls, the ones like me and Mia and Rose and Suze, who had high school diplomas, I mean that besides no lessons in algebra or English, there were also no lessons on pregnancy, no news about what was happening to your body, what would or what could happen to you before you delivered. No speeches on how to prepare. Once a week we went to the clinic and lined up like ducklings to pee in a cup, have our blood pressure measured, and stand on a scale. And once a week we met with our social worker to hear what would happen at the end. My weekly sessions with Mrs. Havermeyer were like a broken record: she would remind me that the baby would be put up for adoption, in case I'd forgotten that I was not supposed to take it home, and then she would ask if I had a preference as to the religious affiliation of the adoption agency, and I would look out the window and study the orange trees and the light in the sky. That was the extent of it. So other than the blood pressure and the social worker pressure, that was our only schooling. No lectures on Lamaze, no instructions on breathing and focal points, no anything. Twenty-eight girls who were going to be mothers for a day and then give their babies away. So what did *they* need to know? Better to keep them in the dark, better to not even discuss that they were pregnant, much less tell them anything, as in no counseling sessions on what was happening to us psychologically, no therapy sessions about loss or grief or pain, so *no* answer to the most horrifying question that would be thrashing around inside each of our heads for the rest of our lives: and tell me, Miss Wayward Thing, do you stop being a mother if you give your baby away?

The only schooling the twenty-eight of us shared was in what labor sounded like. It came from above, and I don't mean heaven; I mean the delivery floor. That's what got me to start speaking—eight hours of lying in the dark listening to Suze give birth.

"Jesus, Mary, and Joseph, why don't they put her out of her misery?" Rose muttered, turning over yet again and smacking her pillow, as the bed creaked.

I watched the moon through the palm leaves outside the open window and started on another fingernail. I had been biting them since the whole thing started, way before midnight, and now it was nearly dawn. I was down to bleeding cuticles and ripped skin. I had never heard anyone scream, and certainly not like Suze was screaming, as if they were sticking knives in her, torturing her with God knows what. Somehow I had never put two and two together and realized how much it would hurt for a baby to come out. Simple mathematics would have clinched it: how does a baby whose diameter at the head is probably four inches, make its way through a one-inch hole? It was too much for me. I broke my vow of silence.

"Can't they do something for her?"

Rose flipped over and sat up, the shadow of her curly head playing in the moonlight against the wall.

"Yeah, they could give her a shot and knock her out, but they won't do that until the end."

Another scream echoed through the garden, raced around the palm fronds, hit the iron gates, and came back at us. Envisioning Suze's face making that scream, I ripped off the last scrap of nail I could get my teeth around. "My God. When's the end?"

"It depends on the doctor, I guess."

I had just met my doctor, after the examination he sat me down for a serious talk, said I wasn't gaining enough weight and why didn't I eat? I didn't answer him. He asked me would I please try, that it was important for the baby, I had to eat so *he* could be big and strong. He called the baby a *he*. A *he* made it into a real person. My heart flew up as if it had wings and tried to fly out through my throat. *He.* Somewhere inside of me I was convinced that I was just at Stella Maris for some kind of indefinite stay, not exactly a holiday but more like a furlough from my life into the *Twilight Zone*. It certainly didn't have anything to do with having a *baby*, much less a *he* or a *she*. I'd tried never to think about what was moving around inside me, except as a sensation, something to get used to, like a headache or a sudden attack of vertigo, something that would eventually go away but certainly nothing that had to do with a real person, a real person who was going to come out of me, a real person with fingers and toes. I hated every inch of that doctor for making what was happening to me a *he*.

"How can she stand it?" I said.

"I don't know."

Rose got up and walked to the window, lowered her head, and sank to her knees. I watched her fingers move across the tiny crystal rosary beads, heard the whisper of her prayers. I got out of bed and stood next to her, put my hands on the windowsill. We kept vigil until way after the morning light. Suze stopped screaming a little

82

before eight. That must have been when they knocked her out with the anesthetic.

All babies were born at Stella Maris with the patient unconscious, then, when they woke up they were told they had a baby and they could say whether they wanted to see it or not. Suze chose not. We were not told if the baby was a *he* or a *she*, and if Suze knew, she didn't say anything when she kissed us goodbye. My first goodbye at Stella Maris. I stood at the edge of the room watching tears and kisses, scraps of paper with hastily written addresses shoved into hands, as if there hadn't been time to exchange numbers in all the months beforehand, as if no one had known there would be a good-bye. Bonds and friendships made during abnormal captivity are like getting close to the rest of the kids in detention in school, getting bound to the rest of the people on your cell block in jail. A peculiar, powerful tie, but one that doesn't go anywhere. What did we know about each other? Next to nothing. What would we have in common after we had served our time? Nothing except a bad memory, because no matter how close we became, how many tender moments we shared, how much laughter, each of us left Stella Maris with a sick taste in her mouth. Always remember, at the end of your tour in the Twilight Zone, you had to give away your *he* or *she*.

In September we tried to get over the loss of Suze by having a picnic on Labor Day. We "inmates" made all the food, but Mary, from Eagle Creek, Indiana, clearly didn't know how to barbecue, and the chicken was bloody at the bone. Of course, I wasn't eating it anyway. I was basically existing on Pepsi-Cola, potato chips, and crackers, with an occasional bite of a Baby Ruth. Rose, on the other hand, was huge. It was clear that Buster was already bigger than she was. Three new things were happening to me: One, I was talking to people, not

a lot of talking but more than "yes" and "no" and "thank you"—
Suze's labor had had a permanent effect on my reserve. Two, it was
getting more difficult to think of the sensation inside me as just a
sensation. The movement was definitely separate from me—I went
one way, it went the other—and whatever was in there clearly had a
life of its own. I did my best not to think about that, though. I tried,
in fact, not to think. If I'd had to face the past and how Will had
left me, I would clearly be looking for aspirin again, maybe even a
rope, or maybe I would even have resorted to something messy; and
if I had to face the future . . . somehow that was even more frighten-
ing, as I had no idea what was going to happen to me. And that led
to the third thing: a piece of me began to question whether it would
be better to be a Catholic than a Jew.

Looking back, I know it had to do with falling in love with the
sanctuary. Just being in there was heady: the hush, the beautiful cushion of quiet, the perfume of dead roses and candles and incense, the
colors of the stained glass—the red of the blood of Jesus, the gold
of the crown, the blue of the sky—reflecting on the skin of my arm
as I sat motionless while the sun made its way around the room. I
could hide in there forever, my hands quiet on the cool, dark wood
of the pews; sometimes it was the only place where I could breathe.
I did not discuss my newfound love of the church with anyone, but
Rose saw. She took it upon herself to give me instruction—she and
Mary and Cookie and Mia began my catechism class.

"If you aren't baptized you can't go to heaven, you can't be in the
kingdom of God."

"Where do you go, then? Hell?"

"Limbo," they all answered, including Mia—the word must have
been the same in Italian.

"Limbo?"

"Anyone who hasn't been baptized goes to limbo."

"It must be a *really* big place."

"Jenny, I thought you were serious," Rose said.

"I *am* serious. I just can't picture it."

Mary pushed herself up from the chair with both hands behind her. "What is there if you're Jewish?"

"There is no heaven or hell if you're Jewish; you just die and they bury you." The four of them watched me, waiting. "Well, I don't know . . . maybe they plant a tree for you in Israel, and certainly they say prayers, but there is no afterplace, not as far as I know."

"But what about your soul?"

"Uh . . ."

"My daddy says when Jews die, their souls go to Miami," Cookie said, laughing. We all looked at her. "Of course, he's a redneck bigot; everybody in Georgia is."

Nobody spoke.

"Well, not *me*," she said.

Rose sighed. "You don't seem to know very much about being Jewish, Jenny."

"I know, isn't that strange?"

"Did you go to Sunday school?" Mary took another cracker out of the open package at the foot of my bed and then waddled back to the chair.

"Uh huh."

"Well, what did they teach you?"

"Uh . . . well, let's see . . . I remember some of it, like the burning bush and Moses coming down with the tablets and parting the Red Sea, and oh, there's this holiday I always liked called Purim, where the rabbi tells this story about Queen Esther—" I stopped.

"What?" Rose said.

"Oh, my God . . ."

"What?"

"Nothing . . . it's just my mother's name is Esther."

"So?"

"Well, they've got it all wrong. They tell this story about Queen Esther and King Ahasuerus and this bad guy named Haman, and every time the rabbi says Haman's name in the synagogue, all the kids get to make a lot of noise with these noisemakers like you have on New Year's Eve."

Cookie's eyes were wide. "Noisemakers right in church?"

"Uh huh."

"Oh, I like that part."

Rose tilted her head, watching me, waiting.

"It's just that they should do the noisemakers when they say my mother's name. It would be so much more appropriate. . . ."

Mia had no idea what any of us were saying; I could tell by the look on her face.

"What did your mother do?" Rose said.

And then I realized that I'd gotten myself into something that I didn't want to get into, and Cookie said, "What else?" so I ignored Rose's question and just went on.

"Well, there's the big things like eight nights of candles for Hanukkah because they only had enough oil for one night but it burned eight and . . . uh, let's see. . . . Passover, when they put the lamb's blood on their doorposts so the angel of death would know they were Jewish and pass over, not take their firstborn . . . and . . ."

Cookie brightened. "Oh, you have angels? *We* have angels."

"Angels," Mary said, yawning. "The messengers from God."

Cookie went on as if she were reciting: "The archangel Gabriel was the one who came and told the Virgin Mary she was with child."

"Yeah," Mary said. "I wish he would have been the one who came and told me."

Rose stood in front of me. "Did you have a confirmation?"

86

"Yes."

"Oh, I loved confirmation," Cookie said, jumping up. "What name did you take?"

"Name?"

"You didn't get to pick another name?" Mary asked, chewing a cracker.

"No."

"I took Elizabeth," Cookie said.

"So did I; I already had Mary," Mary said, laughing, and she looked at me. "Most people take Elizabeth or Mary."

"Or they take Anne," Cookie said.

"Who was Anne?"

"The mother of Mary," Rose answered.

"Who was Elizabeth?" I asked. "Her long-lost cousin on her father's side?"

"Oh, my goodness, she *was* her cousin," Cookie drawled. "How did you know that?" and Mary was laughing, but Rose shook her head. "Jenny, I thought you were serious."

"I am serious, but maybe there's just too much to learn."

"She would probably have to do an awful lot of penance to make up," Cookie said, straightening the bedspread where she had been sitting. "Probably a million novenas and go to mass fifteen times a day."

"*Dio,*" Mia said. She definitely understood "mass" and "fifteen."

After several theological discussions, including one where we explored the differences in angels—the seraphim versus the cherubim and how they were lower on the ladder of angels than, say, the archangels—and Mary and I got into a discussion about which angels sing, as in "Angels we have heard on high, sweetly singing o'er the plains," and I said that possibly the lesser angels were more like the chorus, little song-and-dance-man angels, and Mary and Cookie got hysterical laughing, it was decided by Rose that in the final analysis there wasn't enough time to convert me and I should for the time being remain Jewish. It didn't matter so much that I hadn't become Catholic; at least I had laughed. I hadn't laughed for such a long time. Aren't you supposed to laugh when you're young?

In October we said goodbye to Jane, from New Haven, Connecticut, and then waited for the leaves to turn—that's what people do who are in Los Angeles for the first time, novice out-of-towners, but there is no leaf-turning in Los Angeles, it is the land of constant green, so instead of looking to a red and gold autumn to cheer us up, Rose decided we had to go trick-or-treating for Halloween. In order to do this we had to defy the nuns, they didn't think it was such a good idea to have twenty-eight very pregnant girls parading around the neighborhood in costume. I didn't think it was such a good idea either, but Rose did.

"What are you going to be?" Rose asked me, her eyes lit up.

"Rose, I don't think we ought to do this."

"Why not?"

"Because we're not supposed to."

"But, Jenny, that's why we should."

There was no stopping her once she had a plan. Petite Rose, our version of Mighty Mouse. And when I thought that, I knew it was something Will would have said. And don't think I wasn't thinking about him. I had somehow lost my desire to kill myself, but I hadn't yet converted that to a desire to live. Rose tried to push me to talk about what had happened to me, but I couldn't. It was the same problem I had with eating: I couldn't get words up or food down; everything got caught halfway. Instead of talking about me, I listened to endless stories about Rose and the astronaut, Mia and her Salvio, the English teacher, Mary and her mother's dentist, Cookie and the boy next door. There are a million stories in the naked city; this was just twenty-eight of them. Unfortunately, there was a ghost baby in each one.

We didn't get very far in the trick-or-treating; we were caught before we even made it to Mr. Bernstein's grocery store. Because of the difficulties in rigging up costumes, Rose had talked us into all going as the same thing. Twenty-eight pregnant witches, in stolen nun's habits, were rounded up heading for the corner, heartily reprimanded, and sent to their rooms.

Cookie had her *he* or *she* sometime in early November, but she refused to say goodbye to us before she left. Sister Berl said she was feeling too sad.

"Do you think you'll ever see him again?"

"Oh, Rose, I don't know."

"Yes you do."

I looked at her, propped up against the pillows. I'd told her. *Everything.*

She'd finally gotten to me. I'd never divulged any of my story when I had to sit and talk once a week with my social worker. I couldn't—Mrs. Havermeyer's eyes were so sad, I was sure that if I told her anything she would just dissolve. And I'd never said a thing to Sister Berl. That would have been even harder: who'd want to undermine that heavenly smile? But Rose had finally gotten to me. Not that she had to really wangle it out of me; she just knew the right things to ask. She'd never forgotten what I'd said about my mother, so she asked how I felt about my parents, how I got along with the wicked witch and her trusty sidekick, and the cork came flying out of my mouth. Remember, I'd never told anybody, I had so much to tell.

"I don't believe that's why Will left you."

I stared at her.

"I just don't believe it," she said again.

I traced the chenille flowers across the bedspread with my finger. "Well, that is why he left me," I said.

The nuns were in the chapel, doing evening chant; you could hear *Panis Angelicus* and Sister Mary Julia's heavenly soprano floating through the orange trees.

"You'll see him again," Rose said, and she got off her bed and picked up her towel for the shower. At the door, she turned and looked at me.

"Jenny, you mustn't ever do anything again to hurt yourself."

I didn't say anything.

"Please. For me."

She opened the door but just stood there. "First of all, I couldn't take it, and second, it would really be stupid."

I smirked.

"Besides everything else," she said, "it's a mortal sin, and you know how I feel about that." She made a funny face at me and walked out of the room. Who would have thought that at such a place as Stella Maris I would find my first true friend?

"'And I love you and I miss you, *chérie.*'" She folded the letter, grinned at me, and kissed the pages.

She had a whole drawerful of letters from the astronaut; it seemed when he wasn't doing simulated flights in mock spaceships he was writing Rose.

"I love it that he calls you that."

"I'm his *chérie.*" She looked down at herself. "A big, fat *chérie.*"

"Will he be there when you get back?"

"Christmas. He'll be in Fond du Lac for Christmas"—she looked at me—"and so will I."

End of conversation. We always avoided talking about leaving; we avoided talking about anything that had to do with why we were at Stella Maris and what would happen to each of us before we were through.

Rose went into labor the day before Thanksgiving. I had kept her up practically the whole night, talking.

"I don't have anybody I feel close to the way you have the Virgin Mary."

"I know."

"It's not like I don't believe in God, Rose. I do."

"I know you do."

"But you have specific people to pray to, and I just have—I don't know—this whole thing. . . ."

We listened to the wind move the palm fronds against the screen.

"Jenny," Rose whispered, "you could pray to the Holy Mother if you wanted to."

"Oh, I don't think so."

"Sure you could. She doesn't ask you if you're Catholic; she listens to whoever needs her, whoever prays."

I smiled in the darkness. "I'll have to think about it," I said.

"Okay."

We didn't drift off until about dawn. And then a couple hours after breakfast, she appeared in the laundry room as if she were a vision. I looked up and there was nothing, and then I looked up and she was there, a female in shadow rising out of the steam. I was sure it was the Virgin Mary, making herself known to me between the wet sheets. I was sure she was going to speak to me, tell me that I could pray to her, that she would see me through.

"Jenny," the vision said, "I think my water just broke, and if that wasn't my water, then there's something awfully wrong with me."

They wouldn't let me stay with her, they wouldn't even let me go in and see her during any of it—they wouldn't let me talk to her, they wouldn't let me hold her hand. Nurse Rae Lee informed me that at Stella Maris, you didn't *see* labor until it was happening to you. "That will be time enough to see it, Jennifer." I hid on the stairway closest to the delivery room, with my foot wedged in the door so it couldn't close totally; that way I could see a bit of what was going on. When the dreaded doctor himself arrived, I knew it was the beginning of the end.

She refused to sign the paper. She took one look at Buster and all hell broke loose.

"I'm not doing it."

"Rose, you have to."

We were whispering again.

"They can't make me."

I was on the floor in the dark of her room. I'd done a pretty good job, I thought, slithering down the hall when I was sure Sister Angelica was asleep. Have you ever seen a seven-months-pregnant person slithering?

"Your parents are coming. Mary said she heard Sister Angelica tell Sister Berl. Father Vincent called them, and they're coming on the next plane."

"I don't care if the good Lord Jesus Christ Himself comes. I'm not letting them take my baby from me."

"Your parents aren't going to let you keep him."

"Then I'll run away."

Tears from both of us. I squeezed her fingers, stood up, and sat tentatively on the edge of her bed.

"Oh, Rose, how will you take care of him? What will you do for money?"

She wiped her nose with the sheet. "I'll get a job. The Holy Mother will help me."

"Oh, Rose."

"I can do it, Jenny. I can type, I can take shorthand—I took all of that shit in school."

"But where will you go?"

"I'll go home, I'll go to Fond du Lac; I have to go home."

"But what will people say?"

"I don't care."

"But they'll know." I began to sob; I couldn't help it. "They'll go crazy if you go home. Everyone'll see the baby, they'll know, they'll know you weren't married and you got pregnant . . . they'll talk about you, they'll say terrible things."

"I don't care, Jenny. I won't give Buster to anybody. I don't care what anybody says. I won't."

And she didn't. Her parents arrived, there were lots of powwows, Thanksgiving came and went in a cloud of whispers, and Rose stood her ground. Her parents tried to be as stubborn as she was, but in the end they fell apart. They didn't want to lose their daughter. They agreed to let her bring the baby home. She could live with them until she got a job and was able to put away enough for three months' rent; then she was going to be, as Rose put it, "thrown out into the snow."

"You have no idea how much snow there is in Fond du Lac, Wisconsin, Jenny."

We were allowed to say goodbye to her, but we weren't allowed to see the baby. I saw him, though, because I did a little more slithering. I also hid when they went out the gates to get into the taxicab: I stood behind the orange trees so I could kiss them goodbye between the bars. Buster had black curls, just like Rose, but long fingers and long, skinny feet, feet that might someday walk on the moon, astronaut feet. He was wearing a little blue hat with matching blue bootees. He was five days old and practically as big as Rose.

"If I could get him through the bars, you could hold him."

"It's okay." I let my finger drift across his cheek.

"You promise to come to Fond du Lac?"

"I promise."

"Don't worry about having it—you don't feel anything once it's over."

"Okay."

"You'll be all right, Jenny."

"Okay."

"You have to have faith."

"Okay."

She leaned her head forward, the tip of her nose touching the bars. I was dizzy with the smell of baby powder. "The Virgin Mary will watch over you. I promise."

"Rose," her mother said from the open door of the taxicab.

"I'm coming," she said over her shoulder. "I love you, Jenny."

"I love you too, Rose."

We clutched fingers through the iron bars of Stella Maris. I thought I was going to die. Long after the taxi had gone and the lights had spilled yellow across the dark garden and it was too cold to stay out there anymore, I stood up. My legs were stiff, and I reached for the statue of Saint Robert Bellarmine to hold on to, but there was something wrapped around my fingers—Rose had wound her tiny crystal rosary beads into my hand. As if they were the only hold I had left on life, I clutched those beads until they made marks on my fingers. I believed

Rose and I would see each other again. I didn't know how long it would take, but I truly believed. After all, her baby was named Buster Jaffe Hufstedler. That's what it said on his birth certificate. Hufstedler was Rose's last name, the Jaffe was for me.

I told Mrs. Havermeyer I wanted the adoptive parents to be Catholic.

"But you're Jewish, dear; don't you want your baby to be raised by a lovely Jewish couple?"

I shook my head in the negative. "No, ma'am," I said. "I want the baby to be Catholic." At least the baby would be covered: it would have the Virgin Mary and Jesus and the saints and all the angels and everybody else I couldn't have.

"Well, if you're sure, dear, I'll call Blessed Children, even though I've already contacted Vista del Mar."

I had no idea what she was talking about. As long as the baby was Catholic, I didn't care who she called.

December 4, my birthday, was a far cry from the previous year. No fancy shindig at the country club; just a yellow cake with white icing and twenty-seven other pregnant girls singing "Happy Birthday" to me. My birthday present was a new roommate, Sugar Dawes, who "hailed," she said, from Gun Barrel City, Texas. She wore a cowboy hat and was true to her name, sweet as sugar, but I didn't care. I didn't want to hear her story. I didn't want to hear anybody's story ever again; I had lost my heart for stories. I didn't talk to her much, which I'm sure wasn't very helpful, but I didn't care about that either.

I spent most of my time in church, hiding, trying not to be afraid. I spent hours staring at the statue of the Virgin Mary, but she didn't say a word. I had thought she'd send me a sign, some kind of clue. No matter how long I watched her, she held steady, her eyes lowered, her hands clasped, her toes at the bottom of her blue and white china gown motionless. My biggest problem was Buster; I saw him everywhere. When I shut my eyes I saw him; when I opened my eyes I saw him, blue eyes and blue bootees, his little fist waving wildly in the air. I'd spent eight months pretending that what was inside me was just a sensation, and now, because of Buster, I couldn't do that anymore.

I made it through Christmas. I don't remember much of it, except being a big hit with Sister Mary Julia; because I'd been in chorus all four years of high school, I knew all the words of all the carols. There were eight angels painted on the ceiling behind the main altar, above Jesus and above Mary, above everything, eight angels with golden halos and silver wings, floating in formation in shimmering pastel gowns. Father Vincent said they were unknown angels, that they didn't have names. They were just a chorus, he said, a chorus of angels, and after Christmas and all the singing, Sister Mary Julia said I was one of *her* chorus of angels, and Father Vincent looked at me with love in his eyes and said, "Our very own Jewish angel," and he smiled. I was overwhelmed, drowning in too many emotions, and my knees gave way. They carried me out of church and took me to my room. I had a fever, I felt "blouky," which was one of Rose's words, and "crampy," which was one of mine, and the whole thing was obvious, I told them, I had the flu. I went to bed with flu; I woke up with something else.

Pain. Terror. Panic.

More pain. More terror. More panic.

More pain.

Could there be more pain? There was no one with me. Nurse Rae Lee walked in and out to check on me, and Sister Angelica came once or twice, but I don't think anyone else came. It went on forever, until I thought I would rip and be pieces lying on the table, until I was biting Rose's rosary beads, until the doctor himself came and they hit me with the anesthetic. And then I woke up, they woke me up, they were calling my name. And they told me.

Five pounds, eleven ounces. Eighteen inches. That's what they told me, but they were just words. I could hear them, but nothing registered—there was only the look of a baby, the feel of a baby. They handed me a baby. An incredibly small baby. A *she.*

Sister Angelica put her into my arms.

I couldn't speak, I couldn't breathe. I had gotten my sign from Mary.

Ten so tiny fingers and ten so tiny toes and tiny kneecaps in perfect replica of big ones and tiny heels and elbows and little shoulders and little ears and one little freckle on the tip of her right earlobe and one little freckle on the bottom of her left foot and the sweetest nose with a little dip in it and the sweetest pink mouth and one dimple where the angels had kissed her at the bottom of her left cheek and wisps of blond hair that were so fine and so light they were practically invisible and soft curling brown eyelashes around pale-blue almond-shaped eyes. A plastic bracelet strapped to one tiny wrist: *Female. Jaffe. December* 30, 1960. 2:40 P.M.

I couldn't stop looking at her, I couldn't believe that she was real. Quiet, incredibly quiet, looking up at me with Will's eyes. Still. Not wiggling like Buster; calm and silent in my arms. I touched her little hand, and she wrapped her tiny fingers around my big finger and held on.

Disbelief.

They would never let me see her alone. One of them always stayed in the room with me, stood near the bed or sat in the chair, and they would only bring her to me at feeding time, the rest of the time she was in the nursery under lock and key. Feeding time was with a bottle, no breast feeding, they didn't want your milk to come in, of course they didn't, what would I do with milk in Kansas City without a baby to feed? They bound me with big white bath towels held together with diaper pins, my entire upper body encased in tight terry cloth, but that wasn't what was making it so hard for me to breathe. I was to stay in the clinic five days, the normal procedure for a normal delivery. The abnormal thing was that after the five days I would go home alone.

How could I leave her? I couldn't leave her, I wouldn't leave her. But, Jenny, wake up to reality, oh, yes, you will, the wicked witch said. There was to be "no discussion" about keeping her. I tried on the telephone. Sister Berl sat next to me and held my hand.

I tried when my mother arrived from Kansas City. Father Vincent at the foot of my bed, his head bowed, his voice low, Mrs. Haver-meyer by the door, her mouth open, and my mother pacing the room in open defiance, her eyes screaming *no*. I remember her pocketbook, my mother's pocketbook on her arm, black leather with a double handle and a gold clasp, her elegant gray wool crepe shirtwaist dress, moving about her knees, one strand of pearls swaying over her breasts as gray suede pumps charged back and forth across the floor.

"There is no reason to discuss this. I will not waver and I will not change. Jennifer will not come home with a baby. The baby will be put up for adoption, as we agreed when we sent her to you. I can't imagine that you even want to discuss this with me."

"But, Mrs. Jaffe," Father Vincent said.

"There is nothing more to say, Father. I'm furious with the lot of you, that you would allow Jennifer to think she could change her mind. I would assume the Church agrees with me that adoption will be better for the child in every way."

"I never agreed, I never said anything, I never even thought there would be a baby, somehow . . . I don't know what I thought." I was sobbing. Sister Berl put her hand on my knee.

Father Vincent reached out as if to touch my mother. "Couldn't there possibly be a way that you could help her, since Jennifer so clearly wants to keep this child?"

"I could get a job . . . please, Mom, I could get a job."

She whirled so fast, the pearls leaped up and made a scallop over her left shoulder.

"Doing what? You never had a job in your life!"

"I could, though."

"Could what? What could you be, Jennifer, with your high school diploma—a clerk in a dime store? How much do you think you would make?"

"I could . . . I could work in a dime store."

"Listen to you! Do you know how much it costs to raise a child? Of course you don't! You don't know anything! And you will not live with me, Jennifer. I promise you, I will *not* help you and you will *not* live with me, *not with a child, you won't*. I *won't* have everyone talking about us behind our backs, and I *won't* let you ruin your life. *I won't*."

The words echoed around the room and fell among us as if they'd been walloped high into center field with a bat.

Nobody said anything.

I slipped sideways and fell softly against Sister Berl. "Daddy will help me."

"Daddy? Now you think of your daddy? Your daddy can hardly stand up. The doctor is certain he'll have another heart attack from what you've done."

Father Vincent cleared his throat. "Mrs. Jaffe, there are organizations that can help her. If you and your husband decide not to be involved, there are people we can call. I will get in touch with the Catholic diocese in Kansas City—"

She cut him off. "She won't be able to do it without me, Father."

"If you could look into your heart—"

"She won't be able to do it without me. She isn't capable and she isn't strong."

Father Vincent stood up and locked eyes with the dragon. "If Jennifer is determined, she can do it—with the Lord's help."

She stared at him. "And will the Lord be there when it's time to feed this baby? Tell me that, Father: will the Lord be there when it's time to put food in her mouth? And patent-leather party shoes on her feet and fancy pink dresses and pediatricians and braces and toys? The Lord won't be there when it's time to take care of everything. *And neither will I,* I can assure you. I do not care what Jennifer *thinks* she wants. The baby will be adopted as planned. This is what is best for her, best for the baby and for Jennifer. I will not be swayed. This is my daughter we're talking about. With all due respect, Father, I don't need anybody to tell me what to do."

Father Vincent took a step toward her. "Mrs. Jaffe, I—"

"No. There is nothing more to discuss. Jennifer will come home and go to college. She will put all this behind her; she will forget about it in time. I know what is best for her. I will not let her be burdened with an illegitimate baby and no future at eighteen. I will not let her ruin her life. I will not let my daughter be the talk of the town."

It was no one's favorite New Year's Eve. There was no champagne, there was no "Auld Lang Syne," and there was no merriment. There was only anguish and tears.

Forget about it.

Put it behind me.

But the "it" was a baby. The "it" was my daughter.

And you'd think that I would have been strong enough, you'd

think that I would have stood up and told the wicked witch Esther to go fuck herself, or at least slapped her hard across her evil face. But I didn't. God forgive me, I didn't do anything. Mrs. Havermeyer tried to talk to me; she said I didn't have to go back to Kansas City, there were people right there in Los Angeles who could help me find a decent place to live and a job. I remember that word "decent" hitting me in the face. What did that mean—a bathroom down the hall, a hot plate instead of a kitchen, no running water? Me and my baby living in a decent place in Los Angeles—I tried to picture it, but my mother's words colored everything: I didn't know one person in Los Angeles, I'd never even left the grounds of Stella Maris to see Los Angeles, and where would I leave the baby while I was working at this phantom job in a dime store? Would I leave her with some fairy the angels would send me from above?

Sister Berl tried to talk to me, Father Vincent tried to talk to me, about how the Church would help, and I listened to them—oh, how I listened, how I wished and I wanted, but somewhere in the deepest part of me I knew my mother was right: I couldn't do it without her. Unlike Rose, I would be out there flying solo from the start, just me and my baby without a net, and if I tried to envision the realities of it, me heating a bottle in a little dented pan on a hot plate, all I could see was overwhelming blackness, a curtain of blackness descending over me. I wasn't Rose, I was just Jenny. I didn't know how to fight, and in the end I guess I didn't want to, because if you really want to do something you do it, don't you?

In the end I proved to be what I always had been, a coward. I didn't try to keep my baby. I hardly held on to her, I let her slip through my fingers and fall right out of my life. In the end, God forgive me, I proved my mother was right.

•   •   •

You were not allowed to sign the paper at Stella Maris; it was against the rules, since they were the middlemen for the adoption and you could say they coerced you, held you captive, made you sign at gunpoint or at the end of a witch's broom. I don't know, I don't remember, I only remember you had to leave the grounds. I don't know what they did with my mother; maybe Father Vincent held her at bay. If only he could have hit her over the head with the incense, lit her with the candles, nailed her to a cross. Whatever happened to crucifixion anyway? If only we could have had it brought back—just for my mother, of course. We went to Mrs. Havermeyer's office. In a car; I don't remember who drove. I don't remember her office, except I threw up in the wastebasket that was by the door. Mrs. Havermeyer held my head, sweet Mrs. Havermeyer of the sad face and the thick ankles, and she introduced me to Mr. Stanley, Mr. Stanley from Blessed Children, the Blessed Children's Agency, that's what she said. He would arrange the adoption, he would place my baby— that's what he said, *place*—with a lovely Catholic couple who would raise her, but first she would be in a foster home, probably just for a week or so, he said reassuringly, because they had lots of lovely Catholic couples who were just waiting to get a baby of their own; they just wanted to find the right lovely Catholic couple, he said, nodding his head positively. And then he said he had to ask me questions, he had to ask me questions before I could sign the paper. I was sitting in a chair by then.

"Has anyone forced you to do this?"

That's what he said. I was holding on to the desktop, and Mr. Stanley was standing on the other side of the desk. He was tall, very, very tall and painfully thin and balding—you could see the bones in his head— and he said, "Jenny?" And Mrs. Havermeyer said, "Are you all right, dear? Are you going to be sick again?" and she had her hand on my shoulder. I was thinking he looked like Ichabod Crane, from the headless horseman but I couldn't remember if Ichabod Crane was a good guy or a bad guy, and Mrs. Havermeyer patted my shoulder. I could smell her perfume, it was gardenias, and Mr. Stanley ran his tongue across his upper lip and he said the words again.

"Has anyone forced you to do this?"

He leaned forward, tipped forward from the waist over the desktop like a wooden stick doll, and Mrs. Havermeyer squeezed my shoulder. Maybe it wasn't gardenias, maybe it was freesias, but I didn't know when I had ever smelled a freesia, and in a soft voice she said, "Jenny?" and I looked up at Mr. Stanley and I said no, no one had forced me to do this. That's what I said.

Because I hadn't been forced, had I? Let's face it: I was sitting there, nobody had a gun on me, I wasn't tied to the chair, I'd walked in under my own power, on my own two feet and of my own free will. Hadn't I?

I don't remember the rest of the questions. I don't remember signing the paper, physically writing my name. I remember the word "relinquish." I remember blinking, seeing the word "relinquish" swimming around in front of my eyes. "I, so and so, do hereby relinquish my baby . . ." "I, Jennifer Jaffe, do hereby relinquish . . ." Relinquish as in give up, as in abandon. God forgive me, I do remember holding the pen. I held the pen, I must have signed the paper. I gave my baby away. Excuse me, *relinquish*. I *relinquished* my baby; let's call a spade a spade.

Sister Berl waited on the other side of the door. It was the only time they had let me be alone with her, the one and only time. It was in a little room on the delivery floor, a room at the end of the hallway, which I'd never seen before. Of course I hadn't, none of us had, because it was saved for only these very special occasions: it was the room where you and your baby said goodbye. An overstuffed chair and a window and the smell of orange blossoms. You'd think it would have been raining, but it wasn't; the sun was in full parade, and there was a lovely breeze:

I felt it play on my skin when I unbuttoned my dress. She couldn't deny me everything, not this memory of my baby at my breast.

My sweet baby.

Her little fingers held my finger, her eyes were open, and her little mouth sucked at me, but I had no milk and she'd already had five days of a bottle, so of course she cried. There was no underestimating the reach of the witch: she'd fixed everything; even this I couldn't have.

I buttoned my blouse and I rocked her, I tried to tell her everything. What had happened, what would happen, how some wonderful mommy and daddy would take care of her better than I could, how I wasn't a force to be reckoned with but I knew she would be, because she was half her daddy. I told her all about Will, about the first time I saw him standing there at the Texaco, about all the times, about how I loved him, about how I knew he had loved me. I told her that it didn't matter how we had ended up, that she was a baby who had come from love and that's what made her special.

And then I told her what it said on her birth certificate: that I had written her daddy's name even though we weren't married and that I had named her Cole Jaffe because I wanted her to be named for both of us, that even though he had left me I felt it was right somehow, she would forever be a part of Will and me. I told her that her other mommy and daddy would probably change her name, but somewhere deep inside she would know who she was. I kissed every part of her, every bit of the silk and down of her, and then I stood up and held her out in front of me and looked in her eyes. I promised her that someday I would see her again, that no matter how long it took or how difficult it would be, I would. And then I held her close to me and I wound Rose's beautiful crystal rosary beads around her tiny wrist. It was the only thing that meant anything to me, the only part of me I could give her to take. I looked at her one more time, in one last look I tried to drink her in and tell her everything I could, and then I opened the door.

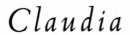

Claudia

"Read me, Mommy, one more, one more," Lily said.

She slid off Claudia's lap and ran to the basket of books at the end of the small blue sofa. Claudia moved back and forth slowly in the rocker, her bare feet made squeak sounds on the hardwood floor as she rocked up and down and looked out the open window at the night sky.

"Look at that, Lily—isn't that beautiful?"

Chunky white stars and planets were actually visible in the Los Angeles sky. For the first time in two months, the desert Santa Ana had blown the smog away. As Claudia turned, the white lace curtains jiggled on the wooden rod above her head, and a gust of hot air moved around the room.

"That's a hawk moon, baby," Claudia said to Lily. "See how it's just a skinny little sliver? That's called a hawk moon." Claudia studied her three-year-old daughter, the little body squatted by the basket, the pudgy dimpled baby legs, the sweet toes, the poof of Lily's last hold-out night-time diaper clearly visible through the seat of her pink jammies, the wisps of light-blond hair curling softly around the child's neck and earlobes. Claudia ran her hand through her own hair, smiled at her little daughter's back, and then pulled at the silk of the old peach nightgown where it stuck to her thighs.

"It's hot tonight, isn't it, baby?"

"This one, do this one," Lily said. She ran back and wiggled herself up and onto her mother. "Read me, Mommy, do the baby bird."

"The baby bird, huh? Well, I don't know about this baby bird. . . ." She held the book out in front of the two of them in the rocker, tipped her chin down and rested it on the top of Lily's damp curls and breathed in. Lily scooched her bottom around in her mother's lap and then settled, one chubby baby hand on top of Claudia's, the other clutching the cherished piece of blue satin from the edge of her blanket to her nose. Claudia felt her shoulders release and lower, as she held the little girl and rocked.

"That's not just a hawk moon, Lily, it's yellow. Do you see that, how it's yellow? A skinny yellow hawk moon is very special. You could make a wish on it, you could—"

"Mommy . . ."

"What?"

"Read me."

Claudia smiled. "Oh . . . read you. Sure . . . so what is this new book we have here?"

"Grandma Margaret got it for me while you and Daddy were in *the* New York."

"She did, huh? And you like it?"

"Uh huh."

"Well, okay, so it got a great review here." She opened the book and turned to the first page. "Let's see. 'A mother bird sat on her egg,'" Claudia read. "That's a good beginning."

"'The egg jumped,'" Lily said eagerly.

"You know it already, huh, cookie?"

"Mommy, read."

"Oh, sure. Sorry . . . 'The egg jumped. Oh oh! said the mother bird.'"

"'Oh oh,'" said Lily.

Claudia's face softened; she moved her chin against Lily's curls.

" 'My baby will be here!' " Lily said emphatically.

" 'My baby will be here!' " read Claudia. " 'He will want to eat. I must get something for my baby bird to eat! she said. I will be back. So away she went.' "

Lily wiggled in anticipation. " 'The egg jumped,' " she said, giggling.

Claudia laughed. " 'The egg jumped. It jumped, and jumped, and jumped! Out came the baby bird!' Oh, my goodness, he was born, wasn't he? That cute little baby bird was born."

Lily patted her mother's hand.

"Okay, okay, cookie. 'Where is my mother? he said. He looked for her. He looked up, He did not see her. He looked down. He did not see her. I will go and look for her, he said. So away he went.' "

" 'Down, out of the tree,' " he went. Lily squealed.

Lily moved her back against her mother's breasts, moved her head under her mother's chin.

" 'The baby bird could not fly, but he could walk,' " Lily said. "Mommy, read."

But Claudia had stopped reading. Her eyes were focused somewhere out the window, somewhere in the black sky to the side of that hawk moon.

Lily went on with emphasis, as if she could read what was on the page in front of her. " 'Now I will go and find my mother.' " She patted Claudia's leg. "Read me, Mommy. 'Now I will go and find my mother,' the book says."

" 'Now I will go and find my mother,' " Claudia repeated softly.

The tears swelled suddenly, surprising her, sliding down her face and into her daughter's hair.

" 'Now I will go and find my mother . . .' " Claudia said, but then the words stuck and she could say no more.

•　　•　　•

She stood and looked at her face in the mirror, wiped toothpaste with a wet hand from the sides of her mouth. She'd put Lily to bed right after that book, rocked her a little, and the child sang in her lap, " 'Night and day, you are duh one . . .' " Oliver thought that was a riot, that Claudia had taught Lily every song Fred and Ginger had danced. "What about 'Twinkle, Twinkle, Little Star'?" he'd asked.

"You're kidding. Don't tell me you want to compare 'Twinkle, Twinkle' to 'Night and Day'?"

Claudia frowned in the mirror. First the damn dreams again, and now this. " 'Now I will go and find my mother,' " she mouthed, and she bent her head, splashed more water on her face, and reached for a towel. She would go down to the kitchen and get herself a big glass of white wine. First she'd talk to him, and then she'd go. Or maybe she'd get the wine first. . . .

"Ollie?"

There was no answer from the bedroom, only an announcer on the television, screaming out plays from the Knicks game. Claudia moved away from the sink and stood in the doorway, watching her husband watch the game. He had propped a lot of flowered chintz pillows back against the king-sized headboard, but he wasn't leaning on them; he was perched on the edge of the bed in his boxer shorts, pitched forward, ready to jump in. If signaled by the Knicks coach, all he needed were shoes, a numbered jersey, and a basketball. Oliver James Morgan, social studies teacher and part-time Saturday-morning soccer coach for the tenth and twelfth grades of Canyon High School, now stripped of his chinos and chambray button-downs, wearing only striped boxers and white socks.

"Ollie, I've been thinking about something. . . . Something happened while I was putting the baby to bed, and it really threw me, and . . ." She put her hand on the doorframe. "I've been having the *other mother* dreams again . . . actually, for some time now—"

"Come on, Ewing!" Oliver yelled at the television.

"Ollie?"

No answer.

She studied him carefully; he wasn't listening, it was absolutely clear he wasn't listening. ". . . and I think I'm going to go to China," she said.

No response, nothing. It was amazing.

"Okay?"

"Hmm?" he said. He didn't look at her. He could just tune her out. Was it her or was it anything? If someone else were standing there, would he be watching TV?

"I'm going to study bound feet and the history of porcelain from the Shming dynasty and maybe how to make mu shu pork just like they do at Little Bill's Old China."

"Defense! You sack of shit!" Ollie yelled at the television.

"Oh, and the other thing I forgot to tell you is I think I'm going to look for my parents, the real ones—" and she stopped. "No, that isn't right, is it? Not the real ones, the *other* ones," she said softly, "not Margaret and John."

She leaned her head against the doorjamb. "Maybe I've finally made up my mind—"

"What, babe? You want Chinese?"

There it was, a perfect example of what she used to point out to her patients: creative listening, you see that—the only thing that got through to him were the words "mu shu pork."

"Come on, Ewing, you moron!"

Oliver shifted his eyes from the TV and looked at his wife, poised in the bathroom doorway. Sand-colored, unruly, wavy hair, bright blue eyes, a thin, tall body through a peach nightgown, broad bony shoulders, freckles, tan skinny legs, tan arms. He liked what he saw, and he beamed in appreciation. "What?"

Claudia shook her head. She couldn't tell him; it seemed she'd lost all her energy—it had oozed out of her and was somewhere on the floor. "Nothing. I'm going down to the kitchen."

"Okay," Oliver said, looking back at the Knicks game. "So hey, we ordering Chinese?"

It wouldn't be difficult. At least, that's what they had told her.

"It isn't difficult to find your birth parents, as long as your birth parents are looking for you."

But why would they be looking for her if they gave her up in the first place? It didn't make sense, and more important, why would she be looking for them? That was the real question; it always came back to that.

She stood in front of the cutting board perched over the kitchen sink and stared out at the next morning, she listened for sounds of Lily waking up from her nap. Hearing nothing, she turned on the faucets, then turned them off again. Then she picked up the table-spoon she'd been holding, poked it inside the Jif jar, filled the spoon with peanut butter, and put it in her mouth. The baby would be up soon, she wanted the baby to get up soon. Maybe she'd go upstairs and make a lot of noise in the hall. If she woke her, then she could play with her, she wouldn't have to think about this stuff anymore. Claudia ran her hand across her face. She was tired from the dreams, that's what it was, but it would be okay. They would eat all the little squares Claudia had made of peanut butter and jelly and she'd let Lily make those things she liked, peanut butter with raisins on top pushed into celery sticks—ants on a log. They'd dribble Fox's U-Bet chocolate syrup into white milk, magically turning it chocolate. Look at Mommy, Mommy's a magician, isn't she great?

A hummingbird poked himself into a pink geranium.

She should just forget about this whole thing anyway. It was ridiculous. It had come out of nowhere, and there was no reason to even consider it; why look for trouble when your life is working? Isn't that what she would tell a patient? Of course. If you're perfectly happy, if your life is perfectly happy, why mess it up with . . . what? unnecessary parents? The hummingbird dashed back to the Iceland poppies; he'd been alternating between the poppies and the geraniums.

"Take it easy, fella," Claudia said.

She took a glass from the drainboard and walked to the refrigerator, removed an open bottle of white wine, popped the cork, tipped it over the glass, and then stopped. She corked the wine and put it back in the refrigerator, set the glass in the sink.

Unnecessary parents. Real parents. *Birth* parents? Yes, that's what the woman had said. She remembered how those words had thrown her—no, more than thrown her, they'd practically catapulted her out of the chair. The words had come out of the lady's mouth, the smiling, very fat lady in the very chintzy red dress at EDNA, where Claudia had gone ten years ago. It was the first time she had ever heard the term. If birth parents were the ones who gave birth to you but didn't keep you, then what were Margaret and John? The afterbirth parents? No . . . that was disgusting. The number-two parents? That was worse. She did not say any of that to the lady; she just sat on the edge of the yellow plastic chair with her feet planted in front of her, her damp hands clamped firmly around her purse, and she thought, what was she doing? what was the matter with her? she had never thought about doing this before. . . .

And now she was doing it again.

Ten years ago she'd gone, right before she'd married Oliver. And it was because of something that had seemed so ephemeral really, until you analyzed it, something that seemed so insignificant that had made her even consider going in the first place.

She'd been sitting in her parents' dining room in the house in Hancock Park where she'd grown up, she and her mother, Margaret, sitting next to each other in the beautiful butter-yellow room with the high molded ceilings and the heavy flowered drapes, smiling at each other at the mahogany table, as Margaret addressed the thick cream wedding invitation envelopes with one of her fountain pens with its permanent black ink. And that's when it had gotten to her. She had to figure out later exactly *what* had gotten to her; she had to figure it out for herself and she had to figure it out for her sessions, she was still interning at the clinic then, so she had to know. "You, as a therapist to you, as a person," Dr. Turner had said, "in order to be a good psychologist, you have to know." Her as a patient, okay, so what had gotten to her? It was the word permanent, the word *permanent* written on the ink bottle, she wanted to get married for *permanent*, this would be her one and only wedding as far as she was concerned, the only time that she would ever march down that aisle, *permanently* attached to Oliver, her *permanent* personal pick. Somehow that was the catalyst, that and the fact that she couldn't address any of the envelopes because her handwriting looked as if she were a paraplegic while her mother's looked as if she had taught penmanship at Miss Hickey's Finishing School for Girls and now got paid a lot of money to do calligraphy on the side. Another way in which she wasn't like Margaret, didn't look like her and certainly didn't act like her, patient and genuinely kind and soft-spoken, always soft-spoken; she couldn't even remember hearing her mother *really* raise her voice, not even at her father; even when it was clear that she was losing her temper, Margaret seemed to be able to hold on to herself and breeze right through. If her parents fought, they must have done it some-where else or when Claudia was sleeping or maybe they did it in sign language, maybe only their fingers flew around in silent fury or maybe Margaret just never fought, maybe it was something she didn't do,

114

and although Claudia tried to copy Margaret's sweet demeanor, it always felt as if she had been horribly miscast in Olivia de Havilland's role, keeping her teeth clamped together until she thought her eyes would pop. And if she wasn't Miss Mellie, then who was she? Scarlett? No, she wasn't that defiant; and not Mammy, ever-giving . . . then who was she? She didn't have the swagger for Rhett Butler. Ashley Wilkes? All these thoughts collided into a dream-wrenched night for Claudia. Over and over, like a back and forth instant replay from one of Ollie's basketball games, Claudia marched up and down that aisle in her wedding gown, but the mother who was watching her in these dreams was not Margaret; this *other mother* was not small and dimpled and rosy like Margaret; this *other mother* would never wear a moss-green lacy dress, like Margaret; this *other mother*, smiling behind the candles and the white roses, was wearing black. And she looked just like Claudia. She had light-brown wavy hair and was tall and thin, with a smattering of freckles; and rotten penmanship. It was hard to know how you could tell about her penmanship from a dream especially one where she didn't *write* anything, but it was clear to Claudia that long night as she lay punching her pillow, that this *other mother* wrote just like her. And looked like her and walked like her and talked like her. And this *other mother*, this dream mother, Claudia knew, was not a dream.

And shouldn't this *other mother* get to see Claudia become *permanent?*

"Well, shouldn't she?" Gena said, and looked up at the waitress. "Could we have a knife to cut this thing?"

"Sure, honey," the waitress said. She had a brass-framed pin on the breast pocket of her pink uniform; under the frilly white handkerchief, it said *Judy*, in script.

Gena pushed at the enormous Reuben sandwich with her finger.

"It's not a big deal. After you find her it could be a big deal, a very big deal, it could possibly change your whole life, but this part is easy. You just go there and they put your name on a list and they see if her name's on the list; they connect you with your real mother . . . and that's that." She popped a french fry into her mouth.

"That's that, huh? Very funny, ho ho ho." Claudia ran her hand through her hair and took a sip of cream soda. "Why do I feel like I want to scream?"

"I don't know. Because you're hungry?"

"Pass the pickles, Maury," said the woman in the booth next to theirs. "And get your elbow out of your brother's side, Tiffany—I see what you're doing over there."

You could hear everything in Nate 'N' Al's, it was always packed on Sunday mornings; they started lining up at dawn for lox and bagels and cream cheese and before it was over the sun was setting and they were still standing there for chicken-in-the-pot.

Claudia leaned in closer to the table. "Gena, you don't understand. I haven't thought about this stuff since I was little; I haven't had these dreams for years. The 'brown-haired-other-mother' dreams, I used to call them when I was a kid."

"Gee, I didn't know you used to dream about her."

"Oh, yeah, and not just her either. I used to dream about him. Of course, I was never sure if it was him or Hopalong Cassidy. Some guy running around in a black cowboy hat, with silver hair."

"Hopalong Cassidy? God, I haven't heard that name since I was a little kiddo. Thank you, Judy," Gena said to the waitress as she reappeared with a knife.

"Sure, honey. You girls want anything else?"

"No, thank you," Claudia said. "Yeah, silver hair and a silver mustache."

"Hopalong Cassidy didn't have a mustache," Gena said.

"Yes he did."

"Nope," Judy said, taking three dollar bills from under the sugar bowl and shaking her head. "No mustache. Of course, I was more a Gene Autry fan myself. See, he could sing and Hoppy couldn't. That was probably what did it for me. I never could get over a man with a guitar." She sighed.

Claudia and Gena gazed up at her.

"Well, okeydokey," she said, putting the tip in her pocket and patting her yellow teased updo. Then she turned and left.

"Okeydokey," Gena said, and gave Claudia a look. She sliced the sandwich into two perfect rectangles and gave Claudia one. "Don't let me eat too many french fries."

"When I was little, before you moved here, I had all this Hopalong Cassidy stuff, guns and a hat and a holster, I have no idea why, and I used to run around the house wearing all that stuff and shooting imaginary bad guys from under the dining room table and pretending I was Hoppy's girl. I don't even know if he had a girl. . . ."

"We could ask Judy," Gena said, taking a big bite of the sandwich.

"Anyway, when I would dream the *other father* dream, which is what I called it, the *other father* had a black cowboy hat and silver hair—à la Hopalong Cassidy, see? And the *other mother* looked just like me."

"Oh," Gena said, chewing. "Mmm, this is deliciously greasy, isn't it?"

Claudia slumped and put her face in her hands. "I know, this whole thing is ridiculous. What's the matter with me?"

"It's not ridiculous; it's normal. Eat your sandwich—your blood sugar's low."

Claudia sat up and made a face. "Why don't I just forget about it? Chalk it up to premarriage heebie-jeebies."

"Why shouldn't you want to know who your parents are?"

"Why *should* I? I have two perfectly wonderful, loving parents. What do I need more for? Isn't two enough for any girl?"

"What does Dr. Turner say?"

"She says it's up to me."

"Well, that's helpful."

"No, it's true—it *is* up to me."

"Okay, so what do *you* say?"

"I say . . . I just don't know. That's what's so awful: I want to know who they are, but I don't want to know who they are."

"Falling into the don't-make-waves category."

"Yeah." She exhaled. "You know those things they use in the movies, where it looks like it's a real house but it's only cardboard and when you walk through the door there's nothing there? What do they call that?"

"A facade." Gena put down her sandwich. "A false front."

"Yeah . . ." Claudia leaned back against the red vinyl. "That's me."

"You are absolutely not a false front. Okay, wait a minute . . . what does Ollie say?"

"He says I should do what makes me feel comfortable." She laughed. "It's the same thing he says when I ask him what I should wear."

That was true, but it was more than that. Anything about parents was an opening for Ollie to make a bad joke or leave the room. His father had died the summer Ollie turned thirteen; the ball-playing, happy-jock Pop whom Oliver had worshiped waltzed out the door one August morning and later that day fell across his thermos of coffee from a stroke so massive they said his heart had literally burst. Oliver was left with a mother as shattered as he was, and as if they were characters in a Pinter play, each of them secretly blamed the other for Mike Morgan's death. Ollie hardly spoke to his mother and was not interested in any discussion about the whys. "I don't want to know about that part of my psyche, Claud. Don't *psychologize* me; leave well enough alone." Fixed and serious and angry. Claudia hadn't seen that part of him before.

"Leave him alone," Gena said, "what do you care if he doesn't like his mother—I don't particularly like mine either, as you well know—and other than that he's relentlessly perfect. Isn't he allowed to have a weak spot or two?"

She was not about to push Ollie into helping her find the *other mother,* so it was Gena who found out there was this organization called EDNA. EDNA, Gena decided, was the perfect name for an organization that helped people find their parents, because it conjured up an image of a farmwoman, "very stoic, very black-and-white, like that lady who was Henry Fonda's mother in *Grapes of Wrath.* Don't you remember her, Claudia, how she sat in the truck all sober-faced with her hat on, tears shining in her eyes, brave and strong but yet so 'motherly'? It's a perfect name for a place where you go to find your mother; it's the very image of a mother—so fitting, so apropos, so *Edna,*" Gena said. Gena thought of everything in terms of movies, usually obscure movies that Claudia had never heard of, because Gena saw *everything.* And Gena explained what she thought in terms of movies. Ollie, she thought, was very Jean-Paul Belmondo, but from his earlier films, she said—Jean-Paul Belmondo with a touch of Gary Cooper's hair, the way it went in a wave, and maybe just a trace of John Garfield, especially in the boxing film. Claudia had never seen the boxing film, she didn't know if she'd ever seen John Garfield, so she just shook her head. Claudia thought Ollie was very Ollie.

"And it's not just because it sounds so motherly," Gena said. "There are other organizations that help people find their parents, but this one seems so perfect. Listen to this," and she read aloud from the pink brochure: " 'EDNA is named for its founder, Edna Jean

119

Malone, who found the graves of her parents after an exhaustive thirty-three-year search.' Can you imagine? She finds her parents after all those years, and they're dead?"

Claudia slumped back against the sofa cushions. "Wonderful."

"Well, I didn't mean that would happen to you. Yours aren't going to be dead; don't be ridiculous. I just love the way they put it—it's so dramatic, don't you think?"

"Gena, I don't know if I really want to do this."

"Oh, come on, think of it as an adventure. If you don't like it, you can leave."

Claudia made a face.

"Okay . . . I'll go with you."

"Oh, that would be good."

"I'll go with you, but you have to stop being such a chicken. We're not still at Saint Mary Magdalene, Sister Anne isn't going to catch us and smack us with her goddamn ruler across the hands." Gena shrugged and shook her head. "Boy, I hated that . . . I wonder if she's finally dead."

"Don't say goddamn," Claudia said. She lifted her foot to put it on the coffee table and then put it down. One long curl fell over her face and moved as she breathed out. "I wish *you* could go and pretend you're me."

"Ooh, that would be wonderful, just like in a movie. . . . Can I, Claud? Would you let me? Do you want me to?"

"No." She stood up. "*I* have to do this; *I* have to go."

A plain brown door down a hallway, the fake brass letters, EDNA, stuck on the brown door, a plain white square room in a low stucco building on a side street close to the freeway—it was there that Claudia had a quiet conversation with the very fat lady in the chintzy red dress.

"But what if she *isn't* looking for me?"

"Well, then she won't have put herself on the list saying that she wants to be found, and he won't have either."

"He?"

"Your father," the lady said.

"My father," Claudia repeated, and she had a vision of John, her father, tall and dear and gruff and conventional, the lawyer lumberjack, to quote Gena, penned from the forest by a pin-striped suit and a navy silk tie. Claudia smiled at the vision of her father, and the lady smiled back at her, a very big smile, with lips that matched the red dress. Claudia turned to Gena, but Gena was seemingly engrossed in a magazine, her lanky body slung low in an orange plastic chair, one blond wave seductively covering half her face (very Veronica Lake, Gena said), her long legs stuck way out in front of her and crossed at her ballet shoes.

What did Gena care? She knew who her mother and father were, she didn't have a problem with feeling undefined; that blond wave over her eye was an exact replica of the one in her mother's hair, her *real* mother. Gena had a real mother, *one* mother . . . will the mystery mother sign in, please . . . and how come, Claudia thought, Gena could wear ballet shoes with anything? How come if Claudia wore ballet shoes she looked like a bag lady? It was probably because Gena was Theater Arts and Claudia was Psych, but that was probably a mistake too: Claudia should have been the one who'd gone into theater, she should have been the actress—actresses have to be blurry, false fronts that can fill up with the parts they play.

"And your name, dear?" Claudia turned her head. The lady's pudgy fingers were poised over the paper, holding her pen.

"Claudia. My name is Claudia. . . ."

"Claudia, my sweet angel," she could hear her mother saying to her, with that look of pure adoration on her face. Margaret, sitting next to her at Saint Mary Magdalene, touching Claudia lightly on the knee, her mother's soft fingertips patting one kneecap of her swinging legs, her mother's head bent to hers, all that pink skin, the cloud of Chantilly, the wintergreen breath of her whisper. "Stop kicking the pew in front of you, my sweet angel; you're disturbing Mrs. Vallely."

And now the sweet angel grows up and looks for another mother. Where's your devotion, Claudia? Where's your loyalty? What's the matter?—the pink mother isn't good enough for you? Doesn't look like you? Is shorter and rounder and—what—kinder? That's right, she was good enough to raise you, wasn't she, knowing you belonged to somebody else, somebody who didn't want you, threw you away. . . .

"C-l-a-u-d-i-a. And your last name?"

The fat lady's lipstick was smeared. She had caught her lip between her top and bottom teeth when she was writing, and now she had released it and the red had smeared practically up to her nose on the left side. Claudia had a flash of Margaret, was flooded with the sweet smell of Margaret, Margaret sitting at her dressing table, her hands poised over her perfumes and creams as Claudia explained it all over Margaret's shoulder in the mirror: "I just want to see what she looks like, Mommy, that's all," and Margaret's face getting all soft and smudgy, but smiling, still smiling, while she nodded her head valiantly. "Of course you do. I understand, I love you, that's all right, dear."

No. She couldn't do that, she couldn't say that to Margaret, that she wanted to find her *other mother;* she would never want Margaret to think that she wasn't mother enough for her.

"Oh, my heart," Claudia said, exactly the way Margaret did, and realized she was clutching her purse to her chest.

"Excuse me?"

Claudia blinked and looked at the lady. "Excuse *me.* I can't do this," she said, and stood up so fast the chair crashed to the floor. "I'm sorry. Gena, please, we have to get out of here."

•   •   •

So the *other mother* didn't get to see Claudia become *permanent*. And neither did Hopalong Cassidy. Just Margaret and John.

"Margaret and John, my *parents*," Claudia said, out loud.

She ate another tablespoon of peanut butter, and then the hummingbird nearly crashed into the window. "Hey, watch yourself, sweetheart," Claudia said. He turned and flew up into the orange tree.

Ten years ago, ten years since the pathetic EDNA trip. She and Gena had run out of there like bank robbers, springing to their getaway car. And then Claudia had tried to forget about it, buried herself in wedding presents and honeymoon plans and Oliver. Ten years since she had walked down that satin aisle and knelt in front of Father O'Malley and said her vows, Oliver's knee in a black tuxedo solidly banging against her knee behind yards of ivory silk, and for six years she had been blessed with no more *other mother* dreams and no more *other father* dreams. They came back when she was pregnant. Ollie thought that all the not sleeping was *because* she was pregnant; Claudia *knew* it was because she was pregnant, but the wakefulness wasn't physical, it was mental. It was about babies, dreams of floating babies: babies people wanted, blurry women holding blurry babies wrapped in blurry blankets to their chests; and babies people didn't want, graphic images too hard to sleep through, detailed and explicit squashed babies in garbage cans, balloon babies plummeting through blue skies, babies that looked as if Picasso had painted them, hanging upside down like ornaments on Christmas trees. . . .

Claudia banged the tablespoon hard against the jar of grape jam and closed her eyes.

Not that she didn't think about it. Well, not exactly think about it: you don't *think* about the fact that you're adopted; it just crosses your brain every now and then.

She made a design in the jam with the tablespoon.

She had to tell Ollie that there was something the matter with the orange tree; the oranges were splitting before they had a chance to grow. Splitting like somebody had wounded them, sliced through their centers with a razor. She threw the spoon down, and it skidded across the counter and fell into the sink.

"You're adopted," they had said to her—she couldn't even remember who it was who said it. Adopted. Who said the word first? Margaret? John? Some rotten, stinky boy in her catechism class? Billy Shelton, perhaps? Creepy Brucie Baum? Brucie's sister, Becky, of the droopy eye and the looming space between her two front teeth? Claudia absolutely did not know.

Repression. She was a psychologist, after all, she certainly knew about repression. Repression, Psych 202, lecture hall 17, Thursdays at two. "Holding back"—a definition.

"No, I'm not holding back. I just can't remember."

"And that's what we call repression," Dr. Turner had said.

She had questioned her parents repeatedly, and they had told her the story in minute detail: how they sat her down, where they sat her down. "We were going to tell you in the living room, but Daddy thought your bedroom would be better," and Margaret looked at John with such love in her eyes. Her bedroom, her frilly bedroom with its yellow dotted swiss ruffles covering everything, including the lamp. She remembered every inch of her bedroom, but she couldn't remember how they sat her down.

"On the club chair under the window?"

"No, sweetheart—we all sat on the floor."

She looked at her parents, and John laughed. "She doesn't remember, Margaret, that we were once young enough to sit on the floor."

"No, Daddy, it's just that I don't remember."

They were patient; they tried to help her remember. "It was in the afternoon," her mother said.

"It was on a Saturday," her father said.

"You could hear Billy Shelton and all those children in the street on their bicycles," Margaret said, "and there were buds on the peach tree, weren't there, John?"

She saw the peach tree and she saw her mother's rose garden in the big green expanse of their backyard, she saw the tree-lined streets and the looming gracious houses of the Hancock Park neighborhood, she pictured Billy Shelton and Brucie Baum and even his ugly sister Becky, all waiting for her, perched on their bikes just waiting to pedal, the front wheel of each Schwinn stopped and tilted, each kid's weight shifted and steady on one leg firmly planted on the ground. Claudia listened back to that day but she couldn't hear anything, no bike riding, no buds budding, she couldn't hear anything and she couldn't see anything; it's as if she hadn't even been there. Are you sure it was me you were talking to, she wanted to say—me, Claudia? but she didn't, she kept her mouth shut.

How had they told her, what words had they used? "Well, I don't remember who started it exactly, dear," Margaret said, turning to her husband. "Was it you, John? Or was it me?"

How had she reacted upon hearing the words? "Did I cry?"

"Of course not, sweetheart. Why would you cry, when we told you how we had picked you from all the babies?"

Claudia had an image of Margaret and John walking through a huge hall crowded with bassinets, holding up babies one by one.

Do you like this one, dear?

I don't know. Take its bootees off, let me see its feet.

And the questions that came afterward, all the questions that flooded her, popping up week after week.

125

"You mean I don't belong to you?"

"Of course you belong to us, Claudia. You just didn't come out of me; everything else is just the same."

"It is?"

She knew about how babies came out of you, she knew from Billy Shelton, because when his big sister Valerie had a baby, it had been inside her *upside down* and Billy had told Claudia all the gory details he'd heard his mother telling his aunt Soochie about how the baby was stuck and how they had to stick their hands up there and turn it around. It was disgusting.

She eyed Margaret. "Everything else is still the same?"

"Of course it is." Margaret smiling at her from across the kitchen table, Margaret's reassuring face above the milk and cookies. "I'm your mommy just the same."

She's my mommy just the same: Claudia's new mantra, one saddle shoe in front of the other; she's my mommy, step on the crack and you break your mother's back; she's my mommy just the same, crossing the blocks to Saint Mary Magdalene, the hem of her uniform swishing against the scabs on her knees.

"But what happened to the mommy I came out of?"

"What, sweetheart?" John's eyes over the top of his newspaper as he sat in the squeaky leather wing chair, drinking his gin.

"The mommy I came out of. Not *Mommy:* the *other* one—what happened to her?"

The newspaper descending. "Ah, well, Claudia," and he looked at her and she took the scrap of satin her mother had given her and covered her dolly in the little dolly bed. "Well, I don't exactly know what happened to her, sweetheart, except to know that she couldn't keep you and we wanted you so much and so we got you, you see?"

"Oh."

Quiet. Quiet on the outside but loud on the inside, so many questions battling for position in her little head. She tucked her dolly in carefully, especially down at the bottom so her feet wouldn't stick out, so the boogeyman couldn't grab her toes and pull her into his evil kingdom under the bed.

"Uh huh," John said, his hand unconsciously patting the editorials but his eyes locked on his daughter's face.

"She didn't want me, Daddy?"

"Oh, no, I'm sure that wasn't the case, absolutely not. I'm sure she wanted you very much. There must have been a reason, a very good reason, why she wasn't able to keep you. When you're older you'll understand that there are sometimes reasons in people's lives that prevent them from doing what they want, reasons that—"

Claudia interrupted. "Maybe she wanted a little *boy* instead."

A faint smile crossed John's lips; he folded his newspaper. "You know, I was thinking maybe we should take a walk around the block before supper, huh? You and me, maybe I'll walk and you can ride your new bike."

"Really? But it's suppertime. Mommy'll be mad."

"You go tell Mommy we have to be a few minutes late for supper; tell her it's imperative that you and I take a walk."

So she learned the word imperative and stopped thinking about who wanted who, while her father encouraged her to pedal her bicycle up and down curbs and fly through the leaves.

"That's it, Claudia—you can do it, right over that curb! That's the way!" John's enthusiasm catching up with her, making her brave on her two-wheeler, the wind pushing her hair back, until she laughed at her old fear of falling off, because her father was cheering her on.

"But why was I the one?"

Margaret turned from the bathtub, where she was sponging the bubbles down the drain.

"Take another towel for your hair, dear."

She rubbed Claudia's slender shoulders with the big white bath towel.

"Huh, Mommy?"

"What?"

"Why did you and Daddy pick me out of all the babies?"

Margaret's arms encircling her with the terry cloth. "Because you were the sweetest one, my angel, you were the most special, and we didn't even have to discuss it: we just looked at each other and we both knew."

Special, she was the most special. That was the word that joggled her memory. *Special* was the key to what she *could* remember: skipping around the schoolyard of St. Mary Magdalene, hair flying, her ribbons untied, skipping in her white blouse and pleated plaid uniform, bragging to everyone how she was so special.

"I'm better than you are. I'm *adopted.* I'm *special.*"

Right. You're so special, somebody gave you away.

"Well, it's good they didn't hang me upside down on an orange tree," Claudia said out loud.

She walked to the wall phone and dialed. She could picture the phone ringing in Gena's New York apartment. Actually, Gena's phone didn't ring, it made a *chirp* sound, like a bird. A bird caught in a tomato, Claudia remembered, and she laughed to herself. That's what Ollie had said when they were in New York and saw Gena's apartment. She'd redecorated three times since she divorced Joe, and her latest scheme was red, *everything* red: the walls, the drapes, the furniture—stuffed or painted, it didn't matter—all in different shades of red. "Very Diana Vreeland," Gena had said. "Very trapped inside a tomato," Ollie whispered to Claudia as they followed Gena down the hall.

The phone got answered on the third ring: "This is Gena. I'm out, I'm in, I'm very busy, I can't talk to you, leave me a message, try something funny, I might be in a bad mood. Wait for the squeak. . . ."

Claudia took a breath. "Hi, it's me. I can't tell you anything funny; I'm the one in the bad mood. Why is it always later in New York when it's earlier here? I hate it. You'd think they'd have figured out a way to fix that by now. You're probably finishing lunch at Le Cirque or something, and I'm cutting the crusts off Lily's peanut butter and jelly. I've actually eaten most of the peanut butter and jelly, and every-thing I own smells of apple juice."

She stopped talking and twirled the phone cord with her finger.

"Gena, I have to talk to you. I seem to be having a little problem here . . . but don't call me back later, because I'll be dealing with the baby and then I'll be making supper and then Ollie will be home and then it will be bathtime for the baby and then being with Ollie and then being with the baby and being with Ollie and on and on until I'm old. . . ."

Claudia paused and looked out the window. Was this true? Was this what her life was now? The hummingbird was gone.

"Gena, why haven't I gone back to work? After all, Lily's three. What am I waiting for?"

She slumped against the refrigerator.

"The answer to this question is . . . okay, so I guess it's clear here,

I really need to talk to you. Please call me tomorrow morning after I get back from dropping Lily off at nursery school. Okay? Tomorrow morning at tenish, my time, okay? That's one o'clock for you. Don't forget or I'll kill you—and look, how convenient: you'll have the threat recorded on tape."

She took a big breath.

"I'm using up all the space on your answering machine . . . I'm sorry." Claudia stopped and put her hand over her mouth. "No, I'm not sorry," she said. She was so dizzy, she thought she might fall down.

"I bet you miss me, huh?" she said, and hung up the phone.

She got a glass out of the cabinet and walked to the refrigerator, filled the glass with ice, took out the bottle of white wine, splashed some over the ice, and sat down in a kitchen chair.

"The hell with it," she said defiantly at the clock and took a deep drink of the wine. "I sounded like a two-year-old. Gena'll think I'm deranged."

"What, missus?"

Claudia turned. Santos stood at the sink, her arms loaded with a stack of fresh laundry: folded, oversized white towels and Ollie's big white socks.

"Oh, nothing, Santos, I was just talking to myself. It's this thing I do."

Santos looked cautious. "I put these upstairs and then I do the *colores* and then I do the bathrooms and then I go."

"Okay."

"The baby sleeping."

"Yep."

"So a sweet baby."

"Yes, she is."

"She look just like you, but no the hair."

"Right."

"Jellow."

"That's right."

"Mr. Oliver, he no have jellow hair."

"Nope—nobody in whole family have jellow hair."

Santos smiled. Claudia smiled.

"I go upstairs," Santos said, and left the room.

Claudia picked up one of the little squares of peanut butter and jelly she'd made for Lily and smashed it between her fingers as if it were Play-Doh, squashed it until it was small and put it in her mouth.

Jellow. Great. How was Santos supposed to learn better English if Claudia kept talking to her like she was Tonto? She took a big swig of the wine, stood up, walked to the counter, opened the Wonder bread package, took out two slices, and whacked off their crusts.

Gena called the next morning as Claudia was drinking her fourteenth cup of coffee, or at least it seemed so, maybe only her twelfth. She'd already done her entire wake-up routine:

"Oliver, get out of bed, you're going to be late. Oliver! I said move it!"

"Hello, my sweet baby. Oh, look at that—such a big girl, you've already put your shoes on. . . . Let's just try them on the other feet, okay?"

"Ollie, the coffee's ready. Do you want raisin bran? What did you say? I can't hear you. . . ."

"Taste, Daddy." Lily held out her little spoon, having decided to try her Cheerios in her orange juice. "It's a spearamint."

"A what?" Oliver looked at Claudia. "Hey, did you want to talk to me about something last night?"

"A *sper-a-mint*," Lily said carefully, in a tone that signified her daddy didn't know anything. "It's when you cook something new."

"Uh huh," he said, tasting. "Extraordinary. If this continues, Lily, you will grow up to be Wolfgang Puck."

"No! I don't want to be a wolf when I grow up. Wolfs are mean."

"Oh, I see. Claud, did you want to talk to me? I thought you said something. I gotta go."

"No, it's okay."

"I want to be a boy when I grow up," Lily said, "or maybe just a people."

"Did you hear that, honey?" Ollie said to Claudia, and kissed her. Lily clapped her hands.

"Are you okay?" he said, one arm around his wife, the other scooping up his books and papers.

"Sure."

And he was gone.

And she was fine. What did she have to not be fine about? She had everything, that's what she had. She buckled Lily into the car seat of the gray Volvo and drove her to nursery school, watched her little people march into the sandbox with the other children, her piece of blue satin tucked firmly under her arm. Claudia's heart surged. Look at her, look at all that moxie; definitely not like me.

She followed the other mothers out of the nursery school driveway, a caravan of women separating themselves from their kids. Most of them looked joyous, as if they couldn't wait to run to their other lives. Was she the only one who wanted to hang around and watch her baby from the car window, the only one who didn't want to let her kid go? She remembered the first morning she took Lily to nursery school: she couldn't believe that *her* baby would leave *her* arms to go with that stranger she didn't know, that Miss Ruby. Where did she get the courage? It was the moxie.

Claudia pushed her hair off her face and turned on the radio. And where did Lily get it, this moxie; was it Ollie's moxie? Whose?

Enough, stop it, look at the surrounding countryside, check out the hideous strip malls, the ugly traffic, the angry motorists, mind your manners, miss, shut up, go home. She left the car in the driveway, unwound the garden hose from its tight green coil by the side of the garage, kicked off her sneakers, and watered the rosebushes on either side of the path up to their door. The Santa Ana was still at it, everything in its path scorched and dry. Including me, Claudia thought. She bent and took a drink from the hose before she shut it off. She wiped her hands against her jeans, picked up her shoes, leaned against the front fender of the Volvo, and looked hard at their house. Small but friendly, neat and tidy, red bricks, cream stucco, tan shutters, white trim. "The Beaver would be happy here," Gena had said when they showed her the house after they bought it. Claudia laughed, walked up the front steps, and unlocked the door.

She made the bed, leaned the large flowered pillows against the big headboard from right to left, and then she put them back the way she usually put them, from left to right. She moved into the baby's room, she folded a quilt and placed it on the arm of the sofa, put the books that had been left on the rug back into the basket, except for the one she'd been reading to Lily. She held that one out in front of her.

"*Are You My Mother?* by P. D. Eastman," Claudia read out loud. Her eyes filled. Her mother had bought this. But Margaret wasn't her mother. But she was.

"Oh, for goodness' sake." Claudia ran her hand across her face. She tossed the book into the basket; it missed and plopped on the rag rug. She turned and walked to the doorway and then paused, her back to the room. She retraced her steps, scooped the book up off the rug, placed it gently in the basket, and left the room. She picked up the photographs on the table at the top of the staircase. In the black-and-white one, of her and Margaret, she was sitting on Margaret's lap, she was around three years old, her hair pulled tight into pigtails and tied with plaid ribbons. In the color-photo, Lily was two and sitting on Claudia's lap, smiling a big smile, one tooth visible on top, two on the bottom. Claudia looked from one photograph to the other and then put them back in place on the table, running her finger along the top of the wood grain and checking it for dust. There was none.

She went downstairs and washed the breakfast dishes, sponged the countertops three times, then glared at the telephone. She walked in a circle, counting the brick-colored vinyl tile squares in the kitchen floor. Thirty-four, thirty-five . . . she placed one Ked in front of the other on the lines between the big squares, heel, toe, heel, toe, white canvas touching white canvas, Hail Mary, Mother of God, thirty-six, thirty-seven, heel, toe. . . .

She had planned to talk about it with Ollie last night, he did hear what she had said, she'd planned to talk about it after the veal and peppers but before the nonfat marble swirl, preferably during the Pinot Grigio, and she'd had to work on how she was going to get into it, a plan, some enticing way that would make him more accessible to her need to talk about it *again.* Ollie was almost always accessible, except for very few subjects: one was politics—he wouldn't discuss politics unless you promised you were ready to be serious, throw caution to the winds, stand up and fight no matter what the odds, no matter if you wound up throwing things at each other, no matter if you slept in the other room—and the other subject was this.

"I just don't get the big deal, honey," he'd say. "Find them or don't find them, but why do you let it plague you? It's not like you don't see all the aspects . . . and if you find them and you don't like them, you can just tell them to take a hike."

You just go take a hike, you *other mother,* and take the *other father* with you when you go. She could see herself, her hands on her hips, the tilt to her head defiant, showing a lot of moxie for once in her life. Like Lily; she could be like Lily. . . . But it didn't matter how she'd decided to approach him or how ingenious her plan, because she'd had to scrap it. One of the girls in Ollie's tenth-grade class had come to school whacked-out on a couple of things she'd swallowed from her parents' medicine chest and had collapsed in front of Ollie's desk. He'd ridden with the girl and the paramedics in the ambulance, stayed with her while they pumped her stomach, spent the whole day holding her hand. He was shaking and pacing and furious, carrying on about a mother and father and how could they have such a loose rein on their kid. How could they be so oblivious? What did the girl have to do to get their attention—die?

"Ollie, I wanted to talk to you about something."

She was going to start with why she wasn't working; that was her plan. Why hadn't she gone back to work? She'd had a practice, after all, patients she had given to others for a pregnant leave of absence only until her baby was big enough, she'd promised, and then she'd be back. It was time now, more than time; just look how Lily could swagger around, with only her piece of satin; she was definitely ready to give up her mommy for at least part of her day, was doing it already, marching into that nursery school without looking back. It wasn't Lily who was having trouble separating. Claudia ran her hand down the white plastic of the wall phone. Anyway, she probably didn't even have a practice anymore, her patients had probably forgotten her. What was stopping her? It had something to do with leaving this house. Maybe she could reopen her practice at home, like GPs did in the old days; she could put a shingle out on the front porch, could see people . . . where? In the living room? In the kitchen? she only needed a chair not an examining table. It could be very cozy, very homey, she could even serve tea. They could sit here at her kitchen table and talk to her . . . but would the patients mind if she had Lily on her lap while she listened? if Lily was coloring or playing ponies while they told her their tales. . . . What if they wanted her to leave Lily in the next room? No, that wasn't it: it wasn't leaving the house; she used to enjoy going to work. Wait . . . maybe it was the work. Maybe she didn't want to be a psychologist anymore, maybe she'd made a mistake. After all, what kind of a psychologist was she if she couldn't figure all this out!

"Oliver, please, honey, help me look at this, what's wrong with me, why am I wandering around like a lost puppy? Why haven't I gone back to work?" That was what she was going to say, and he would get into that, he would talk to her; Ollie was good about such things. And then somehow, they would be discussing her state of mind, how instead of working she'd been sitting around watching everyone else work—she'd watch Santos fold the sheets or scrub the bathroom floor, and she would stand there watching and then realize with a start that she was standing there watching, just standing there as if she were wrapped in fog. And sometimes, while Oliver got ready for work, she'd clutch the pillow, trying to figure out how to get out of bed—of course, part of that was because she was so tired from the dreams. . . . And that's how she could get into it, she could slip it in right there: Hey, remember that *other mother* thing that used to walk around with me in my unconscious? Well, it's leaped to the forefront . . . and she'd explain how the dreams kept waking her up at night, how she'd been reading a book to the baby and this thing had overtaken her, this urge . . . more than an urge, really—a passion? an obsession—and now it was everywhere: awake, asleep, she couldn't seem to let go of it. . . . "Ollie, it's practically all I can think about— it's making me want to bash my head against the proverbial wall. No, I take that back—not the proverbial wall, the real wall, the goddamn real cement wall." Claudia Ellen Magers Morgan, did you say "goddamn"?

But it didn't matter how well she had planned her approach to the discussion, because she never got that far, she never got anywhere; he didn't even look up at last night's dinner table when she said she wanted to talk about something—his mind was totally on that kid—and she said "Ollie" two more times, and then he said, "What?" but it was that "what" that went with that look on his face, and she said, "Never mind," and he said he needed an aspirin and left the room, and she sat there and waited for him to come back and then she heard the television in the living room and she hung there motionless at the kitchen table, shredding crusts of bread into anthill-sized piles until she'd finished the Pinot Grigio. Maybe she would never talk to anybody; maybe Gena wouldn't even call today.

Circling the squares of the floor of her kitchen, one Ked in front of the other . . . thirty-seven, thirty-eight . . . or was it thirty-eight and thirty-nine? She was thirty-five years old, for pete's sake, she was a grown-up, why was she acting like such a kid?

At ten o'clock—the big hand had barely hit the twelve—the phone rang. Claudia pounced on it and had the receiver to her ear before the ring stopped. Gena was practically yelling on the other end.

"How could you do that to me? I'm going to kill you. Call and tell me you have a problem and you need to talk to me but *I'm not supposed to call you back until now?* For crissakes, Claudia. . . ."

"Gena Allen Thornton! Talk about blasphemy! You'll do five Hail Marys and five Our Fathers, young lady, and maybe an Apostle's Creed."

"I'm going to give you an Apostle's Creed right on your head, Claudia. You're pregnant, aren't you?"

"What?"

"You're pregnant—that's the *little* problem."

"No."

"You're not? I was sure you were pregnant; you certainly sound like you've lost your mind. Okay, tell me—and this better be good. I'm supposed to be meeting with this unknown swish miss playwright from—you should pardon the expression—Iowa, who writes like a dream. They're all waiting for me at the Palm, no less, this wasn't exactly the best time for me."

"I'm sorry. How can you go to the Palm? I thought you didn't eat meat anymore."

"I eat everything else. Tell me."

Claudia sat down on the kitchen floor, her back up against the refrigerator.

"Well, I . . . Gena?"

"Yes?"

Claudia looked up at the clock, watched the big hand make it to 10:03.

"Claud?"

"Yeah . . ."

"If you don't tell me, I'm going to scream."

"Do you remember when we went to EDNA?"

"Who?"

"EDNA, that adoption place. Remember we went right before Ollie and I got married, right off the San Diego Freeway in the valley—"

"It was the Ventura Freeway; I drove. Of course I remember. What about it?"

"Well, I . . ."

"Claudia, if you don't stop this, I'm going to spring through the telephone wires and punch your lights out."

"Oh, sorry . . . okay."

Gena waited. She could only hear breathing. "*Claudia!*"

Claudia took a big breath. "Gena, what I want to know is . . . do you think you could fly out here and be with me, so I could go again?"

•   •   •

After all was said and done and they'd talked way past lunchtime in New York and probably even in Chicago, it was clear that Gena couldn't go with her. First off, she was in the middle of rehearsals, and "Didn't you remember I was opening in only two months, if you can believe that, and weren't you and Ollie coming in? I thought you were coming in for the opening; you promised, Claudia." And besides rehearsals, she had to work with the swish miss hotshot playwright from Iowa she had mentioned, on a play that he wanted to write for her—"Did you hear what I said? Write *for me*, as in, with *me* in mind while he's putting paper to pen?"

"It's pen to paper, I think," Claudia said.

"Whatever."

So as much as she wanted to, she couldn't leave New York now; she was just way too over her head.

"What happened that you decided to look for them?"

Claudia moved the phone cord to her left shoulder. "I don't know."

"Of course you know. You're a psychologist; you have to know."

"Yeah, you'd think so, wouldn't you . . . but I don't."

"Hmm, it must have something to do with you having the baby."

"The baby, Ms. Godmother, is already three."

"I know how old the baby is. Maybe you're just a little slow on the realization. . . ."

Claudia laughed. "I thought *I* was the psychologist."

"Well, *I'm* the actress. I mean, if I was playing you in this particular predicament, deciding at this particular time why you wanted to get into this, suddenly wanting to find your parents, after you were so clear all these years about how you *didn't* want to find them, I'd have to know, I'd have to know my motivation, my whys, I'd have to know who you are so I'd know how to behave to play you, so it would be real."

"To play me, huh?" Claudia sighed.

"What?"

"Nothing. Maybe I don't know who I am."

"What? What don't you know?"

"How to play me, I guess."

"What? Claudia, you're mumbling. I hate it when you mumble."

"I know. Sing out, Louise. I know."

Gena laughed. "I miss you. I wish I could go with you, you know I do."

"Yep, I know."

"So are you coming in for the opening?" Gena said, in a little voice. "You are, aren't you?"

And now Claudia sat in her car in the driveway of her parents' home, the motor running, one hand on the steering wheel, her elbow bent and resting on the ledge of the open window, the fingers of her other hand spread across her mouth. Two o'clock, and she'd left the baby with Santos, she'd been playing with Lily and then had this overwhelming urge to call Margaret, to rush over and spill everything: oh, nothing, I just have this plan, Mommy, to find my *other mother*, you know, the one that isn't you. I don't know. The urge just kind of blew in with the Santa Ana . . . so what do you think?

No, she couldn't say that. What *could* she say?

She'd twisted the telephone cord through her fingers and watched Lily coloring with Santos, the child zigzagging her purple all over the page, and Santos meticulously confining her pink in the lines. Claudia had always kept her color within the lines too, hadn't she?

"Oh, nothing, Mom, I just thought I'd come over . . . could I come over, are you doing anything?" She opened her hand flat across her ribs at the top of her breasts; her skin was warm. "Anything special, I mean?"

"Of course not, sweetheart. I was thinking about doing the closets, but of course I don't want to; the idea of seeing me in what doesn't fit me anymore was not something I was looking forward to. I'd love for you to come over, I'll make us lunch."

Sweetheart. And will I still be her sweetheart when I tell her what I want to do?

Claudia turned off the motor and got out of the car. The big pine in the front lawn had just been trimmed; she could see the circles of sap where the branches had been sliced, the limbs trying to repair themselves with their own juice. It was the tree she had looked out on every day as she grew up, every morning when she opened her eyes and every night when she knelt next to her bed and whispered her prayers. My tree, she'd told her parents; it's mine because it's outside my bedroom window and that makes it mine. It was the tree she'd sat in and dreamed in, read in and hidden in, held on to in little-girl exuberance, happy or sad: her haven tree, her climbing tree, her swinging tree: she'd even fallen out of it, breaking her arm in three places, when she was six.

She ran her hand down the bark of the trunk. Would Margaret have enough sap to repair herself after she sliced her with the news? Claudia frowned and looked up at the blue between the pine needles. Oh, Lord, was she going to turn everything she saw into a goddamn metaphor now? "Don't say goddamn," Claudia whispered as she turned the key in the front latch.

"Mom?"

"I'm in the kitchen."

The large rooms were hushed and beautiful, and Claudia was flooded with a sense of peace she hadn't felt in some time. It was something about the sunlight, the way the gold picked up the thick yellow cream of the stucco and made the living room and dining room quietly shine. Spotless mahogany, oak floors, the absence of sound as your feet moved across the rich Chinese carpets; Kiwi furniture wax and pine needles and spice. It was the way she'd felt each time she came home, home from school and home from riding her bicycle and home from her first and every date, home from college and home from grad school and home after she'd married Ollie and after she'd had Lily and now.

"I thought we'd have 'Two Girls Tuna,'" Margaret said gaily, as Claudia walked into the kitchen. She held the mayonnaise jar up in one hand, as if she were doing a commercial, and extended the other hand to her daughter. "We haven't had it in such a long time."

Two Girls Tuna, a recipe Margaret had retained from her home ec class some forty years ago, Margaret's beautiful grade school penmanship in perfect symmetry, the ingredients listed one by one on a yellowing index card: one-half can "fancy" tuna, two celery sticks, finely chopped, one tablespoon mayonnaise, and one dollop of sweet pickle relish that had (optional) printed next to it in parenthesis.

"Oh, Mom," Claudia said. "Two Girls Tuna," and she folded the five feet nine inches of her bones and angles into Margaret's five feet one inches of soft roundness and was overcome with tears.

"It's all right. I've just been waiting," Margaret said, her hand covering her daughter's hand. They sat at the table in front of Two Girls Tuna atop Boston lettuce, thin slices of tomato, radish roses and even carrot curls that Margaret had made as if it were still 1957. Iced tea in tall, thin Waterford glasses, lemon wedges resting on the ivory Lenox with the gold borders, roses from the garden in an Italian painted bowl, Porthault luncheon napkins in the fruit and vegetable pattern folded under the Gorham Buttercup sterling by each of their plates—all part of Margaret's philosophy: Don't save anything for "good," use everything if you're lucky enough to have it, let life be beautiful, because "you never know."

"We're going to Europe because of my wife's 'you never know' theory," John used to say to his cronies as they smacked golf balls in the valley at the driving range.

"My mom is having the whole, entire family over for a picnic even though it's not even a holiday," Claudia would tell Gena at school. "She says we better have it while the old ones are still here, because 'you never know.'"

And now she sat across from her mother at the kitchen table and wondered: was that why she suddenly wanted to find these strangers, because that's how Margaret had raised her; was it a part of "don't wait if you want it, because you never know"? Did she think she was going to die? is that what this was? Claudia had a vision of both sets of parents watching as they lowered her coffin into a grave. The *other mother* was wearing a black veil and sunglasses, à la the newspaper photos of Jacqueline Kennedy. Margaret was openly weeping, crumpled against John's pinstripes like a lump of cookie dough. John towered like her pine in the front yard, his face mashed into . . . what? what was that? some kind of bruise? . . . And wait, who was that over there behind that headstone, sitting on the white horse and wearing the black Stetson? Was that the *other father*, and more important, did he have a mustache?

Margaret's hand touched Claudia's. "I've been preparing for this day for a long time."

Claudia blinked away the vision. "You have?"

"Of course. I always knew in my heart that someday you'd want to find them. We both did. Daddy's just been a little more nervous about it, a little skeptical—you know how he is—but we knew since the day we told you that you were adopted. My goodness, you asked so many questions. . . ." Margaret shook her head. "I think I've prepared myself. I was just waiting for you to want to know." She smiled, but the smile seemed breakable even though it was a smile. "I'm not afraid, Claudia. I've been a good mother, I know I have."

Claudia leaned forward. Oh, sure, that's what she was saying, but in the saying of it, so much else was said. Claudia knew she had to reconsider now; she was not interested in making Margaret doubt herself.

"You've been a perfect mother. I don't know why I'm even doing this. It has nothing to do with you, or Daddy. I just . . ."

"I just hope they turn out to be what you're looking for, what you want them both to be."

Claudia's skin got cold. "Mom, I'm not doing this. It's ridiculous. I'm not going to."

"Of course you are, now that you've decided. I'm sure it's perfectly natural for you to want to see them, especially since you've had the baby. You just want to see a little piece of yourself, and you certainly can't see that when you look at me."

She smiled that fragile smile again, and Claudia closed her fingers over the edge of the table. What had possessed her to do this? This was not what she wanted to do.

Margaret laughed brightly. "Of course, nothing about me is a *little* piece, is it? My backside is getting as big as Grandma Mae's."

"Mom, please . . ."

Margaret pushed her chair back and stood up. "Come upstairs. I want to show you something."

Claudia followed her mother's rounded backside up the carpeted staircase and into the bedroom, her hand trailing along the banister. She felt that uneasy bewildered feeling she used to get, heady with excitement but sick to her stomach, just like when she was little: she wouldn't be able to sleep the night before they went someplace special

144

and then in the morning losing her breakfast before they'd go. But she wasn't seven anymore; who needed this?

Margaret and John's bedroom was aqua, still aqua after all these years: the watered silk bedspread and matching tie-back draperies, the W & J Sloan top-of-the-line carpet, the brocade sofa and two small English pull-up chairs, all in different shades of aqua; and the Irish lace sheers behind the draperies were the same soft ivory cream as the walls. No matter how many times Margaret redecorated, the bedroom always turned up aqua and cream. Claudia found this reassuring; she loved being in Margaret and John's bedroom. Over the bed was a crucifix, silver inlaid with mother-of-pearl, and tucked behind it was a small twig of palm left over from Palm Sunday, which Margaret replaced from year to year. The crucifix had a tiny piece missing from its left-hand corner, the piece that had chipped off when Brucie Baum had convinced Claudia that her mother's bed could surely double as a trampoline.

The box was Chinese lacquer, a saddle-brown color with a flower design in black and white and deep red. Claudia had never seen it before. Margaret lifted it out from under her lingerie; Claudia could hear the rustling sheets of tissue paper her mother used between the folds of her gowns.

"This was Great-Grandma Nellie's," Margaret said. "She got it at the Panama-Pacific International when her parents took her when she was just a girl, San Francisco in 1915—that was the last world's fair before the war—and she gave it to my mother, and when Grandma Mae died . . ." Her voice trailed off.

Claudia was having trouble breathing. Margaret's mother, Mae, had died a year ago. What did it mean, all this history? Was it right, then, that someday Claudia should get the box? After all, she wasn't Margaret's *real* daughter. But if she didn't get the box, then how could Lily get it?

Margaret walked to the brocade sofa and sat down with the box on her lap; Claudia followed and sat next to her. Neither of them said a word.

There should be music, Claudia thought, that mystery music that comes out of nowhere in a movie and you flinch and your hands spring up and you inadvertently smack the person sitting next to you, because even though you can't see anyone, you know someone is waiting to attack the hero behind the door.

Margaret raised the lid and placed it gently on the painted table in front of her. Under it was a separate piece of thick black lacquer, cut to fit inside the box. She lifted it, placed it next to the lid.

And the music swells, and inside is . . . what . . . her mother? Holy moly, the *other mother* has been freeze dried. Just add water and . . .

Inside the box were papers, it looked like that was all that was in there, a few folded papers, a small notebook, and then Margaret pulled out something from a creased envelope, but it wasn't a paper, it was something that caught the light coming through the lace sheers. She put whatever it was into her daughter's hands.

"This is what your mother sent with you," Margaret whispered, and Claudia looked down. In the cup of her palm lay the crystal rosary beads that Jenny Jaffe had so lovingly wound around her baby's tiny wrist.

She could make jokes in her head, try to make jokes to keep herself from screaming, but now she couldn't make anything . . . this was tangible, these rosary beads, she could feel them, touch them, this was something *real.* Claudia's breath caught that this actually existed, that this *other mother* had actually existed, that she wasn't a dream, she was *real,* she had physically held these beads, the same beads Claudia was holding now, she had sent them with her. Claudia looked up at Margaret, but Margaret was sorting through things in the Chinese box.

"Mom . . ."

"Daddy and I named you Claudia, but you see here"—she held a piece of paper out in front of the two of them—"you see, that wasn't your real name. They didn't name you Claudia; they named you Cole. Or *she* did, because as far as I know, he wasn't with her—but of course, we weren't supposed to know that, that just slipped out. They were very circumspect about what you were allowed to know and what you weren't, and we certainly weren't supposed to know anything about him or her, except the very peripheral things: if she'd finished high school, if she was a good student, what she looked like, things like that. I wrote it down . . . everything. I have it all written down. . . ."

Cole? Did she say Cole? The facets of the crystal beads cut into Claudia's palm as she leaned forward to read the words:

> *Amended Birth Certificate*
> Claudia Ellen Magers
> Date of Birth: December 30, 1960
> Time of Birth: 2:40 P.M.
> Original Name: Cole Jaffe

Original name: Cole Jaffe. Cole Jaffe, I am Cole Jaffe, Claudia said to herself in her head.

". . . but we certainly weren't supposed to know your real name, I know we weren't, they were so terribly careful, all of them, but Mr. Stanley especially, he was the man who brought you to us from Blessed Children, and he was very careful about not slipping any information, especially after he'd let slip that she wasn't with him, that they weren't married, I mean . . ." Margaret's face was pink; she was very excited. Claudia touched her arm. "Mom . . ." But Margaret went on, the words running together. ". . . and then all the times we had to meet with him after we had you, in those months when they kept checking up on Daddy and me to make sure they hadn't made some horrible mistake giving us a baby, that we weren't dope fiends or crazy people." She lifted her hand and patted her upper lip with her finger. "Goodness, every time he came to our house I would ask him things just to see what I could wangle—Lord knows what else he knew—but he was very close-mouthed after that, and then the state just up and sent *this* right along with the adoption decree, and there was your other name, your first one, and I knew we weren't supposed to see it, some poor clerk must have accidentally mixed it in, and I told your father, I was so worried, and he said, Well, just put it away, Margaret, it doesn't matter now, it's official, they can't take her away from us, she's ours." Margaret lifted her head and looked at Claudia. "And you were, you know . . . you were ours."

"I still am, Mom."

"Well, I certainly hope so," Margaret mumbled.

"I still am, Mom, I promise," Claudia said, and she wrapped her arms around her mother, one hand squeezing Margaret's shoulder, the other hand closed around Jenny's rosary beads.

Cole Jaffe. Claudia wrote it again across the sheet of paper. What kind of name is Cole? It's a man's name, isn't it? She studied the paper. She'd left Margaret after a couple of hours, left her sitting in the aqua bedroom, and driven home in a kind of fog. She actually didn't remember the driving. Cole . . . Cole . . . ol' King Cole was a merry old soul . . . Cole . . .

She wrote it again and looked at it. *Cole Jaffe.* She'd never heard of anyone named Cole; it had to be a last name. Something Cole. Maybe it was his name . . . that's it, it was his name, his last name, that's

what it was, maybe it was *his* last name and *her* last name was Jaffe. . . .
Cole Jaffe . . .

Claudia looked up from the paper. But Jaffe is Jewish, isn't it?

Didn't she know a girl at Columbia named Jaffe? Jaffe, sure, what was her name? Marsha Jaffe, she was in her dorm, she was on the second floor, and roomed with whatshername, the one from Buffalo with the teeth. . . . Marsha Jaffe, she was beautiful and had that wonderful laugh and all that big hair that she never pinned up, and she dated that boy who worked on the newspaper, she married him, didn't she? journalism, he was in journalism, going to be a reporter, he said, for *The New York Times*, just watch me, I'll be the next Abe Rosenthal, he said . . . funny, fast and funny, and he'd taken her to his aunt's house . . . for Passover. Claudia nodded. That's right, for Passover, he took us to his aunt and uncle's house in Scarsdale, her and Sharon Stefanoni with him and Marsha Jaffe, he said his mother needed two token gentiles besides the stunning Jewess to his right, and he pointed at Marsha when he said it, Marsha in the front seat next to him in the Volkswagen, a Volkswagen that sounded like it wouldn't make it up the Henry Hudson, and she laughed that wonderful laugh . . . Henry Weisman, that was his name, Henry Hudson, Henry Weisman, and she and Sharon were in the back, and it was fabulous, it ended up fabulous, like in a Woody Allen movie, everyone passionate and standing up at the table fighting with each other about Moses, and his uncle was yelling at his father, something about the Red Sea and a staff versus a rod, what was it? and eating matzoh-ball soup, and they fought and then they were laughing, his uncle's arm slung over his father's shoulder, and the light caught the gold cuff links in his French cuffs, and he raised the glass and you could smell the peppermint.

"Do you want a taste, Ms. Magers?"

"Claudia," she'd said.

"Right, Claudia," he'd said, Henry's uncle, his eyes gleaming, as he extended his glass to her.

Schnapps, he'd called it—clear, strong whiskey in short, stubby glasses, which smelled like peppermint and burned your throat. And there'd been fish with a funny name, chopped and shaped into ovals, much like her grandma Mae's quenelles, only not in a white-wine butter sauce, dear, grandma Mae would have said, but in purple horse-radish that singed your nose. . . .

Claudia smiled, envisioning her grandma Mae at the table with Henry Weisman's family, having a heated discussion about Moses versus her beloved Jesus, drinking schnapps and eating scalding horse-radish, her head tilted, her soft beige hair caught in the backlight, one hand clutching her pearls. . . . Claudia shook her head, remembering her grandmother, who had a passion for shocking. "This is how they did it in my day, girls," she said, and Gena and Claudia practically fell off the sofa because Grandma Mae put her cup and saucer on the end table, got up gracefully from the wing chair, placed her deli-cate hands on her ample hips, and launched into an impromptu cheer.

"Ohjahdeeebah, ohjahdoughbah, how's your catatowbah?" she yelled across Margaret's living room, down on one knee in her tea-length lavender silk jersey, Claudia's grandmother in Bullock's Wil-shire's best suede pumps, diamond earrings and her rope of pearls, springing up in perfect form into the air.

Claudia laughed. Grandma Mae had a lot of moxie. Grandma Mae would have liked Henry's Weisman's family. Claudia liked him, she liked his whole family, and Marsha had loved him, Marsha Jaffe. She had married him, in fact, and now somewhere she was Marsha Jaffe Weisman. . . .

Claudia studied the name she'd written on the paper. Jaffe is definitely a Jewish name. . . .

"Mommy?"

Then what was she doing with the rosary beads?

"Mommy?" Lily gave Claudia a little punch in the elbow.

If Jaffe was her last name, then the *other mother* was Jewish, and if she was Jewish she wouldn't have sent rosary beads with her baby, she would have sent a Star of David or a little gold replica of that thing they put on the door—

"Mommy!"

"A mezuzah . . ." Claudia said out loud, thinking of the word. Then maybe it was *him*, maybe *he* was Jewish, maybe his name was Jaffe and her name was Cole. . . .

"Mommy! I can't do this!"

"What, sweetheart?" She turned and there stood Lily, naked except for fuchsia socks and tiny black tennis shoes that had a little embroidered Tasmanian devil on each of the high-tops. She was holding a pink leotard, the lower half of which was a net tutu, and she was hopping around, trying to get one foot and one Tasmanian devil through one of the leg holes.

"So what happens now?" Ollie said.

"I don't know."

"We can get a detective."

"What?"

"We've got the name; we can get a detective, if you don't want to go to one of those places like you went to before."

"Don't be silly."

"It's not silly. I bet people do that." He gave her an encouraging look from across the table, laid his silverware on his plate, and put his hand on her arm. "So how are you?"

"I don't know." She sat still for a moment and he waited, his eyes on hers. "It was just this paper with the name on it, that's what was so unbelievable; all these years she's just had it. . . ."

"Hmm."

"Yeah, that's what I mean."

"Are you mad?"

"No. I don't think so. I don't know."

"Cole Jaffe."

"Uh huh."

He reached up and touched the tip of her nose with his finger. "So you want me to call you Cole?"

"Ollie."

"What?"

"I don't know."

He cupped his palm under her chin. "How 'bout I give Lily a bath?"

"Okay."

"How 'bout I give Lily a bath and 'read her' and after she's asleep I wash the dishes?"

"My goodness."

"In honor of the occasion. And you can just sit in the living room and contemplate your new name."

"Okay, I guess."

"Okay," he said. He stood up, moved to her chair, bent at the waist, and kissed the side of her face by her left ear. His lips felt good against her skin; she wanted to lean back and sink into him.

"All right," Ollie said, moving away from her. "So should I clear the table, or can you just leave it till I get done?"

"I'll leave it—no, I'll put the dishes in the sink."

He pushed his chair into place at the table. "Okay, but don't wash them; I want to do it. Go sit." He stopped at the door and looked at her. "I love you, whatever your name is."

Claudia smiled at him. "Okay."

Whatever her name was, whatever she was, who was she?

Cole Jaffe. Maybe it *was* Jewish, maybe she was really a Catholic Jew. Now, that would be something. My heart, Claudia thought, all that Sunday school, all those prayers . . . what if she really should have been lighting a menorah when she was busy putting the angel on top of the Christmas tree? What if she shouldn't have been one of the wise men in the Christmas pageant, what if she should have been a Maccabee? Claudia snickered at her kitchen table. Wouldn't that throw Sister Anne? She'd drop her ruler over that . . . if she was still alive. Wait till she told Gena. . . .

And hadn't it occurred to Margaret that the name might be Jewish? And why would they give a Jewish baby to a Catholic couple to raise? The thoughts crashed around in her head. She remembered how she used to make her mother crazy when she was little, telling everyone that she wasn't *really* Catholic, she was *really* Episcopalian—only because she liked the sound of the word. "E-pis-co-pale-eee-annnn," Claudia would say, and Margaret would stand behind her, shaking her head.

"Sweet angel, we're Catholic, you know that."

"I know."

Well, this would really be something, then, wouldn't it? Claudia Ellen Magers Cole Jaffe Morgan, the Catholic Jew. No, wait a minute—the lapsed Catholic Jew. She moved the rosary beads from one hand to the other, letting them slide like water into her palms, and then lifted them up in front of her. All this guessing wasn't getting her anywhere; she had to find out exactly what else

153

Margaret knew. What else was in that box? What was in the little notebook? She said she'd written everything down: what else did she know? Claudia studied the cross, held it between the fingers of her right hand, moved it to her lips and lightly kissed it, touched it to her forehead, her heart, her left shoulder, her right. "In the name of the Father, the Son, and the Holy Ghost," Claudia whispered. "I believe in God the Father Almighty, Creator of heaven and earth; and in Jesus Christ, His only Son, our Lord, who was conceived by the Holy Spirit. . . ." And in the quiet of her kitchen, Claudia held the rosary beads, and for the first time in a very long time, she began the Apostles' Creed.

She decided she would go to the Hall of Records. She would try to get a copy of her birth certificate, the original one. You never knew, maybe they'd just give it to her, hand it over as simply as Margaret took her name out of the Chinese box. You just lift the lid and you become Cole Jaffe, one two three, and just like that, your life has changed.

The Hollywood Freeway into the San Bernardino into the 710 South. Get off at Caesar Chavez Boulevard, go down the off-ramp and turn left. She thought it would be downtown in a tall gray building, telephones ringing and computers tapping and people in suits and ties standing erect and quiet behind velvet rope in zigzag lines. It was a squat tan stucco building that resembled someone's forgotten bungalow, red bougainvillea climbing up and across the overhang; children were running in and out the doors, and everyone in the line was wearing blue jeans and speaking rapid Spanish except her. She wore high heels and stockings and the beige Armani suit that Margaret had surprised her with on her thirtieth birthday, her jacket off and over her arm. What had possessed her to get all gussied up? It was hot. She took a step forward, ran her hand under the curls that had fallen across her forehead, and looked down at her shoes.

The conversation with Mrs. Veliz—a supervisor, it said on her tag—was through a hole in the plastic shield that separated the people in the line from the people who knew.

"No, because ju were born before 1964."

"Yes."

"So we doan have it here."

"I see." Claudia moved forward, her lips closer to the hole in the shield. Maybe if Mrs. Veliz could hear her better, she would understand how imperative all this was for her. "What do I do?" She smiled.

"Ju haf to write Sacramento." Mrs. Veliz did not smile, her expression more than suggesting she would rather be eating her lunch.

"Sacramento . . ."

"On de jellow form."

Jellow? Did she say jellow? Claudia felt a knot of hysterical laughter jump in her throat.

"What? I'm sorry . . ."

"De jellow form," Mrs. Veliz said, and pointed to a stack of open boxes on a long table behind Claudia. The paper in one of the boxes was pale yellow.

Claudia held on to her bottom lip between her teeth for a minute. "You mean there's nothing I can do here?"

"No, we are not able to provide ju because ju were born before 1964."

"Uh huh."

Claudia felt the sweat that had collected under her breasts, one drop broke free from the barrier of her beige lace brassiere and ran gleefully down her side until it collided with the top of her panty hose. She had a powerful desire to take off one high heel and smash it into the plastic by Mrs. Veliz's face. Then she would laugh until

155

she shattered too, and they would take her away in a truck. She cleared her throat.

"There's no one else I can talk to?"

"Ju haf to write Sacramento."

"Could you give me the name of someone in Sacramento?"

"Ju jes write to de address on de jellow form."

"Not to anyone? Not anyone in particular?"

"No."

Claudia shifted her weight to her other foot and tilted her face at the shield. She could feel her breath bounce back at her from the plastic. "You see, Mrs. Veliz," she said softly into the round hole, "I'm adopted and . . . uh . . . I'm trying to get a copy of my original birth certificate"— what was that lump in her throat? It was making it so hard for her to speak—"my original birth certificate, so I can see, well, who I am." Claudia smiled bravely.

"Ju haf to write Sacramento," Mrs. Veliz said with authority.

Claudia studied the yellow form on her kitchen table.

County of Los Angeles
Registrar-Recorder/County Clerk

The Recorder's Office is not able to provide you with a copy of the record requested, or, is unable to amend a previously recorded document as directed. The Office of the State Registrar may be able to assist you in this regard.

304 "S" Street

P.O. Box 730241

Sacramento, CA 94244-0241

She took another sip of white wine from the glass, turned the form over, and read aloud:

County of Los Angeles
Registrar-Recorder/County Clerk

La Oficina de Actas no puede proporcionarie la copia del acta solicitada, o como se ha indicado no puede enmendar el documento registrado anteriormente. La Oficina del Registrador Estatal tal vez pueda ayudarie en este respecto.

Claudia put the form down. "Ju haf to write Sacramento, dummy," she said, in a very bad Spanish accent. She ran her hand across her face. "I should have taken Santos with me; she could have explained it better to Mrs. Veliz," she mumbled and finished off the white wine in her glass.

"Did you find them yet?"

"Very funny," Claudia said into the telephone, moving it with her to her dressing table. She sat down on the striped bench and opened the mascara she had in her other hand.

"So," Gena said, "what's happening?"

"Nothing." Claudia looked in the mirror and applied mascara to the lashes of her right eye. "Nothing, nada, period, stop."

"But what did you hear from Sacramento?"

"They said no."

"No? That's all? Just no?"

"They said it was sealed. That's the big word in this line of business: 'sealed.' Those records are sealed, madam; too bad for you."

"Uh huh."

"Uh huh," Claudia repeated. She dabbed at a tiny blotch of mascara she'd left on the skin under her right eye and then moved the mascara wand to the other eye.

"You sound a wee bit angry there," Gena said.

"Uh huh. How's the play coming?"

"You don't want to talk about this?"

"I'll talk about it. What do you want to say?"

"Are you going to go back to EDNA?"

"I don't know."

"Why don't you hire one of those whatchamacallits—you know what you told me."

"A search consultant, Gena."

"Yeah."

"A private search consultant."

"Yeah."

Claudia didn't say anything.

"Why don't you hire one of those?"

"Maybe."

Gena waited. "Claudia, don't you want to talk to me?"

"How could my mother have done this all these years? Kept my name hidden away?"

"I don't know. Well . . . you know Margaret—she probably figured she was doing the right thing, you know, until you asked her. I guess."

Silence.

"What are you doing?" Gena said.

"I'm getting dressed, I'm putting on mascara, I'm supposed to be somewhere with Ollie ten minutes ago, and I'm walking around in my underwear."

"Where is he?"

"In the driveway, probably banging the steering wheel with his hand."

"Where's the baby?"

"With my mother—somebody's mother—*my* mother . . . oh, for crissakes . . ."

"Claudia, get ahold of yourself."

"Have you ever thought about what that means? Picture it: people standing with their arms wrapped around themselves, other people saying, Get ahold of yourself, mister, but I don't think they think about what it means."

"Claud."

"I've got to go, Gena. Ollie will start honking."

"Oh, dear, we wouldn't want that, would we?"

She waited for Claudia to laugh, but there was only the sound of nothing. "I'm going to call you tomorrow," Gena said.

Claudia put the mascara on her dressing table and blew upward. The curls lifted and settled back on her damp forehead, a little to the left. She sighed and stood up, tilted her head to one side and tried to push her fingers into the place where it hurt on the back of her neck.

"It's so goddamn fucking hot here," she said quietly into the telephone and at her face in the mirror.

"What? I didn't hear you."

"It's probably snowing in New York, right? It's so stupid to be hot this time of year. I hate the Santa Ana. I always thought I loved it, but I don't."

"Jesus, Claud."

"What?"

"Take it easy, okay?"

Claudia moved her mouth away from the receiver and breathed out. She walked a little circle around the middle of the bedroom, stepping back and forth over the telephone cord, skimming it with her bare toes. She kicked at her shoes, lying on their sides by the foot of the bed.

"Are you okay?"

"Yeah, I guess so."

"Claud?"

"What? I'm just pissed off, okay?"

"Okay."

She got back in bed after she put Lily down for her nap. It had been two days, two days since she'd talked to Gena and four days since she'd gotten the letter from Sacramento, the two-sentence letter that had informed her that her life was "sealed." Claudia hadn't gotten *back* in bed since she was a teenager, except when she had the flu. She didn't fold the spread down, just slipped under it with all her clothes on. That was after she'd thrown the phone book against the bathroom wall, and *that* was after she'd ripped out pages 403 and 404 and shredded them into long, thin strips. So much for walking through the yellow pages to unseal your life.

> *Detectives, detective agencies* . . . Armstrong, Carl . . . Baker and Associates . . . Connor Investigations . . . Enterprise . . . Stop! Don't be fooled by big or expensive ads. We can do the same job for you as they can. We are a qualified group of private investigators specializing in all aspects of investigations. Don't hesitate, investigate now without paying an exorbitant price! . . . Criminal Analyst Arthur Mandell, A Private Agency Specializing in Covert Operations

Covert operations? What did that mean? spies? How ingenious, how modern—countries could now hire spies right out of the yellow pages. Who knew?

"Jellow pages, excuse me," Claudia said out loud.

RRR Biosearch, missing persons. We are sworn to silence. Background checks. Most searches only $89.95.

Cheaper than a pair of Ferragamo shoes.

If only she could get in touch with Columbo, but he wasn't still on the air, was he? Well, only in reruns, and besides, Columbo probably cost a lot more than $89.95. Anyway—wait a minute here—why did *she* want to hire someone to find *them? They* weren't the ones who were missing persons, after all; *she* was the one who was missing. Why hadn't they hired Columbo to find her?

Claudia slid down deeper into the bed.

But they hadn't, had they? Nope. They hadn't hired anyone to find her. She hadn't discussed that part of it with Margaret; she'd only discussed what Margaret knew. Yesterday at Margaret's kitchen table, after she's dropped Lily off at nursery school.

"Tell me everything, Mom, please don't leave anything out. I want to know."

"You must look like her, I think, Claudia. Of course, he didn't say anything about freckles like you or if she had a dimple, no details, but you have to remember, Mr. Stanley was a man, and men don't notice the same things that women do. But she was tall like you, with brown hair, he said that . . . oh, there were so many little things I asked him, so much I wanted to know, but he would just sit there with this blank expression and occasionally shake his head and say he didn't have that information. 'I don't have that information, Mrs. Magers,'" Margaret mimicked in a low voice. "Very nice, mind you, but stuffy and, I don't know, so exasperating . . . he knew things like her height and weight as if he had actually been the one who measured her, but I'm sure it was just written on some paper, and I wrote down everything he said so I wouldn't forget." She clasped the small notebook in both hands. "Not that I would have forgotten. I remember . . . maybe *he* had the dimple like you." She searched her daughter's eyes. "Not Mr. Stanley, I don't mean Mr. Stanley, but you know, your . . . uh . . ." Margaret hesitated. "The young man."

Claudia just gazed at her mother; she would scream if she had to discuss what she was going to call him. "I got the dimple when the angels kissed me, Mom. Don't you remember?"

Something old, something family, something between the two of them . . . Margaret smiled. "Oh, that's what Grandma Mae used to say, didn't she? Goodness."

Claudia stayed where she was now, under the covers; she didn't make a move to answer the ringing phone.

So let's see, what did she have here? What was the lowdown? One baby girl, one Cole Jaffe, born one California December day at two-forty in the afternoon, one five-pound-eleven-ounce, eighteen-inch-long baby with a dimple . . .

She reached up and punched the pillow, making a new dent for her head. Born of one girl and one boy. So who were these people? The phone rang. She closed her eyes tight and crossed her hands over her chest. Okay, she didn't need Columbo; she'd just go over it again and see what she had.

"Tall," Margaret had said, "you're tall like she was . . . and like him, for that matter—he was six two." Claudia's hands on the edge of the table as her mother read from the notebook. But her eyes were brown, not blue like Claudia's; maybe the blue eyes came from him. Had Margaret told her the color of his eyes? No.

What else? She clenched all the muscles in her body and then let them go.

High school, Margaret had said; she'd completed high school and she was eighteen. . . . Claudia thought about eighteen, about when she was eighteen and a delirious freshman at Columbia, running around inhaling New York, drunk on everything: the streets, the

162

noise, the people. . . . She saw herself standing at Seventy-second and Lexington in her new camel-hair coat, kissing Matt Fanucci from English 129, icy wind whipping around the corner and nearly blowing her off her feet, sleet and rain. He was holding her; she could feel his hipbones and his fingers pushing in between her ribs and her wet hair stuck across the side of her face. Claudia smiled. Matt Fanucci's eyes were brown, with whisk-broom lashes, and he had an accent like Marcello Mastroianni's and wore jeans that were two sizes smaller than Claudia's, the top of his black curls just reached her eyebrows.

The phone stopped, took a short break, and then started up again.

Okay, so maybe *his* eyes were blue like Claudia's and *her* eyes were brown like Matt Fanucci's and she was eighteen like Claudia was once, but not eighteen and carefree and happy, ditching class and kissing boys on street corners; no, eighteen and in Los Angeles and having a baby—all alone and having a baby without the blond "young man," as Margaret had called him.

Sweet Jesus, a baby . . . what would Claudia have done with a baby when she was eighteen? What if she had gotten pregnant with Matt Fanucci? What if the lapsed Catholic's birth control pills hadn't worked? She remembered her hours of anguish trying to make peace with the unholy birth control pills. . . .

Claudia turned over on her side.

Would she have had it? Left school and had a baby? Left Columbia? And all her dreams? Holy moly.

Well, what were the choices? You either have a baby or—what— you have an abortion. That's never changed. Mother of God.

And then she remembered: it came to her and she sat up. The last bit of information, the other thing Margaret had said. What was the matter with her—was she unconscious? Margaret, sitting in a flood of backlight at her kitchen table, pale-pink reading glasses at the end of her nose, gripping the cherished notebook filled with her perfect penmanship. "A five-foot-nine-inch-tall, eighteen-year-old, brown-haired, brown-eyed Jewish Caucasian girl, sweetheart—that's what Mr. Stanley said."

Jewish. The *other mother* was Jewish; she had to be the one named Jaffe. Claudia had something; she didn't need Columbo—she had a clue.

They met at Marie Callender's; it was Dorothy's choice. "Oh, just call me Dorothy," the woman had said on the phone. She'd wanted to do everything on the phone, but Claudia said please, please, she'd really rather meet now, and Dorothy had explained how she could just fax her the "nonidentifying" information—that's what it was called; that's what she'd taught her the first time they'd talked. "You can call them, but they'll make you put it in writing, so you might as well just save time right off the bat and write them, and, honey, don't tell them you have your birth name—you just play dumb." Claudia was to contact Blessed Children, say she was the adoptee, give her date of birth, and ask for all the nonidentifying information about her birth parents, and then, when she got that, call Dorothy back. That's when she'd asked Dorothy, please, could they meet.

"You'll see the Marie Callendar's as soon as you get off the free-way. It's right there at the end of the ramp."

"They have good pie," Ollie said.

"Uh huh."

He changed lanes and glanced at her. "Do you think she'll be wearing a trench coat?"

"What?"

"A trench coat and a fedora, like Mickey Spillane."

"Ollie."

"What?"

164

"She's a search consultant, not a detective."

"I was making a joke."

"Yeah, but I'm nervous."

A wiser choice than saying she was thinking of pushing on the door handle and falling out of the car so someone could run over her before they got there.

"Why?"

Claudia turned. "What?"

"Why are you nervous?"

"I don't know."

"She doesn't know anything yet; she hasn't even started."

"I know."

Oliver punched the radio buttons. "Dorothy Floye from Tarzana, search consultant extraordinaire."

Claudia turned her head away and looked out the window. Her name had not come from the shreds of a phone book; it came from someone Oliver knew at school, someone who knew someone who had used Mrs. Floye to find someone less than a year ago. She was not wearing a trench coat and looked nothing like Columbo or Mickey Spillane; she looked like somebody's aunt Evelyn from Pasadena or, for that matter, somebody's aunt Dorothy from Tarzana. She looked like someone whose living room smacked of *Good Housekeeping* and smelled of cinnamon spice cake. Round and short, with a big shiny black pocketbook and wearing an upscale sweatshirt in royal blue with rhinestones in the shape of a galloping horse across her ample bust, Calvin Klein jeans at least one size too small, and white Nike walking shoes. Her hair was copper and teased and sprayed into a feathered helmet; she had snappy, gorgeous, big green eyes, wore burnt-orange lipstick and, if Claudia was not mistaken, at least one coat of Max Factor pancake makeup, or something very much like it that you could still buy at your local drugstore.

"Oh, I don't just do lost birth mothers, honey," she said to Oliver. "I do lost loves, lost relatives of any kind. I'm kind of the queen of the lost."

Ollie laughed, took a swig of his iced tea, and polished off his second piece of cherry pie. Claudia opened a packet of Equal and added it to her coffee. Her hand was shaking; she refused to look at it, but she could feel it move.

Dorothy raised her eyes from the papers. "What we have here is an out-of-state search, honey."

"Is that harder?"

"Yeah, but that's okay." She patted Claudia's hand as if she'd known her forever. "We've got some good stuff here. Don't worry, we're on our way."

Claudia had read the *nonidentifying* papers over and over—in the kitchen, in the bed, in the bathtub. She could recite them verbatim:

Your birth mother was described by the social worker as being pretty, obviously quite intelligent but very independent in her thinking and reluctant to talk. She had decided against relinquishment of the child after its birth but then changed her mind and consented that the child be put up for adoption. She requested that the adoptive parents be Catholic and not of the Jewish faith as she was. Your birth father was not involved in the planning. Your birth mother declined to speak much about him or their relationship, she declined to give any information regarding his family, education, or special interests. He was in good health. The attending physician reported that your birth mother was in good health and physical condition and there were no complications during the pregnancy or delivery. (See attached report.) You were reported to be in good health. There were no birth injuries or defects. (See attached report.) The parents of the birth mother were in good health. The birth mother had no siblings and was born in the state of Missouri.

And on and on: the ages of the birth mother's parents, her father's occupation, the physical description of the birth mother, which Claudia partially had from Margaret . . .

"Jaffe was *her* last name, since it says she was Jewish." Claudia smiled at Dorothy. "Don't you think?" Claudia's cheeks were stiff from smiling—why was she smiling? She made a desperate effort to rearrange her face.

"Maybe."

"Do you think his name was Cole?"

"It's hard to know. I try never to second-guess; you never know what went on in their heads, those poor girls. Ostracized, shamed—not like it is now, let me tell you. Nowadays anybody and their uncle can have a baby and bring it up all alone, it's perfectly acceptable; nowadays you have a baby by yourself, la-di-da, you're a *single mother*, ain't she sweet. In those days, if you tried a stunt like that, you were a fool and a whore." She touched her cheek by her mouth with one finger, the nail perfectly painted the orange flame color of her lipstick. "A disgrace, you were a disgrace to yourself and your family, and a lot of girls didn't have the courage to be a disgrace, or the guts, the wherewithal, the money—oh, don't get me started; I definitely do go on." She took a sip of her coffee, her green eyes shining over the top of the cup.

"Is that what *you* did?" Oliver said.

Claudia couldn't believe it, she couldn't believe what he'd said.

Dorothy laughed. "Yep, I guess I wasn't too circumspect just then, was I? That's what my husband says, *circumspect:* 'You gotta be circumspect, Dotty'—what a word. That's how I got into the business, I guess. Well, actually I *know.* That's how most of us got into the business, most of us searchers: we either gave up our babies or faced the music and kept 'em, or we were the ones who were adopted—most of us, I'd say." She took the last bite of her chocolate cream pie, pushed the fork against the crust crumbs, and raised them into her beautiful full mouth. "That's why I usually do my business over the telephone. When I'm face-to-face I'm more apt to get riled up." She shook her head. "All those years ago and look at me, I still fly off the handle—what a hoot." She blotted her lips with the paper napkin, not disturbing the orange color one bit. "I didn't put my boy up for adoption; I was in the fool/whore category, don't you know. I kept my 'little bastard'—that's what my father called him: 'You want to keep that little bastard, you do it on your own.'" She pursed her lips. "I went to live with my aunt Henrietta; she took me in."

Claudia was speechless.

"You do what you gotta do. Of course, from the time he turned thirteen until he was twenty, I was sure I'd made a mistake." She laughed. "I wanted more than to have just put him up for adoption—I wanted to crack him in the head with a bat." She flashed her big green eyes at Ollie. "How old is your baby?"

"She just turned three."

"Oh, I've got a grandson that's three; they're still angels then. You got a picture?"

"Sure," Oliver said, reaching into his pocket for his wallet.

Dorothy looked at Claudia. "Sometimes they just made up names and put 'em on the birth certificates, honey, names that didn't have anything to do with anything, names they read in a book or heard in a song, could be anything. Then it's really hard, then you don't have any clues. We'll just hope she came to Los Angeles, had you, named you with her last name, and went back home to Missouri and stayed there; that's what I'd like."

"Sure," Claudia managed to get out. "But Missouri is a big state, isn't it? How will you know which city?"

Oliver held out a color snapshot of Lily, and Dorothy took it.

"Oh, a little towhead, what a cutie. Lily, huh?"

"Uh huh," he said.

"She's a honey." She handed Ollie the photo, picked up the pages Claudia had brought her, tapped them together against the tabletop until they became one. "You know, *you* can do this; you don't really need me."

"Oh, no; I do," Claudia said. She'd have to smack her if she wouldn't do it; she'd have to figure out a way to tie her to the booth and convince her.

"Don't think for one moment that I don't want to. I just want to make sure you know you can search on your own."

"No." Claudia couldn't find more words; she was terrified. She could see herself walking through the state of Missouri. She'd never been to Missouri and had no idea what it looked like; she imagined a flatter version of upstate New York, envisioned herself criss-crossing the state by foot, stopping in every village, no . . . what did Missouri have? farms? asking every tall, brunette, Jewish-looking farm woman, "Are you my mother?" just like the baby bird. Claudia looked at Dorothy. And what if she wasn't brunette anymore, what if she was gray? or what if she'd dyed it? What if the *other mother* had copper-colored hair like Dorothy's? She looked down and moved her hand across the seat of the red vinyl booth. Her palm was sweaty; she could see its trail. She turned to Oliver; she didn't say anything, but just turned.

"We'd like you to do this, Dorothy," Ollie said, rising to the occasion like Sir Lancelot.

"You got me, then," Dorothy Floye said.

"She said there were no guarantees, Dad. She said she's had cases where it's taken her two weeks and cases where it's taken two years. Are you sure you don't want wine?" Claudia said, holding the bottle up in front of the open door of the refrigerator.

"No, I'll just have my gin." He studied Dorothy Floye's business card.

Claudia poured herself some white wine and filled a martini glass with Bombay Sapphire gin she kept in the freezer for her father. She carried both glasses to the kitchen table, set the gin in front of him, and sat in the opposite chair.

"What if they're bad people?"

"What?" She didn't think she'd heard him correctly.

"Not everyone's respectable, Claudia, let's be realistic here. Just because it said on a piece of paper that she was a very nice girl in 1960 doesn't mean she's a very nice girl now." He took a sip of the gin. "And most *nice* girls who weren't married then weren't getting pregnant, but I'll give her the benefit of the doubt." He put the glass down. "And we don't know a damn thing about *him*, do we? How do you know one of them won't see the way you were raised, what you and Oliver have put together here." He extended his hand around her spotless kitchen. "Nice house, nice cars, professional people, nice everything . . . How do you know that they aren't hurting? How do you know that they won't see all of this and want some of it, take you for a goddamn ride?"

"I can't believe you're saying this."

"You can't? Well, think about it. I am not all gung ho about this big reunion, like you and your mother. I think it's a big mistake. I think you should leave well enough alone. Where are your olives? In the refrigerator?"

"I thought you liked those horrible little onions. When did you start using olives?"

"When I want a martini instead of a gibson—and you never have my onions here. Do you?"

"No."

He walked to the refrigerator. Claudia trailed her finger around the rim of her wineglass. It had never occurred to her that they could be bad people. How could her very own birth parents be bad people?

"Are you thinking?" He returned with the olive jar. "I thought I always taught you to think things through." She watched John Magers's big hands unscrew the lid of the olive jar. "Your mother's all upset about this, you know. She won't let on she's upset, but I know better." He poked a spoon around inside the olive jar, clinking the sides of the glass. "I know what she does in that bathroom when she stays forever and comes out like a little prune. Cries under the sound of the running water. Nobody has to tell me. I know."

Claudia looked at him. She had no idea what to say.

"Damn right." He plunked two olives into his martini glass. "I just don't get it. Didn't we do enough for you, that you have this need?"

"Oh, Daddy . . . it's not about a need because of something you did or didn't do; it's a need because of me."

"Love you enough, give you enough. Explain it."

"I . . . I can't. I'm sorry, I can't."

"Well, there you have it." He took a swig of the gin. "I say if you can't explain it you better leave well enough alone. We don't know who these people are, Claudia, *if* you find them. How are you going to protect yourself? Have you thought about that?"

"No, I guess not; no."

"You see? You and your mother, all emotional, running willy-nilly into finding them, you'd think this was one of those talk shows, that trash they have on in the daytime. Are you planning on having this reunion on Oprah Winfrey?"

"Daddy, please."

"Well, how the hell should I know?"

"Grampa!" Lily screamed. "Grampa's here, Grampa, Grampa, Grampa!" Lily ran in from the opened back door ahead of Santos and threw herself across her grandfather's knees.

"Hi there, my little Lily," he said, scooping her up in his big arms. "How's my little Lily today?"

He looked over the top of the child's blond curls. "Why open up Pandora's box, Claudie? I think you should let it be."

"Canyon four, Ardsley nothing!" Oliver yelled, slamming the front door. "Hey, Claud, we walloped 'em, we tromped 'em to smithereens, we nailed 'em to the you-know-what." He looked around. "Claud! Where are you?"

"Upstairs!"

His soccer cleats made smacking *squoosh* sounds as they crossed the living room floor and clomped up the steps.

"You walloped them, huh?" she said, as he entered the bedroom.

"We creamed 'em, you should have seen it—my boys were great!" His T-shirt was damp when he grabbed her; he smelled of sweat, Mennen aftershave, and pepperoni pizza from the Shakey's near the park.

"You look cute," he said, kissing her on the mouth and crossing to her earlobe. "And why are you wearing only this delicious short piece of terry cloth? Lucky me. What's going on?"

"Nothing. Listen, Daddy was here and"—she pushed him a little away from her—"he thinks I should forget all this."

"All what?" Ollie backed up and pulled his T-shirt over his head. "Boy, I stink. I am so glad we won. I hate that jack-off Cubby—you

172

know how much I hate him, the pompous rich potbelly, strutting all over their trimmed grounds with that golf club. I'd like to stick that golf club down his throat."

"What golf club?"

"Oh, he walks around their school wielding a golf club, pokes the air with it when he's making a point. I should have made him swallow it, considering. . . ."

Claudia loved the way he told a story. Waving his arms around as if it were just happening, he looked about eighteen. "The boys were good, huh?"

"They were magnificent." He pinched the edge of the bath towel she was wearing. "What happens if I whisk this off?"

"Ollie . . ."

"Hey, where's your sense of adventure, kid?"

"Lily and I are about to take a bath."

"Oh, I see. Timing is everything." He kissed the hollow at the base of her throat, one hand encircling her, pulling her hard against his chest, and the other hand up and under the towel.

"Ollie . . ."

"I love it when you call me Ollie."

"He thinks I should forget finding them. He thinks—"

"I also love it when you call me Oliver. In fact, you could probably call me anything, and I would . . ." One hand cupped her bare ass and the other hand tilted her chin up. He closed her mouth with his.

"Daddy! You want to take a bath with me and Mommy?" Lily stood behind him, naked, her arms loaded with floatable toys. Ollie released Claudia and turned.

"Miss Lily, how nice to see you again."

"I'm not *Miss* Lily, I'm me. You want to take a bath with me and Mommy? We're going to have bubbles."

"I don't think so; I think I'll have a shower. I don't think you want me in the bathtub with you."

"Why not?"

" 'Cause I'm stinky."

She giggled. "No you're not."

"Oh, yeah, I am. Ask your mother."

"I would let you play with my ponies. You could even be Winkle— she's the pink one with the sparkly mane and the shooting start."

"Shooting start, huh?"

"Not the whole time. You could only be her till the water comes in."

"Oh, well, then." He squatted and kissed Lily on the top of her head. "I think I better have a shower, as much as I would like to have a bath with you and Winkle."

"And Mommy."

"Right," he said, looking up at Claudia. "I would like very much to have a bath with Mommy, but some other time."

"Come on, Mommy." Lily skipped into their bathroom.

"I'm coming. Don't get in, Lily, wait for me. Call me when the water's high." She turned to Oliver. "So did you hear what I said?"

"He thinks you should forget about finding them."

"Yeah."

"Why?" He sat on the edge of the bed and unlaced his soccer shoes.

"In case they want something, in case they're bad."

Oliver laughed.

"That's what he said."

"John's just afraid of the competition."

"Come on."

"I'm not kidding. Who knows who the other guy might be? He might be—I don't know—F. Lee Bailey, or William Rehnquist." Oliver laughed and stood up. "On the other hand, he might own the Galaxies or the Knicks—now, that I would like."

"The *other guy*."

"Well, I don't know—what do you call him?"

"Mommy, there's so many bubbles!" Lily shrieked from the bathroom.

Oliver patted Claudia's ass through the terry cloth. "Your father's afraid of the competition, honey. As your mother would say, mark my words."

She sat motionless in the bathtub, lingering while the water turned cool, listening to the sounds of Ollie playing with Lily in the next room. She remembered the nights of her childhood, when John would talk her to sleep. She saw him last in the day; it was not her mother who gave her her good-night kiss, it was John. John, who spent most of his life in a book-lined office or a crowded courtroom—he was the one who claimed the evening's final moments; it was her father's face that she saw last before he turned off the light. The width and depth and height of him squeezed into the small yellow dotted-swiss-covered chair by the side of her bed. Her big father surrounded by ruffles, while they played Chinese checkers or Go Fish or he told her stories or they sang. His tie would be loosened, but he would still be wearing his white-on-white shirt, his cuff links, his pressed suit pants, his suspenders, and his gleaming hard shoes.

" 'Someone's in the kitchen with Dinah, someone's in the kitchen, I . . .' "

" 'Know-oh-oh-oh,' " Claudia would sing, her back snuggled up against the pillows.

" 'Someone's in the kitchen with Dinahhhhhhh,' " John would follow in his booming baritone, " '. . . strummin' on the ol' banjo.' "

175

And together: " '. . . singin' fee fi fiddlee i oh, fee fi fiddlee i oh oh oh oh . . .' "

"John, it's time for her to be sleeping," Margaret would say from the doorway.

"One minute, Margaret," he'd answer, but he wouldn't turn to her, and she'd wait there for a moment, hovering. Claudia would hold her breath, feeling the presence of her mother's frame in the doorway, but her eyes were glued to her father, no one moving, and then her mother would finally leave and they'd wait together until they heard her slippers go *klop-klop* down the hall, and then he'd whisper, " 'fee fi fiddlee i ohhhhhhh . . .' " and he'd point to Claudia.

" 'Strummin' on the ol' banjo,' " she'd shriek from her pillows, and they would laugh together, Claudia and her father, Claudia and John.

"There are two ways to do everything," he'd said, towering over her when she was thirteen, the pages of her book report lost in his hand. She wanted to get out of there, she'd told Gena she'd meet her at Hudson's in Larchmont, they were going to buy sandals and have pizza and spend the whole afternoon hanging out. It was Saturday— why did she have to do this on a Saturday?

"Did you hear me?"

She shrugged. "Yes."

"Two ways. The right way and the fast way: you always have a choice."

She bent down and scratched her leg. It was nearly noon already; how long was this going to go on?

"You'll have that choice all through life, in everything you do."

"Uh huh."

"You don't understand that now, but you will."

"Dad, I'm supposed to meet Gena."

"I'm sure she'll wait for you."

"I'll do it over."

"It's not about doing it over; it's understanding *why* you should do it over. Do you?"

"Yeah, I guess so—'cause it isn't good enough . . . I don't know."

"It's why painters work for years on a painting, revising, fixing, painting over what they've already painted; why writers rewrite . . . Claudie?"

"What?" She was staring at him but she didn't see him; her eyes had glazed over. She wanted the sandals that had the two straps over her toes, not the thick ones but the thin ones, but she couldn't decide if she should get tan or white. Gena would probably get white.

"You can turn it in this way."

"I'll do it over, Dad."

"Why?"

"Uh." The curtains on her bedroom windows moved. There was something growing in the garden that she could smell—it wasn't orange blossoms, it was more spicy; was it stock? She looked at him. Why do it over? Was that what he said?

"You don't have to do it over; it's fine the way it is. It's good, it's passing, it fits the bill, you might even get a B on it."

She held her ground with him. "Because I can make it better."

He nodded.

She moved her foot on the carpet. "Do I have to do it now?"

"I don't care when you do it. It's your work, it's your choice."

"I'd like to go meet Gena and hang out and work on it tomorrow after church."

"That sounds reasonable. It *is* Saturday, after all."

She relaxed. "Yeah, it *is* Saturday."

He put the papers on her desk. "Have a good time," he said. "Tell Gena to come back with you. Your mother's making lamb chops for supper—Gena likes lamb chops, as I recall. Unless you girls have other plans."

"Thanks, Dad."

He smiled as he passed her. "Anytime."

Claudia reached forward now and lifted the drain lever, releasing the water from the tub. She scooped up three tiny rubber horses that were floating near her breasts and balanced them with the others on the edge of the bathtub, their tails dripping water down the porcelain. She stared at the light-blue one with the silver mane; it was a little bigger than the others; Lily said it was the boy.

She took the tiny blue pony and moved him as if he were galloping through the scum of melted bubbles along the top of her wet thigh. Could he be bad? The *other father?* The *other guy*—was that what Oliver had called him? The *young man,* her mother had said. Claudia had a vision of the two of them having a shootout: the smoke cleared, and there was John, large and luminous, silver guns flashing, all in white, with a ten-gallon white Stetson and a big white horse, and the *other father,* lassoed and broken, her fantasy Hopalong Cassidy, defrocked, dusty, and wounded, stumbling behind John's horse, and John turning to him in the saddle. "You be good to my daughter, you hear me, whoever you are," and the *other father* meekly saying, "You got it, yes, sir."

The pony floated out of Claudia's hand toward the drain.

"I love you, Daddy," she had whispered as John raised her wedding veil, and he had nodded, that same nod of total devotion she still looked for now, his nod of approval and acknowledgment and complete love; he nodded, and he turned her gently with his big palm on the small of her back to face her groom. "You be good to her, son," he said to Oliver, and Oliver looked John square in the eyes and said, "Yes, sir."

Laughter and shrieking from Claudia's bedroom. Claudia could hear Lily and Oliver from the bathtub. "I'm gonna get you, Daddy," Lily squealed.

She had handed her little Lily to him, her tiny new baby Lily, lost in John's big arms. It was the first and only time she had seen her father speechless. John, who had something to say about everything, the grand orator stunned and silent, his hands trembling as he held the small pink bundle, saying everything in his silence, he'd nodded at her.

Claudia sat motionless and felt the air on her skin, she closed her eyes and leaned her head back against the porcelain, she listened to the water snorkle its way out of the tub.

"It's called a Consent for Contact form, honey. They didn't send it?"

It was a week later, and the first time Dorothy had called Claudia since they'd met at Marie Callender's.

"I've never heard of it." Claudia moved the phone to her other shoulder. "What is it, Dorothy?"

"You're sure? There was no mention of it existing?"

"No. What is it?"

"It's strange is what it is. You write them and you ask them. Those red-tapers, sometimes I think nobody uses their brains."

"What do I say?"

"You say you want to know if either of your birth parents ever signed a Consent for Contact form, honey, that's what you say."

She wrote and she asked them. And she washed the dishes and she drove Lily to and from nursery school and she made chicken with yams.

If it took two days for them to get her letter and two days for them to see if they had this Consent for Contact form . . . She made the beds and she drove to the beach alone, trudging up and down at the edge of the waves, watching her footprints get erased with water. . . . And two days for them to write her back. . . . She went shopping for nothing, tried on hysterically expensive spike-heeled shoes and designer dresses and left them hanging neatly in peach dressing rooms, saying nothing to the clerks. She painted Lily's cheek with a rainbow. She trudged around the grocery store, touching everything in the produce department, tomatoes and bananas, picking only the flat onions, as Margaret had taught her—"The flat ones are sweeter, Claudia"—and she would teach Lily, because that's what mothers do, pass on thousands of tiny bits of ordinary and extraordinary information. Claudia stared right through the checker. What would the *other mother* have taught her? Did she know how to pick the onions that were flat? She went to the movies with Ollie, she debated cutting her hair short, she made veal piccata with rice. She wrote Blessed Children to see if the *other ones* had signed a Consent for Contact form, and she waited and she walked through her life.

"What about we make another baby?"

"Hmm?" Claudia opened her eyes. Dawn light colored their bedroom. She rolled over, yawned.

"I think it would be good for you." Ollie turned his face to her, kissed her shoulder; she felt the morning stubble against her skin. "Give you something else to think about."

Claudia stared.

"Lily's three." He punched a pillow behind his head. "Wasn't that our plan?"

"A baby?"

He stretched up against the pillows. "Yeah," he said, and grinned.

"I can't believe you."

"What?"

"You want to talk about having another baby? *Now?*"

She swung her legs out from under the scramble of sheets and stood up. She was naked; she grabbed at the quilt and pulled it around herself.

Ollie got out of bed on the other side and stood naked across from her. "This search thing has become a goddamn obsession with you. Is finding them all we're supposed to talk about now?"

"I'm certainly not going to talk about having another baby."

"Maybe you should go see somebody and talk about what's going on with you."

She clutched the quilt around her breasts. Ollie didn't move.

"I mean it, Claud. You're walking around here like a piece of driftwood. Is this all you're going to do with your life now? Wait?"

She stood there, didn't answer. Ollie studied her from the other side of their bed.

"Claud?"

Her hands were icy.

"Claud, say something."

"I can't do this now."

"Which part?"

"None of it."

"Great." He turned and walked into the bathroom. Claudia watched the door shut behind his naked back, lowered her shoulders, and tried to take a breath.

Have another baby. He'd hit her with it out of nowhere; it was like waking up and getting hit in the face with a pie. And it wasn't so much about having another baby; it was that he'd brought it up now. Didn't he understand what she was doing? She'd thought about finding them practically her whole life, and now that she was in the middle of it, she couldn't do anything else. Didn't he understand?

Claudia yanked at a shopping cart in front of the market; two of them were stuck together, their silver flip-up parts entangled. It was as if they were doing it on purpose. Anything to annoy her—first Ollie, now the shopping carts . . . and Gena in between. She never should have called Gena, but she'd walked around with the argument in her head all morning and then finally picked up the phone. Of course, Gena had turned the whole thing around, just like she always did when it came to babies.

"You're not, are you?" Gena had said.

"Well, not now, but that's not what I'm talking about. I'm talking about him bringing it up *now*."

"You mean you're *going* to have another baby?"

Claudia ran her hand across her face. "Oh, Gena, someday."

"Why?"

"*Why?*"

"Yeah, why?"

Claudia gave up her hold on the jammed shopping carts and moved to another group. She knew what would happen now—now she'd get one with a crooked wheel, one that would keep trying to return to the frozen foods. She never should have tried to discuss it with Gena.

"You already experienced having a baby. What's the need to do it again?"

"Gena, it's not an acting exercise."

Claudia shook her head. Gena had never understood anything about Claudia wanting to have a baby. Gena didn't have any, she didn't want any, and she certainly didn't understand why anybody else would. End of discussion. They had made their peace about that when they were just little girls.

"You can be the mommy, and I'll be the star," said Gena.

"Okay."

She did *adore* Lily, though. That was her word, *adore*, but from afar. Gena looking slightly pale as Claudia extended a bundle of newborn

Lily wrapped in a blanket. "Holy mother—she's so little, Claud. I don't know . . ."

Gena's eyes wide when a toddling Lily took the chewed potato out of her mouth and put it lovingly into Gena's hand.

"I think I'll be better at this godmother thing when she can at least hold a knife and fork, order from a menu, preferably while wearing high heels."

Claudia pushed her cart to the array of fruit in the produce section, lifted two plastic baskets of strawberries, checked out the ones on the bottom, discarded one basket and put the other in the cart next to her purse. This shopping cart didn't have a wobbly wheel; it was behaving just fine. Actually, the shopping cart was the only thing that was behaving fine in her life right now. All she needed was a god-damned Consent for Contact form. Why didn't anybody understand?

By signing this form, I voluntarily give my consent to the State Department of Social Services or licensed adoption agency to arrange contact with my adult biological child who was placed for adoption.

So simple. How could it be? As simple as having your name in a box. A box your great-grandmother gets at a world's fair and hands down to your grandmother, who hands it down to your mother, who uses it as a treasure chest hidden under her lingerie.

Claudia scanned the creased papers she'd pulled from the envelope when she'd returned from the grocery store. Her eyes traveled down the lines of type, she read them, said the quietest "Oh," and sat down, one bag at her feet tipping, a parade of oranges rolling across the floor. *Jennifer Jaffe Glass,* Claudia read. *Jennifer Jaffe Glass, 28 East 82nd Street, New York, N.Y. 10028, 212 388-0681.*

There was nothing else; nothing from the *other father*; only this. Yes, you may let my adult biological daughter contact me, love and kisses, Jennifer Jaffe Glass. Claudia traced her finger around the letters of the black-ink signature. It was messy; it looked like doctor's handwriting, loopy and loose and practically illegible. Claudia brushed the tips of her fingers across her wet cheeks. Nobody could understand this feeling she was feeling, this undeniable euphoria. She knew what this handwriting looked like; it looked like *hers*.

She would write, not call, she finally decided.

"It's up to you, hon," Dorothy Floye had said. "I'll send you an initial-contact guide for calling and some samples for writing—it's six of one and a half dozen of the other. If you call, they can hang up; if you write, they can throw the letter in the trash and never answer. You never know how they'll react."

"Uh huh."

"Hey, don't fret, hon. You're way ahead of yourself and once we have her, we'll find him. Don't think for a minute I thought it would be this fast." She laughed. "What a search, huh? You got what you wanted—you found your birth mother. Aren't you thrilled?"

"Sure, absolutely." Claudia put her hand on the wall and steadied herself. "I'm thrilled."

" 'I would like to speak to you about something, but it's very confidential. Can you speak freely?' " Claudia read off the paper. She turned to Oliver. "I can't do this. I sound insane."

"No you don't. Here." He offered her a piece of the apple he was eating.

"No . . ." She looked down at the paper in her hand. "Uh . . . 'I need to ask you a few questions to make sure you're the person I've been looking for—' Oh, Ollie . . ."

"It's okay. Go on."

"Uh . . ."—She looked back at the paper. " '*My name is So-and-so, and I was born on, you know, December the thirtieth,* 1960, *and uh,*"—She looked up. "And then what? 'Did you happen to have a baby that day? Around five pounds, eleven ounces, with a dimple and brown hair, a little baby? I mean, do you recall?' Oh, I can't . . ."

"Okay." He laughed. "You're right, I'm wrong. Write, don't call."

Her mother's shoulder bumped against hers as Margaret returned from communion. Claudia turned and Margaret smiled; they sat back together. It had been a long time since Claudia had felt the hard wood of a pew at Saint Brandon's beneath her knees. Father Maynard stood. "Bow your heads for a special prayer," he said, looking at his congregation. Margaret's head lowered, Claudia's eyes scanned the church. It was hard to know what she was doing there, not that Margaret hadn't more than suggested on umpteen Sundays that maybe she might like to go to church with her and Claudia had said no time after time. . . . So why this Sunday? Why after all this time did she feel the need to come here? It wasn't just Margaret pushing. Why? To get help for her rewrites? From Jesus? Claudia shifted on the bench, folded her hands, held them steady. Better she should try to find Arthur Miller. Or Sam Shepard or David Mamet. Allen Ginsberg. Claudia smiled to think how differently each would write the letter. Dear Mom, Dear Mother, Dear Occupant. . . . Claudia caught her lip between her teeth; all she needed now was to start laughing in church. She pushed her backside hard against the pew. Anyway, why was she limiting the field to male writers? What about May

Sarton or Lillian Hellman? She opened her eyes and settled on the statue of the Virgin Mary. Maybe she could connect with the spirit of Sylvia Plath . . . Dear Mother, Please write me before I put my head in the oven. . . . Placing her hand over her smile, Claudia tried to focus on Mary—the white alabaster folds of her gown, her serene face, her head lowered, her crown—and then she remembered what had always gotten to her. Mary's arms, Mary's beautiful arms, frozen forever, in statue after statue, from Los Angeles to Rome: Mary's arms always and forever open, open to enfold you, to take you into her embrace. Claudia's eyes flooded with tears; she shut them.

O sweet Mary, she prayed silently, sweet blessed Mother, it is to you I cry, it is to you I turn. Please look on me with your eyes of mercy, please hear my prayer. She could hear her mother breathing beside her, smell Margaret's Chantilly, the spray net in her hair. Sweet Mary, you who were united with your Divine Son in the glorious Assumption, please remember, please remember and please help me in uniting with my—Claudia took a little breath—my birth mother, please help me to . . . Margaret touched Claudia's clasped hands with the tips of her fingers. "Are you all right, dear?" . . . Please help me, blessed Mary, Claudia prayed, to do the right thing. She bowed her head. Thank you. Amen.

"Did you finish?" Gena said.

"I'm working on it." Claudia wedged the phone between her neck and her shoulder, took the wine out of the refrigerator, and poured herself a glass.

"I can't believe you're doing it. What are you saying?"

"I don't know; I keep changing it."

"I'd be rewriting until next Christmas, I'd be hysterical, I'd be drinking—"

"I *am* drinking."

"I can't believe she's in New York. I could just walk over. Well, I couldn't *walk* over—she's all the way uptown—but I could take a cab. Do you want me to go park myself outside her building and wait and see what I can see?"

"Gena, I'll kill you."

"I was kidding."

"Promise me."

"I was kidding!"

"Promise me!"

"Mother of God, I promise you."

"That what?"

"That I won't go anywhere near Eighty-second, I won't even go above Fifty-seventh, and I'll stay on the West Side. Okay?"

Claudia took another swig of the wine. "Okay."

Neither of them said anything.

"Unbelievable," Gena said.

"Do you realize how many times I've been in New York? Four years of school in New York, four whole years, and all the times since then? Do you realize?"

"You could have been walking on the same street as her, you could have sat next to her on the subway, in the park, your shoulder inches from hers, been across from each other in a restaurant, looked at each other—oh, Claud, you could have looked at her, you could have seen her. Jesus, Mary, and . . ."

"Yeah," Claudia said.

"Un-fucking-believable."

"Yeah." Claudia sat down at the kitchen table.

"What about him?" Gena said.

"Nothing. I guess he didn't sign one."

"Maybe he doesn't even know."

"What?"

"I don't know—that you were born."

Claudia frowned. "I never thought of that."

"You didn't?"

"No."

"Well, we don't know what he knows. Maybe she didn't tell him, maybe he doesn't even know she was pregnant, maybe they only saw each other once."

Claudia didn't say anything.

"Well, it's possible. Maybe they were in love, maybe it was nothing; there's no way to know."

"I'd hate to think it was nothing."

"Why? What difference does it make, as long as you were born?"

"I don't know. I'd hate to think I came from a nothing."

Gena laughed. "Hey, lest we forget, I came from a nothing."

"Oh, Gena."

"Well, it's true. It doesn't matter how long they are married, my darling parents—their relationship is a nothing, and I am their one and only offspring."

Claudia got up and circled the kitchen. "Well," she said.

"Yeah, well. Listen, call me when you finish writing it, when you send it, okay?"

"Yeah."

"Don't forget."

A nothing, could they have been a nothing, Jennifer Jaffe and Whoever-he-was? She'd always assumed they were a something, more than a something, a romance, a real love. . . .

"Aren't you sleeping?" Ollie mumbled.

"No."

She had been lying there in the dark, making lists of what she knew about herself, a list of ingredients like Margaret wrote on her index cards. Who was she? Mother of Lily, daughter of Margaret and John—oh, right—*and* daughter of Jennifer and Whoever-he-was, wife of Oliver . . . one five-foot-nine-inch skinny psychologist—no, lapsed psychologist—a lapsed psychologist and a lapsed Catholic, except for one Sunday, one prayer, one morning: did that count? She'd been lying there in the shadows listening to one bird sing, and then, half awake and half dreaming, she'd imagined them, Jennifer Jaffe and her Whoever, tall and sweet and young and beautiful. Could they have been a nothing, those two out-of-focus figures, her birth parents? Could she possibly be only the leftovers of a one-night stand?

Oliver rolled over and slipped his arm under her shoulders; she turned to him, one leg bent across his thighs, her head on his chest; he pushed her hair away from his mouth, kneaded her back near her shoulder blades, curved into her.

"What's up?" he said, yawning.

"I don't know. I've been up about eighty-two times."

"The letter?"

"I guess so."

"Maybe more than the letter? Maybe the everything?"

Claudia laughed softly, her lips against his skin. "Yeah, I guess so."

"What time is it?"

"I don't know . . . five-thirty, six . . ."

"A little early for biscuits and gravy, huh?"

"Yeah."

She felt his cock getting hard under her hand. He moved against her, she lifted her mouth to his, he ran his fingers along the inside of her thigh and lifted her leg up and over the curve of his hip. He put his hand next to hers on his penis, he rubbed the tip of it against her, and she moved closer and she was wet. She raised up a little and he moved into her, just a little ways, just the beginnings, the way she liked it when she wanted him so much and he kept himself back, and the more he held back the more she wanted him, she needed him, she ached for him to be deep inside her, so deep, and now she moved up against him and he moved a little more inside her, just a little, and she lifted and said "Ollie" and he came forward and he was in deeper and she said, "Oh, Ollie," and he whispered, "What, baby?" and she said, "Ollie, Ollie, Ollie," and then she turned, he was still inside her but she had her back to him now, she pushed back against him, he was in her all the way, she wanted him in her all the way, she could hear herself breathing, a rush in her head, and he slipped his hands around her, his breath and his lips hot against the back of her neck, the fingers of one hand gently pulling on her nipple, the fingers of the other hand softly moving against her clitoris, and she moaned and Ollie was deep inside her, deep and hard and moving, he banged into her hard like she wanted—he knew what she wanted, deep and hard—and she grasped the edge of the night table as the darkness faded into blue-gray, the bamboo blinds made slats of charcoal, and she was wet, so wet, and he was touching her and he was in her and he whispered, "I've got you, Claudia," and she didn't know if she said "Ollie," and she came.

Dear Mom,

Claudia stopped writing and looked at the sheet of blue paper. She laughed, pushed the page aside, and put another piece of stationery in front of her.

She put her pen to the paper and scribbled fast:

Dear Whoever-you-are
Dear You-know-who-you-are-and-I-don't
Dear To-whom-it-may-concern

Oh, really . . .
Claudia pushed the paper off the table.

Dear Mrs. Glass,

She stopped, her pen poised on the paper.
Okay. Go ahead. You can do this. It's like the Nike ad.

Dear Mrs. Glass,
I guess you're wondering why I'm writing to you after all this time. Well,
it's not such a big deal.
I was just wondering—how come you gave me away?

No.
She ripped the blue paper into halves and quarters and dropped
the pieces on the floor.

Dear Mrs Glass,
Fuck you.

That'll make her want to answer me! She shook her head and
exhaled. Okay, okay . . .

Dear Mrs. Glass,
I have brown hair that isn't really curly; it's more wavy, you would say,
except for this one horrible spot in the back at the top of my head where

191

it frizzes up no matter what I do and it looks like shit. Does that happen to you?

Claudia sighed and got up. The odds were Jennifer Jaffe Glass wouldn't be able to read her handwriting, so what difference did it make what she wrote? She walked to the window and stared out at the orange tree, leaned forward until her nose touched the pane. "Dear Mrs. Glass," she whispered, "remember me?"

Maybe it didn't matter what she wrote; maybe Jennifer Jaffe Glass wouldn't answer her even if Claudia turned into John Updike and wrote like the wind. Maybe she'd changed her mind. Maybe she'd thought better of it and decided, *Who needs a daughter? Not me.* Claudia closed her eyes and imagined her. Jennifer Jaffe Glass at the opera in a black silk suit, Jennifer Jaffe Glass walking up Park Avenue, the edges of her raincoat blown open, Jennifer Jaffe Glass stepping out of a cab, laughing, a flash of pale leg, a turn of the head, Jennifer Jaffe Glass opening the letter from Claudia and falling in slow motion to the floor.

Claudia made a little cloud of breath on the glass. Maybe she wasn't even there anymore; maybe it was an old address; maybe she'd moved away and forgotten to write Blessed Children. Maybe she'd died and no one had told Blessed Children. Maybe the letter would come back marked *Occupant Unknown.* Did they ever send a letter back stamped *Occupant Dead?* What if she was dead and he was lost forever? No, even better . . . what if she answered her letter and they met and Jennifer Jaffe Glass took one look at Claudia, threw up her hands, said, *Oh, my goodness, look how you turned out,* and walked away.

Pathetic, she was getting pathetic. Just write the thing, Claudia. Shit or get off the pot, like Gena says.

She turned back toward the table, poured more diet Coke from

192

the can into the wineglass, sat down, and picked up the pen. She wrote slowly and as clearly as she could.

Dear Jennifer Jaffe Glass,
My name is Claudia Morgan and I'm your daughter. I would like to hear from you. Please call me at 213 322-8217 or write me at 76228 Woodrow Wilson Drive, Los Angeles, California 91684. Thank you.

Thank you? Did she need the thank-you? Yes . . . leave the thank-you; let her see Margaret and John had raised her right.

Claudia studied the sheet of blue paper, stood up from the kitchen table, circled it twice, touching the back of each chair as she passed, took a handful of potato chips out of the bag and stuffed them into her mouth, wiped her hands on the back of her jeans. She signed the letter, folded it into perfect thirds, inserted it into the already stamped and addressed envelope, licked the flap, hurried out of the kitchen and across the dining room, and opened the front door.

She slid the thin blue envelope halfway into the mail slot, slammed the door shut, turned the lock, and leaned back against the wood. Then she stood there for fourteen minutes with her hand covering her mouth, until she heard the mailman take the envelope with him as he delivered the mail.

Claudia and Jenny

Jennifer Jaffe Glass tossed her keys and the mail into the antique blue-and-white platter on the dining room table, ran both her hands through her wavy hair, and stepped out of her high-heeled lizard shoes.

"Ron? Are you home, honey?"

She turned her head to listen. Nope, he's not home, honey. Of course he's not home; he won't be home until . . . when did he say? She made a face as she pulled off her suit jacket and placed it perfectly shoulder-to-shoulder across the back of a dining chair. She hadn't been listening. She could call the OR and find out . . . seven, eight? Damn. She'd have to make dinner. Or she could order in—no, not after last night.

"I stand in surgery for six and a half hours to come home to cold pizza stuck to the box?"

Angry; disgusted and angry.

"I'm sorry," she said, her eyes on his. "Did somebody die on your shift?"

"Jenny."

"Okay, okay, not funny. I'm sorry. No more ordering in."

There was no way.

"Damn."

She walked into the kitchen and opened the refrigerator door, bent and stood there, looking inside. She moved a few things around, pulled out three zucchini and three yellow squash, and put them on the sink. She needed to go marketing. She could have done it that afternoon instead of walking up and down Madison, all dressed up, coming home with another pair of expensive gloves. She took a big pot, filled it with water, a dribble of olive oil, a sprinkle of salt, put it on the stove, and lit the gas.

"Pasta, pasta, pasta," she mumbled as she walked out of the room.

She circled the dining room table, pulled off her earrings, and began unbuttoning her black silk blouse. She scooped the mail out of the platter and took it with her as she went up the narrow staircase of the brownstone. Entering the third-floor bedroom, she threw the mail and the blouse on the bed with her earrings, stepped out of her suit skirt, peeled down her panty hose and pulled them from her feet. She got a hanger out of the closet and hung up the skirt. She un-hooked her bra and let it fall to the floor, next to the pantyhose. Then she padded barefoot and naked across the thick Aubusson rug and pushed a switch on the wall by the desk. Music came from unseen speakers, country music; she played it only when Ron wasn't home. "He stopped loving her today," George Jones sang over the muffled New York traffic, covering up the taxi horns with a sad refrain.

She walked back to the bed and picked up the mail. She ought to call him and tell him something lovely, perk up his day. She thumbed her way through the bills and the letters to "Occupant," a *Vanity Fair*. What could she tell him—that she was making dinner? That wasn't what he wanted to hear; she knew what he wanted to hear. I love you, come home to me. She couldn't say that. She turned over a postcard and read aloud: "Dear Ron and Jenny, Positano ain't the same without you. Piss in my ear—oops—wish you were here. Love, Susan and Bernie, the humble ones."

Jenny laughed. She'd call and read him the postcard; that would have to do. She slid back across the bedspread and leaned against the big pillows propped on the headboard. She put the magazine against her raised knees and opened the front cover, and the blue envelope fell onto her skin. She picked it up and squinted at the handwriting.

"What have we here, Dr. Watson?" she said as she slipped her finger under the envelope flap.

When Ron came home, the apartment was dark and there was less than an inch of water left boiling in the big pot.

"What is it? My God, Jenny . . ."

He found her upstairs in their bedroom, the length of her pulled into a half circle on the rug, her body curved into a comma, naked and motionless in the dark. He'd thought she'd had a heart attack, his hands on her pulse, her chest, her eyes, the big surgeon brought to his knees in fear.

"Jenny, listen to me—tell me, where does it hurt?"

She couldn't stop crying, a flood of tears she would have sworn couldn't exist anymore. ("There's no tears left in me, kid. I'm the Sahara.") She would have bet anything, but there they were. Tears, sobs racking through her, joyous sobs tearing through her body, shaking it as if she were coming, as if a cork had been pulled out of her, releasing the pain. And poor Ron's face hovering above her, his body bent over hers as she tried to speak, and he held her and she clutched the thin piece of crumpled blue paper to her breasts, the letter that had become both a lifeline and the open gate that had released the flood.

"My baby, my baby wants to see me, my baby, Ron. . . ."

•   •   •

Claudia was holding Lily when the phone rang, washing her face and hands clean from mud from the garden, dipping Lily's little fingers under the running faucet in the kitchen sink.

"I want to plant, I want to plant."

"Okay, okay."

They'd scooped holes in the mud with their garden spades. Claudia shook the fledgling pansies from their plastic nursery pots, showed Lily how to put in the roots.

"You have to be careful, sweetheart."

"Let me, let me."

"Push the dirt around the roots gently—that's it, gently."

And they'd watered them. "Not too hard, Lily."

"I know, Mommy. Pansy babies," Lily had sung.

And now she'd set Lily down on the sink—one hand holding on to her, one hand grabbing the phone—expecting Ollie. She'd told him to call back in a few minutes; she was washing off mud.

"Joe's Bar," she said into the telephone, Lily giggling and Claudia said, "Joe's Bar" and there was silence, and then a woman's voice said, "Oh, I'm sorry, I must have the wrong number," and Claudia said, "Oh, no, *I'm* sorry. I was just—Lily, wait a minute." The baby was splashing her, wet tiny fingers patting her face with water—"You have dirt, Mommy"—and the woman's voice said, "I was calling 322-8217."

"This is 322-8217," Claudia said.

And there was silence, another couple of seconds of silence, air on the line, and the woman took a breath, Claudia could actually hear her take a breath, and the woman's voice said, "Is . . . this . . . Claudia?"

And she knew.

"This is Claudia."

"I . . . uh . . ." the woman said, and then she stopped and there was a moment of nothing, and then, "I'm Jenny . . . I mean, this is Jenny. Oh, God . . ."

"Mommy, you're *squeezing!*"

"Oh." Claudia loosened her grip on Lily. "I . . ." She scooped Lily up off the sink and lowered her to the floor. "This is Claudia," she said again, because she didn't know what to say, and her heart was beating too fast and she couldn't get her thoughts straight, but the woman didn't say anything; all Claudia could hear now was sobbing on the other end of the phone.

"Mommy, you said you'd color."

"In a minute," she whispered, and handed Lily the crayons. "You start, go ahead." Lily folded down to the floor at Claudia's feet with paper and crayons.

"Hello?" Claudia said into the receiver.

"I'm sorry, I thought I was all cried out." She was sniffling and trying to catch her breath. "—You'd also think I'd have a Kleenex, wouldn't you"—and then there was a crash. "Oh, shit . . ."

"Are you okay?"

"I just knocked over everything on my end table," and then Jenny laughed and blew her nose and laughed again. "This is not happening the way I planned it. It's not like they have a handbook, *How to Talk to Your . . .*" She took a breath. "But I don't know what I'm doing anymore. I haven't been the same since . . . since yesterday. It's in shreds, your letter. I carry it around with me, I can't put it down, it's crumpled and"—she took another gulp of air and blew her nose again—"wrinkled and"—she laughed—"wet. . . ." And then she was quiet.

They were both quiet. Claudia caught her lip between her teeth.

"I can't think of anything to say except I love you," Jenny said. "Me saying I love you, you probably want to hang up"—she was crying again—"but I just . . . I never stopped loving you, no matter what you think. . . ."

Claudia's eyes were focused somewhere over the top of Lily's head, somewhere on the refrigerator, blurry and white with no edges, like snow.

"I keep seeing your face as if you were still a baby. You were the most exquisite baby. . . ." She sniffed. "I tried to picture all the birthdays—tried to send out messages as if I had powers: 'I love you, baby, please know I love you, baby, wherever you are. . . .'"

A flood of words, a runaway faucet, fast, breathless. Claudia nodded, her fingers unconsciously moving through Lily's hair.

"Did you have clowns at your birthdays? Balloons? I tried to imagine . . . your face with braids. . . ."

Lily looked up at her mother, but Claudia didn't seem to see her. All Claudia could see were her birthday snapshots, pink icing and pink candles, Margaret's glowing face above her cake. "Make a wish, sweetheart, blow out the candles and make a wish."

Lily searched Claudia's faraway eyes. "Hi, Mommy," Lily said.

". . . braids or a ponytail," Jenny went on. "Did you have a ponytail? . . . Halloween, Christmas, the prom, I tried to imagine you . . ."

She was a mummy; John had wrapped her round and round with white gauze because she wanted to be a mummy. "Don't you want to be a ballerina, sweetheart, or a fairy?" "No, I want to be a mummy, Mommy, please." A small mummy holding a pumpkin with a face cut out. She didn't go to the prom her junior year because nobody asked her, and she went to the prom her senior year with Mike Zindell and she didn't even like him but Gena said they could double and she wanted so to go.

". . . high school, college . . . There must be pictures—do you have pictures?" Jenny sniffed and tried to catch her breath. "Oh, God, I'm sorry, you haven't said a word." She cleared her throat. "But I didn't let you, did I? I'll shut up, I promise. This isn't like me, it isn't; I just can't believe you're really there."

Claudia realized she was standing; her eyes refocused, and Lily was looking up at her. Claudia smiled at the child, smiled to reassure her, to reassure herself. She sat back down in the chair. "I went to Columbia."

"Columbia?" And then a shuddering sigh, "You went to school in *New York?*"

"Uh huh."

"You were *here?*"

"Yes."

"For four years? You were *here* in New York at Columbia for *four* years?"

"Uh huh."

"My God." A few seconds of silence. "I taught a class there once."

"At Columbia?"

"Yes."

"In what?"

"Dance; dance theory."

"Oh."

Jenny laughed. "I'm about to have a heart attack here. Did you take dance theory?"

"No."

"Oh."

"Is that what you are, a dancer? Or a teacher?"

"A dancer. Well, I was a dancer; I mean, I still am a dancer—once a hoofer, always a hoofer—but you know, I'm a little long in the tooth now to be dancing where anybody can see me. I try to confine my dancing to my bathroom . . . less crowds."

"Did you?" Claudia said.

"What? Dance where anybody could see me? I'm afraid so."

"Really? Are you famous?"

Jenny laughed again. "How did we get into this? No, absolutely not; I'm absolutely not famous. I was just in the chorus—you know, a chorus girl."

A chorus girl. Claudia imagined someone who looked like her, the image of Claudia, but the image wasn't sitting in an office, calmly listening to a patient; she was parading around on a stage to blaring trumpets, dark hair piled up in a tumbled mass, miles of leg in fishnet stockings, a skimpy costume, feathers, sparkles. . . . "I never imagined you as a chorus girl."

Hesitation. And then, *"Did* you imagine me?"

"Of course."

"You did?"

"Yes." Claudia could have told her then about all the dreams and all the images, about how it always seemed as if everywhere she went she was searching, scanning face after face to find *the* face, the one that looked like her face. The tall one, the skinny one, there's a brunette over there. . . . That nagging feeling that she'd left something, lost something, a haunting feeling that something was always missing but she couldn't remember what it was. . . . But she didn't say any of that, she couldn't say any of that. "Were you on Broadway?" was all she said.

"What? Oh, Broadway, sure."

"Really?"

"Broadway, stock, road companies . . . whatever there was."

"What if I saw you?" She leaned forward. "I could have seen you. What were you in?"

"Oh, I was probably off Broadway long before you got here, waaaaay off Broadway. I was probably all the way to Indiana before you . . ."

Claudia laughed.

"Oh, God, I made you laugh. I will never believe this is happening, never in a billion years."

"It's okay," Claudia said, "don't cry," and then the tears covered her own face, and Lily said, "What's the matter, Mommy? Don't cry, Mommy," and she climbed up into Claudia's lap and put her arms around her mother's neck.

They talked for an hour—no, more than an hour, maybe an hour and a half: important things, stupid things, cocktail party conversation, a Ping-Pong ball going back and forth. "A *doctor*? You're a *doctor*?" Jenny amazed. "No, just my master's; I never went for my Ph.D." And, "*Lucky Lady*? You were in *Lucky Lady*?" Claudia amazed. "Yeah, but I was in the back."

"She's funny," Claudia said to Oliver.

"Well, you're funny," Ollie said.

She stared at him as if he'd lost his marbles. "No I'm not." She knew she wasn't funny: she was . . . what? Nice? Well, that was pathetic. Pleasant? Oh, Lord. Adaptable? Yeah. That was it—adaptable. Comfortable and adaptable, and what was wrong with being adaptable? Then you could fit in anywhere.

"What else?" he said, from the sofa.

She wanted to tell him everything in sequence, but she kept forgetting things, and then she'd remember and she'd run in to tell him. He was sitting in the living room, watching a game on television and preparing a soc. test. He was surrounded by books and papers.

"She likes country music."

"So much for following in her footsteps."

"I know, I know."

And she'd leave and then come back. "Did I tell you she likes her steak really rare, like I do?"

"Yep. Now you can order together at Ruth's Chris, two women cutting into warm dead cows."

Claudia laughed. "Right."

"How did you get into steak anyway?"

Claudia made a face. "I guess we were talking about food." She laughed again. "I don't know."

Jenny was coming to Los Angeles.

"She said if I wanted her to, if it was okay."

"And you said?"

"I said it was okay."

"Okay."

"Unless I wanted to go there. She offered to send me a ticket to New York if I wanted."

He gazed at her.

"I'd rather she came here, I think."

"Your turf," Ollie said.

Claudia gave him a weak smile.

Should she go there, should she come here? Did it make a difference? Jenny had suggested that they meet in the middle. "How do you feel about Chicago?" They were both laughing by then, getting comfortable, the initial hysteria having settled. "Or we could pick someplace wildly memorable—the Top of the Mark in San Francisco, under the clock at Grand Central, so romantic, or where they were supposed to meet in *An Affair to Remember*, you know, when she got hit by the car."

"The top of the Empire State Building," Claudia said.

"Right. But I've got to warn you, I look much more like Cary Grant than Deborah Kerr."

"I know," Claudia said. "I think I know what you look like."

But did she? Would the *other mother*, in reality, look like Claudia's dreams? Silence. The important things crept into the funny things, and then they would both stop. Did she look like her? Would she be like her? What if she hated her? Then what? You go back to New York, you *other mother*, you, and take that *other father* with you . . . but she hadn't said a thing about him, neither of them had even mentioned him, as if he didn't exist. There was this star in the east, Claudia imagined Jenny saying. The angel Gabriel came to me and said . . .

"What did you say?" Gena said. "When?"

"A week from Thursday."

An intake of breath from Gena, and then, "Have you told Margaret?"

"No. I'm waiting for the right moment. I haven't told her anything."

"Not even that you talked to her?"

"No."

"Uh huh."

"Was that a judgmental uh huh?"

"From me? Of course not. How could you say such a thing?"

"Okay, okay, I know I have to tell her. I was just kind of waiting. . . ."

"For what? Godot?"

"I don't know. I kind of just wanted to *feel* this without having to deal with Margaret feeling it, you know?"

"Okay, you're right. I take back my judgmental uh huh."

Claudia leaned forward and turned on the hot water.

"Don't drop the phone in the tub, okay? All we need now is for you to turn to toast."

"How'd you know I was in the bathtub?"

"I know you practically my whole life. Where else would you be?"

They both listened to the roar of the water.

"What does she do?"

"Uh . . ." Claudia frowned. "I don't know. She said she doesn't dance anymore, but that was all she said."

"Did she mention him? Your . . . hey, what are we going to call him?"

"I don't know. . . . She didn't mention him."

Claudia pushed some of the hot water to the back of the tub.

"Did you?"

"No." Claudia slid down, her breasts half covered by the water. She leaned her head back against the white porcelain.

"Is she married?"

"Uh huh, that's the Glass. Dr. Ron Glass; he's a surgeon."

"What kind?"

"My heart, Gena, I didn't ask."

"Okay, okay. God, I can't wait to hear what happened with her and your—Hey, so what did you call *her*?"

"Nothing. No, I never said her name. . . . Jenny—she calls herself Jenny. . . ." Claudia's voice trailed off. She leaned forward and closed the hot-water tap. They were both quiet for a few seconds.

"Did you ask if she had any other children?"

"No. She brought it up; she said she has two boys, but they were his when she married him. They're grown now; they don't live with her."

"God, Claud, she never had any other babies."

"No."

"She just had you."

"Yeah, she just had me," Claudia said.

• • •

She stood in the bedroom, discarding outfits, trying on everything she owned. There was no use asking Ollie—if it were up to Ollie, everyone would face life in shorts and a T-shirt; and Gena was too far away from Claudia's closet; and Lily was only three and out of the question; and she really wasn't close to anybody else . . . was she? How did that happen? Didn't she have any friends? Any acquaintances? Well, there was no one she wanted to discuss this with. . . . Had she always been a loner? Disconnected? Maybe after she met Jenny she wouldn't feel disconnected anymore. Claudia stared at herself in the full-length mirror. Bare-legged in a pair of high-heeled pumps, wearing only underpants, she backed up a couple of steps and struck a pose, one hip tilted, her arms flung out above her head. She sucked in her cheekbones and thrust out her breasts, and then she did a version of what she thought was a sexy strut, caught a glimpse of her backside as she turned in the mirror, covered her breasts with crossed arms, and sat down laughing on the edge of the bed. She could ask Margaret what she should wear, but then she hadn't even told Margaret yet. Santos?

"Ollie?"

"Mmm?"

"What should I wear?"

He looked up. "Are we supposed to be someplace?"

"No; when I meet her."

"Who?"

"*Ollie.*"

"Oh. Oh, sorry. Uh . . . I don't know."

She stood there.

"Uh . . . how 'bout that black thing, you know, the tight one I like, with those skinny straps, the short one."

"That's a cocktail dress. Are you kidding?"

"Oh." He shook his head. "Oh, okay. Well, why can't you just wear jeans?"

"Jeans? How can I just wear jeans?"

"Uh"—he looked at her—"uh . . . a whatchamacallit, a skirt?"

Claudia laughed. She walked across the room, bent to where he was sitting.

He looked up at her. "Not exactly my area, huh?"

"Not exactly. Excuse me, I lost my head."

"I really don't think it matters. From what you've told me, I'm sure she wouldn't care if you were naked. I wouldn't."

"Thank you very much."

"You're welcome."

She sat down next to him on the couch. He pulled her to him, and she put her head on his chest.

"So how do you feel?"

"Elated, frightened, happy, apprehensive, panicky, thrilled . . . should I go on?"

"A to B, huh?"

"Yeah, but it's better."

"What?"

"It's better knowing—it *will* be better knowing—because not knowing was just getting too hard."

In the end she wore a skirt. But first she told Margaret. And John.

"She's coming."

"Oh, my goodness." Margaret turned from the sofa. "When?"

"Thursday."

John sat down, put his big hands on the arms of the wing chair. Claudia studied him, tried to read his face.

"Is she coming alone?" he said.

"Yes, I think so."

Nobody spoke. Margaret repositioned herself on the pillows, looked to John.

"Where's she staying?" he said to Claudia.

"The Beverly Wilshire."

"Well, I guess she has money."

Claudia didn't say anything. Margaret looked down at her hands, tucked them under her. "I have to get my hair colored," she said.

"What, Mom?"

"Oh, nothing. I was just . . . Nothing."

Claudia reached across the cushion and touched Margaret's shoulder. "Are you worried? Please don't be worried."

Margaret managed a smile.

"Where are you going to meet her?" John said.

"At the hotel."

"That's good."

"Do you want us to go with you?" Margaret's eyes on her.

"Don't be ridiculous, Maggie," John said.

"I don't think so, Mom. I think I have to go alone."

And they sat there, the three of them.

There were so many things to say, and there was nothing. She had been their baby since she was two months old. First she'd gone to foster parents: "That's how they did it then," Margaret had told her. "The babies would go to a foster family, and as quickly as possible they'd match them up with their real parents—oh, dear, their *adoptive* parents—and then we took you home."

She'd heard the story a thousand times.

"You had colic."

"You told me, Mom."

"Yes, and we thought it was the formula, and Dr. Charlie switched you three times, but nothing helped. They said it wasn't anything we were doing wrong, it was just the way it was; some babies' little insides just aren't ready yet, they said. Oh, you would wail and wail from around four in the afternoon, off and on, into the night."

"How did you stand it?"

"Oh, I didn't. I cried right with you. Every second."

"She nearly drove me crazy," John said. "I used to put you in the car. If I could get you away from your mother, I'd pop you in the car and drive you around the neighborhood until you'd finally cry yourself to sleep."

"There were plenty of nights your father slept in the driveway. He didn't want to bring you in, for fear he'd wake you, so he'd sleep in the car with you all night long and then at dawn he'd tiptoe in and put you right next to me and he'd take a shower and go right to court, didn't you, John?"

"I got enough rest, Margaret."

"Well, I didn't think so. I never could understand how he could work all day after sleeping all night sitting up in a car."

"You just wanted me in bed with you."

"Oh, John."

And they looked at each other, and their eyes said everything. She had been their baby, their baby and their toddler, their little girl and their big girl, their teenager, their young lady, and now their woman, all grown up. Their daughter. There was no sharing to be done, she'd belonged to them completely—and a week from Thursday all that would be over, a stranger was coming, and as John had said to Margaret as he held her, "You had better prepare yourself, Maggie. The party's over, just like they said in the song."

Claudia, they'd named her Claudia. Had she ever known anyone named Claudia? Jenny picked up her drink.

Dorothy McGuire. That's all she could come up with, Dorothy McGuire was Claudia and Robert Young was David, and they were ugly, weren't they? Not ugly, disfigured . . . an automobile accident?

Something, scars and ugly, only not to each other, not in the cottage; when they were in the cottage they were beautiful—*The Enchanted Cottage*, that's what it was, or no . . . was that *Claudia and David:* she had the two movies mixed up. . . .

Ron was saying something, his mouth was moving, something about a patient. Who was it? when had she stopped listening? Four days ago—no, that was when she'd called her. . . . Five days ago—it was five days since she'd gotten the letter, the letter that had fallen into her lap and changed everything. The blue letter that she wouldn't let go of, and Ron thought she'd had a heart attack, so concerned, his face all beaten, cradling her in his arms until she could get up, sitting with her while she babbled into the night as if she'd lost her mind. She smiled now at Ron across the table. She did love him, she knew she did. Make a list, think of all the good things. His passion for his work, she loved that; his freckles, his long, gangly arms; she loved how good he was. She took a sip of her martini. She loved him, of course she did. She smiled at him and at Bernie and Susan; they weren't paying any attention to her, but she smiled anyway, took another sip of the icy drink and leaned back in the chair. The restaurant was crowded, filled with pretty people, theater people after the theater, talking too much, too fast, smoking, drinking, eating pasta primavera and downing espresso when they should have been flat in their beds. After midnight in New York but only after nine in Los Angeles. She knew without thinking; she automatically looked at her watch now and subtracted three. Three hours earlier, and in three more days she would see her. She ran her finger around the stem of the cold glass.

California . . . she'd never dreamed the baby would end up in California, stay in California right where she'd left her; she'd never thought of that. Minnesota . . . Montana . . . Texas; some remote place. A farm or a ranch—she always pictured that whoever got her lived on a ranch, this lovely couple who had horses and chickens and a puppy, always a puppy, the baby in red corduroy overalls, running after a puppy through waves of grass. . . .

Jenny refolded the napkin in her lap one way and then the other, like a Chinese fan. She hadn't asked her if she ever had a puppy; she had to remember to ask her that. . . .

"Do you want to know who the couple is?" Mrs. Havermeyer, bending to Jenny, her eyes all solemn in her cookie-dough face. "Dear? When we pick? Do you want to know? You could even meet them if you want."

"Oh, no—no, thank you."

The couple: they were always a couple to her, a nice Catholic couple connected at the hips or was it at their fingers—she couldn't tell in the dreams—forever smiling across their Formica, squeaky-clean Formica table, which was tipping over with bowls of happy food, no, family food, that's what it was, mashed potatoes wallowing in pats of melting butter and fresh steamed green beans cut on an angle, you could see the little squiggles of steam rising from the bowl. The baby had one in her high chair, one little green bean in one little chubby baby fist, the wife behind the husband, the percolator in one hand but her other hand somehow attached to his shoulder, and the smell of apple pie, always the smell of apple pie . . . where did they get all the apples? *Do you want some more coffee, dear?*

"Hey, Jenny, here's your coffee, kid, one regular and one prune Danish . . . and I got a bear claw here—hey, who the hell gets the goddamn bear claw?" Some guy muttering backstage in a darkened theater a million years ago, and Susan saying, "Are you watching? We gotta get this," and Jenny shook her head yes and touched her lips to the hot cardboard cup to try and burn away the image of the baby in the high chair and focus on the combination, mark it in her little place offstage . . . stop thinking about the goddamn green beans,

214

watch the steps, you don't need green beans, you don't need a baby, where would you put her—in your dance bag, under your shoes?

Do you want to know who the couple is? No, Mrs. Havermeyer, no, thank you, no, no, no.

"If you love her you'll give her up," Nurse Rae Lee said from the foot of Jenny's bed. "That's the only way you can prove you love her, let her have a life where she'll have a mommy *and a daddy* and they can give her *everything.*"

Love, Jenny thought, I could give her all my love. . . . Okay, love and what else? A farm like the nice couple? No, not a farm, not even a house, not even an apartment. No job, no money . . . what did she have to give her? Just love. But if you love her, you'll give her up— wasn't that the manifesto of the nursing staff? Absolutely. The nice couple can give her love as good as you have *and* green beans *and* mashed potatoes *and* a puppy *and* a farm with grass and trees and maybe even a pony, and "If you don't stop thinking about whatever you got on your mind, kid, you'll be dancin' on a funny farm, instead of on this stage. You got that?" Yes, sir, O dance captain, sir. Yes, she would dance through the images of Stella Maris, dance them right out of her head. You will forget this, you will move on with your life, you hear me? Hey! Did you forget yet?

White sheets, white pillowcases, white napkins. She could smell the laundry, the wet, the steam, orange blossoms drifting in through the windows, twenty-eight pregnant, frightened young girls, their faces shining, candles burning at the altar, Rose's shoulder next to hers in chapel, their fingers entwined through the gates of Stella Maris when she took Buster and said goodbye, and *her* baby, *her* baby's face when she left her, when she handed her to Sister Berl, and . . .

Jenny lifted the remaining olive out of the martini and put it in her mouth. So long ago. She hadn't been to California since Stella Maris. She'd refused to go whenever they'd asked her. *Sweet Charity* in

San Francisco, a couple of television specials in Los Angeles in the seventies—what was that show. The Hollywood . . . Palace: that's right, they'd wanted her for the Hollywood Palace from the very beginning, and that thing with Michael Kidd, and, oh, *Hallelujah, Baby*—wasn't it?—in Long Beach. When was that? Well, it didn't matter; if it was California and they'd asked her, she always said no.

"You want another drink, Jen?"

"Oh, no, thanks, Bernie, I'm fine." Bernie's face close to hers: curly gray Brillo hair, stubby eyelashes, blue eyes . . . Jenny took the napkin and touched it to the sides of her mouth. Blue eyes . . . she wasn't going to think about blue eyes. A blue letter, but not blue eyes. She'd been trying all week not to think about it—his eyes, his hands, his face, his hair. It was more than thirty years ago, it was forever ago, and it had all tumbled back onto her; it was ludicrous that she could still remember it all the way she could.

And what if his child looked like him? Not only his blue eyes, *if* they had stayed blue—most babies' eyes change, don't they? Okay, so maybe her eyes were still blue, but what if she also had his long, skinny legs and his hair and his cheekbones and the way he walked across a room and his hands and . . .

Bernie's hand touched Jenny's shoulder. "We'll have a check, please, then," he said, looking up at the waiter.

"Hey, wait a minute, it's our turn," Ron said.

"Like hell it is."

She'd said she would never go back to California, she'd promised herself that she would never go. She would never go to look for him, she would never try to find him, she would never see him again. She'd promised herself the day she put the baby in Sister Berl's arms. She would never go back to California, never. And she never did. Big promise for such a chicken to make, for such a nothing, an ineffectual nothing, a will-o'-the-wisp nothing, who couldn't even keep her own baby, hold on to the only baby she would ever have. Do you want to have a baby? Who, me? No.

Jenny shut her eyes. She would never go back to California . . . until now.

"Are you okay?"

"Hmm?"

Arpège. Susan still wore *Arpège* when nobody wore *Arpège.* Susan always had a lot of class.

"You look funny. Are you okay?"

"I am funny."

"I'm serious, Jenny."

"I'm fine. I was just, you know, off in the stars." Susan held her eyes, but Jenny laughed. "A case of too much martini."

"Lucky for you," Susan said, and smirked.

Susan didn't drink. It didn't have anything to do with being an alcoholic; it had to do with getting kicked in the gut by a horse when she was eleven and some cockeyed damage it had done to her liver, the doctors said. Susan knew all about the letter and the phone call; she was the only one of Jenny's friends who knew, but Susan had been there since forever, Jenny's first friend in New York, her first roommate; they had been fledgling "Broadway babies" together, pounding the pavements to get a show. Jenny didn't talk about her life before New York with anyone else, as if she had no life before New York, as if she'd been plunked down at the Barbizon Hotel for Women at the age of eighteen, like Athena right out of Zeus's head, only in ballet shoes and a leotard instead of a helmet and a fancy robe. The only part that was the same as the myth was the headache. Athena had been her father Zeus's headache, and Jenny had made it her business to be her mother Esther's headache in every way that she could. Her mother's headache, not her father's be-

217

cause she knew her mother was the one behind everything, her mother was the one.

She would never tell Esther, not that she talked to her anymore, hadn't in years, but oh, wouldn't it have felt good to wallop her with the news? Hi, it's me, your daughter, your only child, remember? And remember that thing I was supposed to get over, Mom? That . . . what was it? Oh, right, that *baby*. The one I never forgot, no matter what you said. Well, listen to this . . .

If she longed to tell anybody about the blue letter, it was Rose, and she was trying her best to tell her, had sent her messages all week. February would be eight months since they'd buried Rose, and every day since the blue letter she'd been camped out, third row, on the aisle, in the back of Saint Patrick's, lighting an abundance of candles at the feet of the Holy Mother, sitting there quietly joyous in the dim light, pouring her heart out to the Blessed Virgin and Rose. It was Jenny's place, this place in the church where she had gone for solace since she'd hit New York, where she'd worked out everything, the good, the bad, and the ugly, as Rose had said. It was also the place where she'd sat at each and every one of the baby's birthdays. *I love you, baby, I love you as much as the nice couple, please remember I love you, this is me.* Please let her know, sweet Mary, I pray to you, please let her know I love her, please let her hear me. Messages shooting out of her head like ticker tape, billowing across the rafters of Saint Patrick's through the stained glass and across the sky like Sister Mary Julia singing evening chant, the messages would have the power of floating song. If she could just pray hard enough, they would.

"I called you three times; have you been hiding out at Saint Patrick's?"

Rose and Jenny spoke at least once a week, all the years since Stella Maris, until Rose died.

"I'm getting more Catholic than you are, Rose. Maybe I should just convert already."

"We've gone through this umpteen times. You don't want to be Catholic."

"Why not?"

"Beats me." She laughed. "Maybe you don't want to give up Hanukkah."

"Are you kidding? Hanukkah doesn't hold a candle to Christmas."

"Eight candles, miss."

"Rose, there's no way you can compare eight measly candles and some nine-pound potato pancakes with a star in the east and tinsel. . . ."

"Tinsel is not Christmas, remember?"

"Okay, okay, but Mary and Joseph and the baby—you take them and the manger, and what with the wise men and the star and the shepherds . . . just look at it: the Maccabees fall right on their ass."

"Hey, you don't have to sell me. . . ."

"And it's not just Christmas. Think of Easter, the pageantry, ash Wednesday, a smudge of ash on a pale forehead, the drama, the penance—"

"I'll tell you the drama—you have to give up something."

"What?"

"For Lent, something that means something to you, something important. You have to give it up."

"I did that, didn't I?"

Giving up a baby, she'd come to think, was like a death with no body, no official mourning, no graveside service, no place to go.

Silence, and then, "Oh, Jenny, I'm sorry, I didn't mean that. I meant . . ."

"I know, I know. So how's Buster? Is he taller than me yet?"

219

She never stepped foot in a synagogue and was in and out of Saint Patrick's, but somehow Jenny never found whatever it took to convert. Rose was her confessor; they talked weekly, traded lives with each other by phone.

Endless auditions, and Buster teething and screaming. "I put booze on his gums just like my mother said and everything, but it's not working."

"Try the booze on *your* gums," Jenny said, "if all else fails. You won't hear him, you'll be drunk."

Rose finally moved out of her mother's house, and Jenny finally got an apartment with Susan and Luba, who needed a roommate. "It's a fifth-floor walkup, and I sleep on a ratty wool couch, just me and a few cockroaches, but they're very nice." "Who? The cockroaches?" "Yes." "Sounds perfect."

Rose screaming into the phone from her kitchen in Fond du Lac: "He's *standing*, Jenny, he's *standing* and banging on the table with his pudgy fists, can you hear him?"

"Are you kidding? They can hear him in Jersey."

And Jenny weeping into a filthy pay phone on Forty-fourth Street, frost coming out of her mouth, tears freezing under her nose: "So he moves me from this group to that group, up and back, and then he finally says, 'Okay, all of you—I say your name, you go backward: Iva, Katherine, Jenny, Maxine, Maryalice, backward; the rest of you stay front.'"

"Holy Mother," Rose said, and Jenny said, "Yes, and we stand there, 'cause it could go either way, and I think I'm going to keel and we're in the back so you think he'll let the back go because you never think you're going to get it, ever, and he says, 'Okay, everybody in the back, you stay, and everybody forward, you can go, thank you very much.' I got the show, Rose," and Jenny is weeping and Rose is crying right with her, and she says, "Well, all I can say is thank you,

Jesus, because if I had lit one more candle for you, Jenny, Saint Agnes would have gone up in smoke."

Sometimes they shared their lives in person: Rose beaming up at Jenny from front row center; Jenny stretched out on a towel in the August grass of Fond du Lac, Buster shrieking with glee as he drenched her with his watering can; Jenny meeting the astronaut, watching his eyes follow Rose around (he never left his wife, and he never left Rose either, and Rose said that was just fine with her, and although Jenny questioned it, the years went by and it *was* fine with Rose, by the looks of her), Rose blissfully sniffling into Jenny's shoulder as they clutched hands and watched Buster graduate from kindergarden and then junior high and then high school; and Jenny and Rose at Saint Patrick's, sitting in Jenny's place together, their heads bowed, their shoulders touching—just the way they did in chapel at Stella Maris—the afternoon two years ago when the bigshot specialist at Sloan-Kettering said Rose's cancer had spread from her breasts to her bones. If only she could have lasted a little longer . . . No. God, she didn't mean that; how selfish; how could she have wanted Rose to endure one more second of pain? No, it was all right—Rose knew that Jenny had heard from the baby. If there was a way to send a message to the other side, she'd certainly tried.

All this week, Jenny kept having the fantasy: She would be driving crosstown in blocks of traffic and the car phone would ring and she'd grab it and say hello and it would be Rose. *Oh, Rose, she's alive, my baby's alive and she wrote me and I'm going to see her. Oh, Rose.* Embracing the cell phone through the taxi noise as she braked at the corner of Fifty-seventh and Madison and, amid the mass of crushed fenders, Jenny crying, "Oh, Rose . . ."

Jenny smiled to think of it. Well, if anybody had the power to dial direct from heaven, it would surely be Rose.

•   •   •

Margaret stood looking up at the boxes in the closet. They were taped and stacked and on the top shelf, and she would have to stand on a chair if she wanted to reach them, and she knew she wasn't supposed to do that, not with her knees, she knew. She took the chair from behind Claudia's old desk and dragged it into the closet under the shelf. She put one hand on the wall and the other on the back of the chair, gingerly lifted one leg and then the other until she got up there, but she still couldn't reach, so she rose up on her tiptoes and stretched and stretched until she got her hand on one box. By the time she came down she was shaking and wet with sweat, but she had jiggled that one box back and forth until it crashed to the floor. She got off the chair and pulled the box into the room with her and sat down next to it on the floor. She rubbed her fingers across the disfigured knuckles on both her hands, caught sight of them, and turned her head away. She blotted the wet above her upper lip and pushed at her hair, pulled out the handkerchief she had tucked into the cuff of her blouse, and dabbed at the sweat caught between her breasts.

"Goodness," she exhaled in the quiet.

Margaret looked at her own handwriting in thick black marker. She took the paring knife she'd brought up from the kitchen, sliced through the tape, and lifted the box flaps. Tissue paper, folds of tissue paper, and then there they were. Lifting her hand to her chest, she sat there a moment before lowering it into the box. Tiny white cotton gowns, thin satin ribbon running in and out through the hemlines so you could tie them up and the little infant feet wouldn't come flying out. Margaret could hear John: "What is that thing, Maggie? You've got her decked out like she's Olive Oyl."

"Swee'pea, John; it was Swee'pea who wore these."

"Swee'pea . . . such a swee'pea. Give her to me."

Cotton bonnets and knitted bootees and pink all-in-ones. She'd tried to give it all to Claudia for Lily.

"Mom, they're too beautiful. I'll wreck them."

"Don't be silly. Let the baby wear them; you wore them."

"Mom, you have to *iron* them; you know I can't iron."

There was no talking to her once Claudia got it set in her head, so Margaret gave up. But she could never bear to pass them on to anyone else, to give them to charity; she would give other things to charity, not the things her baby wore.

"Margaret, it's one too many miscarriages, and this last one caused too much damage, I'm afraid . . ." Dr. Braverman, shaking his head. "Margaret, I'm sorry, you'll never carry a baby to term." The last one had been on the staircase, halfway up and halfway down, bleeding there, a gush of blood as if she'd been cracked open, as if someone had attacked her with a crowbar, knocking her to her knees. One hand on the railing—she would make it—and the other hand holding herself there, she tried to pull herself up, and what was that in her fingers, that couldn't be, oh, no, sweet Jesus, was that *the cord?*

"We have a baby," Mr. Stanley said. "Do you think you and Mr. Magers could come by sometime at the end of this week and see her?"

Her.

John, white at the foot of her hospital bed. "We will adopt a baby, and I mean it, Margaret: you won't go through another second of pain, that's enough of it, we will not try again. I mean it. Maggie—please, no more."

She had a dimple, one deep dimple at the bottom of her left cheek, and blue eyes like those tiny flowers by the side of the road, and she was sleek and soft and so beautiful. Margaret had prayed long and hard for a baby; she hadn't even asked for one that was beautiful, just a baby—*Can't there just be one little baby for us, please, Father*—and here was this one with the grave blue eyes and the kicking feet and the little fingers curled around Margaret's thumb.

Three sweaters with matching hats knit by Margaret's mother, Mae, in aqua, pink, and cream, the tiny stitches still as strong as rope. A yellow snowsuit—John had insisted on taking her to see snow. "She won't remember, dear; let's wait till she's older." "Bullshit, I'll remember. We're going." More tissue paper, and delicate, thin undershirts with minuscule snaps at the shoulders, and a white lace christening gown that Margaret lifted and held to her face, and then, in the bottom of the box, Claudia's first pair of shoes. Stiff white leather and still smelling of shoe polish, the laces tied with bows, and wrapped with the shoes, the fuzzy snapshot the salesman took of her wearing those new shoes, Claudia's hand raised and lost in John's, her smile wide, her blue eyes shining. "See if they can run, sweetheart, try them," and the salesman and Margaret laughed together as John in a tie and a buttoned suit jacket ran with the baby round and round Harry Harris Shoes.

Margaret took the shoes in her hands. She prayed to Jesus that He would let her keep this baby, this baby that was all grown up now, no more colic or chicken pox or first day of school or not making the team or not getting the boy to ask her or losing her lunch money or putting all the answers in the wrong boxes or not wanting to wear her coat, this grown-up woman that Margaret knew had not been sent to her from the angels, had not been dropped to her from the stork's mouth, but had been born to a dark-haired mystery girl who couldn't keep her and now was coming to town. She prayed to Jesus that He would let Claudia keep loving her; she sat on the floor and held the stiff white little shoes in her hands and whispered, "Just let her keep on loving me, Father, thank you. Amen."

"Goodnight moon and goodnight . . ."

"Where's the little mouse, Mommy?"

"Ahh, let's see . . . is he on the cereal bowl? No . . ."

"I know, I know." Lily was wiggling around in Claudia's lap.

"You do? Well, let's see . . ."

"I see him."

"You do? I forget where . . ."

Lily giggling. She loved this game, this ritual, this pretending each night as they turned the page that they wouldn't be able to find the tiny moving mouse.

"Claud, your mother's on the phone. What are you guys doing, looking for that rotten mouse?"

"Come see, Daddy. I know and Mommy doesn't."

Oliver moved from the doorway, scooped Lily off Claudia's lap, and took her place in the chair. "Go talk to Margaret—I'll find the little fella. Where is he, Lily? Are you sure he's here?"

"I see him, I see him."

"You do, huh?"

Claudia went into their bedroom, lifted the receiver from the end table.

"Hi, Mom."

"Hi, sweetheart. Were you busy?"

"No, just reading Lily a book."

"*Goodnight Moon* again?"

"You got it."

They both laughed.

"So," Margaret said, "how are you doing?"

"You mean about tomorrow?"

"Tomorrow, yes."

"I'm okay, I guess, maybe. . . . I don't know, I feel like I'm going to jump right through my skin."

"Well, I guess so."

Claudia didn't say anything.

"You'll be fine, and she'll be thrilled to see you."

"Oh, Mom."

"I'm so proud of you. She couldn't get a better daughter, Claudia, nobody could."

Claudia's eyes filled. "Oh, Mommy, thank you."

"Don't be silly."

"I love you so much."

"I love you too, my sweetheart," Margaret said, and paused. "You'll call me?"

"Of course."

"Well, I'll let you go. . . . All right, good luck."

"Thanks."

"Bye, sweetheart," Margaret said, and the line went dead.

Claudia put the phone down and sat motionless on the edge of the bed.

Margaret put the phone down in her house, pushed the desk chair back into place, closed the curtains, and shut the door to her daughter's old room.

The plane had been practically empty. Jenny had been in business class, and she had her seat and all the surrounding seats practically to herself. She had a vodka instead of the airplane food; she'd already had a vodka at the airport, but she didn't care.

"Ron, you've never driven me to an airport before."

"Well, I don't know. It seems right." He smiled.

"But I ordered a radio car."

"Well, cancel it."

They looked at each other.

"Well, thank you."

And he said, "Okay."

He got out of the car to say goodbye, walked around and kissed her on the cheek and left his hand on the small of her back for longer than it had been in some time. "I hope everything goes all right."

"I know you do."

"It will. You okay?"

"Sure." She laughed. "I guess so."

"Okay. You'll call me?"

"I'll call you."

"As soon as."

"Okay."

So she'd had a vodka. The letter had been like a white flag, not only a truce but a possible postponement of whatever was going on between them, and Jenny wasn't even sure what that was. If she'd had to put it in words, what words would she have used: boredom? monotony? It would have been easier if they hated each other, it would have been easier if they screamed. Tepid, that was the word for it, like sitting in three inches of lukewarm water with no desire to stay and no desire to go. She had never had a passion for Ron; that much was true, and he knew it. She had never pulled any punches; she'd told him straight away when he'd asked her to marry him.

"I love you. You're a wonderful man and I love you. I love so many things about you—the way you are, the things you do—you know that, but I don't feel the same way as you do about me. Do you want to live with that?"

"You bet."

But maybe she shouldn't have; maybe it was her lack of passion that slept in the bed between them.

She'd married him. Thirteen years ago, she was a forty-year-old first-time bride. Before Ron, she had accepted the fact that she would never marry, she had made it her business to find a reason to walk away from any relationship, but he was so determined that he'd eventually worn her down.

"Of course you have to wear a gown," Rose said.

"I'm too old for a gown."

"You're never too old for a gown. It doesn't have to have a train, Jenny, just a simple gown"—she smiled—"with a veil."

"The only train I'm taking is to Jersey. Why can't I just go on being an old maid?"

"Jenny."

The wedding consultant at Bergdorf's smiled graciously.

Jenny looked up. "How about a white suit?"

"Black tie with a white suit?" Rose shook her head.

"Why not?"

Rose glared. "A gown."

"It would be more appropriate, madam. It *is* an evening wedding, and the gentlemen will be in tuxedos"—the consultant tilted her head—"the women in gowns."

Rose smirked at Jenny.

It was a gown. Simple and elegant and ivory, or "eggshell with a touch of the palest pink," said the Bergdorf consultant. "The color of your skin, madam," she gushed, and Jenny jabbed Rose in the ribs and lifted the heavy silk to stand on the round carpeted step so two women could kneel at her feet and push pins through the hem of the gown. She gazed at herself in the mirrored dressing room.

"What am I doing, Rose?"

"Getting married."

"Why?"

"Could you turn a little to the left, please," said one of the kneeling ladies, and Rose made a face at her in the mirror and Jenny lowered her hands and moved her satin shoes in a slow two-step to the left.

The astronaut flew in with Rose and Buster from Fond du Lac, and

Susan and Bernie, for sure Bernie, since Ron was the magician who had remade Bernie's shot knees, and some friends from the theater, some friends from the old days, some friends from the new days, but that was it for her, certainly not her mother, and her father was long gone; twenty-two invitations for Jenny and one hundred ten for Ron.

He wanted everything. Jenny was sure that if she'd let him, Ron would have had a billboard on Broadway, klieg lights and a marching band. Cracked crab, the smaller ballroom at the Saint Regis, a cathedral's worth of candles, piles of roses, oysters and caviar, an orchestra; he even wanted Jenny to walk toward him in the gown.

"Down an aisle? Like a bride?"

"You *are* a bride." He laughed and pulled her close to him.

"Oh, my God."

She walked down the aisle, her hand trembling on Buster's arm, the only child Jenny had ever known—Rose's twenty-two-year-old beaming, hulking boy in a tuxedo—and as he whispered, "I love you, Aunt Jenny," in the blur of Buster's eyes as he leaned in to kiss her, she saw herself standing in front of a dancing school, the dead dream of a wedding in Oklahoma, and Will's face. She stopped short for just an instant, and then Buster lifted her hand from his arm and put it in Ron's hand, and Jenny turned, and in the candlelight the dream melted away.

Ron had a passion for her from the very beginning. She'd always thought it had something to do with her once being a dancer, some cockeyed unrealistic mix-up of her and glamour, but the passion had continued long after she'd hung up her dance shoes.

"Do your audition song."

"Come on, Ron."

"Do it. I love to watch you."

"You're nuts, you know that?"

"Do it, Jenny, please."

And she'd tilt her head and smile like she used to, from behind the footlights, one hand at her waist, the other straight above her head, her left hip stuck out toward the refrigerator, she'd sing and dance her way across the kitchen floor.

He had the passion and she didn't, but she told herself she was lucky, because, as Rose said, "He adores you and you've been alone long enough. I was getting worried you would end up with cats."

"Better then being in *Cats*," Jenny said.

In the deal, she got Ron and part time with his two boys, fourteen and sixteen then, in and out, back and forth to boarding school. They didn't really need her—they had their own mother, whom Ron had divorced when they were little—but they liked Jenny and allowed her to mother them any way that she could. They were too old to tuck in, too large to cuddle, so she gave them straightforward answers always and opinions shot right from her hip. That seemed to please them. Now they were grown up and on their own—one of them was married—and they looked to Jenny as . . . a what? a mother? no, not a mother . . . a good friend? She'd never been a mother, for as she'd put it so bluntly to Ron years ago when he'd asked her if she wanted to have a baby, "Being a mother just ain't in my cards." He'd asked her about babies when he'd asked her to marry him: his babies were big, but did she want a baby? *At forty? No, thank you.* He looked at her. She didn't? *No.* Really? Was she sure? He was serious. It wasn't too late, lots of women were having babies at forty, he could show her the statistics. *No.* She was sure. A tilt of the head—he studied her. But why? Ah, why. . . . Well, you see, Ron, *when I was seventeen . . .* and she'd told him—oh, she'd told him, but not quite everything: all about the baby but not all about Will.

Jenny stepped out of the huge marble bathtub in her suite at the Beverly Wilshire, wiggled her toes on the thick white cotton rug, and studied her long, wet body in the mirror. Angles and hipbones and—she leaned forward and peered closely—shadows under her eyes. She'd hardly slept. She had taken a cab from the airport to the hotel the evening before, checked in, circled the room like a zombie, and then gone out for a walk. She'd wandered the streets of Beverly Hills, meandering in and out of the stores until it got dark; she wound up buying Claudia a very cuddly white stuffed bear. He had a big brown nose and tufts of eyelashes, and Jenny couldn't put him down once she'd taken him off the shelf. She took him back with her to the hotel, opened the box and peeked at him in the tissue paper at least three times that evening, and it never occurred to her any of these times that she'd bought a stuffed animal for a woman who was thirty-five years old. She had room service bring up her dinner, washed her face, put on silk pajamas, and lay down on top of the spread. She spent most of the night trying to recall every second she'd ever had with the baby. She had been sure she would never see that baby again, and now she would. She fell asleep just before dawn.

Jenny took a sip of the room service morning coffee, let the towel slip to the floor, poured body cream into her palms, and ran her hands down her long legs, up her arms, across her breasts and her stomach. She studied herself in the mirror. One baby girl that she'd given away, two abortions that she never allowed herself to think about—two abortions because a woman who could give up a baby should never be allowed the joy of having another baby—and then Ron's boys. That was the extent of Jenny's mothering. Until now.

The valet took the Volvo. Claudia put the car-park ticket into her jacket pocket and then took it out and slipped it into her purse, behind her wallet. The sun was bright. She walked up the three steps from the driveway to the Beverly Wilshire, through the brass doors, and down the corridor to the lobby. She kept her eyes focused on the toes of her shoes as they hit the white marble. It had occurred to her as she got out of the car that she might run into somebody. *Oh, Claudia, how nice to see you, what are you doing here? Uh . . . I've come to meet my mother. Margaret and you are having lunch? Oh, how lovely. I wish my daughter didn't live so far away. Well, give your mother my best. Okeydokey.* Jenny, let me give you the best from this woman who thought you were Margaret or actually she thought I was meeting Margaret, you see . . .

"May I help you?"

"Oh . . . uh . . . the house phones?"

"Right over there, madam."

"Thank you."

"Certainly."

Her hand was sweaty; she nearly dropped the receiver.

"Operator."

"Uh . . . Mrs. Glass, please. Jenny Glass."

"One moment, please."

"Hello?"

She knew the voice now, low and rich.

"Hi."

"Hi."

"I'm . . . uh . . . in the lobby."

"Should I come down and meet you?"

"No, I'll come up."

"Good because I don't know if my legs will work."

Claudia smiled. "Me neither."

"I'm in 907."

"Okay."

She watched her face in the mirrors of the sumptuous elevator, tried a few smiles, but she could feel a knot of hysteria about to rise from her throat, so she turned away. She decided she looked as best she could under the circumstances. She'd been dressed since eight-thirty; she'd seen herself from every angle of every mirror in her house. Ollie was long gone when she left, and Santos had just come back from taking Lily to nursery school. "Oh, missus, ju look just like a lady." Claudia was wearing the same suit she'd worn to the Hall of Records, the beige Armani Margaret had given her for her birthday. She smoothed her skirt and adjusted the lapel of the jacket, and it occurred to her that she was wearing a suit from one mother to go see another. . . . No, she'd better not think about that. As Claudia ran her hand through her hair, the bell went *ting* and the big elevator doors slid open. The hallway was hushed, the carpeting soft yellow and jade roses, and the walls cream. The door to 907 stood open.

Claudia saw Jenny's hand first: pale long fingers, oval short nails with dark-red polish, and a wedding band of tiny diamonds that seemed to go all the way around. The door moved; the person behind it took a step forward and came into full view.

She was smiling, wearing a simple black sheath dress that had what Margaret called a bateau neckline. Claudia couldn't believe she could hear Margaret's voice in her head saying "bateau" as she looked at Jenny. Her hair was gray and wavy and chopped off bluntly at her chin. Her face was clean except for mascara and a stain of cherry lipstick, and there was a spray of freckles across her cheeks and her nose, but what somehow mattered more than anything was that Jenny was the very same height as Claudia: they looked directly into each other's eyes. The reality of that was staggering. Claudia had to steady herself.

"You're beautiful," Jenny said, and she put her hand to Claudia's face, and Claudia felt her anxiety melt away just a little and taken totally by surprise as she looked at her birth mother, she said softly, "I look like you."

• • •

233

Lily loved the white bear; she named him Mash. No one had any idea where that name came from, but Lily was very positive; she looked at him, said his name was Mash, and fell asleep holding him, along with her beloved rabbit and her piece of satin. It never occurred to her that the bear could possibly belong to her mommy, she was sure it was for her.

"Did you want to sleep with Mash?" Ollie whispered in the shadows as they looked at their daughter. "You can tell me. I'm not the jealous type."

Claudia smiled, her face against his bare chest. She turned, and he could feel her lips curve against his skin. He was being very sweet to her, but there was also a carefulness, as if she'd just gotten over an illness and it was her first time on her feet. In the light of the reunion, no one knew quite how to behave. John was right: it could have been taped for Oprah—how Jenny's arms just opened and Claudia walked right into them with no hesitation, how they stood there not speaking, two female strangers who were connected by their mere being, arms wound around each other hard and tight in the open doorway of room 907 of the Beverly Wilshire Hotel. She had tried to tell him, but she was too tired, spent in a good way; if Claudia had had to put a word to it, she felt relieved. It was like a soothing balm, this glimpse of Jenny. The dreams could stop now, the vision was real, it was as if the hole in her was patched now—not filled, but patched—with this tiny taste of Jenny, and maybe, Claudia thought, as she gazed at her sleeping child from the shelter of her husband's arms, maybe it was more than just relief: maybe, for the first time, Claudia felt free.

"It was something," Jenny said into the telephone.

"Tell me," Ron said.

"She's lovely. Tall and thin and—"

"Like you."

"Different. Her hair is lighter than mine was, and her . . . everything is lighter. She's kind of . . . golden," Jenny said, and she laughed, an exquisite, full laugh, and Ron said, "Oh, honey, I'm so happy for you," and she said, "I can't tell you what I'm feeling, it's all jumbled, but it's good, I know that."

She couldn't tell him because her mind was moving faster than her lips could, but more than anything she couldn't tell him because she was flooded with Will, images like a color slide show. Will in the Mercury, Will behind a counter, flipping pancakes, Will's face so close to hers that it was blurred. Claudia was golden like her father; she had his light. She was a combination of both of them, but she had his stance and his shoulders, and her eyes were Will, startling blue and intense and steady, and she had his frown, the one he had when he was thinking, and she did this thing with her hands, this little something that stirred a memory so deep in Jenny. Claudia's face superimposed on Will's face, the blue and the gold, and the lamps were all on in the room of the Beverly Wilshire—she fell asleep in the chair without supper. She was going to get up—and she slept slumped in the chair, still wearing her black dress, and she dreamed all the dreams she had long ago buried, all the shut-away dreams of Will.

Ollie came into the bedroom from his morning run around the neighborhood. "Who is it?" he whispered at Claudia, who had the phone wedged in the crook of her neck.

"Gena," she mouthed.

"What?" Gena said into the telephone.

"I was telling Ollie it was you."

"Ah, the return of Florence Griffith-Joyner. Tell him hello."

"Hello," Claudia said to Ollie. He nodded and kissed her, peeled his wet T-shirt over his head.

"So what else?" Gena said. "Tell me."

"Uh . . ." Claudia yawned and punched the pillow behind her. Ollie sat on the foot of the bed and pulled off his shoes and socks.

"You didn't talk about what happened? I mean, how you came to be?"

"No, nothing. She didn't seem to want to get into that yet." Claudia cradled the receiver between her chin and her shoulder and pushed the hair back from her face. "She told me stuff about her life in New York a little, and I told her some stuff about me, but there's no order, you know; it's a skipping, random, stream-of-consciousness conversation." She frowned. "It's catch-up, but you don't know what you're catching up on, so you don't know where to go."

"Like my grandmother said, a lot of years under the bridge."

"Yeah." Claudia frowned. "What? I thought it was water."

"Claud, that's the point. She got it wrong, see? Never mind."

"I get it, I'm just not up yet."

"Shower," Ollie said, tossing his shorts on a chair and walking out of the room naked. Claudia appraised his naked backside and smiled.

They were quiet.

"I gave her the rosary beads."

"Oh, Claud, what did she say?"

"She wouldn't take them, said they were mine, and she got very emotional, really emotional. They were from her friend Rose, who died last year; she was Catholic, and they'd been together since Stella Maris."

"Who?"

"The home for unwed mothers where she had me."

"Holy Mother, is that what it's called?"

"Yeah."

"Is it still there?"

"No."

Neither of them spoke for a few seconds.

"Gena, I couldn't stop looking at her."

"Oh, Claud."

Jenny rolled over on her side and adjusted her cheek on the pillow. She'd awakened in the chair and moved to the bed at dawn. She was having a hard time shaking the dream, and the dream had brought up all the memories. They had leaped to the present and were parading in front of her eyes.

She pushed open the door of the dancing school. It was hard, hard to get to the door, harder to get past the spot where she had stood. *Six o'clock in front of Lala Palevsky's, six o'clock, my little sweetheart, I'll be there.* She pushed open the door. Eight girls in leotards, young and gangly, so young, it seemed to her—a carefree set to their shoulders, an untroubled toss of the head—but maybe that wasn't age she was looking at.

She turned away and walked into the girls' dressing room, leaned against the lockers across from the bench. Lala Palevsky knew she was there; she hadn't lifted her hand from her cane or her eyes from the pirouetting leotards, but Jenny knew that she knew. She caught an image of herself in the mirrors. Was it obvious that she'd had a baby? Was it written like invisible neon across her chest? Jenny felt the cold of the locker against the back of her neck. The girls swooped in, excited, laughing, and then the voice said, "Miss Jennifer?" and they were instantly hushed. Jenny turned. Lala Palevsky stood in the doorway.

"Come," she said.

She would call New York for her. She had people.

"There is nothing to discuss now. You will go to New York and dance."

"What if I can't? What if I'm not good enough?"

"Then you will come back."

"No, I'll never come back here."

"Then you will be good enough," Lala Palevsky said.

She sat up in bed now, reached for the telephone.

"Room Service, dis is Julio, please hold on."

Somewhere deep in her, she'd thought there would be something when she returned from Stella Maris, a letter, a note. No, she *knew* there would be something; he would have found a way, no matter what he had done and how he'd left her. Will would have rethought it while she'd been away in California, and he would have left her a message, a note, something, with someone— with anyone—or maybe he would be there himself. Standing defiant, ready to battle her parents, ready to take her in his arms. All the feelings Jenny had suppressed at Stella Maris flooded her when she returned to Kansas City, but there was no message and there was no Will; there was nothing.

She remembered now and held the receiver tightly.

"I have to leave here, Daddy. I can't stay in Kansas City." Esther opened her mouth to protest, but Moe silenced her with his eyes.

"Room service, dis is Julio," the voice said.

"This is Mrs. Glass in 907," Jenny said into the telephone, but all she could see in front of her was an eighteen-year-old girl, thirty-five years ago, getting on an airplane alone for New York.

Claudia pulled up the hotel drive and Jenny stood waiting: a tall, lean woman in sunglasses, stacked-heel sandals, a white silk T-shirt, narrow black linen pants, a black cashmere cardigan on her arm. Claudia felt the relief slide over her; she wasn't about to tell Jenny the terrifying thought that had hit her: how she would ask for Mrs. Glass in 907 and they would say she had checked out and gone back to New York.

They were coming at seven. First it was lunch and then it was cocktails, and then John said they should go out, after she'd already convinced Claudia that she wanted to make the dinner at home.

"You just be with her, sweetheart, and I'll take care of the food."

"But, Mom, it's too much for you. I can do it here."

"No, it's right that it's at our house. Please, dear, let me."

And then, after all that, John was insistent that they go to a restaurant, and Margaret had to carry on with him until she won.

"It's much easier at home."

"No it's not."

"Yes it is. Everyone will be much more relaxed. I don't know why you're making such a fuss, John. You don't have to do anything except mix the drinks."

She was making chicken, what John called her standby chicken. He said she could make it cross-eyed and drunk, with her hands tied behind her back, she'd made it so many times. Chicken with crumbs and rice with mushrooms and sweet peas, and a green salad with cherry tomatoes, and a coconut cake, but first, salmon in the living room, thin slivers of smoked salmon on tiny toasts of pumpernickel, with a mustard mayonnaise sauce with fresh dill, and that's what Margaret was doing when the pain in her knees nearly toppled her— she was chopping handfuls of fresh dill. She leaned against the counter, nausea rising in her throat.

"Sweet Jesus," she whispered, and bent her head; the green fragments of dill blurred, and she shut her eyes.

"What are you doing, Maggie?" John said as he entered the kitchen.

"I'm looking at my recipe," she said, pushing the index card in front of her.

"I'm calling the liquor store. Do you need anything?"

She gripped the edge of the counter. "Cream. No, half-and-half; nobody drinks cream in their coffee anymore, I don't think."

"That it?"

"Mm hmm." *And knees and hips and fingers—could you ask them please, dear, if they could send those from Gotti's Liquor Store with the gin?*

"You look peaked."

"What a silly word." She picked up her chopping knife.

"Are you all right?"

"Yes."

He glared at her, his lips pursed as when he was making his closing argument. "You're overdoing it."

"John, I'm just making dinner." She tilted her head. "Do you want to help me?"

"Are you kidding?"

"Absolutely." She winked at him.

"Very funny," he said as he left the room.

Margaret put the knife down; she moved to the sink and got a glass of water, drank it and then had another one. She let her hands hang under the running faucet and then wet her face. Shaking, she tried to get the cap off the Advil. *All right, Margaret, you're not going to call him to help you; open it yourself.* She twisted the cap with her swollen fingers, hit it against the sink and twisted it again, twisted and pushed it until it opened. She shook out three caplets and swallowed them, walked back to the chopping block, straightened her shoulders, and blotted her upper lip with the back of her hand. She would do this, knees or no knees, crone's hands, crippled fingers, and all, she would make a lovely dinner and she would put her best foot forward. After all, she was Claudia's mother; it was her place. Margaret took a breath and steadied herself, and then, with the flourish of a sushi chef, she picked up her knife and attacked the dill.

A grandchild. A daughter and a granddaughter. How could that be? Jenny sat wedged into the little chair at the little table in the child's room. It was the end of the day, and the light was rose coming in through the windows, a soft butter-cream rose touching the mounds of pillows and stuffed animals on what Lily had explained to Jenny was her new "big-girl" bed. "Big girls don't have cribs, only babies." The *big girl* stood next to Jenny, all three feet of her leaning into the table, intent on moving her yellow crayon in a lopsided oval and then in a kind of fast zigzag line across the page. The yellow was darker than the child's hair; her hair was like spun light. She hadn't seen that color since Will's. Jenny wanted to touch it, she wanted to reach out and touch the tumble of curls that had fallen across her face.

"That's a zeba," Lily said.

"It is?"

"Uh huh," she said, her eyes fixed on the paper, "and he's growling because he wants his supper. He likes Cheerios." She looked up at Jenny. "Aren't you going to make anything?"

"Oh, I'm sorry." She took the purple crayon the child had given her and drew a small circle. "There," she said.

"It needs eyes."

"Oh. Of course." She put two dots in the circle.

The child's torso brushed up against Jenny. She could smell her; she was up against her arm like silk: baby powder, it smelled like, and cookies—oatmeal cookies?—and shampoo.

"Do you have a little girl like me at your house?"

"No."

"A little boy?"

"No, I . . . uh . . ."

"I'm going to have eight babies," Lily said.

"Really."

"And a puppy and a kitty and ducks."

"Ducks," Jenny said.

Lily looked up from her picture, her face serious. "I love ducks," she said.

"Oh."

"What do you like?"

"Animals? Well, let's see . . ."

"So anybody here ready to go to Grandma's?" Claudia stood in the doorway.

Lily hurled herself into her mother. "Me, me!"

"I'm sorry, I didn't mean to leave you. My mother was—" She stumbled on her words. "Margaret was on the phone."

Jenny untangled herself from the tiny chair and stood up. "We were fine. She's just . . . wonderful. I don't seem to have the right words."

Claudia bent down and scooped Lily up into her arms. "*Woman* doesn't have any babies, Mommy," Lily said, her arms circling Claudia's neck.

Claudia and Jenny gazed at each other over the top of the child's head. Lily swung around to Jenny. "Do you have ducks?"

"I'm afraid not."

"Is *woman* going to Grandma's?"

"Her name is Jenny."

"Is she?"

"Yes."

Lily gave Jenny a stern look. "Don't run in the living room."

Jenny hid her smile. "Okay."

• • •

She lingered at the table of framed photographs in the upstairs hallway while they thought she was in the bathroom. She picked each one up off the table: Lily, Lily and Claudia, Claudia and . . . Margaret—this must be Margaret—a short, plump woman with round cheeks in a lively face, a blond teased hairdo and a drop-dead smile. Margaret, with her eyes on Claudia. Claudia was looking straight into the camera, but the woman's eyes were on . . . her daughter. Claudia and Margaret, Jenny thought, Claudia and her mother . . . Margaret . . . the mother of my child. She stood for a moment, leaning against the table. Where was she in this family picture? Did she have a place? Jenny's fingers had made smudges on the sterling-silver frame. She wiped the marks away against the sides of her linen slacks, returned the photograph to its place, and went downstairs.

"You've probably been in Los Angeles lots of times," John said.

"No, only once, a long time ago, when"—she wasn't quite sure what to say—"when I was young."

"Always lived in New York, have you, since Kansas City? We were in New York last April—wasn't it April, Margaret?"

"May. We went with Claudia and Oliver to see Claudia's dear friend, Gena; she was in a play."

"A goddamn boring play."

Ollie laughed. "You can say that again."

"Lily, sweetheart, please put that down," Margaret said.

"Lily, don't touch that. I told you." Claudia took the Baccarat candy dish away from the child. "It wasn't boring."

"Okay, not boring . . . stupid."

"Ollie."

"What?" He turned to Jenny, who was next to him on the couch. "It was boring and stupid, I promise you."

"It was just . . . ," Claudia went on.

"What?"

"I don't know—New Age?"

"It was a goddamn travesty," John said. "Give me a musical any old day. That's what you were in, right? Musicals?"

"Yes."

"So are you going to dance for us?"

"John," Margaret said.

"I was kidding. What can I get you to drink, Mrs. Glass?"

"It's Jenny."

"Jenny."

"Do you have vodka?"

"I have everything. How about a martini?"

"I'd love a martini, Mr. Magers."

"If you're going to have a martini, you'd better call me John."

The *nice couple* came to life before her, they stepped out of Jenny's dreams alive and kicking, and if they weren't connected by hand to shoulder, they were indeed connected by years of love; it was as plain as the food on their table. John raised his glass to Margaret, and it was as plain as the look on his face. There were no guarantees when you signed that paper. You gave your baby to a fantasy *nice couple*, but in reality, it was all a crap shoot. They could turn out to be ax murderers—how would you ever know? And now she knew, and except for an uneasy wash of loneliness, she nearly slid to the floor with relief.

"Can't I help you?" Jenny said.

"Oh, my goodness, no," Margaret said. "I've got it." She smiled at Jenny and backed out of the dining room, through the swinging door into the kitchen, the remainder of the coconut cake on the silver tray in her hands. She put the tray on the counter, poked her finger into the white icing, and scooped a fingerful of icing and coconut into her mouth. The woman looked like a French movie star. Angles and bones and that haircut, stunning, like you see in a film. Margaret ran her finger under the faucet, dried it on a dish towel, and stood there. Then she stuck her finger back into the cake. Of course, *her* hair would never do that, wave like that without rollers and a hair dryer and Michael combing it out, and then still it didn't wave, no matter what you did to it; it just lay there like a flattened soufflé. And gray, she'd let it go gray, how brave. Margaret would never dream of giving up her color. Of course, she happened to know that under her blond there was no gray, she was as white as a snowstorm; if she didn't have color, she would look older than George Burns. She sighed, pushed her finger through some icing, and put it in her mouth. And charming, she was charming . . . or was it disarming, something underneath the charm: a what? an edge? Well, that probably came with the life; she was sophisticated, worldly, a whole other life from Margaret's, all those stories about all those shows she was in, so exciting and important. She hadn't seen John laugh like that in years, especially when she told the one about how she tried out for that show where everyone was Oriental, but she went anyway and danced for them as if she could get into the show, as if they would think she was Chinese. That took spunk, Margaret thought; she couldn't have done that. Of course, how could she pretend she was Chinese? You had to be mysterious and willowy to attempt Chinese, and she'd looked like a hamburger bun from the time she was three. Margaret tugged at her tunic. Well, it was just a whole other way of living—a carefree young dancer on her own in New York while Margaret was in California training to be what? A wife. It was true, she'd never had dreams to be anything else: a doctor, a lawyer, an Indian chief; it didn't matter—it had never occurred to her to be or do anything except what her mother had done before her and her mother

245

before that, to be a homemaker, a housewife. She'd certainly never done anything sophisticated. Well, marry John: she'd thought that was pretty sophisticated at the time. An up-and-coming young lawyer, seven years older than she was, the top of his class and starting out with such a solid firm, her father said, and big and handsome, her mother said, and he had such presence and wherewithal, her grandmother said. Of course, things were different then—but that wasn't why she hadn't been daring, she knew that; she hadn't been daring because it wasn't in her; she was about as daring as this coconut cake. She couldn't have gone on her own to New York to be a dancer any more than she could fly. She licked some of the coconut off her finger. With or without a plane, Margaret thought, and she smiled. Of course, she couldn't have given up a baby either. How in the name of heaven could a woman do that? "Could you have done it, Mom?" Claudia's sweet face asking. "Could you have done it? Could you?" It was all Margaret could do to remind herself that there were always circumstances; as her own mother had scolded. "If you don't have all the details, Magpie, you mustn't ever try to put yourself in the next man's shoes." And it was another time, wasn't it? In 1960 no one was raising a baby without a husband—it was a scandal, a terrible scandal—and if a girl did it she needed her mother and father to help her, she couldn't have done it alone, and maybe Jenny's parents couldn't help her or maybe they wouldn't help her or maybe this or maybe that, and oh, my goodness, on and on she'd gone, trying to think of all the circumstances that might have made Jenny bring herself to sign such a paper, to give her child away, but as much as Margaret tried to think of all those unknown details, as much as she knew that if Jenny hadn't signed the paper Margaret wouldn't have had Jenny's very own child to love as her own, as much as she didn't want to color anything and certainly didn't want to cast any stones, she knew. Margaret had lost too many babies, sweet babies that hadn't made it to this side; she knew that if she had ever had a baby, nothing could have made her give it away.

"May I come in?"

Margaret turned. It was Jenny.

"Oh, I was just coming out, I'm sorry. . . . Well, if the truth be known, I was picking at this cake, which of course I certainly don't need."

"It was delicious. You baked it, didn't you?"

"Yes."

Jenny crossed the kitchen and stood next to Margaret. "I'm a nitwit in the kitchen; I'd rather board it up and paint it black." Her perfume was exotic; not a floral, something more spicy and strange.

"Well, I can assure you I don't do anything adventurous; I just follow the recipe. It's not like I attempt anything on my own."

"I wouldn't attempt it even with the recipe. There's a story out about how I once *broiled* a cake."

Margaret laughed.

"Everything was beautiful . . . lovely. You have a lovely home."

"Thank you."

"This was all very kind of you. I couldn't have done it."

"Don't be silly."

"No, I couldn't. Here I am, a total stranger, and you let me in."

"I'm sure you would have done the same, if the shoe had been on the other foot."

"But it wasn't, was it?"

"Well, no."

They stood looking at each other. Margaret was suddenly aware that her finger was full of coconut; she wasn't quite sure what to do with it, she let it rest on the tray. There were a few seconds of silence. It didn't seem to be her place to begin anything; after all, they didn't know each other; she couldn't very well say to a perfect stranger all the things she wanted to say.

"Is the hotel all right for you?"

"It's wonderful."

"That's good. I hate it when I'm staying somewhere and I don't feel comfortable."

"Do you do a lot of traveling?"

Margaret laughed. "Oh, no . . . I don't do well on the return part. John says I have trouble with reentry. I see all the things that need fixing—they glare at me." She made a face. "The living room furniture needs recovering and everything in the drawers needs rearranging and there's a crack in the ceiling that I never saw before, and because it's everything at the same time, I go into a tizzy." She smiled and gestured with her hands. "John says it isn't worth going anywhere with me unless he can drug me on the return." She could hear her own voice, yards of absurd chatter, but she was certainly not about to strike up a conversation about giving a baby away, and then Margaret realized her hands were poised in the air between them; she could see the wad of coconut icing waving around on her finger. "Oh, look at me—I'm so sorry." She turned, but Jenny stopped her, her cool fingers on Margaret's arm.

Jenny took a sharp breath. "I have to tell you, Margaret . . . I have to . . . thank you. She's just the way I would have wanted her. Claudia . . ." Jenny stumbled for the words.

"Oh, my dear . . ."

"Mom? Are you washing the dishes? You said you weren't going to do that, just take in the cake." Claudia walked into the kitchen, and the two of them turned to her together, and she stopped still in her tracks.

Page after page of photographs, all the picture albums on the shelves of Margaret's bedroom, the three of them side by side on the brocade couch, turning the pages. Ollie finally left with a sleeping Lily. "You take the baby," Margaret said. "Claudia can take my car."

"Yeah, well, I can see that you guys don't really need me." He was laughing when she kissed him. "Hey," he said, "have a good time."

Memories, bits and pieces of Claudia's childhood . . . Jenny was greedy for everything, and Margaret was delighted to tell. "She didn't scratch that chicken pox, I know for a fact she didn't, I was with her every minute," Margaret said, "but look how it left a scar."

Jenny's eyes raised with concern to the tiny cavern above the arch of Claudia's left eyebrow. "I see that," she said.

John had fallen asleep on the couch in the living room. Claudia covered him with a throw when she went down to get the brandy because Margaret had decided the three of them should have a drink. She had a sense of being in another time zone; what was happening was far too unreal.

Jenny had slipped her shoes off, she had one leg tucked under her, and Margaret leaned toward her, her face flushed. A history, Margaret had the history, and here was Jenny, latching onto the details like a fish on a hook. Claudia handed each of them a crystal stem of brandy. They were talking about her as if she wasn't in the room. No, she didn't break out from strawberries—do *you* break out? Oh, dear. And yes, she can ride horses, but not jumping—Margaret couldn't bear to let her jump, for fear . . . and no, she never really loved swimming.

"Me neither," Jenny said.

And yes, she was always better in English than in math, and yes, she loved stories, and yes, she certainly did have a sweet tooth. Margaret laughed. "It must run in the family," and then she caught herself. "Oh, how silly; it would have to come from you, her sweet tooth, not from me."

"Not from me either," Jenny said, laughing with her. "I'd rather have potato chips."

"Well, maybe her father," chirped Margaret. "Did he like sweets?"

"Pie, he loved pie," and then the smile abruptly faded and she stood up and the crystal glass of brandy tumbled silently over onto the thick ivory rug.

"Oh, God," Jenny said, "I'm sorry. What a jerk."

"It's all right, it's nothing. Let me get a towel."

And Margaret struggled to her feet and there was a scramble for towels and soda water and mopping up the amber stain and Margaret didn't want Jenny to do it but Margaret couldn't get to her knees and Claudia was saying, "I've got it, Mom," and Jenny was saying, "No, wait, let me," and the spell was broken. There was no way they would ever get back to that conversation, and Claudia knew she would have to bring it up, she would have to ask Jenny, if she wanted to know anything about her father besides his love for pie.

"You don't need him," Jenny said, and walked into the bathroom of her suite at the Beverly Wilshire.

Claudia followed. "That's not for you to say."

"Oh, yes it is." Jenny scooped up lipstick and mascara and moisturizer and tossed them into a makeup bag. She didn't look at Claudia; she kept her eyes on the sink.

"You're not being fair," Claudia said.

"Life's not fair."

"Don't say that to me."

Jenny picked up her hairbrush and the makeup bag; she faced Claudia. "I won't help you on this."

"I can't find him without his name, you know that."

Jenny walked out of the bathroom, her shoulder brushing Claudia's as she passed.

"You're the only one who knows," Claudia said.

"Don't ask me, Claudia." She squeezed the things she was holding into the corner of the suitcase.

"Would you stop what you're doing?"

"No. I don't want to miss my plane."

"What is it? You think you're protecting me?"

"You don't want him in your life."

Claudia stood next to her at the suitcase. "My God, what did he do to you? Did he rape you? Was he someone you didn't even know?"

"No."

"Did you love him?"

Jenny said nothing; she pushed at things in her suitcase and zipped it shut.

"I'm a grown-up. Why won't you tell me? Look at me, goddamn it!"

Jenny raised her eyes. Claudia's face was white.

"*I found you, Jenny, you didn't find me.* It took me years to decide to do this, off again, on again. I nearly made myself crazy, always stopping because of everybody else's feelings. *Why make waves, Claudia? You already have a mother and father, be a good girl.* . . . but I couldn't shake it; I knew I had to find you even if I made trouble." Her eyes were steady on Jenny's. "And I did it, I found you, and I let you into my life . . ."

"I know that."

". . . and you have no right to stop me from finding him." Jenny shook her head, but Claudia went on. "This secret doesn't belong to you; it isn't just your secret."

"Claudia."

"No, I need this; don't you see how I need this?"

Jenny turned. "My plane's at noon. If you don't want to take me, I'll get a cab."

"That's the way you do things? You get a cab?"

"I guess so." She took a breath. "I shouldn't have come here."

"I can't believe you. . . . How can you say that?"

"You should be happy you don't take after me, if you don't like what you see." Jenny took a step, but Claudia got in front of her.

"Take after you? I don't even know you, I don't even know who you are."

"I can't help that."

"But you could have. Couldn't you?"

The high color drained from Jenny's face. She tried to get around Claudia, but Claudia stopped her. "How could you give me away?"

"I had to."

"Why? Did he make you? Did he want you to?"

"Please, I don't want to do this now."

"When do you want to do it? Thursday? Next Christmas? May?"

Jenny shook her head. Her mouth opened, but nothing came out.

"I'm asking you to tell me his name. It's the only thing I've ever asked of you. You've never given me a goddamn thing!"

"I can't give you this. Ask me for something else."

"Ask you for something else?" Claudia's shoulders fell; she laughed softly. "And you say you're my mother."

"I *am* your mother."

"No, you haven't earned a right to say that. Margaret would give me anything."

The words hung in the air between them.

Jenny's eyes dropped. "I'm going. I'll take a cab." She turned, but Claudia grabbed her arm. "Claudia, please, stop it." Jenny tried to pull away. Claudia's fingers were digging into her.

"This isn't about you. It's about me," Claudia said, her face close to Jenny's.

"I won't tell you."

"You have to." Claudia leaned back a bit so her eyes could meet Jenny's. "*You owe me.*"

"Flag on the play," Ollie said. "I didn't think she was going to tell you, I thought you were going to have to get on the plane with her and go all the way to New York."

Jenny missed her plane; she missed two planes; she wound up staying another day. *You owe me.* Words that Claudia didn't even know were in her, words that Jenny had never wanted to hear. An umbrella of words that covered: how could you leave me, how could you hand me off like a football and walk away, how could you not know what happened to me and not care, how could you be my mother and never try to find me in all these years?

"I made myself believe I had no right: I don't know how else to explain it to you."

"But how could you live without knowing?"

"I made myself."

"*I* couldn't live without knowing what happened to Lily."

"Well, I guess I'm different than you."

And they saw each other with their veils down. Not being tentative anymore, not being careful, stepping all over each other's hearts with their words.

Why did you leave me? how could you go?

How did they raise you? what did they say?

Is there a place for me now?

Is there a place for me now?

You owe me.

And Jenny stopped where she was and stared at Claudia, lowered her hand from her mouth and said the words.

"His name was Will."

And her eyes filled and she stumbled backward and fell into a chair. "Will McDonald. William Cole McDonald," Jenny said.

Jenny wouldn't tell Claudia anything more than the bare bones; she refused to get into what Gena called "the gory details." She loved him, she was supposed to marry him, he left her waiting by the side of the road.

"Gena, I didn't say '*by the side of the road.*'"

"Okay, on the sidewalk somewhere."

"You always go straight to the dramatic."

"Hey, you've got to admit it was pretty dramatic without me beefing it up. He gets her pregnant, he's going to marry her, he takes *money* from her parents, and he leaves her without so much as a word. Jesus, Claud."

And they were quiet on both ends of the connection, taking it all in.

"And on top of that, she named you for him."

"Yeah . . ."

"I bet she thought he'd come back."

Claudia wrote *Cole* on the pad next to the telephone.

"She never found out anything?"

"No."

"She never knew what happened to him? He just left her standing there and never contacted her again?"

"Yes."

"And she loved him?"

"Yes, she loved him."

"No wonder she didn't want to tell you."

Claudia didn't say anything.

"Son of a bitch."

"Gena, please."

"Well, wasn't he?"

William Cole McDonald, Claudia thought, my *father*, who we shall deem henceforth, the *son-of-a-bitch*.

Will

She left before sunrise. She backed the Volvo down the driveway, holding on to a hot cup of coffee, some of which splashed over when she shifted from reverse to drive. She didn't care; she wasn't going to stop to mop up the coffee; she wasn't going to stop for anything. The sky stayed black through Palmdale and Lancaster, it was just turning to navy as she hit the edge of Mojave, and by the time she came out of the Chevron with fresh coffee, it was a bright royal blue. Claudia watched the stars disappear as the royal turned to azure, felt the morning chill on her face and stretched her legs. She hadn't driven this many miles alone since she was in college. She realized she was smiling as she got back in the car.

"Do you want me to take you?" Ollie had said.
   "No, I want to do it. It's only—what—three, four hours?"
"That's what it looks like on the map."
"Piece a cake."
He laughed and kissed her.
"Kiss *me*, Daddy," Lily said, pulling on Ollie's hand.

•   •   •

"Lone Dove. It's so romantic," Gena had said when she'd told her. "You'd just know he'd live someplace romantic, wouldn't you?"

"Lone Tree, Gena, not Lone Dove."

"Oh. Is Ollie going with you?"

"No."

"You're going by yourself?"

"Yep."

Gena hesitated. "You're not going to stay with him, are you? If you find him."

"No, of course not. I'll get a motel."

"How do you know they have motels in Lone Dove?"

Claudia laughed into the phone. "Gena . . ."

"Lone Tree. Lone Tree."

"I don't know, I just assume they have motels."

"It might just be a sign and two barns and a tractor; for all you know, *that* could qualify as a town."

"If they don't have a motel, I'll drive back, or I'll sleep in the car."

"Oh, I'd like to see that. . . . I can't believe you're doing this."

"Well, it's only 'cause Ollie said he'd buy me a fedora and a trench coat."

"Very funny. What if you don't find him?"

"I don't know. I'll cross that bridge when I come to it."

"You sound like Margaret."

"Yeah," Claudia said, and smiled into the phone.

Five months, give or take a week—it had taken five months and a million phone calls between Claudia in L.A. and Jenny in New York, but Dorothy Floye had come through.

"Well, I'd say it'll take me . . . oh, three to six months, 'cause I don't let my files sit, but it's not like we have a lot to go on here. Mrs. Glass is not

258

exactly a wealth of information." She heard Claudia's sigh. "Don't you fret, hon; you just live your life and let me go do what I do."

It wasn't only that Jenny didn't remember; there was a lot she didn't know. He was born in Bishop or was it Kernville and he was raised in Burbank or was it Darwin and he went to jail in—

Did she say jail?

Claudia looked down at the slip of paper tucked under her leg on the seat: *William Cole McDonald,* she read for maybe the hundredth time in Dorothy Floye's slanted scrawl, *General Delivery, Lone Tree, California.*

"Oh, Dorothy," Claudia had said, clutching the slip of paper and trying to keep breathing. "Thank you."

Dorothy laughed. "Anytime, honey. Whenever you're lookin' for a daddy, just come to me."

"How did you do it?" Ollie said.

Dorothy gave him a little tilt of the head and fluttered her lashes. "Oh, we have our ways."

Ollie laughed. "No . . . really."

"You want me to tell you the tricks of the trade? I'd have to turn in my card."

"C'mon, Dorothy."

"Oh, old phone books, honey, old records, old anything . . . just like me," and she laughed.

"General Delivery?" Claudia said, looking at the paper.

"That's all I got so far."

"No street?"

Dorothy shook her head.

"And no phone?"

"Unlisted"—her big green eyes twinkled—"but I'm working on it."

Claudia knew she wasn't going to wait for Dorothy to work on it.

She had something, and that *something* would have to be enough for her. It had been five months since she'd gotten his name, and now that she had at least a kind of address, she was going to Lone Tree.

"Those post office people aren't going to tell you anything; they're not allowed."

"I know that, Dorothy."

"Well, then, what are you going to do? Pretend to be a mailman? Or just sit around in the post office and wait for him to saunter in? You don't even know what he looks like."

"I have an idea."

"Honey, I don't care how well she described him—none of us look like we did in high school, take it from me."

"I have to go, Dorothy. I can't just sit here now that I know where he is."

"You're going to end up disappointed, I'm telling you. It's one big, fat wild-goose chase."

"You might as well give it up, Dorothy," Ollie said, smiling at Claudia. "She's going—look in her eyes."

Claudia took a swig of the lukewarm coffee and popped an Etta James tape into the deck. The sun in the sky was gold now. She shrugged off her jacket and opened the window. Clean air filled the Volvo and blew her hair around.

Jenny didn't know how old he was—he'd hated birthdays, she said—so she knew the date but not the year; she remembered his mother's first name but not her last, and she couldn't remember his father's first name at all. She didn't know why he'd come to Kansas City. No, it wasn't to see family; he didn't have any family there. She didn't know much about his family anywhere, except there was an aunt named Cleo who'd taken care of him—no last name, just

Cleo—who had a beauty shop in . . . no, she couldn't remember where.

"Siblings, ask her if he had any siblings, hon, that's what I need."

"Siblings?"

"Brothers especially, with the same last name."

Brothers, yes, there were brothers, and sisters, but he wasn't close to any of them, Jenny told Claudia . . . no, wait a minute, there was one she remembered, what was his name? Jim? Tom? With Jenny it took a lot of probing before anything valuable came out. As in: What did he do before her? Where was he before he came to Kansas City? What did he do?

"San Quentin?" Dorothy Floye said, leaning forward in the booth at Marie Callender's. "Well now, honey, that's what I call a clue."

A robber. Armed robbery, Jenny had said, and in Claudia's fantasy, her beloved Hopalong Cassidy tossed off his white hat, leaped from Topper to a dark appaloosa, and mad a dramatic turn from the good guys to the bad.

The brown dirt spread out from the narrow two-lane highway on both sides of her. California brush and brown dirt and mountains with snow on top—the whole thing looked like a backdrop from MGM. She nosed her wheel out and decided to pass the camper and pickup in front of her. " 'Time after time, I tell myself that I'm . . . ,' " Claudia sang with Etta, and pushed the gas pedal to the floor.

"I don't think you ought to drop this on John right now," Ollie had said.

"What? That I'm trying to find him?"

"No, the San Quentin part."

"I guess not," Gena had agreed, "unless you're prepared to watch John have a cerebral hemorrhage."

Claudia decided not to tell John anything about finding him and not to tell Margaret and not to tell Jenny. Most of all, not to tell Jenny. They spoke nearly once a week. *How are you? Fine. How's Ron? Good, thank you. How's Lily? Oh, she's fine. And Ollie? Great.* That kind of volley, and then the conversations would drift. It wasn't that Claudia didn't enjoy talking to her, but what did they really have to say? What did they really know about each other? Four days of swapped information about what had happened to each of them since Claudia was born. Not a shared history, but individual pasts. Jenny had sent Claudia a sweater from Barney's, an expensive, thick black cashmere sweater with a beautiful note. Claudia didn't have the heart to tell the woman who could have known everything about her that she was allergic to wool.

There was so much each of them didn't know. After the hellos and how are yous there wasn't much to say except questions, and "Have you found him?" was not a question Jenny ever asked. Maybe because of what had happened between Will and Jenny, Jenny would never ask. Claudia decided this was her own personal wild-goose chase; she didn't have to tell anybody anything, not yet, and if it came to pass that there was something to tell, she'd tell Jenny face-to-face in three weeks, when she came to L.A.

"Are you sure?" Jenny had asked on the telephone.

"It would be wonderful."

"I don't have to go through Los Angeles. I can connect in Texas—Dallas, I think."

"No, come here."

Jenny was going to meet Ron in Mexico City. He was at a convention and she was going to meet him when it was over, then they would have a little holiday together, she'd said.

"You'll stay with us this time," Claudia said.

"Oh, I don't think so."

"Why not?"

"It's much easier at a hotel."

"Jenny, really, you said it was only for two days."

"Okay, I'll think about it," Jenny said.

If there was anything Claudia had to tell her about the wild-goose chase, she'd tell her then.

Claudia pulled off the highway into something called Brady's Place and bought two bottles of mountain spring water, which she took back to the car. The sun was hot; she pulled her T-shirt out of the damp Levi's waistband and lifted it to get some air on her skin. She took a swig of water and leaned back against the car. Blue sky that went on forever, the particular quiet of nowhere: the buzz of the Coca-Cola machine behind her, the drone of a bee, the whiz of an occasional car, and heavy shoes moving across the gravel.

"You need gas, little lady?"

"No, thank you; I did it."

"All right." He pulled a handkerchief out of his pants. Claudia smiled.

"Where you headed?" he asked, taking off his glasses and mopping his face.

"Lone Tree."

"Nice place."

"Is it?"

"Used to live there."

"Really."

"Yeah, till I moved here. Got hot today, didn't it?"

"Yes."

"Well," he said.

Claudia lifted her backbone away from the Volvo. "Did you . . . uh . . . happen to know a man named William McDonald? In Lone Tree, I mean."

"William McDonald . . ." He pushed his glasses back up onto the bridge of his nose. "No, can't say that I did."

"Oh."

"Course, that don't mean nothin'," he said, nodding.

"Well, thanks anyway," Claudia said.

He looked at her, shoved the handkerchief back into his pants pocket. "There's a highway patrol car with a speed trap, sittin' 'bout two miles north. You look for it. Side of the road."

"Thanks a lot, Mr. Brady."

"Oh, I ain't Brady." He laughed. "I'm Garris. Brady's been dead for years." He turned, his dusty work-shoes crunching on the gravel. "Watch out for that patrol car," he said, with his back to her.

Three hours out of L.A., and Claudia felt like she'd walked into *Bonanza*. As she pulled back onto the highway, the man stood at the gas pumps, one hand lifted in a kind of half wave. She never saw the patrol car, but she did keep her eye on her speed, and then there was a long stretch of nothing, and then the road did a slow curve and the limit went from 65 to 55 and then to 45, and up ahead, the dirt that was stretched out on either side of the road turned from brown to green. *Welcome to Lone Tree,* the sign said, and Claudia laughed out loud, her hands holding tight to the wheel.

"I've got a deuce openin' up any minute, honey," the waitress said. She had black holes on either side of her smile, where her teeth came abruptly to a halt. Claudia nodded and let her eyes scan the crowded restaurant; maybe everyone in Lone Tree had breakfast at the same time.

"Here we go." The waitress gestured to Claudia with a menu and walked her to a small booth. "Coffee?"

"Yes, please."

She brought coffee in a big mug and cream in a little pitcher, jutted her hip out, and held her pencil poised over her pad.

"Oh," Claudia said, looking up. "I'll have . . . uh . . . eggs, scrambled, and . . . toast, I guess, wheat, and . . ." Claudia's eyes moved to the four people in the booth across from her, shoveling in large quantities of food, and it occurred to her that she'd never been so hungry. ". . . and bacon—"

"You want the Mount Whitney," the waitress said, touching the menu with the eraser tip of her pencil. "Two of everything—two eggs, two pancakes, two strips of bacon—"

"I don't need pancakes."

"Why not? Everybody needs a little sweet in the morning, honey. Give it to yourself."

"Okay," Claudia said, laughing. "I'll have the Mount Whitney."

"That's the way."

She stirred sugar into the coffee. What if he was sitting right there in the restaurant? Blond, he was blond, Jenny had said, a towhead. . . . She moved her eyes around the room. Well, that guy was blond . . . no, too young; and that one . . . no, he looked really little. . . . Six feet two, she'd told her . . . well, she couldn't tell how tall someone was, hunched down over his breakfast. "Cornflower-blue eyes, Claudia," Jenny'd said softly, "the same as yours." The same eyes and the same name—but she didn't call him Cole, did she? She called him Will. The man in the corner booth grinned at her; she had been staring at him. She dropped her eyes to the tabletop. She would have to stop it before they called the sheriff and had her arrested for flagrant flirtation in a restaurant. Claudia smiled at the salt and pepper shakers; they would lead her out into the street in handcuffs. Handcuffs . . . had *he* been in handcuffs . . . ?

"Here you go, honey," the waitress said, and Claudia picked up her fork.

• • •

The post office was a block down from the restaurant, a block off the main drag. The main drag went right through town: it was highway and then it was Lone Tree and after about ten blocks it was highway again. The town spread on either side of the main drag, just like the waitress said, one way toward open land and the other way right up into a range of mountains called the Alabama Hills, which were the edge of the Sierra Nevadas, most famous for the mountain that had the same name as Claudia's breakfast, Mount Whitney. The post office was a square stone building with big windows; the doors were propped wide open. The front room was a sea of brass post office boxes covering three walls, and the second room had a counter. A young woman stood there in thongs and shorts, a baby perched on her left hip, a young child sitting next to an open package on the counter, and a toddler asleep in a stroller, his little head tilted back.

"Well, I don't know what you wanted me to get her," the woman said to the postman.

"Hell, Mary, you know my mother doesn't like knickknacks."

Claudia got in line behind the young woman.

"That's not a knickknack; it's a cup."

"How can you send somebody *one* cup?"

"It's a teacup, Marshall, an English teacup; it's for nice."

"Well, she's not gonna like it."

"Well, how am I supposed to know what she likes?" She sighed, shifted the baby to her other hip, and looked at Claudia. "Isn't a teacup nice?"

Claudia hesitated.

"Mary," the postman said.

"Oh, don't hassle me, Marshall," she said, lifting the cup out of the tissue paper and extending it to Claudia. "Isn't it nice?"

It was English bone china, ivory with tiny yellow flowers around the border. "It's beautiful," Claudia said.

Mary tilted her head at Marshall. "See? What do you know?"

The postman shook his head. "Nothing, I guess, except my mother doesn't drink tea."

The child on the counter grabbed at the tissue paper and flung a piece of it around his head. Mary scooped him up with her other arm and lowered him to the floor, where he immediately began to scream. "You stop it, Marshall junior," she said to him, "and if *you* don't like it," she said, narrowing her eyes at the postman, "then you can go get your mother something else." The baby in her arms started to cry in concert with the child on the floor.

"Oh, for Pete's sake," the postman said.

"If you don't stop that, Marshall junior, we are not going to the Dairy Queen." She held the crying baby in the arm that pushed the stroller and grabbed Marshall junior with her other hand. "You hear me?" she said.

"Mary . . . ," the postman tried.

"See ya," the young woman said to Claudia. She turned her back on the postman and pushed her screaming entourage out the open doors.

"Mary," he called again, but she was gone. He rubbed his forehead, looked at Claudia. "A teacup," he said.

Claudia tried a smile. He exhaled. "What can I do for you?"

It was definitely not a good beginning. Should she just buy stamps and come back later and try to talk to him? Should she tell him the whole story? Any of the story? Should she call him Marshall? Should she pretend she was living in Lone Tree? Should she move to Lone Tree?

"I was . . . uh . . ." Moving her weight from one foot to the other, she tried to remember her plan and smiled at him, what she hoped was an ingratiating smile. "I was . . . uh . . . wondering about general delivery. . . ."

He squinted. "Yeah?"

"I mean, if you were getting general delivery"—she looked at him, but he didn't say anything—"for instance, like Will McDonald . . ."

"Yeah?"

"He gets general delivery, right?"

"Yeah."

It was working, he was buying it; wait till she told Dorothy Floye. "So that means you don't deliver to him, right?"

"We only deliver to rural routes."

"Uh huh."

"Up in the Alabama Hills."

"Uh huh."

"Everybody else has a post office box, except a few who have general delivery because they don't want a post office box, don't ask me why. Course, they don't get much mail, the general deliveries."

"I see."

He waited. They looked at each other.

"So Will McDonald," Claudia went on, "for instance—because he's somebody who gets general delivery, he has to come in here to get his mail, because you keep it here for him, right? Until he comes in?"

She sounded like she did when she spoke to Santos.

"Right there," he said, pointing to a compartmented wooden box on the table beside him. "Alphabetical, just like it says, A to Z, general delivery. Thirty days I keep it and then return to sender." He squinted at her again.

Marshall was also beginning to sound like she did when she spoke to Santos.

"Uh huh," Claudia said. The conversation had somehow gotten away from her; she suddenly couldn't remember her plan.

He leveled his eyes at her. "Are you one of those postal inspectors?"

"What? Me? Oh, no."

"Because if you are, I do it just like they trained me, and I been doing it that way for nine years, and if somebody's got a problem—if Will McDonald's got a goddamn problem about coming in here to get his goddamn mail—he can just tell me face-to-face, he doesn't have to call up the goddamn United States Postmaster General to send out some spy."

Claudia held out her hand. "Oh, no, really, I'm not a postal inspector, I promise. I'm just a . . . I'm"—she took a breath and looked him right in the eyes—"I'm just looking for Will McDonald, that's all."

He squinted again.

"I need to find him . . . and I only had General Delivery for his address, and I knew if I asked you, you wouldn't tell me his real address, because you're not supposed to, so I was trying to . . . I don't know . . ." She made a face. "I flunked as a detective."

He pursed his lips.

"And we got off on the wrong foot anyway, because of the teacup. Didn't we?"

"My mother's gonna hate it," he said. He took a step back away from the counter, studied her, his chin down. "You an ex-spouse of Will's or something?"

"No."

" 'Cause I don't want to get mixed up in anything. I sure as hell don't need Will McDonald walkin' in here with a gun."

A gun? Did he walk around with a gun?

She kept her eyes on his. "No, really."

"You're not gonna serve him a paper? You sure don't look like the law."

"No, I'm . . . a relative. I'm just . . . a relative."

"What kind of a relative?"

His long-lost sister from China? His half-cousin from Toledo?

What could she say? Claudia looked at him, and he rubbed his fore-head and pursed his lips at her again. *Veracity, Claudia, it'll get you farther. What's veracity, Daddy? Look it up, John said.*

"I'm his daughter," Claudia said to the postman.

He looked her up and down. "I didn't know Will McDonald had a daughter."

"Well, Marshall . . . there's a possibility that he doesn't know either."

"Goddamn." His eyes lit up. "Talk about a doozy."

Claudia laughed.

"You just gonna surprise him?"

"I haven't quite figured that out."

He chuckled. "Boy, I'd sure like to see that."

Claudia smiled at him.

"Well, I'll tell you," he said, giving her a wide grin. "He lives right up Owens Road."

It was the road that wound up the mountain to the Sierra Nevadas, horses grazing on either side, wide fenced fields, waving stretches of green, huge terra-cotta rocks, and no addresses. He'd told her what to look for, and she'd driven slowly; she didn't want to miss it—a little bend in the road to the right, and then, before the sharp left, you look for it; there'll be a driveway nearly closed off by trees. "He loves trees," Marshall had said, and smirked. "You won't see his truck, you won't see anything, for all the goddamn trees."

She wasn't sure where to put the Volvo; it didn't look like you could just park by the side of the road. She went up a ways and turned the car around, came back down slowly, across from what she thought was the hidden driveway, and stopped. No, that wouldn't work; somebody would hit her going around the curve. She turned again and came back up, pulled off the road as far as possible, parked, killed the motor, and got out. She stood with her back to the Volvo and tried to see through the trees. Nothing. She tucked her T-shirt into her Levi's and ran her hands through her hair. She bent down and checked her face in the side mirror, debated redoing her lipstick, decided against it, and stepped away from the car.

She could go back to L.A. and get her hair cut, she could put on the jeans that made her look thinner, she could come back when she was forty, maybe fifty . . . she could just tell her head to shut up and go. Claudia pushed through branches until she got to it. A crude log fence hidden by foliage that went across a gravel driveway in between the trees. She paused; there was nothing but quiet, a bird singing, wind in the leaves. She put her hand on the fence to lift the latch. The smaller of two rottweilers began a low growl.

"Sweet Jesus," Claudia said under her breath. She stayed where she was but took her hand off the latch. "Hi, puppy," she said, and the larger rottweiler curled his lip. "Okeydokey," Claudia whispered, as she took a slow step backward. The dogs didn't move, they just rumbled, glaring at her from the other side of the fence. She took another step and then another and another, all backward, her eyes on the dogs. She kept going even when she couldn't see them anymore, slamming into branches and brush until her ass finally collided with the fender of the Volvo. She slid along the warm steel, opened the door, and got in the car. Her heart was throwing itself up against her rib cage. She checked her face in the rearview mirror—it was wet and pink. She blotted the sweat off her upper lip and her forehead with the back of her hand, pushed the damp hair away from her face. Well, so much for the surprise theory; as much as it would disappoint Marshall, she wasn't about to get eaten by dogs. *I found these shreds of a unknown woman on my property,* Will could say to Marshall. *Oh, yeah,* Marshall could come back, pursing his lips and grinning. *Well, I know who she was.*

Claudia started the motor, turned the car around, and began down the hill. She couldn't get up to the house if she had to fight rottweilers; she would have to figure out something else. She took a deep breath. Okay, so she didn't know how to be Columbo, but she wasn't about to give up. She would go back to the post office. No. She would go to the restaurant and have a Coke. No. She would go back to the post office and ask Marshall if there was any mail for Will McDonald in that box. Then she would plead with him to let her buy a small rollaway bed and sleep behind the counter until Will came in to get his mail, and if that didn't work she would plead with Marshall's wife, Mary; after all, she did side with her about the tea-cup. She was halfway down the hill when she saw it. "A seventy-two Ford with a short bed," Marshall had told her. "He's got a lot a vehicles, but he mostly drives that truck; it's a half-ton, green." She had no idea what a half-ton was, but the truck that was coming up the hill was definitely green. It passed her; she couldn't make out who was driving. Claudia stopped short in the middle of the road, waited a few minutes trying to make her heart slow, and then turned the car around. He was shutting the fence behind his truck when she pulled up. The dogs began barking. He stood with his hand on the latch and eyed her car. Claudia turned off the ignition and got out.

"That's enough," he said to the dogs, and they were instantly quiet.

She didn't have to ask anybody; she knew it was him.

Tall, with wide shoulders, a white T-shirt visible at the neck of a stained blue work shirt, the sleeves rolled. His skin was tinted nearly chestnut, he had the beginnings of a gut above long legs in worn blue jeans and big feet in scuffed boots, prominent Indian cheekbones like off the face of a coin, a shock of thick silver hair, a silver Yosemite Sam mustache, and Claudia's blue eyes.

This must be what it feels like when you're about to pass out, she thought. She kept one hand on the fender; he took his hand off the fence. All the words were lost in facing him. Hi, you don't know me, but I'm related to you. Ho ho ho. She should have asked Gena to pull up something from one of her scripts. No, she should have written. What had possessed her to think that she could just walk up to somebody and say what she had to say? No, don't write, Claudia; better you should drive four hours into *Bonanza* country and then stand frozen with your foot in your mouth.

"Beautiful day, isn't it?" he said. His voice had the same timbre as the rottweilers.

She hadn't known she'd stopped breathing until she felt herself inhale. He took a couple of steps toward her. There was something wrong with his right leg; either he'd just hurt it or he had a limp.

"Are you lost?" he said.

"No."

"Well, at least we've got that settled." He smiled. Lots of lines around his eyes, deep ones, like cracks on the moon. Blue eyes, the exact shape of hers.

Claudia's eyes filled.

"Are you all right?" he said.

She could feel herself breaking. She shook her head sideways, felt the tears fall, and then shook her head up and down.

"Not sure, huh?" he said softly.

Pieces of the puzzle, all the pieces of the puzzle, the last piece of the puzzle slid into place. A little piece of her that she had seen in Jenny and now a little piece of her that she could see in him.

"I'm Claudia," she said, "my name is Claudia"—breaking like the news footage she'd seen of floodwaters crashing through barricades; she was cracking like a tree splintering into tossed twigs—"but that isn't my real name. My real name is Cole. . . ." His eyes on hers, a small frown gathering on his forehead. "She named me Cole . . ." as if she'd been holding it in since the onset, behind her rib cage, in front of her heart. *You're adopted,* Margaret and John had said to her, ever so gently. Adopted. To take into one's family and raise as one's own. Hadn't she looked it up over and over? Hadn't she told herself over and over since she was six. Where do babies come from? That's what had started it. Babies come from inside their mommies, from something their mommies and daddies do; that's what Billy Shelton said. Is that where I came from, Mommy, inside your tummy? she asked Margaret, and Margaret looked at John. Special, you were special, Claudia, they told her in her yellow room. Special, as in adopted, as in take in. Someone threw her out, and they took her in. Jenny, with her legs tucked under her on the sofa at the Beverly Wilshire: "You can't understand how it was then. I didn't know what else to do." And what about him? Did he even know she existed? "I had no way to tell him. I had no idea where he was." Well, *she* knew where he was now: he was standing in front of her in the middle of nowhere, on the other side of a log fence. Claudia slipped back against the fender. "I'm your daughter," she said to Will.

The frown broke into a dazed look of astonishment. She remembered that but not too much after it, which was probably due to the fact that she couldn't seem to get her legs to work. There was a creek and an overgrown cabin, more trees than her fantasy of Sherwood Forest, and what Claudia thought was probably a fleet of trucks. "Nah, I steal from one to keep another one running," he'd said. "Not all of them work." There were redwood chairs and a table, which looked like they had grown right out of the earth.

"Did you build these?"

"Afraid so."

He gave her water until she got her color back and then lemonade with cracked ice. He'd had his arm around her when he walked her in. His hands were big; strong fingers spread around her waist above her hipbone, and he was solid, she could feel his muscles move under his shirt; he smelled of some long ago aftershave she'd inhaled once in a drugstore and soap and sweat. He put her in a chair and stood next to her until she got control of the shaking. He didn't say anything, he just stood there, his big hand on her shoulder until she was still. Then he went away and came back with the lemonade. He set some packets of Equal down next to the pitcher. "I watch my sugar," he said. He took the chair next to hers; the dogs circled until they saw he was settled, and then they collapsed under the table, as tranquil as lambs.

He stretched his right leg out in front of him, opened a packet of Equal, and sprinkled half in his glass. He folded the open end of the packet neatly and set it on the table between them, took a long drink from the glass. He reached up and smoothed his mustache.

"Hard to know where to begin," he said.

Claudia took a breath, put her hands on the chair arms. "You knew about me."

He took her in with his eyes. "I knew a baby had been born," he said, and then he nodded, smiling. "I didn't know you were a girl."

His eyes were bluer than Claudia's, his smile was disarming; she was having a hard time believing this was real. "How did you know there was a baby?"

"Jenny was pregnant." His face changed. "We were going to get married, did you know that?"

"Yes."

He picked up the folded packet of Equal and turned it around in his hand.

Claudia took a breath. "You knew that a baby had been born?"

"I knew."

But he didn't say more.

"You didn't know what happened to me?"

"No."

"I was adopted."

275

His eyes flickered up to hers.

"In Los Angeles. I grew up in Hancock Park."

He leaned forward. "Los Angeles."

"Uh huh."

He set the packet of Equal back on the table, ran his hand across his face. "That's not what I pictured."

He pictured? He had images of her?

He spread his thumb and fingers out across the ends of his mustache; the tips of three fingers on that hand were missing right below the nails. "I thought she kept you," he said. "I thought you grew up with her."

"No . . . I just found her. This year."

He sat back in the chair; he folded back as if she'd punched him in slow motion. "You just found her," he said.

"Yes."

He didn't move.

"Are you okay?" Claudia said, watching him.

"When?"

"About five months ago, in L.A."

"She lives there?"

"No, I live there. She lives in New York."

The smaller of the rotts got up from under the table, came to his chair, and sat by his leg. She put her paw on his knee. He lifted one hand to the back of her neck, and she moved her head to make it more convenient for him to scratch her ears.

Claudia shifted in the chair. He turned to her. "Are *you* okay?"

"I think so. . . . I don't know what I am."

"You're tellin' me," he said. His face softened. "You look like my mother."

"I do?"

"Your mouth," he said. "What I remember. I don't remember

much . . . but you don't have Jenny's mouth." He lifted his hand, gestured toward the sides of Claudia's lips with his fingers. "My mother," he said, "definitely . . . here and here." He didn't touch her; his fingers floated about an inch away from her, and she moved her head forward until her cheek collided with those fingers. She couldn't stop herself: she tilted her face and leaned her cheek into his hand. She was flooded with the scent of him, his rough fingers grazing her skin, and they sat there for a full minute, Will cradling Claudia's face in the palm of his hand.

The dog's front paws slid out in front of her; she dropped at his feet and plopped her big head on the toe of his boot. They both laughed. Will dropped his hand and they sat there, neither of them speaking. Claudia was stunned by the touch of him. It was different from Jenny; she didn't know what this was, but she was feeling some kind of connection that made no sense.

"I went there." He shook his head and gave a quiet laugh.

"I'm sorry . . ."

"I went to New York."

Claudia had an image of a giant cartoon redwood in cowboy boots walking through clogged theater traffic, horns blaring and taxis screeching as an American Crocodile Dundee with branches and a mustache made his way crosstown. "What were you doing there?"

"Looking for her, her and the baby—you," he said, slowly shaking his head. "Of course, I didn't know where . . ." He stood up. His eyes had shifted off Claudia; they were focused somewhere beyond the cabin. ". . . long time ago; it doesn't matter. . . . You want to see the creek?" The dogs moved to his side, and he stood in front of her, extended his hand.

Claudia sat there. "You were *looking* for Jenny?"

"Sweet baby girl," Will said, his voice low, "I've been looking for Jenny all my life."

Will ran his hand over his eyes. He had to get up and turn on some lamps; it was pitch dark; he'd fallen asleep in his chair. He pushed the lever on his lounger, disentangled himself, stood up straight, and stretched his back. The dogs looked at him. Babe kept her head up, followed him with her eyes as he moved about the cabin, but Sarge fell back to the hook rug immediately and resumed snoring. Will turned on the kitchen light, cupped his hands under the faucet, and had a drink at the sink. He stood at the window, studied the night sky, ran water through his hair and across his face. Talk about a day! That she should be standing there, that he could pull into that drive-way like he'd done a million times and she could be standing there. A full-grown woman. He couldn't imagine it. He had long ago given up hope that he would ever see the child; if they had paid him a million dollars he would never have believed she could be standing there. A girl. Tall as Jenny—nearly as tall as him, for that matter— but different from Jenny: she had a softness, fewer angles, more light. Beautiful. The most beautiful thing he'd ever seen. And Jenny had named her Cole. Will frowned, walked back through the cabin and into his bedroom, sat down at the foot of the bed, and pulled off his boots. He caught his image in the mirror above the oak chest and scoffed. Thirty-five years ago. No telling what Jenny looked like now. He unbuttoned his work shirt, tossed it on a chair by the door, pulled his T-shirt over his head. He ran his thumb along the scar and stared at himself in the mirror. JENNY, he'd carved with a hot 16-inch penny nail he'd hit with a blowtorch. JENNY, he'd burned into the soft flesh on the underside of his upper arm. Will leaned forward. Jenny was out there. He put his head in his hands.

•　　•　　•

Claudia walked across the parking lot of the Frontier Best Western, the finest motel in Lone Tree, the sign said.

"I have room here," he'd said as they left the cabin.

"No, I'd better . . ."

He nodded. "I'll follow you down."

"I can find it, really. I passed it, I remember, right as I came into town."

"I'll follow you."

"But you don't have to."

"What'd I say?" he said, gazing at her.

She smiled. "You said you'd follow me down."

They had dinner at the Lone Tree Café. She had enchiladas rancheras because it was the special and Al, the owner, said he made great rancheras. Will laughed, said he didn't have a hankering for enchiladas, rancheras or no rancheras, and ordered the buffet. She had a glass of wine, he said he didn't drink alcohol; he had iced tea, which he didn't have to order because Stefanie, the waitress, brought it to him as soon as he sat down. Everyone who came into the restaurant acknowledged him.

"Will . . ." A tip of the head from the short man as he passed their table. "Jim . . . ," Will said, tipping back.

"Evening, Will," from a couple in the corner. "Ruth, Brock . . . ," Will said.

"Hey, Will," Al shouted from behind the counter. "You ever get that head for your Corvair pickup? Hoot Clarence said you mighta found somethin' in Markleeville."

"I got it," Will said.

" 'Sixty-two and everything?"

"Yep."

"Well, I'll be."

"Whatcha gonna have tonight?" Stefanie said, giving Claudia the up-and-down.

"This is my daughter, Stefanie," Will said with a sly smile.

She gaped at him and then looked to Claudia.

"Yep," Claudia said.

"Well, you old closed-mouth," she said to Will, laughing. "Hey, Al, guess who this is?" she yelled over her shoulder, and punched Will in the arm.

Claudia circled the small oval swimming pool and plopped into one of the chairs on the tidy stretch of trimmed lawn at the front of the motel. The air was soft, the night was gentle, but her brain was flying and there seemed to be no way to put a cap on it, no way even to stay in the room or try to sleep. He had looked for her and Jenny—it was like neon flashing off and on—he had looked for her: Claudia could see the words lit up next to the stars in the sky.

She sat in the darkness, her mind connecting all the details of him like a line moving from dot to dot. He'd finished everything on his plate and swiped at the last trace of gravy with the last scrap of bread. He put his silverware on his cleaned plate and his empty salad bowl and the small plate that held the bread and butter, and his glass and his napkin, stacked everything by size on top of his plate. With his spoon, he ate the remainder of the salsa Stefanie had brought for Claudia's enchiladas. He added that spoon and the empty salsa dish to the top of the pile, tidied up the table crumbs with another napkin, refolded that dirty napkin and placed it on top of the rest, sat back in the chair. He ran his thumb and his fingers out across opposite sides of his mustache, gazed at her, and grinned.

"We got a lot of years to cover," he said, rocking back on the chair legs. "Tell me about when you were a little girl."

•　•　•

Claudia leaned her head back against the metal lawn chair, slipped her shoes off, and plunged her bare feet into the cold, wet grass. A vast black sky and dazzling fat stars close enough to climb on, some kind of crickets, and cows. Claudia grinned. Who knew cows mooed at night? Cows with white faces and Maybelline eyes. The cows were fenced up to the parking lot, and she'd actually stood there mooing back at them until Will laughed.

He'd walked her to the room and come in with her; he checked the bathroom, took a chair, and brought it with him to the door.

"After I leave, you put this here like this." He leaned the chair over on its back legs and wedged it underneath the knob.

"Are you kidding?"

"You see what I did?"

"Yeah, but . . ." She looked at him. "Is there a lot of robbery in Lone Tree?"

"No."

"You really think I need a chair stuck in the door?"

He didn't say anything.

"I'm a grown woman."

"I see that."

"I thought this was Lone Tree's finest."

He didn't say anything, just stood there.

"That's what it said on the sign," she tried, grinning. "Lone Tree's finest . . ."

He didn't move, just looked at her, his hand on the chair.

"Okay," she said.

Claudia smiled under her hands, which covered her face. She ran them back through her hair and squinted at the moon until she couldn't see it anymore.

She'd told him about when she was a little girl. Sister Anne, she'd told him, and her first communion and how she threw up all over her white dress, and about when Gena transferred to her school and they both got stung by bees and how she woke up at night for months afterward, thinking bees were in her room, and how she was afraid to put her fingers on the escalator railing at Bullock's Wilshire, no matter what Grandma Mae said, because she knew the escalator would take her with it when it slid back into the floor, how her yellow room looked and all the ruffles, and how her bed was so high that Margaret had a little stool for her to stand on but the needle-point flowers on it itched her feet so that when she stood on it she had to wear socks, and how she loved to read from the moment she'd put the letters together, and about her rabbit, Captain, which was a name for a dog, but they wouldn't let her have a dog because some-body was supposed to be allergic but she never could find out who that was, and how Margaret would let Claudia eat all the crusty cara-mel *and* the cherries off the top of her pineapple-upside-down cake before anybody else, and how after Margaret had read the last good-night story and given them the last drink of water she told her and Gena they would go to Sleepytown, up out of their beds and over the tops of all the houses, flying on baby angels' wings to what Marga-ret said was the only place where Jesus slept, and how John taught her to swim without water wings and taught her how to ride her bike without training wheels and taught her how when it was a grounder to go down on one knee to block the ball so it wouldn't get past her and *then* scoop it up, and how the first time she saw Ollie he was shooting baskets in New York and his hair fell over his forehead and he was allergic to pecans and that was the first thing she'd made for him, pecan pie, and he said he'd nearly eaten it because he didn't want to disappoint her, wasn't that sweet, and the first time she saw Lily, when Dr. Brooks pulled her out and how she wasn't crying, her big eyes wide open and still attached to Claudia, her little hands punching the air, and how she'd always pictured him, Will, that is, how she'd always pictured him from the time they told her, sat her down in the yellow room and told her, Margaret and John . . .

. . . And Al was standing, silent and patient, at the corner of their table; she didn't realize he was standing there until Will put his fingers quietly on her arm.

"Sorry, Will," Al said. "Betty's rented herself some lovey-dovey movie." He made a face. "I gots to go. . . ."

"Sure, Al," Will said. He left money on the table, and when she opened her wallet he gave her a steady look and she closed the wallet and put it back in her purse. It had turned dark while she was talking, and the restaurant had emptied. Even Stefanie had vanished. Just the two of them and Al.

He held the Volvo's door open for her, took the key out of her hand and unlocked the door and held it, stood there while she got in and relocked it, then followed behind her in his truck to the motel. Claudia watched his headlights in her rearview mirror. She hadn't stopped talking, he hadn't stopped listening. He'd never interrupted, he'd never made a comment, he'd just let her go on and on. An occasional smile, a nod, a grimace, depending on what she had said, his face when she talked about Lily. "She looks like you." The smile that touched his eyes. "She does, huh?" He'd laughed hard when she tried to imitate Gena, but he hadn't spoken, he'd just listened, to every word.

He stood next to her while she registered and then went with her to the room. He said he'd pick her up in the morning, eight, was that okay? Didn't want to waste the day away. They'd have breakfast and then he had some things to show her, maybe she'd like to go up Mount Whitney, maybe he'd take her to Darwin, well, wait a minute, he didn't mean to be pushy, could she stay?

Stay? Was he being funny? Of course she could stay.

"What about your family?"

"They'll be fine."

"The baby and everything? your husband?"

"Ollie."

He nodded. "Ollie."

"They're fine." She paused. "Darwin?"

He stood at the motel door. "Where my mother was born." He reached his hand out, his fingers grazing her shoulder. "She was an Indian, you know, half Shoshone." He stood there, buying time, choosing his words. "I'm sorry I missed everything when you were little," he said, and took a step backward, hooked his thumb into the top of his jeans pocket. "Good night, baby girl," he said as he shut the door.

Claudia pushed herself up out of the lawn chair, yawned a big, wide yawn, kissed the palm of her hand, and blew the kiss off her palm to the Seven Sisters. She took her shoes in her hand and walked back to the room, barefoot across the asphalt. He wouldn't like it, she thought, if he knew she was walking around out there alone. She mooed at the cows. They mooed back. She shut the door and locked it, and then she shoved the chair under the doorknob, and then she laughed out loud. She stripped off all her clothes and left them in a heap on the floor, pulled back the bedcovers, threw herself across the sheets, and rolled over on her back. She wasn't going to brush her teeth, she decided. She wasn't going to wash her face. She wasn't going to do anything. Claudia pulled up the covers, reached for the phone, and dialed Ollie. She couldn't stop smiling. She felt six years old.

Will got up at five, fed the dogs, and began his watering. He started with the poplars, worked his way back through the cherry trees, and ended up hosing down the truck. Then he showered and shaved, got dressed, and went to get her. He had to pace himself, because he'd wanted to pick her up hours ago, call her and say, "I'm coming now." To look at her, to hear her . . . he couldn't get over it; he felt as high as if he'd won megabucks in Vegas; no, richer, Will thought, because he'd gotten back something he would have sworn was forever lost to him, he'd gotten back his child.

She was waiting by the cows when he pulled up and got out of the truck. "You like all animals, or are you just partial to cows?"

She laughed. "I've never been this close to cows before."

She was holding a plastic coffee cup and wore jeans and a pale-blue T-shirt with a V at the neck. Her skin was golden. The sun had come over the mountains and painted everything a rich red-gold; it filtered through her hair and hit her smile. She took Will's breath away; he didn't move.

"I should have brought Lily," she said.

He didn't answer.

"To play with the cows." She watched him. "Is something the matter?"

"No."

"Good morning," Claudia said, and she leaned forward and kissed his cheek by the side of his nose.

They ate breakfast at the same restaurant where Claudia had eaten the day before. It was just as crowded, and nearly everyone gave a nod or a hello to Will. The same waitress sashayed up to their table, held her pen poised over her pad.

"Whatcha gonna have this morning, honey?" she said to Claudia, and then her eyes shifted. "How ya doin', Will?"

"Fine, Leona."

"Basted? Splash a gravy?"

"Yep."

"Toast or an English?"

"I'll have an English this morning, Leona."

She tilted her head at Claudia.

"French toast," Claudia said, "*with* syrup."

"Atta girl," Leona said. She winked at Claudia and walked away.

Claudia put sugar in her coffee, stirred it. "Everybody knows you."

"Been here awhile."

"How long?"

" 'Sixty-eight."

"You moved here in 'sixty-eight?"

"No; bought the first piece of the property, still lived in L.A., came up bit by bit."

She lowered her coffee cup. "You lived in L.A.?"

He nodded.

"We *both* lived in L.A.?"

"Afraid so."

"My God. Where?"

"Burbank."

"What did you do there?"

"Drove for the pictures."

"The movies?"

"That's right."

She shook her head. "I can't believe it—we both lived in L.A."

Brown dirt and California shrubs and nothing, miles of nothing—an expanse of flat, brown nothing that jammed abruptly into jutting, dark-bronze, huge round rocks.

"It goes on forever," Claudia said.

Blue sky, wispy streaks of clouds, and dry wind; the truck kicked up a lot of dust. They were on a rough dirt road winding between the mountains; she could feel the grit on her face and the sun burning her arm.

"Hell of a shortcut," Will said, laughing, and she turned toward him. He took one hand off the wheel and adjusted the side mirror.

"It's gorgeous," she said.

"Most wouldn't use that word."

"What would they say?"

"Desolate, I guess; barren . . . whatever they use when they describe desert."

"I think it's beautiful," Claudia said.

"That's 'cause you come from a long line of desperadoes—you have a feeling for the land."

"So," Claudia said, laughing, "am I an official desperado now?"

"Yep, just like me."

They'd been to Darwin. She seen the leftover shafts of the silver mines, fleeting glints of sparkle nestled in the mountains that flashed your eye and then the boarded-up ghost town where her grandmother had been born, a cluster of wood shacks surrounded by barbed wire. He pulled the truck over, and they got out.

"That's where they made the Indians live," he said, his legs spread, hands clasped behind his back. She watched the set of his jaw.

"Separate from everybody else?"

"Uh huh,"

"Can't we go up there?" She held one hand flat over her eyebrows to cut off the glare.

Will laughed. "When's the last time you broke through barbed wire, honey?"

"Never."

He studied the boarded-up settlement carved into the slope of the mountain. "They probably got some kind of security. . . ."

"If we get caught, I could say I'm an archaeologist—no, that I'm doing a piece for a newspaper . . . a magazine . . ."

"Yeah? Who am I? Your bodyguard?"

Claudia looked him up and down. "No, you're my . . . tour guide."

Will eyes flashed, and he was laughing. "Good girl," he said.

He unsnapped the black tarp cover on the bed of the truck, took out his wire clippers, and they were in. She took his hand and they scaled the mountain; he went first and she made it mostly by putting her shoes into the tracks of his boots. Falling-down shanties, bits of crockery, dirt, dust, bent pots and pans, shredded tufts of bedding on collapsed cots, a twisted spoon, a piece of cup, a rip of photograph, and, in the corner of one square that was possibly a foot larger than Claudia's walk-in linen closet, the remains of a china doll. She crouched and rescued it, cradled it on her bent knees. Will watched her; she looked up at him.

"Do you know which one your mother lived in?"

He shook his head.

"Did you ever come up here?"

"Never."

The only sound was the wind through the empty hovels and his boots on the packed dirt floor.

"What was she like?"

"Oh, honey . . ."

"Anything," she said.

"Honey, I was only five when she died." He wet his lips; the lines around his eyes deepened. "I don't remember much."

She held his gaze.

"Long black hair," he finally said.

"Black? Not blond like yours was?"

"Black"—he took a step—"down to her waist; she kept it up with something. . . ." He raised his hands to the back of his head.

"Combs?"

"Yeah, maybe. I saw her take it down."

"Oh, Will."

"And . . . she'd do anything you wanted." He hesitated. "That's it . . . all my memories." She was quiet, he extended his hand. "Let's get out of here."

Claudia placed the doll carefully back in the corner and reached up for his hand.

Now he was concentrating, maneuvering the truck through the ruts, a piece of silver hair flopped on his forehead, a shine of sweat on the front of his throat.

She touched his arm. "So what's the first thing you did as a desperado?"

"Well, I didn't break into a ghost town. I stole cigars from the corner store."

"How old were you? A teenager?"

"Six."

"You weren't."

"Oh, yes I was."

"Six?"

"Yep, and I never got caught either. The first time I got caught was for a bag of red hots." He frowned. "I think I was eight."

"What did they do to you?"

"Oh, the shopkeeper threatened me, said he'd tell my mother. . . ." Claudia's eyes on his. "He didn't know that she was dead. . . . Hey, I bet you've never been this dirty."

Claudia brushed her hand across her cheek, tilted down the visor and looked at her face in the glass. "Will, Marshall acted like he was afraid you were going to come into the post office and shoot him."

Will moved his eyes to the road.

"Was he kidding?" Claudia said.

"I wouldn't know."

The truck bumped over some bad parts. She pushed the visor back, held on to the window ledge, and watched him drive, his hands on the wheel, his hands that looked like her hands, wide nails with deep beds, a small brown birthmark by the knuckle of the second finger on his right hand, just like hers.

"Did you use to carry a gun?"

"Sometimes."

"Why?"

"I thought I was a tough guy."

"I'm serious."

"Sweet baby," Will said, turning to look at her, "so am I."

"Now *you* tell me about when *you* were little," Claudia said, and he laughed.

"Not much to tell. How 'bout when I was big?"

She turned her head, her eyes on his, slid the porch chair a little closer. "Tell me about you and Jenny."

"Me and Jenny," he said.

"Yeah."

"She was beautiful and I loved her and I messed up. Enough said."

"That's it? That's all you're going to tell me?"

"Right now."

She could ask him, this could be the moment, she could ask him about the money, why he took it, why he left them, she could ask him everything. His eyes were steady on hers. She took a breath. She couldn't; she wasn't ready to see what would happen, not yet.

She moved in the chair. "Tell me about when you were in jail."

His face changed. "You don't want to know about that."

"Yes I do."

"Why?"

She pressed him, said it was part of him; she said she wanted to know, and so he told her, but just a little; he figured he could tell her a little, as long as he skimmed it as he went. Clearing firebreaks high in the mountains, "that was at Preston," working for cigarettes: "They didn't give us any money, kid, just cigarettes." He relaxed a little in the chair. "I haven't thought about any of this for a long time," he said, sitting across from her on his porch, and the truth of it was, this was the first time he'd ever told anybody since Jenny, nobody'd ever been close enough to tell since then.

"Twelve four-oh-four," he said, and Claudia leaned forward.

"What's that?"

He leveled his eyes at her. "That's my number, honey. California Youth Authority number twelve four-oh-four—that's me."

She didn't waver, she didn't flinch in the chair.

Lifting weights, that was harmless, he could tell her about that: "Me and Arnold Schwarzenegger," he said, and flexed his arm like in one of those ads in a magazine, and she laughed. And working on the front gate—"That was at Mira Loma"—and how you had to fight to get a job, fight to hold on to it, always watch your ass. There was nothing wrong in telling her that, that was stuff you could pass on to your kid, and then he remembered and told her about escaping from Preston with this other guy and how they'd hitchhiked all the way to Santa Cruz, free and clear, but when they got drenched in a rainstorm they built a fire on the floor of an abandoned school to get warm, and of course the cops came. "Some desperadoes, huh?" He laughed. "What was I then? Lemme see . . . fifteen?"

"What else?" she said, sitting forward. She loved the way the light caught his face.

Working in the kitchen, he told her. "Hundred-pound sacks of potatoes, baby, a little peeler and me." His boot heels angled into the porch floor, his chair tipping back. "I got so good they let me cook for the brass," and he smiled. "Course, I only know how to cook for a whole lot of folks, if you know what I mean." How he was lucky to have landed a job in the kitchen, how he got it only because he had friends, which wasn't really true, because he wouldn't call those guys friends, he never had friends, he made it a rule never to get close enough to anybody to call them friend. And then he started telling her about D Company, and that led to the football games, not exactly prep school football, he said, and then he remembered, and then he knew he couldn't be telling her any of this, he knew this was wrong, this telling her, and his eyes changed and he leveled the chair. The memories were colliding into each other too goddamn fast, and he was having trouble cleaning them up before they came out. Claudia's eyes on him, blue and steady. He'd better shut up. These were things she didn't need to know, these were things he didn't want her to know, these were things a man didn't tell his daughter, that much he suddenly realized. Football games between the laundry guys and the kitchen guys, how when the laundry guys lost they were so pissed they sent the kitchen guys' shirts back shredded with razor blades, so he and the rest of the kitchen guys shredded up a little glass and put it in their stew. Cut up their insides and put 'em in the hospital. How they got their shirts back looking real nice from then on. Was that a bedtime story daddies told their little girls?

"Will?"

Was he going to tell her about how he saw a man get stabbed over a peanut butter and jelly?

"What's the matter, Will?"

The way the knife handle stuck out of his eye.

"Will?"

The sound the handle made when the guy fell facedown into the slop on his plate.

292

He got up from the chair. Was he going to tell her about the fight he got into at San Quentin, how they'd stamped "Agitator" across the front of his prison file, "Needs Continual Watching," because a guy got hit in the back of the head with some flying bread and he thought it was Will who threw it, so the guy bad-mouthed him and Will couldn't take any bad-mouthing, no way, you better not do anything to cross Will McDonald, so after dinner one night he waited for the guy in south block and when he came through the rotunda Will grabbed him and gave him four blows to the throat. Is that what he wanted to tell his baby?

Claudia studied him, his pallor, the silence, his right hand hovering in the air between them, the fingers locked tight, how the hand was trembling and then he ran it across his face.

Was that one of the fatherly things he wanted to teach her? Here, let me pass this on to you, honey, and you can pass it on to your little Lily; let Daddy teach you how to nearly kill a man.

"Will?"

"That's enough," Will said.

"But . . ."

"It's finished."

"I only . . ."

"Hey. What'd I say?" He lowered his eyes to hers, picked up his iced tea, and went into the house.

"Come home, Mommy," Lily said on the telephone.

Claudia's heart lurched. She was suddenly filled with such a longing for her child, she practically fell down. Will listened from a chair out on the porch, his hand on Babe's head.

"Tomorrow, sweetheart."

"Now."

"Tomorrow, I promise, when you get home from nursery school. Where's Grandma?"

"When I wake up?"

"When you wake up from your nap I'll be there. Where's your daddy?"

"I did all the sprinkles on the cookies."

"You did?"

"Not Gramma, me."

"That's wonderful."

"I'm her number one," and then she was giggling. "Grampa, no, no, no," and then she said something that was muffled.

"Lily, let me talk to your daddy."

"He's not home. Grampa's eating the cookies," and then she shrieked with laughter and the phone fell with a loud clunk and John said, "Hello, hello?" John's voice in her ear and she was looking at Will who was watching her and Claudia said, "Hello."

"Hello, sweetheart, how's the spa?"

It took her a few seconds to recover. Ollie must have told them she'd gone to a spa.

"It's wonderful."

"I bet you're not doing the morning hikes, though, are you?"

"Uh . . . no."

"I knew it. I told your mother you wouldn't get up unless they came into your room with a trumpet."

"Mm hmm."

"So you're being healthy and we're sitting here eating cookies— Hey, Lily, watch out with that."

"So what are you guys doing there?"

"Oh, Oliver had some parent-teacher thing, and Santos's car blew up—something with the radiator this time. She's going to have to get a new car, Claudie, I told you that, didn't I? That damn Nissan is on its last leg."

"Uh huh."

"Lily, not too much icing there. . . . Margaret, get her."

"What's she doing?"

"Putting icing all over my— Lily, no . . ."

"Could you ask Ollie to call me when he gets home?"

"Don't do too much on those weight machines; you'll come back looking like a lady wrestler."

Claudia could hear her mother laughing. "Okay, Dad," she said.

Dad, she said, and hung up the phone, lifting her face to Will's eyes through the window screen.

"This is my favorite time of day," he said, from the purple shadow, "the way the light goes." He stood up. "Come on. We'll take a walk, and then we'll eat. You like barbecue?"

He fixed her barbecued ribs that he'd left marinating since that morning, just in case she liked barbecue, he said. He cooked while she watched, and there were so many things that she'd planned to ask him, but it was as if the quiet in the cabin was a part of him, and all the questions that Claudia knew she had to ask seemed to dim.

"This is all I've got to show you," Will said, as he handed her an envelope.

Her grandmother's hair was dark in the sepia print, and she didn't have their light eyes, but Claudia's mouth was definitely his mother's, he was right—Claudia's mouth and the shape of her face were right there in front of her, frozen by a camera long before she was born. Claudia lifted her eyes to Will and then lowered them to the photograph. She looked at it for a long time, sat on his sofa and studied this little lost piece of herself, and he sat across from her and didn't say a word.

"Guess I'll have to come down to L.A. and see that little Lily of yours."

"You certainly will. What about tomorrow?"

"Tomorrow?" He laughed. "I don't think so."

"Why not?"

He moved his big frame, and the lawn chair creaked. "I don't want to step on anybody's toes, honey."

"Will . . . " She leaned forward. "I have a place for you in my life, Will."

"Well, that's good. I appreciate it." He turned his face into the shadows. "Can't say how much I appreciate it. . . ." His voice trailed off, and then he said, "I'll be down."

"But not tomorrow?"

"Well, maybe I better read up on this grandpa business first; I've never been a grandpa before." She caught the shine in his eyes. "Now look, it's best you leave early enough tomorrow to get through Palmdale/ Lancaster before their morning traffic, or late enough so when you get there it's through. No reason to have to deal with all those people on the road unless you have to."

"Whatever you say," she said. "I wonder where my cows are."

"Probably gone to visit somebody in Bishop."

Claudia laughed. They sat facing each other in the lawn chairs on the square of grass by the parking lot of the Best Western, only them and the night and the stars.

"I reek of barbecue."

"It's no wonder," Will said. "I thought I was the only man alive who could eat a whole slab of ribs without breathing. We'll have to hose you down."

"You have my number."

"Yep," he said, tapping the slim book he carried in his shirt pocket.

"And you'll come down?"

"What'd I say?"

Claudia studied the outline of his mustache and his jawbone in shadow. A cow mooed. "Hey," Claudia said, laughing.

"Those cows got a thing for you."

The movement of the leaves in the poplars, the feel of her bare feet in the grass. "There are so many things we didn't talk about. . . ."

"What?"

"Lots of things . . . everything . . . "

"Okay. Go ahead."

She laughed. "I don't know where to begin now."

"First thing that crosses your mind."

"How'd you lose the tips of your fingers?"

"With a saw."

"Oh."

"Damn thing got away from me is all."

And then she knew that this was the moment. She wasn't sure how to ask him, but she knew she had to, she couldn't leave without asking, she needed to know. "Will?"

"What?"

"There's something I need to ask you."

He was quiet.

"It's hard, but I need to say it . . . I need to know."

"Shoot," he said.

She sat there a moment. "Will, if you loved Jenny so much and you wanted to be with her and the baby—"

"You," he said.

"Me . . . if you wanted to be with Jenny and me, Will"—she took a breath, looked him square in his face—"how could you take the money?"

The creak of the lawn chair, his eyes catching the moonlight as he sat up straight. "What money?"

Claudia stared at him. "The money . . . the money they gave you . . . to go away."

He stood up fast, his bad leg nearly buckling out from under him. He grabbed for the lawn chair and it keeled over, making a soft *plop* in the wet grass.

"Jesus," he said.

"What?"

"Those fucking bastards."

Claudia's heart was slamming up against her ribs. "What?" She wanted to reach for him, but the look in his eyes stopped her. "You didn't take the money? Will?"

"I'll kill them," he said.

He took off across the grass and Claudia ran after him, her shoes left lying on their sides by the fallen lawn chair.

He would pick Jenny up at six in front of the dancing school. He'd already cleared everything out of the apartment—it didn't take long; all he owned was a fistful of clothes. He'd picked up both checks: had worked a double shift at Joe's and asked Joe if he could get his check early—Joe laughed, asked if he was getting ready for a big night—and then he'd stopped by old man Boyer's and gotten that check too. He'd go to the bank and be waiting for her, right out front in plenty of time: when he crossed Seventy-fifth and Ward Parkway, the clock on the tower read ten after five.

He was going to marry Jenny; everything was okay; his life had changed. And he felt okay about the baby too. It would be hard, yeah, to have a baby when they were just starting out, it wasn't the way he would have planned it, but he would make the best of it, better than the best—he would be a dad and a husband and take care of them; that was the way it was. Will's eyes shifted to the rearview mirror, and then back to the car in front of him. He'd never felt about anybody the way he felt about Jenny; just having her look at him, that was all it took. He moved his fingers lightly around the Mercury's steering wheel and waited for the light to turn green. Ought to take about four, four and a half hours to get to Pryor, Oklahoma. They'd get a room, be married first thing in the morning. He wasn't about to take any chances with her parents, especially not with the mother, who was all revved up to make Jenny have an abortion—what kind of a mother would make a daughter have an abortion? Well, she wasn't gonna get her hands on her. That was his baby inside her; he wasn't about to let anybody hurt Jenny or his baby, not while he was standing. No, sir. He did a little drumbeat on the wheel. . . . first thing in the morning, they'd be waiting at the justice of the peace, and by breakfast they'd be Mr. and Mrs. William McDonald. Will grinned into the air and hit the accelerator as the light turned green.

It was one of the few times in his life he hadn't been paying attention. A plain brown Dodge with two plainclothesmen, but Will didn't see them; he had Jenny decked out in a wedding dress in front of his eyes. They got him before he made it to the bank's doorway; they cuffed him spread-eagled, facedown across the dirty Dodge fender. The skinny one laughed when he begged them to at least drive by where she was standing, so that he could explain. "It's only five minutes from here, just five minutes. . . ."

"Well, we ain't got five minutes, buddy, and you're not goin' anywhere except L.A. That'll teach you to violate your damn parole."

They sat for three hours at the Kansas City airport, waiting for the plane to California, and Will never stopped asking them. He tried everything he could think of, until the skinny one finally threw up his hands. "Jeez, Pete, I'm gettin' sick of this kid's sob story; let him make the damn phone call." Pete stayed cuffed to him as Will dropped the money into the pay phone, Pete reeking of peppermint Life Savers and yesterday's coffee, and Will swallowed the flood of nausea and tried to turn his back to the man. His hand was wet on the receiver and his heart was fast and the phone rang three times, and when she answered he said, "Please, Mrs. Jaffe, please let me talk to her," and Jenny's mother quietly hung up the phone. He was standing there sweating, cuffed to that cop, and he knew then that it was them, they had to have done this, her parents. The cops wouldn't tell him anything, but in Will's guts he knew. Maybe Jenny had let something slip, but somehow her parents had found out, because in all the minutes of all the hours, unless somebody tipped them, how could they know to pick him up just then?

They took him back, threw him in L.A. County for sixty days, and then they moved him to DuVal in Lancaster. Dormitories like army barracks, fifty beds to a dorm, and he knew some of the guys from Mira Loma, but it wasn't like when he'd been in before. When he'd got caught the second time he didn't care if he went back, because he truly missed the place, but that was all changed now. He didn't need discipline, he didn't need rules. He had one goal and one goal only: do his time so he could get out; find Jenny and the baby. That was it.

Every letter came back to him—*Return to Sender, Addressee Unknown*—and the next time he was allowed a phone call, the number had changed. He figured that by the time he got out they would have probably even moved. Everything was up to the parole board, and the parole board said one year. One year in DuVal if he was a good boy. One year if he minded his manners and watched his ass. One year if he could keep his head on. The day they told him one year was the day he went for the nail and the blowtorch instead of smashing someone in the head. It didn't matter that he hadn't broken any laws in Kansas City; he'd left California without saying *Mother, may I,* and that was breaking the rules. He'd left California, he'd found Jenny and loved her, and that love had made a baby. So you're gonna have to eat it, boy, you're gonna have to pay big time, because the penalty for wanting love in your life is one year.

He got out of DuVal in August 1961, one year, just like they'd promised. He'd done it, kept his mind focused, got a job in the kitchen, held on to it, and gotten into only two fights. You just had to watch your back, you had to pay attention, and you had to make sure you never let any of 'em know when they got to you, but Will figured that worked for your whole life, not just jail. Don't let anybody ever know when they got to you, no matter what. They let him out on a Monday morning at dawn, just after the light broke, and put him on a bus to L.A.

"Once a month, boy."

"Yes, sir."

"I don't mean phone calls. I want to see your face."

"Okay."

"So you gotta be here. In California. In Los Angeles."

Will didn't say anything.

"I mean it," D. Francis said. That's what the cheap sign said on his cheap desk in the Parole Office in downtown L.A. Will did not ask him what the D. stood for, he just said, "Yes, sir," to the cheap suit and the greasy hair of D. Francis, walked out of his office, and left for Kansas City that afternoon: stood at the interchange, propped his boot on his duffel, and stuck out his thumb. He'd just go there. He'd find her no matter what. He caught a ride to the truck stop in

Ontario and was lucky enough, not ten minutes later, to hitch a lift with a trucker heading for El Paso on the 10. The trucker said he was in a big *mondo* hurry. Will said, "Hey, it works for me." He had one month to find Jenny and the baby. If there was a baby; if they hadn't made her have an abortion: he'd been worrying about that all year. He leaned his head back against the passenger seat of the trucker's cab and closed his eyes. One month to go to Kansas City and find them and bring them back to California so he could make the meeting with D. Francis, and if his luck held, that would be all the time he would need.

They still lived there. Jenny's old man backed the Buick out of the driveway seven-thirty sharp in the morning, when he went to play golf. The old lady didn't show her face until around eleven. She backed the powder-blue Olds down slow as honey and ran over the curb, just like always. Will had to laugh: the tire ruts in the clipped lawn were even deeper than they were the year before. He followed her to the Plaza; all she had to do was look up into her rearview mirror, she would have seen him—didn't she remember the car? Will ran his hand along the dash. Good old Mercury, thanks to Joe, who'd kept it on ice for him the whole time he'd been at DuVal. When he called him from L.A. County, he'd told Joe to drive it, but Joe had laughed. "I wouldn't be caught dead in that heirloom a yours, kid. Don't worry; Becker and I'll drain it, put it up on blocks until you get out." And here it was, just like he left it; Joe and Becker had even got the kid at old man Boyer's to give it a tune-up and a polish for his big return. He'd offered to pay them— he had a little money left from Aunt Cleo; she'd talked to him once a month at DuVal and she'd sent him a little money now and then—but Joe gave him a smirk. "Don't say I never gave you anything, kid." Will was going to surprise Jenny; he would drive up to wherever she was in the Merc.

The old lady parked behind one of those fancy department stores, and it took her about ten minutes to get out of the damn car. She was balancing a purse and gloves and the car keys and trying to put on her jacket, and she was wearing some dumb hat that kept listing over her right eye, and she had a great big present that was all wrapped up with a pink bow and the card fell away from under the ribbon and he moved in front of her, scooped it up off the pavement, and extended it in his hand.

"Oh, thank you," she said, taking it, her eyes glued to the card. She had that soft trace of accent; she was much smaller than Jenny, shorter with a littler frame, everywhere. She had probably been a looker once upon a time, Will thought. He hated her. She touched the hat with the cherries, tilted her chin up to give him a big thank-you smile, full-on.

"Where's Jenny, Mrs. Jaffe?" Will said.

Something came out of her mouth in German—he didn't know, but it was probably curse words. She went white behind her powder and the red on her cheeks and dropped her purse. Will bent down and picked it up, tucked it under his arm.

"You got a little case of the dropsy today, huh?"

"Give me my purse."

It was amazing that she could talk with her lips pulled tight like that; she looked like one of those ventriloquists that made the dummy talk while they drank water—Paul Winchell, in a cherry hat and gloves.

"Where's Jenny?"

"Give me my purse,"

"Hey, I was only going to help you carry. You don't seem to be managing so well yourself."

She kept her eyes down.

And then he couldn't wait anymore. The questions he woke up with every morning and went to bed with every night, the questions that plagued him and were the only thing that kept him going—they were about to blow off the top of his head. "Mrs. Jaffe, please, did Jenny have the baby? Is she okay?"

She didn't answer, her lips still slits, her eyes matching.

"It's my baby, Mrs. Jaffe. I have a right, you know."

"You have no rights," she whispered.

Okay, so it wasn't going to be easy. He had to be careful, figure out his strategy. He took a step and walked around her. He'd take his time, ask her, let her see . . . And then it changed, the air changed, and Will knew it didn't matter what he did, because he could feel her fear. It was thick and coming off her, stronger than perfume. He knew what to do when you wanted something from people who were afraid of you; he hadn't spent a whole year at DuVal for nothing; he'd learned a thing or two.

"It wasn't very nice, your not taking my phone call," he started. Oh, yeah, he started like a real big shot, but then his eyes filled, so fast he couldn't stop it, the memories sharp in his heart. "The one from the airport." He choked back the thing in his throat and tossed his head. "What did you tell her, huh? Tell her I just skipped out? Left her standing there like she was nothing? Is that what you said?"

"I'm not afraid of you," Mrs. Jaffe said.

"Yeah? Well, you sure are doin' a good job of looking like it. What did I ever do to you, huh? Tell me. All I ever did was love her, that's all I ever did."

The parking lot had been pretty quiet, there weren't too many Lookie Lous, but then two broads who'd gotten out of a Chrysler were walking by, pushing a baby in one of those things. They smiled.

"How're you doing?" he said, smiling back at them. Mrs. Jaffe raised her eyes, and he put his hand on her arm. Very gently. "Give me the package, Mom," he said, loud enough for them to hear. "I'll carry it for you."

He waited until they'd moved through the glass doors into the store. Okay, so he wouldn't be a tough guy because he couldn't be a tough guy, but he had to know where Jenny was.

"I don't want to do anything to you. Please. I'm sorry. You don't ever have to see me again. I just want to know where Jenny is, then I'll leave you alone."

She leveled her eyes at him. The hat was crooked; the brim covered her eyebrow, and one cluster of cherries was hanging down. He touched it with his finger, gave it a little push. It was the truth; she would see how much he loved Jenny; she wouldn't say no.

"I'll never tell you where Jenny is," Mrs. Jaffe said. "You'll have to kill me first."

His body froze. He wanted to pitch forward, ram his hand through her face. He staggered. It was just for an instant. "Hey, Mrs. Jaffe," he said, "I'm surprised at you—*you*, of all people, certainly know I'm not a killer, I'm just a thief."

She inhaled, a sharp sound like she was choking; maybe she would just croak right there in the parking lot. He took her purse out from under his arm, placed it delicately on top of the wrapped package with the pink ribbon, and walked away. He drove the Mercury from the Plaza, headed south on Ward Parkway. He would go either to Sherry, Jenny's friend, or to the dancing school.

He hadn't been sure until he got out of DuVal, and he'd practically had to kiss D. Francis's ass to get the information, but in his heart of hearts Will always knew it had to be her folks. Otherwise none of it made any sense. Without somebody meddling, California would have never spent the bucks to go to Kansas City to pick him up and bring him back, not some *nobody* with a few months left on his parole for a penny-ante robbery; they wouldn't have spent the bucks or the time, he knew that, they would have let him go. And then there was the timing: it was just too on the nose that they should pick him up just as he was on his way to get her.

"Alrighty, let's see here. . . . I don't know why I'm doin' this for you, boy," D. Francis had said, moving his greasy fingers through Will's file.

He'd always figured it had to be the old lady; the old man didn't look like he had the balls. Will stayed steady at thirty-five in the left lane. Her, him—what was the difference?

"Let's see here," D. Francis had said, and Will had leaned forward. "Uh . . . Mr. and Mrs. Moses Jaffe, it says here, made the complaint." He frowned and narrowed his eyes. "Hmm, never heard of anybody named Moses 'cept in the Bible. What kind of a thing is that?"

Mr. and Mrs. Moses Jaffe. Well, that blew the suspicion, didn't it? Now he knew for sure. Mr. and Mrs. Moses Jaffe took themselves to some hot Jew lawyer because he'd gotten their baby pregnant, maybe thought they could get him for statutory rape or something, as if Jenny was fourteen, as if he would do that to a fourteen-year-old girl. And as if she was still a virgin, which, of course, she wasn't but they wouldn't have known that, that he wasn't the first. Not that that mattered as far as Will was concerned, he was the first. He was the first one to love her, she was the first one to love him. That was the real first. She was his everything, but who had cared about that? The only thing anybody cared about was getting him out of the picture, and all it took was one little meeting with one lawyer and the lawyer running Will's name through the red tape and there it was. It must have jumped out at them all wrapped up as pretty as the package with the pink ribbon. Their big chance to save Jenny, all because he'd been stupid, because he'd left California, because he'd violated his parole. With that information they could make more than trouble, they could destroy the two of them, wipe him away like chalk on a blackboard. They could have him picked up and sent back to California. And they did.

He had no way of knowing what they had said to her, he couldn't fathom it. As much as he thought about it, he never could. All he knew was that he'd told her the truth in every letter, in every letter that they had returned.

It was a toss-up between Sherry and the dancing teacher; he wasn't about to try and get anything out of Jenny's old man. She'd told him all about the guy's seven million heart attacks, how he carried a little bell around the house with him in case he got up in the middle of the night to get a drink of water and an attack hit him while he was in front of the sink, he could ring the bell. Will took a right off Ward Parkway at Ninety-fifth Street. He sat waiting for the light to change at State Line. Sherry was probably his best bet; he decided, at least he knew her a little bit. The dancing teacher had never even said hello to him, just given him the fish eye whenever she saw him, slithering around in that little pink thing, her hand clamped on her cane.

Sherry had already left for college. The University of Illinois, her mother said, in Urbana. Was he in her class at Southwest? She didn't remember him; she was so sorry; had they gone out?

"No, we were just kind of buddies," Will said.

"Oh, now wait a minute," she said, and got all smiley-faced. Maybe she did remember—was he the William who was on the football team?

Sure, why not? He could have been a football star if he'd had a chance. "That's me," Will said.

"Oh, you were quite the popular one, weren't you?" She crossed her arms in front of her, kind of squashing her breasts. "I didn't know you and Sherry were friends. I remember her mentioning you, but that was only when she went to the games. . . ."

Will kept his hand steady on the open screen door. "Well, we had some classes together, talked on the phone mostly; she kind of helped me out when I was having this thing with . . . this girl."

"You sure you don't want to come in? Have a Coke?"

"Oh, no, thank you. I have to get back to my folks for dinner. My Mom gets really wacky if you're late when she makes lamb."

Sherry's mother nodded her head emphatically. "Oh, she's right; you have to eat lamb as soon as it comes out of the oven—don't I know." She made a face, lifted her shoulders, and shook her head kind of like a poodle, but her hair didn't move, it stayed solid like a helmet—she must've used a whole can of spray stuff to make it stick like that.

"There's just nothing worse than cold lamb grease," Sherry's mother said, "and if you have to put it back in, to warm it, then you might as well just *give up* medium rare," she smiled, "I like to do a leg in mustard, that French mustard . . . does your mother ever do that?"

"Uhhh, I don't think so."

"Oh, I'll have to get her the recipe. Where do your folks live?"

"Off Ward Parkway."

"Oh, how lovely. Out South?"

"No. Uh . . . Sixty-fifth Terrace."

He had picked the richest neighborhood in Kansas City, the hill up above the Plaza, past the curve around the Carriage Club, where they played golf and drank highballs brought to them on silver trays by niggers wearing white gloves. The best, the biggest houses, the widest lawns. Sherry's mother smiled knowingly. In her eyes Will could see what she pictured, and it wasn't his mother making the lamb by a long shot—mothers in that neighborhood never even went into the kitchen—it was his mother's cook.

"I just got in and I was trying to connect with whoever was still home . . . you know, before I leave again for school."

"Oh, where do you go to school, William?"

He clutched the screen door. "Harvard," he said. What the hey, he might as well go all the way; he was already in over his head.

She beamed. "Your parents must be so proud of you."

"Yes, ma'am. Well, you'll remember to tell Sherry I came by, won't you?"

"Do you want to come in and we can call her? She'd be so surprised."

She sure would, Will thought.

"No, I gotta run. You know, the lamb."

She gave him another beam. He had to try it, he was going to try it, what the hell?

"Uh . . . Mrs. Ronne, you wouldn't happen to know if Sherry's friend Jenny Jaffe left for school already, would you?"

"Oh, I don't think so."

"Great, I'll give her a call."

"Oh, no, she's not here. She's somewhere back East, I think." She kind of trailed off. "But not at school."

"No?"

"Well, I don't know. Sherry and Jenny don't speak anymore, not since the situation."

"Pardon?"

"Well, she went away and then she came back and then she went away again." She gave him another knowing look, even raised an eyebrow. "All very hush-hush."

"Oh, right, she was pregnant," he said.

"Uh huh." Sherry's mother had released her arms, but now she hugged herself again, squashing her breasts flat. "I guess all you kids knew Jenny was pregnant."

"I'd heard that," Will said. He had to try, he had to ask her—what difference did it make now? "So did she have the baby?"

"That's what Sherry heard, but Jenny wouldn't speak to Sherry when she came home, wouldn't speak to anyone, we heard, and then she was gone."

There was a baby! He could have flown. There was a baby and Jenny was okay. The relief swept over him so fast he got dizzy, had to close his eyes. And when he opened them, Sherry's mother was watching him.

"Wow, that's too bad." He furrowed his face in concern. "Did she have the baby with her?"

"Oh, I don't know, William."

He nodded.

She did the poodle shake with her head again, touched her helmet hair. "Well, now you'll tell everyone that I'm an old gossip." She uncrossed her arms. "You'd better get home to your mother's lamb."

"Right. Yeah. Well, thanks so much."

"I'll tell Sherry you were here as soon as I talk to her, and you be sure and come and see us when you're home for Christmas."

"Yes, ma'am," he said.

"Good luck at school," she called out gaily.

She watched him as he got into the Mercury, kept one hand on the screen door and waved the other hand wildly as if he was going off to England on a ship or something, instead of just off to Harvard like he said.

"There's a baby," Will said out loud, as he turned the key in the ignition. "They didn't make her have an abortion. I have a baby!" and he let out a yell.

Old Lala Palevsky was one tough broad, he had to admit it; she probably could have made it on the inside. He had to wait until after the last dance class and all the little ballerinas, or whatever they were, left. A flurry of those flimsy costumes and a lot of I'll see you tomorrows, goodbye, goodbye, cars pulling out of the parking lot until it was just him and the Merc. The sun was down but had left its markers, red streaks over the plains of Kansas. Why couldn't life be as simple as a sunset? Will thought. He opened the door of the dancing school and went inside. Crashing music, drums and horns, grating and edgy and very loud. He'd never heard anything like it. He found her in the second studio; that's what Jenny had called it. Will had never been in there before; he'd only been in the front. This was a smaller room, the walls all mirrors, and she was dancing in all of them, alone. Flying around, leaping, her hair down and out of that bun, she was wearing one of those things they wore, flesh-colored, and that was all, her nipples raised hard against the stretch of material, some hair at her crotch escaped from out of the pink thing and her bare feet were slamming into the wood floor. He could feel the vibrations each time she went up and slammed back down. The way the light hit, you could actually see the sweat flying off her. She was dancing like some mad Russian, dancing like she was a young kid, she was *dancing*, she wasn't leaning on her cane.

She knew he was there—she must have felt him, because he didn't catch her seeing him, but he knew she knew. She didn't falter but continued thrashing her body around—that's what it looked like more than dancing, it looked like somebody was hitting her or throwing her, but nobody else was there; maybe she was getting beat up by the Invisible Man, Will thought, but it was too spooky to even smile. It went on for a good ten minutes, him watching and her dancing and the music crashing. He felt like Rod Serling had snatched them up into the Twilight Zone. It stopped finally, with her crashing down from an incredibly high leap. The music came to an abrupt end, and the room somehow got louder with the silence, and she was lying there, motionless, in a crumpled heap, facedown. Will felt paralyzed, but maybe she was the one who was paralyzed—that's how it looked from where he was.

"Uh . . . excuse me, are you okay?"

He could see the dust moving around her motionless body. She seemed barely to be breathing. He took a step forward. "Ma'am?"

She got up slowly, walked across the room, and took a towel off the bench. She ran it around her face and neck, pulled it across her shoulders, and lifted her hair with her hands.

"What do you want?" she said, not looking at him. He felt like he'd been hit with a stun gun. Her cane was propped against the bench. She reached for it, leaned into it, and turned to him. "I am going home," she said.

"Hey, wait a minute."

"What do you want?"

"I'm Will McDonald."

"I know who you are."

She sounded like a Russian in a spy movie, and her eyes were incredible, pitch black; no pupils could be seen from where he stood.

"I'm trying to find Jenny."

"Why?"

"Why?" He kept his gaze steady. "I love her."

She took a step toward him.

"Do you know where she is?" he said.

She didn't answer.

"I figure you're the only other person who cares about her, maybe as much as me. That's true, isn't it?"

A flicker of something. "She is away from here."

"I know that. I need to know where."

"She is not coming back."

"Where is she?"

By now she was in front of him. Her breathing had nearly returned to normal, her hair was all over the place, and he could smell her. "She is a dancer now. Leave her alone."

That was all she said, and she didn't give him time to say anything; she moved past him and left the room. He knew it was useless to try and get anything out of her; he could tell by the way she moved. He got the answer later when he drove back and broke into the dancing school. Three postcards shoved under a bunch of stuff in her top-right-hand desk drawer, no address on any of them but all three postmarked New York City. Will ran his thumb over the "Love, Jenny" and put them in the pocket of his shirt.

"Are you kidding?" Joe said, taking a swig of beer. "Talk about a needle in a haystack. New York's the biggest place you've ever seen, kid." He gave a laugh. "You'll never find her in New York."

He'd never felt such humidity, he'd never been so slick with sweat. As far as Will was concerned, New York was too much noise and too many people all crammed into one small, dense piece of space. Will didn't like New York, and the feeling was mutual.

"Why don't ya find anotha place to put it, bud? I taught we went troo dis yestaday."

It was the day doorman at the Imperial; he had a problem with Will hanging by *his* stage door. Will shrugged and moved his back off the building, took a couple of steps away from the door. He'd already been to the St. James on Forty-fourth and then walked through Shubert Alley; now he was at the Imperial, and then he'd go to the Forty-sixth. He'd already had a coffee at the Howard Johnson's on Broadway and a coffee at the Edison Coffee Shop on Forty-seventh; he was working his way uptown, to be at the Vim and Vigor across the street from Carnegie Hall around lunch. That's where they met, swapped information, ate, drank coffee, and smoked lots of ciga-rettes, in all these places—the dancers, the chorus kids, that's what they called themselves, chorus kids and gypsies, somebody'd said. He'd learned all their haunts and where they went to their dance classes; he'd asked anybody who would listen to him, and he went wherever they told him to go. He'd been to Luigi's and the June Taylor Studio, he'd had a hell of a fight with a skinny broad at Equity, who wouldn't even tell him if she'd ever heard Jenny's name. He knew now which theaters did musicals and which theaters did straight plays. He scanned *Back Stage* and *Show Business* for audition times and stood scanning the crowd as they pushed their way in, he went to Variety Arts and the Showcase Studios, he hovered in the hallways outside Ballet Arts and the International School of Dance, he searched waiting rooms and corners, he lingered in front of Johnny Ray's and Downy's, he hassled every day and night doorman at every theater, he asked every chorus kid who would listen, he pleaded, he described her in meticulous detail—nobody knew who Jenny was. He'd been there going on three weeks.

He had only two days left, two days tops, was what Will figured. He'd been staying in a rat hole on Forty-third Street called the Dixon, and he was down to about eight bucks. He'd left Kansas City with maybe only fifteen, but by the time he got to New York he was up to fifty; it was amazing what you could do to get money when you had your back to the wall. He'd jimmy barred every Coca-Cola ma-chine on every stretch of road between Kansas City and New York

City, picked up any hitchhiker who might have enough change for a tank of gas, and he'd do it all the way back. That, with a seven-foot piece of garden hose so he could siphon at night, and he would make it. It would take him at least six days to drive the Merc back to L.A. to make the appointment with the parole officer. Six days, maybe five if he drove hard and just pulled over to sleep. All he needed was something to go on, just a trace of her, anything. It was at Vim and Vigor that he got his one and only clue. It came from a big blonde, eating a tuna sandwich, who sat next to him at the counter on a high stool.

"You can always tell the New York girls," she said. "They would never get tuna on white bread."

Will was trying to stay calm. He looked at her sandwich. "They wouldn't?"

She shook her head, chewing. "No, only tuna on rye."

He nodded. "So you're from . . .?"

"Michigan." She smiled at him; there was a little mayo on the side of her full pink lips. "That's how we got to talking—she was the only other one having tuna on white." She ran her finger in the crook of her mouth and got the mayonnaise, licked it off her fingernail, and took another bite. "Jenny Jaffe from Kansas City. I remember. Tall as me but skinny, with big brown eyes."

"Big brown eyes," Will repeated. He couldn't find breath for more words.

"They have the best tuna here in the whole city. Are you sure you're not hungry?"

"No."

"So you two aren't still together?"

"Will be as soon as I find her."

"How do you know?"

"I know."

315

"Pretty sure of yourself, aren't you?"

"I love her."

She chewed a bite of the sandwich. "How do you know she still loves you?"

"I know."

"Boy oh boy. Want half of my pickle?"

"No, thanks."

"It's a half-sour—don't you like half-sours?"

"No, thanks. So you two had lunch together. Did you see her after that?"

She giggled. "You sound like Perry Mason. It wasn't lunch together—we were just both *having lunch.*"

He waited.

"I never saw her again."

"Never?"

"No . . . oh, that's not right. I saw her one more time—at least I think it was her—walking into class at Luigi's, but she didn't see me."

"She didn't?"

"Nope." She popped the last corner of the sandwich into her mouth.

Will frowned. "So you don't know where she lives or anything?"

"Oh, no." She pulled on the straw with her puckered lips until all the lemon Coke was gone. "It's not like I knew her. Or know her."

Will ran his hand across his face. He felt worse than before this girl said she knew Jenny; he had a vision of throwing himself in front of a bus.

She wiped her mouth with the napkin. "You don't know where she lives?"

"No."

"You don't know anything?"

"No."

"Boy, you sure are one determined guy." She unzipped her dance bag, pulled out a couple of dollars, and picked up her check. "Well, I hope you find her."

Will's throat closed. She hopped off the stool. He turned, put his hand out, but didn't touch her. "I'm about running out of ideas here."

She made a face. "It sounds like you're doing everything." She cocked her head at him. "There's only three places she could be: Broadway, a national tour, or a bus-and-truck. That's if she got something."

"A truck and what?"

"Bus-and-truck, on tour but not a national . . ." She stuck out one hip. "Dancing someplace where she probably wouldn't be caught dead. I wouldn't."

"Oh."

She touched his arm with her fingers, tilted her chin down toward one raised shoulder. "Maybe she doesn't want you to find her—did you ever think of that?"

He stared at her. "No."

"Well, maybe you should." She leaned her head toward him. "Do you have money? I mean, for a sandwich."

"No, thank you."

"'Cause I could stake you."

He shook his head.

"You sure? I mean, we've *all* been broke."

Will shook his head again.

"Well, if you're sure, I gotta run." She breathed out a cloud of tuna. "I got a class." She bent forward, her pink lips touching his cheek for a moment. "Boy, will you look at me *kissing!* I'm getting *so New Yawk.*" She giggled. "I hope you find her," and she squeezed his arm. "I mean it, Will." Soft hazel eyes and a lot of mascara. "Good luck," she said, and she was gone.

It took him twenty minutes to get his legs to stop shaking. *Maybe she doesn't want you to find her.* That was his one and only clue. He left New York.

"You pushed the car over the mountain?" Claudia said, trying to keep her voice calm, her eyes on Will's face.

"Yep."

"You drove it all the way back to California, and then you crashed it?"

"Yep."

They were quiet.

"It reminded you too much of Jenny, the Mercury. . . ."

Will didn't say anything. Claudia closed her mouth. It had taken her more than an hour to calm him down, to get him into her motel room, to make him drink some water, to insist he sit down. He had been pacing; now he was slumped in a chair by the foot of her bed.

"Then what did you do?"

"Got a job, got married."

"What?"

"Went to work for Warner Brothers, driving a truck."

"Will, the married part . . ."

"What?" He frowned. "I got married, that's all."

"But you still loved Jenny."

He stood up. "You gotta live your life."

She watched him; he looked back at her. "I been married five times, baby. None of 'em mattered much."

Her mouth actually opened, but she didn't say anything. He walked the length of the room and back.

"You never had any other children?"

318

"No."

"Why not?"

"Just didn't happen."

"How long were you married?"

"I was never married to any of them for more than two years." He turned and walked to the end of the room again. Claudia just stared.

He would never find her. That was all he could hear in his head. He demolished the Mercury; it was the closest he could get to demolishing what they'd had. He never took his foot off the pedal all the way to L.A., except when he slept, wedged bent across the front seat, the imprint of the door handle pink across the side of his face. He made his meeting with D. Francis and pushed the car over the crest of a mountain in Stough Park in Burbank that very night. He turned his back and walked away without looking at the damage. He was determined: he would get over the Mercury, and he would get over her.

Claudia made great time going back to Los Angeles. She left before dawn, just as Will told her. She was there when Lily got home from nursery school; they ate cheese melted on tortillas and drank lemonade from fresh lemons that she let Lily help her squeeze, and she consented to play Lily's favorite, balloon ball. She watched her child zwoop around the garden, got caught up in her laughter, at two sticky pudgy hands stretched high into the air. Claudia threw the purple squeaky circle to her daughter, and like background music to Lily's chatter, she ran what Will had told her through her head again and again. How could she tell Jenny on the telephone? She couldn't tell her on the telephone. Three weeks, she would sit on it for three

319

weeks; she called Will after supper and said she would tell Jenny as soon as she got to L.A.

"Let's hope she doesn't kill the messenger," Gena said.

Claudia, stretched out on the kitchen floor, cradled the phone between her chin and her shoulder and yawned.

"Claud, are you yawning? I'm the one who's looking at two-thirty A.M. here. Tell me again."

"What?"

"Everything about him."

Claudia laughed. "What? I told you."

"I know. I just can't get used to it. I already painted him as a blackguard, and now he turns out to be—what—The hero in the blackguard's cape? Why didn't you call me from Lone Dove? I was losing my mind."

"Gena . . ."

"I know, I know. I like calling it Lone Dove. Leave me alone."

Claudia smiled. "Okay."

"Just think, the real villains are your pardon-the-expression maternal grandparents. What did Jenny ever say about them anyway?"

"Her father's dead, that's all I know. When I asked about her mother, she said they'd had a 'parting of the ways.'"

"Well, I'll say."

They were quiet.

"Claud?"

"Hmm?"

"Tell me again—I can't believe it: does he really have a mustache?"

Claudia laughed and rolled over on the cold floor. "Gena. Yes."

• • •

She slid into the bed next to Ollie, curved herself around his backside, her knees into the backs of his knees, her breasts pushed up against his warmth. She curled her arm over the side of him, her arm on top of his arm, her fingers brushing the top of his wrist.

"Uh huh," he mumbled.

"Uh huh what?" Claudia whispered.

"Uh huh."

"Honey, are you sleeping?"

"Uh huh."

"Ollie?"

"Uh huh."

Claudia laughed softly. "It's okay. Go back to sleep."

"Uh huh," Ollie said.

His breath deepened and then found a rhythm. She breathed with him, put her lips against the back of his neck. Soap and Ollie. Claudia smiled, settled her cheekbone against her husband's back, and closed her eyes.

"I'm a little disappointed," he whispered.

"You big phony. I thought you were sleeping."

"Uh huh."

She pinched the skin on his thigh.

"Hey!"

"What do you mean, you're disappointed?"

"I wanted the *other father* to own the Knicks . . . at least the Lakers."

"You did, huh?"

"Yeah, I was already figuring out what I was going to say to Jack Nicholson on the floor."

"What?"

" 'Hi, Jack.' "

Claudia laughed.

"You want to hear what I was going to say to Pat Riley?"

" 'Hi, Pat'?"

"No. 'Hi, Mr. Riley.' After all . . . "

She hugged him.

They were quiet.

"So you like him," Ollie said.

"Yeah."

"That's good, babe."

"It sure is." She yawned. "What a thing."

"Yeah. They never got a chance, did they?"

"No."

"I guess you got to count your blessings."

"Boy, I do."

"All of us," he said.

She pressed herself into him, tightened her arm over his side. "Oh, Ollie, they must have been . . . something."

"Yeah."

She exhaled, her breath warm against the back of his neck.

"You know," Ollie said, "I was thinking . . . "

"Mmm?"

"I've never done it with a woman who has *two* fathers and *two* mothers. . . ." He moved his hand out from under hers and over his hipbone, trailed his fingers across the soft skin of her groin.

She breathed against him, even and warm.

"Babe? Are you sleeping?"

Claudia didn't answer. She knew he was waiting and listening.

"You had a hell of a three days, kid," Ollie whispered, and he moved his hand back over his hip, curled it around Claudia's hand, laced their fingers, and closed his eyes.

"Don't say 'hell'," Claudia murmured, and laughed low.

"You little hussy," Ollie said, and he turned around.

"I wasn't at a spa," Claudia said.

"What, sweetheart?" Margaret turned from watching Lily out Claudia's back door. John had the child out there playing hide-and-seek in the garden. So silly, John trying to hide behind an orange tree—you could see him sticking out from either side. "What did you say?"

"I wasn't at a spa. I went to find Will."

Margaret kept her eyes on her daughter. She could hear Lily shriek, "I see you, Grampa, I see you!"

"And?" Margaret said. She held on to the door, could feel the panic hit her deep in the chest.

"I liked him."

She turned and looked out again, tried to calm herself with a big breath. It was Lily's turn. She was crouched down between the rosebushes, her little bottom stuck up in the air, and John was hulking around, stalking her as if he were a terribly bad actor trying to play Cochise.

"Mom?"

"You know, your father is really a character."

"I know."

Margaret turned and came to the table, sat in the chair next to Claudia, her hands folded in her lap. She waited.

"Mom, you look like you're in church."

Margaret unfolded her hands. "Tell me."

"I liked him," Claudia said again.

"Good."

"Now you look like I just told you I have cancer."

"My goodness, Claudia, don't talk like that. You know I hate that kind of talk."

"Sorry."

"Goodness."

They looked at each other. Claudia smiled at Margaret. "What is it?"

"Oh, it's just"—she sighed—"my uneasiness, that your seeing him will somehow change you and Daddy."

"Did seeing Jenny change you and me?"

"No."

It hadn't, it was true. She and Claudia were the same as they'd always been, and there was also the comfort of the relief. The secret was lifted from her heart when she lifted the lid of her great-grandma Nellie's Chinese box and gave Claudia her real name. All these years of waiting for Claudia to say she wanted to find them, and now she'd found them, and Margaret could breathe. John said it was because the other shoe had finally dropped. Of course, now he would have to face *his* other shoe.

"It didn't, did it? Change between us?"

"No," Margaret said, her face easing into a smile. "It didn't, sweetheart."

Claudia stood up. "I have to tell Daddy."

"You know," Margaret said, "somewhere inside me I knew you didn't go to a spa. It was just so unlike you, so *not* you, that I think I knew. Isn't that funny?"

"You just know me, Mom," Claudia said.

Jenny sat on the third bench in from Central Park South on the way to the zoo. She had her pick of people to watch. The young black couple kissing, one of his legs wrapped around both of hers. They didn't look old enough to be kissing; they also didn't look old enough to be smoking, and they were doing that too. There was a bag lady camped out on the bench across from Jenny, with two filthy ripped shopping bags from D'Agostino and two from Food Emporium leaning up against her legs. Jenny preferred Food Emporium; the bag lady didn't seem to have a preference. She had one smaller bag, from Bergdorf's, which she clutched to her breasts, one of the lavender ones with the line of black cut-out ladies parading up the side. What could she have in that one? Her jewels?

"There but for the grace of God . . . ," she had said to Rose.

Crossing Fifth Avenue at Sixty-fifth Street, Rose and Jenny, just a year and a half ago, making their way to lunch at Montparnasse, three doors in from Madison.

"You're insane," Rose said softly in Jenny's ear. "You will never be a bag lady—how could it happen?"

"I don't know."

A lump of rags, she lay ahead of them, propped up partially by scraps of cardboard.

"If you lost everything, Ron and everything, you could always get a job."

"As what?"

"A receptionist," Rose said, laughing.

They would have to walk around her, her legs spread across the sidewalk, caked sores, dried blood on the wrappings, and no sign of ankles, swollen thick from the knees down. "What?" Jenny said, trying to move her eyes away from the woman's feet.

"I don't know. When I was a kid, my big plan was to escape Fond du Lac and be a receptionist at *Harper's Bazaar* in New York. *Tres* sophisticated, I thought."

"You never told me that."

"Well. Too much Rona Jaffe."

Running eyes and ripped fingers . . . Rose steered Jenny around her, a wave of the stench of her as loud as the garlic wafting through the gap between the buildings, and Jenny had clutched Rose's arm.

"You could teach dancing again," Rose said.

"No."

"Why couldn't you?"

"Because you have to love it to teach it."

"Don't be silly—you were a great dancer."

"I didn't love it, Rose."

And they opened the door of Montparnasse and were hit by the warmth and the light, and the maître d' said, "Good afternoon, ladies," and whisked away their coats.

A year and a half ago, before Rose's killer cancer had returned. Just a year and a half ago, and Rose would have been here with her. Jenny brushed at her slacks, recrossed her ankles. But Claudia wouldn't have been with her. Jenny laughed to herself. What was it— a swap? *Don't ask for too much, kid. I'll give you back your daughter, but I'll take away your best friend.* No. Rose would have said Jesus would never do that.

The bag lady leveled her eyes at Jenny and mumbled something. The scraps of rags wrapped around the woman's legs were like a dancer's leg warmers. Jenny turned her head away.

She could see herself painting her broken blisters with gentian violet, the purple seeping lavender through the white gauze.

"Are you crazy, Jenny? You can't dance like that." Susan yelling at her as she left their tiny apartment to go to class.

But she did it, and she danced on two broken toes shot with Novocain when the new guy who was supposed to catch her in *Lucky Charlie* had missed. She danced with a torn ligament in *Gift of Gab,* she danced

326

on bleeding feet stuffed into orange rhinestone tap shoes in *Chili Gumbo,* and she danced with both knees wrapped in bandages underneath her hoop skirt in *River Belle.* It didn't matter what happened to her; she danced. She went to every class, every audition, and when she got a show she stayed on the floor even during breaks, tucked away in a corner practicing the combinations over and over.

If she danced hard enough and long enough, she wouldn't have to think, she wouldn't have to remember. If she danced hard enough and long enough, she would dance away every memory of her and Will, she would dance away what he had done to her, she would dance away not knowing what had happened to him, she would dance away the image of her baby's face. She worked show after show; she nearly always got hired, because she had become a brilliant dancer, but brilliant as in a hard-edged, shining *thing,* a robot, a dazzling whiz of precision. She dazzled but there was nothing behind it; she knew her love for it was gone. She might as well have stayed what her mother said she was, "the ugly duckling, the gawky big one in the back," because in the end the wicked witch won again, Esther got what she had predicted: Jenny became a real dancer, but she never got her dream.

A man feeding the pigeons had let them land all over him—his shoulders, his arms, his hair. It was disgusting. The black kids had tilted to the left and slid down several inches on their bench. One of his hands was definitely very busy inside her coat. Jenny lowered her eyes and studied her hands in her lap. It was cold enough for gloves, but they were in her pockets and she didn't want to move. She twirled the slender diamond wedding band round and round her third finger with the tip of her thumb.

It had been different when she first got home. Her elation at seeing Claudia swirled in a wide circle, even entangling her and Ron. She'd told him everything, describing it all in a rush of brightness—Claudia,

Ollie, Lily, every second she'd spent in L.A.—and Ron was happy to see Jenny happy, and things were good. But as the months went by, the well-being settled like feather pillows, and everything returned to how it had been with them: flat. The knowledge that she knew where Claudia was and could talk to her with the lift of a telephone filled Jenny with enormous peace, but that peace didn't slide over into her feelings about her husband. Claudia would find Will—somewhere inside her, Jenny knew that, and she couldn't get it out of her head. She didn't ask if Claudia was making progress on the search, she didn't mention his name when she talked to her, but she knew. Claudia would find Will, and for the first time since he'd left her, Jenny would know where he was, and what would she do with that? She lifted the hand with the wedding band and pushed her fingers up against her mouth.

Will edged himself out from under the water truck on his ass and his elbows, leaned toward his good leg, and rolled up. He threw the handful of wrenches on the wooden bench, tried to brush some of the dirt and grass off his back, wiped his greasy hands against his T-shirt, and slid into the truck. He turned the ignition; the motor sputtered and quit. Okay. So it wasn't the starter. He stayed where he was behind the wheel, the truck door thrown open, one foot on the dirt. He ran his hand through his hair. Time changes everything, isn't that what they said? She would be different. They would both be different. Why was he even considering seeing her? To hold on to some childish fantasy was a crock. He turned the ignition again; she gave a little cough and whine. Had to be the distributor; the damn thing was shot. He got out of the truck, took a swig of iced tea from the mason jar, and carried it with him into the shed. He opened a couple of drawers in one of the tool chests, rummaged around, couldn't remember what he'd come in there for, slammed each drawer shut. The bitch had let her think he'd run away. Taken money, for crissakes. And how could Jenny believe that, huh? He couldn't get that part of it through his head. He walked out of the shed and slid back in behind the wheel. Babe barked. She was sitting on the passenger side, waiting to ride. "Not yet, Babe." She panted and barked again. "Not yet, I said." She extended her legs in front of her slowly, lay down across the bench seat, and rested her big head on her paws. He wouldn't have left Jenny no matter what they did to him. Hell, the only way they got him away from her was in cuffs. Will turned the key; the engine sputtered. "God damn it," he said. He had to get a new distributor. He leaned forward and rested his chin on the backs of his hands, perched on top of the steering wheel. Five more days. Claudia would tell her everything, and then Jenny would know. She would forgive him if she was still holding on, she would know none of it was his fault. Will ran his hand around the steering wheel. Claudia would tell her what they had done to him, the bastards, tell her how he'd tried to find her as soon as he got out, tell her how he wanted to see her, and Jenny would forgive him and he would drive down. Will smirked. Sure. Sure she would. He put his hand on the seat next to him. Babe looked at him from under the whites of her eyes. He looked back at her. Nah, it was all right, he would see Jenny. But the picture of her he had in his head didn't exist anymore. She didn't look like that, he didn't look like that, and besides, what he liked then was not necessarily what he would like now. Hell, he didn't even know who she was now, and what was he going to say to her anyway? *Hey, Jenny, why don't you just leave that guy in New York and come live with me?* Will laughed. Babe raised her head. "Talk about a fool," Will said to the dog. " 'That guy' is her husband." Babe whimpered. Right. His Jenny, who looked at him with wide eyes, who believed he was a somebody, made him feel like he was a somebody, not a nothing—she looked at him and he could believe he was a guy who would make it, a guy who was worthy, a guy who was smart. She probably looked at the fancy doctor that way. Claudia had said that guy was a big shot. What was he thinking? Jenny wasn't his anymore: she belonged to some Park Avenue Dr. Glass.

There was no reason to see her; why was he even thinking about it? Wasn't it enough now that he'd have his baby? And his baby had a baby. He could be a grandpa and a daddy—wasn't that enough for him? Thirty-five years . . . thirty-five goddamn years—the whole thing was dumb. He wouldn't see her. Sure, that was the ticket, he wouldn't see her; no use looking like a damn fool. He got out of the truck, walked around to the front, and lowered the hood.

Of course, you never knew. A marriage wasn't always a marriage; he was living proof. As he wiped his hands on a rag, his eyes wandered to the arc of water shooting out from the sprinklers across the green extending from the side porch. He threw the rag on a bench, walked over, and moved the hoses four feet to the left. What did he have to offer her anyway? If she'd even talk to him, if she'd even listen to what he had to say. Seventeen acres at the foot of a mountain, half a dozen vehicles, a rambling cabin, a creek, two dogs . . . what was that to a sophisticated lady? For she was a sophisticated lady now, his Jenny: been everywhere, seen everything, probably wouldn't want to give any of that up, and he was just the opposite—he wasn't interested in seeing anything he hadn't already seen. He liked his life the way it was, he didn't need anything but the essentials. He was—what did Leona call it?—a simple man. "Simpleton is more like it," he muttered. What would he do with Jenny? You had to learn to give up your dreams.

He didn't know why he was sitting there; he had things to do. He had to get a new distributor, he had to fix that piece of side fence, he had to think about what he was going to say to her, he had only five days, he had to make a plan. He took off across the dirt and gravel. The dog made a beeline out of the dead water truck and slid into the green truck with him, practically tackling him as he opened the door. "Hell, Babe," Will said.

"What are they going to do—get on the back of a horse together and ride off into the sunset, singing songs from *Annie?* For God's sake, Margaret, the two of you are being ridiculous," John said.

"Daddy, really."

He looked at Claudia. "What?"

"Don't pay any attention to him," Margaret said, putting down her cup.

"She's married, she has a husband. She lives in New York and he lives in the middle of . . . where?"

"Dad . . ."

"What does he do again?"

"I told you: he's retired."

"Retired," John said. "What does he do—sit around all day and play golf?"

"I don't think so," Claudia said, holding back her smile. It was such an inappropriate picture, Will playing golf.

"He didn't ask you for anything?"

"No, Dad, I told you."

"You never know."

Margaret shook her head. "Nobody said anything about her leaving her husband."

"Well, what are you talking about, then?"

"We're talking about closure, Daddy. They need to see each other."

"Don't use that pop-psychology psychobabble with me."

Claudia grinned. "Are you angry?"

"No."

"He is too," Margaret said, pushing some crumbs from the short-cake to the edge of the table and toppling them into her hand. "You're still angry that Claudia didn't follow in your wingtips and go into law."

"My wingtips?" His face softened. "That's good, Margaret."

"Of course it's good. I'm very funny. I just forget."

He laughed, put his big hand on her shoulder. "*I* don't forget, Maggie."

Margaret tipped her head to the side and raised her shoulder, nuzzled her cheek against the top of her husband's hand. Claudia was caught by the two of them and then dropped her eyes. It was one of Gena's favorite things to carry on about when they were kids. "Oh, if only I had been the one who was adopted! You get to live in Shangri-la with Bette Davis and Paul Henreid, *sans le* cigarette, and I'm being held captive with my *parents*, the fighting Irish, in the middle of the Hundred Years' War."

John looked at his daughter. "I never expected you to follow in my wingtips, Claudie. You picked a fine field. You know I'm proud."

"I know."

"Of course, you could have ended up being a movie driver. That would have beat psychology all to hell."

"Dad, please."

"Okay, okay." He looked at her. "I still think you should get your Ph.D."

"I know."

"Don't push her, John. Claudia, where is he meeting her?" Margaret said.

John frowned, turned his head to Margaret. "Who?"

"Will, Daddy," Claudia said. "My house, if she agrees to; he'll drive down."

"Will," John said, with a smirk.

Margaret put her hand to her chest. "My goodness . . . she'll be beside herself. Just like that, forever ago and now . . . my heart."

John dropped his spoon into the saucer. "Are we back to that again?"

Both women ignored him. "And where are you going to be, sweetheart?" Margaret said to Claudia.

"Wherever. I don't know. Just not there."

"Absolutely. This isn't about you, is it?"

"No, Mom," Claudia said, and she smiled.

"Bunch of goddamn romantics," John said, getting up from the table. "The next thing you know, you'll be discussing what canapés to serve at the *tête-à-tête*. I'm sure you ladies won't miss me. I'm going into the living room and make myself a drink."

It wasn't about her. That's what Margaret had said, and she had agreed with her, but . . . Claudia sat in the parked Volvo in her own driveway, the door thrown open, keys in her hand. This isn't about you, it isn't your story. Oh, yeah? Whose story is it, then? Wasn't it supposed to be hers? Once upon a time, a woman decided to find her birth parents and opened up a big, fat can of worms. Claudia studied the front of her house, ran her eyes along the trim around each window, and got out of the car. A boy and a girl and a pregnancy, a man and a woman and a baby, and everybody's life had changed. Slam. But now it was a slam dunk, because she'd found them. Isn't that what Ollie would say? The case of the missing birth parents. Claudia smiled, bent and uncoiled the hose, ran a slow trickle of water in the bed under each rosebush.

After all, she'd found them, her birth parents, against all odds.

She'd found them, but did finding them give her what she wanted so desperately to know? And what was that anyway? She pinched some aphids off a white bud with her thumb and finger, shut the faucet, and re-coiled the hose. Whose story? She'd thought it would be hers. She sat down on the brick steps, leaned back on her elbows, let the car keys drop into the grass. In finding them, she had revealed *their* story, not her own.

That was true, wasn't it? Claudia ran her hands along the tops of her knees. What had changed about *her* story? That she knew now why her eyes were so blue, why she was so tall, that she knew now that the trace of temper lurking inside her probably came from Will, the trace of edge from Jenny? But those things were there before, weren't they? Did it matter that she knew now where they came from? And what about the stubbornness she'd certainly gotten from John, and Jenny's vulnerability—did she have that besides her height? And Margaret's beautiful sweetness and how she would spray you with Pledge if you stood still long enough. Claudia smiled. She had certainly inherited that. Our Lady of Cleanliness, Gena had called her. "Claudia Magers, stop cleaning *my* room!" And John's bluffness, which she knew she'd picked up and used to her advantage when she was late with a paper at school. And Will's tenderness, did she have that? She hoped she had that, how it caught you unawares, and his hands, and Margaret's patience, please, let her have at least a little of Margaret's patience. . . . And what came from who, and what difference did it make if you could put names on each feature, like when they used to paint by numbers, and she could say okay, all these particular parts of her were blue. Claudia unclasped her knees and dropped her hands to the grass. Who she was hadn't changed by her looking at Jenny, it hadn't changed by her listening to Will.

She raised her eyes.

It hadn't.

She was still Claudia, the Claudia she had been before. What was really different? And then she smiled. Okay, one thing. It was true, as Gena had so cleverly pointed out, that she was the *only* Catholic girl from Saint Mary Magdalene's who was really half Jewish—that was different from before, that would certainly topple Sister Anne if she were still alive, but other than that . . . She scooped up the car keys, tossed them into the air, and caught them in the palm of her hand. And why was she so happy? She stood up. Maybe everything would be clearer in the middle of a long, hot bath. Everything would come clean.

"Oh, really," Claudia said out loud, and laughed.

Just look at that razor-sharp wit of hers—now who did that come from? Or could it possibly be her own?

"What are you doing in here, Margaret?" John said from the doorway. She was in Claudia's old room, sitting on the edge of the bed, surrounded by issues of *Better Homes and Gardens* and *Architectural Digest,* slowly flipping through pages while she scrutinized the room.

"Oh, I didn't hear you. Did you just get home?"

He walked to her, bent, and kissed the side of her face. "I did. What are you doing?"

"I was thinking we might redo this room."

John frowned. "What's wrong with it?"

"Nothing, but we haven't really changed it since Claudia went away to school. . . . I thought maybe it was time."

"It was yellow . . . and frilly." He moved to the desk by the window.

"When she was little. Ruffles, yes; dotted swiss."

John pulled out the desk chair and sat down. "And then she wanted . . . blue, wasn't it?"

"Pale blue. High school."

"And then she wanted to put up all those goddamn posters and you let her. . . ."

Margaret smiled.

"And she and Gena and their cronies were always running up and down the stairs and in and out of the house, slamming doors, everybody's car in the goddamn driveway when I'd get home . . . pizza boxes all over the kitchen and boys and the goddamn stereo—"

"It was nice, wasn't it?"

"Whatever she wanted, you allowed her."

"Well, within reason."

John's face softened. "You were a hell of a mother, Maggie."

Margaret turned the page of the magazine she was holding, focused her eyes on the slick colored photographs.

"You still are," John said.

"Goodness . . ."

"Very brave to go along with all this 'finding them' business."

"Well."

"It's true. You were very gung ho and understanding. I was a little more . . ."

She looked up. "Trepidatious?"

"No, not worried; I wasn't *worried*, I was just—" He caught his wife's eyes. "—Okay, I was a little worried, but you can't be too careful when it comes to your own—" He heard himself and he stopped, looked at Margaret, at how she was smiling at him. He laughed softly and shook his head.

"Oh, John," she said.

He cleared his throat and stood up. "So what are you going to do with the room now?"

"I don't know, dear. I hadn't gotten that far. Maybe a kind of sitting room or upstairs den."

He pushed the chair back into place at the desk.

"Hey, what about you do it in all those ruffles again, for when our little granddaughter comes over to stay with us?"

"What about you come over here so I can kiss you?" Margaret said, her eyes on John.

"Maybe I'll just sit here," Jenny said to Claudia.

She'd arrived the night before, but it had been too late to tell her then. The plane had sat on the runway for two hours with a mechanical something before it even left New York, and by the time they got to the house and by the time they ate something and by the time they dealt with Lily—"But why can't *woman* sleep in my room with me?"—and by the time they could have sat down and Claudia could have found the words . . . But morning was better, wasn't it? Fresh and new, her head clear, she'd tell her after coffee and . . .

"Jenny?"

"What?"

"I need to talk to you."

She'd whipped her head around. "You found him, didn't you?" The look in her eyes.

She thought it was just about Will.

"You can't rehearse for it," Gena had said. "There's no good way; just say the words." The words, she had to say the words.

"There was no money, Jenny, they didn't offer him money, they had him arrested, it was all a lie."

Jenny's face as the realization slid over her, the slam of her body into the chair.

"Do you want me to stay with you?"

Jenny didn't answer, didn't look up at her.

"Okay," Claudia said, scraping the metal chair legs across the brick. "I'll . . . uh . . . be in the house."

Jenny kept her eyes on the hummingbird. She would keep her eyes on the hummingbird. She would not fall from the chair, she would not scream, she would not cry, she would not anything, because what difference would it make? And besides, she'd never seen a hummingbird stop before, but there he was, stopping for just an instant, perched low on an orange-tree branch level with her face; you could actually see the red at his throat. How did his tiny heart not break, keeping up such a pace? She moved in the chair. What should she do now? What *could* she do now? Fly to Kansas City and shoot her seventy-eight-year-old mother? Take that, Mom. And you thought I was bitter. Hold on to your hat, kid—I'll show you bitter close up.

"When did you get to be so bitter, Jenny?"

Shutting the wrought-iron gate, holding their coats close, their heels poised on the packed snow, and Esther's words echoed in the quiet, for the short time that Eighty-second Street could ever be quiet, and that was only when the light had changed and the traffic was stuck on Fifth. But in that tiny wedge of quiet it was suddenly clear to Jenny that she was not going to see Esther anymore. That she would give that to herself. Not see Esther because when she looked at Esther, all she saw was her baby's face. She promised herself, and she didn't care what Ron said or what Rose said or anyone, and only when her father died did she forsake her promise. She went to Kansas City like a good girl, stood next to her mother, threw dirt on the coffin, stayed for three days, and left.

She envisioned Esther now, still stunning, still elegantly coiffed and beautifully dressed, but more-than-her-normal rigid, with a darling red pinhole in the middle of her regal forehead, a pinhole emitting a thin wisp of smoke from the gun that Jenny had shot her with.

Take that, Mom. Jenny ran her hand across her face. What an idea. Shoot old Esther right between the eyes.

No, her *mouth*. She could shoot her in the mouth that had said the evil words. *We offered him money and he took it and he went away.* Jenny leaned her head back, closed her eyes. On second thought, why should she dirty her own hands? She could have it arranged. Who was that guy, that friend of a friend of a friend of Bernie's, whose nose was definitely pushed too far over to one side? *Hello, Joe, can you do me a favor? Nah, it's nothin', just an old lady rattling around her mansion somewhere in the midwest, piece a cake.* Jenny opened her eyes, looked for the hummingbird. No, it was a waste of a good hit man. What difference now? What difference could it make now if the wicked witch was alive or dead? It was all too late, wasn't it? Her father gone, her mother just a dried-up old lady holding on to her meanness with the same voracity with which she held on to her house. She would just let her rot there; no need for violence, not now. They'd all lived their lives, hadn't they? You bet. Besides, Esther had probably done her a favor. Look how he'd ended up. Really, what was he? A loner Marlboro man in the middle of nowhere. Was that the wine country, where he was? Jenny put her fingers to her lips. Could she picture herself in the middle of nowhere? She would have had to give up Broadway, the hoopla of her life, her scrapbook bursting with reviews. The tears raced through her fingers. A trucker, her Will had been a trucker. Just think of it, Jenny Jaffe wearing gingham, raising chickens, saying you-all. And that didn't even touch on the important things, like what would she have done with her closetful of good black suits? She imagined herself as a Dorothea Lange photograph, black-and-white and barefoot and pregnant, standing in front of a dirty pickup in the middle of a desolate stretch of desert, one hand at the back of her waist, the wind whipping her tattered dress back from her legs. Barefoot and pregnant.

I love you, Jenny, you're my girl. She could see him saying it.

Oh, Will.

Jenny ran her hands back across her wet cheeks. She searched the orange tree; she couldn't see the tiny bird.

Wait. Maybe Will could shoot her. Oh, yes, that would be better. Maybe he still had the gun hidden under the car. Maybe he still had the car. Maybe they could go together. She felt her throat catch. Together. They were together and then they weren't. Don't blink now, folks, first you see them and then you don't.

"Do you want to see him?" Claudia's face swimming in front of her, her hand touching Jenny's, Will's blue eyes looking at Jenny out of Claudia's face.

See him? No. Why? What for?

She shouldn't see him. Why mess up her heart and her head, and oh, yeah, what about Ron? Remember? You're married, Mrs. Glass. Aren't you on your way to Mexico to meet Ron? Ron, your husband, who loves you and wants to make this work.

"We can make this work, Jenny. Please, try with me."

Work? Work to love somebody? Don't you either love someone or not? And if you loved somebody and you felt that *something* that touched every part of you, why would it need work?

"I don't love him that way, Rose," she'd said thirteen years ago. Running to Fond du Lac two weeks before her wedding, threatening to run all the way to the moon.

"It's okay."

"No it's not."

"He loves *you* that way."

"It's not enough."

"Every love isn't the way it was with you and Will."

"I'm not talking about Will."

"Yes, you are. Ron adores you."

"Right. I don't adore him. I think he's nice."

"Come on."

"Okay—good, wonderful, a fine man, a great doctor, everything my mother would have wanted—" And she stopped, stunned. "My God, I can't believe I said that."

But it was true, wasn't it?

She'd gone back, she'd gone back and she'd married him and it was thirteen years and it had been okay. What was it supposed to be anyway? Violins? Polka dots and moonbeams? A Cole Porter tune?

She was married and she was meeting her husband in Mexico. That was the reality. There was no reason to see Will. She had spent too many years putting him out of her head; what was the point in seeing him now? Because she knew now he hadn't taken the money? Because there was no money? What difference did it make now? It was too late. Their lives were nearly over. Half over. Three-quarters over.

She wiped her face with the bottom of her shirt.

They had nothing in common.

She smiled. They'd never had anything in common, had they?

They never should have been together in the first place; they were a fluke. He was just the only person to ever look at her and listen to her and make her feel real. And special. And pretty. And strong. And everything. She put her face in her hands.

What do you say to someone after thirty-five years? *Hey, Will, what-cha been up to? Did you miss me? Do I look the same? Oh, no, don't be silly, of course I knew you didn't really leave me. I knew it, baby, don't give it a second thought. Hey, absolutely, sure, you bet, I knew.*

What did you do to my life, Mother?

Jenny got up from the chair, wobbled back and forth on the brick patio like a baby taking her first steps. She couldn't stop the sobs, they'd been such a long time in coming, and she didn't really know how she felt, but did it matter? Would there be some peace in labeling

341

this emotion? Happiness? Sadness? Relief? She didn't know; she was too far caught up in it to even care. She touched the rip of soft, deflated purple balloon that had flattened itself across a branch of the orange tree. Her hand was shaking. She knew only one thing. Did she want to see him? Yes.

Will looked off across the mountains. There was a dry wind coming in off the Sierras, blowing a lot of dust around. He would see Jenny. Claudia had called, and it was for sure, tomorrow. He would leave before the traffic. He debated going into town for supper, tipped back in the porch chair, and ran everything through his head again, his eyes on the sky.

Jenny sat naked on the bed in the dark of Claudia's guest room, she would see Will tomorrow, and what would happen would happen; she wasn't going to think about it anymore. She watched the skinny moon through the open window, let the towel lay where she'd left it across the edge of the bedspread, and let the night air dry the bath-water on her skin.

Lily stood to her full height, her little hands poised on her hips, and looked up at Ollie.

"You made a mess, Daddy."

Ollie turned. "What mess? Where?"

"You're 'posed to put your shoes in the closet."

"Oh."

"You're not 'posed to leave them where people can fall on them."

"Oh."

She eyed him, his big sneakers shed in the doorway, and then looked to Claudia at her dressing table across the room. "Mommy said so," Lily said with satisfaction.

"Well, Mommy's a little anal about such things."

Claudia laughed. "I can't help it. I take after my mother."

"Oh, yeah?" Oliver said, turning to his wife. "Which mother?"

He noted how soft and beautiful her face was as she said it. "Don't be silly, Ollie. Margaret's my mother."

Their eyes met and locked over the head of their child.

"What's a *anal*, Daddy?" Lily said.

Will changed shirts three times, and then it occurred to him that what he was doing was pretty silly, since all the shirts were blue.

Jenny circled Claudia's kitchen, looking down at her shoes.

He took the 395 into the 14 into the Golden State heading south.

She brushed her teeth again, fixed her lipstick, wondered why in God's name she'd let her hair go gray.

He stayed to the right and moved at a good clip from the Golden State into the 170, passed a woman with a mess of kids in the back seat who should have her license taken away, adjusted his side mirror, gave the steering wheel a little pat with his hand.

She touched Rose's rosary beads on Claudia's dressing table, sent up a small prayer, and wandered from room to room.

He got off at Riverside, went west to Laurel Canyon and took a left.

She checked her face again in the hall mirror, went up and down the staircase three times, and then sat on the edge of the top step, her arms hugging her chest.

He took the curves up the canyon, hung a left at Mulholland, caught a glimpse of himself in the rearview mirror, laughed, and then frowned.

She hung her head between her knees, felt the blood rush.

He made a quick right on Woodrow Wilson, like Claudia'd told him to.

She raised her head.

He found 76228.

She heard the truck pull up.

He parked, got out, slipped an Ace comb out of his back pocket, ran it through the wave in his hair.

She did not look out the window.

He walked up the three front steps, his eyes lowered.

She came down the staircase and stopped poised at the closed door.

He hiked up his pants and smoothed the ends of his mustache.

She put her fingers over her mouth.

He rang the bell.

She lowered her hand, exhaled, and opened the door.

They looked at each other.

He handed her the rose he'd cut when he left Lone Tree, and she walked into his arms.

Acknowledgments

A special thank you to those who gave their time to speak to me about adoption: Sonya Menor, Ida Knapp, Ron Ruscillo, Marlou Russell, Ph.D., Lynne Turner, M.S., M.F.C.C., and Anthony Carsola. *Thank you to* James H. Ensz, *who tried to give me a crash course in Missouri and California law.*

To the new believers: Ginger Barber and Claire Wachtel.

To the ones who read and reread, speak their piece and push me: Dinah Lenney Mills, David Freeman, Eric Lax, Denise Worrell, Jean Vallely, Gena Rowlands, Leslie Garis, and David Francis.

To the essential ones who keep me going: Carole, Razie, and Iva.

John Cassavetes,

Tonto,

always and forever, Bob Gottlieb,

and my dearest Eve.